Salvation Blue

Reese Barton

Published by Cross of Grace, 2023.

SALVATION BLUE

First edition. October 2, 2023.

ISBN: 979-8988876618

Written by Reese Barton.

This book is dedicated to all of those out there seeking the truth. Knowing that when you find it, the truth shall set you free. That truth and freedom are summed up in one word. Salvation.

Chapter 1

Friday—July 1, 2010

He sat on the side of the road. Eyes facing forward, focusing on nothing. It was two in the morning, but he had lost all track of time. His knuckles were white from gripping the steering wheel so tight, but he would not feel that uncomfortable soreness until later. He was completely numb. There was only one word echoing in his head over and over. Inoperable. The radio was almost nonexistent tonight, which was unusual for a Thursday, but he could really use a distraction about now. He took a deep breath in, released his grip, and then exhaled loudly as he leaned forward and placed his forehead on the top of the steering wheel.

"Why," he whispered.

The sudden tap on his driver's side window startled him. He sat up straight in his seat and jerked his head around to see who it was. The look of surprise on his face must have been apparent to his visitor, because the man backed away slowly with his hands in the air mouthing the word, "Sorry." He sat there for another moment until his breathing was normal and then rolled down the window.

"I'm sorry officer I didn't mean to startle you," The stranger stated.

Dave took a moment to inspect the unwanted visitor before he finally spoke.

"Is there something I can do for you, sir?"

"I was just wondering if you were okay."

He gave the stranger a noticeable pause before he answered.

"What would make you think I wasn't?"

"You have been sitting here in the same position for over an hour."

He dipped his head slightly and almost seemed embarrassed before he spoke.

"I needed to finish some paperwork."

"I have no reason not to believe you, officer, it's just that," he paused, "you have literally not moved in over an hour."

Now he was getting angry.

"Who are you, and why have you been watching me for over an hour?"

The stranger sensed his anger building and attempted to ease the tension.

"Officer, my name is Bill Dunkirk. I am the senior pastor of the church you are sitting in front of." He pointed to the building that read Faith Bible Church. "I mean no disrespect in my actions sir, it's just that I couldn't sleep tonight." He laughed and then pointed to the house behind the church. "You see, I live right there behind the church in the parsonage. Me, my wife, and my children. I am usually a good sleeper. But tonight, I could not find rest. I tried counting sheep," he laughed once again, "but that did not work. So, finally I decided that if I could not sleep, I might as well work. I walked over to the church around twelve thirty, and I noticed you sitting out front in your patrol car. I thought nothing of it and read from the book of 1 Thessalonians to get a start on Sunday, or maybe the Wednesday night message."

"Wednesday night? I thought church was only on Sunday unless you're catholic?"

"We have a Sunday morning service, Sunday evening, and a Wednesday night service for believers."

"People actually go to church that much?"

He laughed at the comment.

"Some do."

"Anyway, Pastor, you were saying."

"I looked back out here at one thirty and noticed you in the same position. I told myself I would check at two, and if you were still here, I was going to come down and make sure you were okay."

He smiled, and his disposition seemed a bit more at ease.

"I thank you for your concern, sir, but as you can see, I'm doing fine."

Below the window and out of view of the pastor, he was flexing both hands, which were feeling sore at the moment.

"Okay then. I'm sorry to have bothered you, officer..."

"Jackson. David Jackson."

He extended his right hand out the window. The pastor took a step forward and shook his hand.

"It's very nice to meet you, Officer Jackson."

"Please Pastor, call me Dave."

"And you call me Bill."

"Alright Bill. I guess I should be going."

"Dave, before you leave. I know you said you are alright, but is there anything you want to talk about? Anything that's on your mind?"

Dave paused and scratched his chin. Pastor Dunkirk reached into his pocket and took out a business card. He handed it to Dave.

"Dave, if you feel like talking about anything at all. You just call me."

"I hate to burst your bubble, Bill, but you might not get a phone call from me."

"If I don't that's okay. You have the card if you want to talk."

He held the card up and examined it.

"Senior Pastor William Dunkirk, Faith Bible Church.," he whispered.

Dave realized that in these last few minutes since he had been talking to Pastor Bill; he had not thought about his condition once. Dave decided that if the radio would not cooperate by distracting him tonight, then maybe a conversation with Bill would be just what he needed. The shift sergeant had always preached community-based policing. Maybe he could kill two birds with one stone here.

"Actually, Pastor Bill, if you have a moment, maybe we could talk a little."

The pastor smiled.

"I would like that, Dave. Do you want to come into the church or -?"

"That won't be necessary. It seems like a pleasant night to talk outside."

"Very well then. If you would like, you can just pull your car around to the front entrance. There's a bench in front we, or I can sit on while we talk."

"Alright. I'll meet you over there."

The pastor turned and starting walking toward the front of the church. Dave shifted the car into drive and did a U-turn back out onto the road and then made a left into the parking lot. He parked in the spot closest to the bench and exited the car. He stretched. The pastor walked up and had a seat on the bench.

"Would you like to sit? There's room for both of us."

"Thanks, Pastor Bill, but I think I need to stand for a bit."

"Very good. What would you like to talk about? You know whatever is said between us stays between us, right?"

"It is not one of those conversations, pastor. I thought maybe I could get to know you better, that's all. Maybe hear a little about the church and community things."

"Oh. Well, that'll be fine." He smiled. "Ask away Dave. What would you like to know? I'm an open book." Before Dave could speak, he added, "But before I tell you about me, let's put your police experience to the test."

"Okay, Pastor Bill. What did you have in mind?"

"Turn around."

Dave turned his back to the pastor. "Okay."

"I'm a perp who just committed a crime in front of you. How would you describe me?"

This made Dave chuckle.

"A white male approximately 40 to 45 years of age, 5'10 to 6'0, 175 to 185 pounds, short brown hair, clean shaven, wearing a blue polo shirt, khakis and loafers."

"Wow! I am impressed. I especially like the part where I could be 40."

"Well, I guess when you've been doing something for twenty-plus years, you should be good at it. How long have you been a pastor?"

"22 years."

"So, you know what I'm talking about?"

"I do. It seems like just yesterday that I graduated from high school. Time sure flies, doesn't it?"

He sighed, "That it does, Pastor Bill, that it does." He smiled. "So, what made you decide to go into the ministry?"

"Well, my father was a pastor, and his father was before him."

"Ah, the family business."

He chuckled. "It might look like that, but it's deeper. You feel a calling within yourself. Yes, I grew up listening to my father practicing his sermons at home, and we spent a lot of time at the church, but when I read the bible and prayed, I felt a genuine bond with God. Probably the same type of draw you felt toward law enforcement."

"They were hiring. I applied."

He laughed.

"Okay, I was wrong about that one. It drew me toward the love of a God who gave his only Son for my salvation."

The conversation was getting a little more serious than Dave wanted it to, so he changed gears.

"You said you have a wife and kids?"

"I do. I have been married to Marsha for 20 years now. We have four children; Matthew, who just turned 18, Sarah, 16, Brenda, 13, and Seth is 10."

"Wow!"

"I know. Sometimes I can't believe it myself."

"Is the oldest boy going into the family trade?"

"No, He wants to be a history teacher. He has always loved anything to do with history. Mainly American history. Not to brag either, but the Dunkirk men have had their fair share of running into historical figures."

"We'll circle back around to that. Will that make him an outcast?" He raised an eyebrow. "Not going into the family business."

Pastor Bill chuckled. "Not at all." He paused a moment to find the words. "Every father just wants their child to be happy with what they do in life. History makes Matthew happy, and so it makes me happy."

"But he won't be preaching from the pulpit on Sunday's. As a pastor, do you feel some sense of remorse that he won't be following in your footsteps?"

"Matthew is his own man. He must pray and follow God's will for his life. Whether it is teaching history, preaching from a pulpit, or protecting and serving others, that is up to him and God. We, as parents, have them in the nest for a little while. It is our job to instill in them the skills necessary to survive in this world without us. Wouldn't you agree?"

"I would."

"Do you have kids of your own, Dave?"

"I do." Time to shift gears again. "Have you been at this church for 22 years?"

"No. We have been here," he paused and appeared to be counting in his head, "16 years now."

"Are you from here?"

"I was actually born in Green Bay, Wisconsin."

"Ah, so, a Packers fan?"

"No, no, no! A bears fan. We moved to Chicago when I was five."

"So, you grew up in Chicago?"

"I did. I graduated from high school there and then went onto Moody Theological Seminary, where I eventually got my MA in Pastoral Studies."

"Did you meet your wife in college?"

He laughed.

"We met in kindergarten."

"Was it love at first sight?"

"We started eating the same paste, and when our eyes met, it was magic." He got a laugh out of Dave. "We lived in the same neighborhood. We went to the same school. So, we really saw each other a lot. Over time, our friendship developed into a relationship, and four beautiful kids later, here we are."

"How did you make the leap from Chicago, Illinois, to Dargen City, Michigan?"

"The short version is that God sends you where he needs you."

"And the long version?"

"I was pastoring this small, albeit very nice, church just inside the city. It was a wonderful church, a godly church, and the congregation was growing. We had been there for six years, and it had grown by thirty percent."

"That's a lot. So, what makes a man uproot his family and move them four hours away to pastor a church in an area he isn't familiar with?"

"I was sitting in my office one Friday night, going over my notes for the Sunday sermon, when the phone rang. It was late, right around 11:30. I answered, and the voice on the other end was one of my college buddies, Martin Jacobs. Martin and I talked from time to time over the years, but I had not heard from him in a little over a year. He had this big booming voice that I remember only got louder as he got more excited." He paused for a moment and chuckled. "Anyway, his voice seemed weaker. I knew that something was wrong."

"Nice friend. He doesn't call you for a year and then, when something is wrong, he picks up the phone. Let me guess, he needed money? It's amazing how that happens."

"No, nothing like that. He wanted me to come and visit him."

"It's harder for you to say no if he can look you in the eyes."

He smiled and then continued.

"I told him I could come see him in a couple of months when my schedule opened up. We had a lot of things going on at the church that needed my attention. He managed a laugh and then he said, 'I need you to be here tomorrow.' He could be the dramatic type occasionally, so I told him I would see what I could do."

"Was he satisfied with that answer?"

"Just before we hung up the phone he said, 'I'll see you tomorrow.'"

"So, he expected you to jump in your car the next morning and drive four hours from Chicago to see him, just based on him saying, 'I need to see you tomorrow.'"

"Yep."

Dave smiled.

"How disappointed was he when you called him the next day and told him you couldn't make it?"

"He was happy to see me the next morning when he woke up."

"Wow! You actually drove to see him?"

"I left around four the next morning and made it there a little after eight."

"Was your wife angry?"

He leaned in and whispered. "Marsha's the one that made me go."

"Really? How did that conversation go?"

"After the phone call, I wrapped it up for the night and went home. I walked through the front door and Marsha was sitting in the living room. Normally at that hour, she is in bed. Matthew was two and Brenda was about a month old, so she was usually exhausted. I walked over and gave her a kiss, then sat down next to her. Before I could say a word, she said, 'Go see him.' I was, of course, stunned. I asked her who she was talking about, and she said, 'Martin.'"

"You're freaking me out here, Pastor Bill."

"You? It freaked me out."

"Did she tell you why, or even how she knew?"

"It appears he called the house first and talked to Marsha. I guess he was more convincing to her than he was to me."

Dave laughed.

"For a moment there, I thought you were going to tell me she had a dream or a vision."

"No, just a sympathetic heart to the plight of a dying man."

"Wait. He was dying?"

"Yes. He didn't say it over the phone, but her intuition has always been better than any of my instincts. She could hear the desperation in his voice and knew that I would regret it later if I didn't go."

"So, what was the big secret?"

"When I got there, the first words out of his mouth were, 'Thank Marsha for me.' It, of course, made me laugh. He then told me he had developed prostate cancer." He paused and collected his composure. Dave remained silent and waited for him. "Sorry, I zoned out on you for a minute. Cancer. It is a nasty disease that has taken my fair share of family and friends. Anyway, he told me he had little time left, and that he wanted to leave the church in excellent hands. He said he prayed about it day and night, asking God to send him someone who would love and nurture this place as much as he had."

"And that person, was you?"

"According to him, it was. He said he felt led to tell me what God had revealed to him, and I could do whatever I wanted with it. He looked weak. I visited with him for about two hours and then got back in the car and made my way back to Chicago."

"And just like that, you became pastor of this church?"

He laughed.

"No, the process is a little more detailed than that. The church will select a few interested candidates and have them come in on separate Sundays and preach. When all the candidates have gone, then the congregation votes on one candidate to come back and preach again. Then, after that sermon, they vote again. This time to either make him the new senior pastor, or to keep searching."

"Sounds pretty cutthroat."

"No, not really. It doesn't benefit a congregation to choose the wrong leader."

"How can you choose the wrong leader if all of you preach the same thing?"

"Because even though we preach the same message, we have different styles of delivering it. Some pastors, like police officers, relate to others differently. There are many factors at play."

"I guess I never realized that. So, they chose you?"

"They did. It was hard leaving Chicago, and a church with a congregation that I loved and had been ministering to for six years."

"Then why leave?"

He smiled.

"You go where God calls you to be. After my meeting with Martin, things fell into place, and Marsha and I could see us calling this place home."

"So, your friend Martin died of prostate cancer?"

"He did."

"When you spoke with him, did he mention whether there were signs, or did it just come upon him quickly?"

"Like most people, Martin is stubborn. He told me that looking back, there were many signs that he just ignored. He was too involved with work or just pushed off the symptoms as a nagging pain here and there, until the pain was more severe, and he couldn't ignore it any longer."

Dave paused. He smiled and sighed. "Yeah."

"So, we have fully embraced this church, congregation and community as our own." He smiled. "Did you grow up here, Dave?"

"I did. I was born here. Raised here. And I will die here." He looked down at the ground and smiled before continuing. "I have a lot of significant memories here, Pastor Bill. I hope that you and your family have a lot of same."

"So far, so good."

"Do you see yourself staying here and retiring from this church?"

"We always keep our minds open to the possibility that we could be called to move again, but I don't see us leaving soon. Do you have a home church, Dave?"

"No."

"Do you have Sundays off?"

"The way my schedule runs, I have every other weekend off?"

"We have Sunday night services that start at 6 p.m. It is perfect for the people working midnights. Come to church, hear a great sermon, and then grab dinner and relax the rest of the night."

"Sorry Pastor Bill, that's more of my wife's thing."

He smiled. "Well, something to think about."

Dave chuckled. "Maybe."

There was an awkward pause in the conversation, which made the Pastor feel as if Dave had something else on his mind.

"Dave, is there anything you'd like to talk about tonight? Anything on your mind you'd like to get off your chest?"

"Pastor I,"

Dispatch interrupted.

"616 and 612."

He depressed the button on his radio.

"Go for 616."

"Go for 612," Officer Martinez chimed in.

"28747 Lona. 28747 Lona. A neighbor reports yelling from that location."

"616."

"612."

"I'll show both units on the way at 0247 hours."

"Duty calls Pastor."

"I enjoyed our conversation, Dave."

"So did I."

"You have my number if you ever want to talk, or my address if you want to stop by."

"Thanks. I hope you're able to get some sleep tonight."

"Me too. Stay safe out there."

The pastor turned to walk back toward the church, and Dave climbed into his cruiser. He shifted into drive, but then rolled his window down.

"Pastor Bill," he called.

The pastor turned.

"Yes, Dave."

"I'm just being curious, but you said that you were working on a sermon from the book of 1 Thessalonians. What's the message?"

"It focuses on 1 Thessalonians 5:16-18. 'Rejoice always, pray without ceasing, in everything give thanks; for this is the will of God in Christ Jesus for you.' The message being, give thanks to the Lord for everything that happens in your life. We seem to always thank him for the things that benefit us, but we seldom thank him for the calamity that enters our world. Verse eighteen is very clear. Give thanks to the Lord for everything that happens in your life."

"So, you're telling me we're supposed to thank him for our troubles? When we break an arm, or the bank forecloses on our house, or even when we get diagnosed with a terminal disease? That's what you're telling me?"

"It's not what I'm telling you, Dave. It's what God is telling us to do."

"That doesn't seem right."

He smiled.

"There's more to it than that. Come to the service on Wednesday night and find out more."

"I have to get to this call, Pastor Bill, but I'll think about it."

He shifted into drive and headed for 28747 Lona.

2

They came from opposite directions but pulled onto the street at the same time. Dave let dispatch know they were both on scene.

"616 and 612 are out."

"Copy that. I will show both units out at 0255 hrs. Be advised I am showing numerous runs for DV at the residence, but no weapons currently registered there."

"Units copy." Dave responded.

They parked two down on both sides of the house and approached on foot. Martinez took up a position on the side of the front door, and Dave walked around to the side door. As he approached the door, he noticed a light on in the back of the house. The back gate was open, so he walked through to see if he could see or hear anything. He heard voices coming from what appeared to be the kitchen.

"Yap-yap-yap-yap-yap...that's all you do all day long." A male voice screamed.

"Well, maybe I wouldn't have to if you actually did something around here." The female voice shouted back.

"I bust my hump working all week to provide for this family and this is the thanks I get."

"Being a man means more than just working for a paycheck. You also have responsibilities at home."

"Yap-yap-yap, you're like a little bird that won't stop."

"If I were a little bird, it would be, chirp-chirp-chirp, not yap-yap-yap, you idiot."

"Why did you even marry me, Rachel? All you do is criticize me. Do you even remember why?"

"Every day I forget a little more, Joe. Most men take decades to digress into the state you've fallen into, but it only took you a couple of years."

"Well, I'm sorry I'm not Mr. Perfect."

"Mr. Perfect? Joe, right now I'd settle for Mr. Cares. All you do is go to work, then you come home and start drinking the rest of the night before you pass out on the couch and do it all over again the next day. I can't even get you to do anything on the weekends. You just watch sports, yell at the TV, and drink."

"Well, excuse me for trying to find a little pleasure in life."

Dave then heard sobbing. He looked over to see Martinez peaking around the corner of the house at him. He gave him the nod as he started toward the front of the house. Martinez knocked on the door. A second later, the porch light came on.

"Who is it?" Joe yelled through the door.

"Police department sir, open the door," Martinez responded.

"Everything's okay in here. You can go."

Dave had made it back to the front of the house and was standing on the other side of the door.

"You know that's not how this works, Joe," Dave yelled back.

"We have neighbors Joe, open the front door." Rachel whispered loudly to him.

The front door opened. Joe then unlocked the screen and invited them in. Martinez entered first, with Dave right behind him. As he entered the door behind his partner, he whispered to him, "Why don't you take her into the kitchen while I speak to him in the living room?"

"Ma'am why don't we go into the kitchen and speak while my partner speaks to your husband here in the living room."

He followed her into the kitchen while the other two men stayed put. Once they were out of sight, Dave started.

"What seems to be the trouble this morning?"

"Same as every morning," he paused for a second to look at Dave's name tag, "Officer Jackson. Haven't you been here before?"

"I have, but that doesn't mean it's the same problem as last time."

"Well Officer Jackson, it is. She gets on my case about not doing enough around the house. I drink too much, yadda-yadda-yadda, and here we are."

"So why don't you get a divorce and move on with your life?"

Joe seemed surprised by this suggestion.

"Aren't you supposed to tell me to work it out?"

"I'm not a counselor or a priest. I'm a realist. Why prolong the inevitable? You two can keep going through the same song and dance, but the answer is right in front of your face."

"I guess, maybe. I really hadn't thought about it like that."

"Your young, there's no kids yet, so why drag it out?"

Martinez stood across from Rachel as she sat in the kitchen chair and cried.

"We had so many plans, Officer Martinez."

"How long have you been married?"

"It'll be two years next month."

"And how long have you known each other?"

"Six years now. We met our freshman year in college. We took the same literature class, Mr. Fisher. Man, he was a weird duck." She laughed. "We bonded over discussing how weird he was. I discovered this sweet, sensitive, ambitious young man. He was so passionate about life."

Martinez smiled.

"So, the relationship progressed. Then, after four years of getting to know each other, marriage."

"In a nutshell, that's it."

"So, what happened?"

"Beer happened."

"Was he a big drinker during those four years?"

"Not at all. Both of us are social drinkers. We would have a drink or two at a party, maybe a glass of wine with a nice dinner, but never one right after another. We didn't even keep any beer in the fridge."

Martinez spoke softly, and his face revealed a sincere empathy for what the young couple was going through.

"So, tell me Rachel, what happened that changed all of that?"

Her voice cracked, and she dipped her head. She took a moment before she spoke. Martinez saw a box of tissue on the counter. He grabbed the box and handed it to her.

"It's okay. Take your time."

"We got the call on Saturday, July 4th, last year, around six thirty in the afternoon. Joe's mom was driving home after work. She wasn't even supposed to work that day, but she picked up an overtime shift at the hospital to make some extra money." Rachel paused and blew her nose. "She was a nurse. Anyway, she was driving home on Interstate 94. The police estimated her speed at right around 65." She smiled and managed a weak laugh. "It always drove Joe crazy that she stayed in the right lane and drove under the speed limit."

"It sounds like she was just a cautious driver."

"She was." She wiped her eyes and took another moment. "Well, on this day she was driving behind a pickup truck, who also was doing 65. They were moving right along in the right lane when, without warning, the truck swerved to the right and up onto the shoulder. There was a car stalled in the right lane. She never even had time to react. She hit it doing 65. The police told us it killed her on impact."

She cupped her face with her hands and cried. Martinez walked over and put his hand on her shoulder.

Joe tried to look around Dave like he could somehow magically see through the wall into the kitchen.

"Why's she in there crying?"

"She's playing the sympathy card. Did you strike your wife tonight, Joe?"

"No, I wouldn't do that."

"Did you push her or maybe lean into her as you walked by, by accident, of course?"

"No-no-no..." He responded.

"Well, it sounds like she might be communication something different to my partner. Maybe even shedding a few tears to gain a little sympathy."

"Rachel wouldn't do that. If she's anything, she's honest."

"Maybe she knows that when the police go to an address over and over, eventually somebody has to go to jail."

"No, no way. We have our problems, but I would never lay my hands on her. Ever!"

"Does she have any girlfriends who really kind of hate men? You know the one I am talking about? The one that see's men as nothing more than oppressive, and she can't hold a relationship to save her life."

It only took him a second to think before he uttered the friend's name.

"Sydney."

"What's her story?"

"She's a man hater. She cannot hold a relationship because she's an intolerable witch. Sydney's probably been on a hundred first dates over the last five years because no man can stomach a second date with her."

"So, are you sure Sydney isn't rubbing off on her?"

"Sydney." He said it again, this time with contempt in his voice.

Rachel finally regained her composure, and she put her hand on Martinez's hand and squeezed it. He gently squeezed her shoulder and then moved back into his position.

"Thank you so much, Officer Martinez, for being so patient with me."

"Your family is going through a rough time,"

She wiped her eyes with the tissue and continued.

"She was a very sweet lady. My husband and her were very close. His dad walked out on the family when Joe was five and his brother was three. He moved to Texas to do God knows what, and Joe has not seen him since. Joe has a good relationship with his brother, but he is in the Airforce, stationed over in Japan for the last three years. He saw him for the funeral, but then it was right back to Japan."

Martinez stood there with a somber look, nodding as she spoke.

"That's got to be tough on him. A dad that's not a factor in his life, and a brother he loves but can't see."

"It is tough for him, and when his mom died like that, it just sent him right over the edge. About a week after the funeral, he brought home a case of beer. It lasted maybe two days."

"And he hasn't stopped since that day?"

"No. I've approached him about getting help. Going to AA. He has no desire."

"Does he have any friends who can help you convince him to seek help?"

"His so-called friends are the ones who have helped get him to this point. He has superficial friends who refuse to talk about anything that might exhibit feelings. It's not manly to talk about your feelings. Drink your problems away."

"He doesn't have one friend he can confide in?"

"Not one."

Martinez shook his head in disapproval.

"Does your church offer any type of counseling or help in this matter?"

"Church? I haven't been to church since I was a little girl, and I'm not sure he's ever been."

"Have you talked about seeing a counselor or couples' therapist?"

"I've brought up the idea, but his friends have convinced him it's not-"

Before she could finish her sentence, Joe came barging into the kitchen.

"I never touched her," he screamed.

Martinez stepped toward him and extended his arm.

"You need to stay back, sir, and she never said that you touched her."

"Bologna, I heard her in here crying, trying to play the sympathy card so I would go to jail. Well, I've never laid a hand on her." He focused his eyes on her. "And that witch Sydney has completely turned her against me."

Rachel stood up and looked into his eyes.

"Joe, I stopped talking to her weeks ago. I do not agree with the way she approaches relationships. She has a very cynical way of looking at things."

Dave was standing behind Joe with a hand on his shoulder.

"Let's go back into the living room and finish our conversation."

"I just want to go to work now. I don't start until six, but I can sleep in my car in the parking lot until I start my shift."

Rachel stepped toward her husband and placed a hand on the side of his face.

"Let's just go back to bed and you can rest until you have to leave. I won't say another word this morning."

He pulled away and turned to walk back into the living room without saying a word. Dave followed. She sat back down in the chair and looked down at the floor.

"I just don't know what to do, officer."

They stood on the front lawn and watched as Joe drove away. Dave handed Martinez his notes so that he could write the report.

"What did you and Joe talk about in the living room?"

"I told him he needed to get out while he was still young."

"What? Why would you tell him that?"

"Because he needed to hear it. He can sit here for the next couple of years miserable, getting the police called on him once a week, maybe get arrested once or twice, or he can start fresh."

"Did you ask him what the fight was about today?"

"Joe said she won't get off his case about not doing enough around the house. She's constantly making him feel like he's an inferior man."

"Did he mention the fact that everything went downhill about a year ago when his mother died in a car accident? That for six years before that, they never even kept a beer in the fridge."

"No, he didn't mention that."

"So you automatically jump to divorce without even suggesting counseling."

"Here we go with the counseling."

"It works Dave. I have seen it."

"You are a 28-year-old happily married man, Javier, with a kid on the way. Life is good. You are in a good place because you made the right decision. Not everyone has that kind of luck."

"So, were you unlucky when you met Gina?"

"No, and we're not talking about my marriage."

"Your separated Dave, not divorced. You still have hope of saving your marriage."

"With counseling, right?"

"You trained me for two months. We went to your house to eat lunch frequently, and I saw the way you two acted toward each other. Love with a capital L. It wasn't fake or forced. It was genuine."

Dave cut him off.

"You got all the info you need to write this?"

Javier sighed.

"Every time a conversation gets real Dave you-"

"Javier. Do you have all the info you need?"

"Yeah, I'm good."

Javier shoved the notebook paper in his pocket and started walking to his squad car. Dave turned and walked toward his car. Javier sat in the driver's seat and watched as Dave stood outside the door of his cruiser. He could not tell if he was in pain or adjusting his belt, but Dave was taking his sweet time getting into the car. Finally, Dave got in, fired it up, and drove away. Javier grabbed the mic.

"612, radio."

"Go ahead 612."

"You can show both units clear. No assault and the male half will leave for the night. I'll be writing."

"Copy 612. Both units are clear at 0330 hours."

Javier found a quiet spot in town and parked to write the report. Dave made his way back to the church. He drove by slowly to see if there were any lights on. It was dark, both at the church and the parsonage. He heard that word echo in his head once more. Inoperable. He had some serious thinking to do, and he could not do that half asleep. He pressed the accelerator and headed toward the only church a cop knew. Dunkin Donuts.

Chapter 2

The apartment above the garage was there when they bought the house in 1994. It needed some work, but it reminded them of the cozy little studio apartment they were living in currently. Dave's father, Edward, was a carpenter, so at an early age, he taught Dave some very useful skills. Between Dave's carpentry skills and Gina's decorating sense, they had the place looking exactly like their old apartment in no time. It had a staircase that went up the back of the garage to its own private entrance. Inside there was a queen size bed, a fully functional kitchen with a refrigerator, stove, and sink, and a bathroom complete with toilet, sink, and shower. Guests could visit and be comfortable in their own private space.

Dave started staying over the garage roughly four months ago. This is not what they intended the space for, but their marriage was at a crossroads. He believed they had been drifting apart for the last few months. She knew it was the last couple of years. Dave had become distant from the family. He started missing important events, because of working longer hours and working on his off days. He always claimed that it was to "pad the family bank account," but she knew it was more about him and his wants, then it was about their family's finances. The kids always wondered when dad was going to be home, and if he would make it to their school event to watch. When she tried to talk to him about it, he would get angry and it would always end with him on the couch, or above the garage. She also noticed that after he moved into the apartment, the kids acted out at school and at home. On the chaotic meter of life, it was currently at a 9.5.

Gina sat in the middle of the bed in the dark. Her hands clasped together, and her eyes were closed.

"Lord, please help us. I do not know what is going on with Dave, and he will not talk to me. I love him and just want to be a part of his life again. Please help our family."

She could not hold back the tears any longer. She laid down, hugged her knees, and wept uncontrollably. The stress over the last couple of years had finally taken its toll. The kids were both staying at a friend's house tonight, so she was free to cry as loud and long as she wanted.

2

Gina came to know the Lord almost two years to the day. July 6, 2008, to be exact. She remembered the date, because Dave had spent Friday the 4th partying with his friends, and it carried over through the weekend until the night of Sunday, July 6th. In the past, they had driven north and rented a cabin on Higgins's Lake. It was a nice family friendly lake almost 3 hours away, and it was a great way to spend time together and shed the city for a few days. She had proposed the idea in the winter because the cabins filled up quick. He told her to wait a bit because he was not sure if he had to work or not. Even though she pointed out to him he had enough seniority to take any time off he wanted, he always made an excuse to push it off. When the fourth finally rolled around, he told her he had taken the weekend off to bond with the boys. The argument that ensued was one of their worst fights ever. Ironically, he told her they were going up north to one of the guy's cabins to golf, fish, and just hang out. They left at noon on that Friday. She sat in her room with the door closed, crying. The kids, now 13, were seeing the pattern that was developing. Dad did whatever he wanted, whenever he wanted, and mom cried. The man that they had grown up admiring and loving was now the man that consistently made their mom cry and put everything else before them.

Gina continued to sit in the dark and cry when the phone rang. She wasn't going to answer it, but something inside of her forced her to.

"Hello."

"Hi, Gina?"

"Yes, this is Gina."

"Is everything okay? You sound sad."

She pulled the phone away from her, covered the receiver, and cleared her throat. She recognized the voice as Patty King, one of her friends from work.

"I'm sorry Patty, I just woke up from a little nap."

There was a chuckle on the other end.

"The brief pleasures in life. Hey, I know this is last minute, but would you like to come over for a Fourth of July BBQ tonight?"

"Tonight?"

"Frank swore up and down to me he would not do it this year, but he came home early from work and told me to call some friends, that he was feeling festive," she laughed again. "It's one thirty now, so we were thinking six o'clock. Just bring yourselves. Frank stopped at the grocery store on the way home and bought a ton of hamburgers, hotdogs, brats, potato salad, chips, and much more."

"That's awfully generous of you both. But if we came, I would want to bring something."

"No. Just you, Dave, and the kids."

"Dave had to work..."

"Then just you and the kids. Please come Gina. It will be a lot of fun, and a lot of good food."

She then rattled off the name of several of her friends and co-workers that were coming.

"Okay. We'll be there."

"Excellent. We look forward to seeing all of you."

Gina placed the phone back on the cradle and made her way into the master bathroom, and splashed cold water on her face. She opened the bedroom door to find both of her kids sitting up against the wall on either side of the door. Gina sat down in between them, and they placed their head on her shoulders. She told them they were going to a BBQ.

Marc asked, "Whose house mom?"

"Patty and Frank King."

"Awesome. Justin has the best games."

"Yeah, well, we're not going over there on a beautiful summer day to sit inside and play video games."

She pulled him in tight and kissed the top of his head.

"Is dad gone for the weekend?" Melissa asked.

"Dad had a work thing."

"He always has a work thing."

"I Know."

She pulled her daughter in tighter and placed her chin on top of her head.

"But today we're going to eat some hamburgers and hotdogs and see some fireworks and hang out with some really cool people."

"Cool people...if you say so, mom," Melissa responded.

Gina laughed.

"Well, at least you can hang out with Brenna."

"Yeah, that's cool."

"What's wrong? I thought you liked Brenna."

"I do. That's why I said, 'That's cool.'"

"Okay, okay, you just didn't sound all that excited when you said it."

Melissa just sighed.

"I'm going to go make a dessert for the BBQ, and I want you two to clean your rooms, please."

"Ah mom," they said in unison.

"Don't 'ah mom' me. I'm not raising a couple of hobos. I want these rooms to look like a couple of clean, respectful, and neat young adults occupy them."

A double sigh echoed the hallway before they both stood up and went to their rooms. She smiled and stood up. She walked toward the stairs to make her way to the kitchen when Marc poked his head out of his room.

"Can you make rice crispy treats, please?"

"I don't think that we have any more Rice Krispies left. But I know I just got a box of Fruity Pebbles."

"Yes, even better. Thanks mom."

Before she could answer, he closed the door. She continued toward the kitchen.

3

Frank and Patty King were two of their closest friends. Gina and Patty started working together at the hospital fifteen years ago, and they instantly hit it off. When Gina learned that Patty and her husband, Frank, were close in age to her and Dave, they got together for dinner. During dinner, they also learned that their sons and daughters were very similar in age. The men learned they had a lot in common. They both loved the outdoors, Detroit sports, and a good BBQ. As a bonus, Frank owned his own insurance company, and they went through him for all their insurance needs. Over the years, the families bonded through vacations, dinners, and sporting events. Roughly four years ago, that all seemed to change when Frank and Patty declared they had found the Lord. Gina still saw Patty as the friend she had grown to love, but Dave was having a hard time adjusting. It was right around this time that Gina noticed a change in Dave as well. He started drinking more and hanging out with his work friends a lot. Whenever the King's wanted to go to dinner or hang out, he always had an excuse to miss, so Gina and the kids often went alone. Frank also noticed a change in Dave. Whenever they hung out together, his mind seemed a thousand miles away. When he tried to explain his newfound faith, Dave would change the subject quickly, or find an excuse to leave. Coming to know the Lord had excited Frank, and he was excited to share that with Dave. They hung out less and less until they eventually stopped hanging out altogether. This did not hurt the women's relationship. Patty explained to Gina every detail of their transformation. What it meant to be saved, and how she too could find salvation. Gina explained to Patty that she and Dave were okay and that their life was good. Patty respected that, but gave her an open invitation to attend church with them anytime she wanted to. She also expressed to Gina that she was praying for them daily, and Gina told her she appreciated that. Their relationship remained strong.

4

Gina and the kids made it to the BBQ around six thirty. Frank was manning the grill. There was a lot of smoke, and Patty was setting out the side dishes. She stopped what she was doing and gave her a big hug as she walked up. Marc and Melissa had already found Justin and Brenna and were off doing whatever teenagers do.

"Gina, I told you that you didn't need to bring anything."

"I just whipped up some fruity pebble treats. It was no problem."

"When Frank gets wind of these, they won't last long. You know his sweet tooth."

She smiled.

"I do. He and Dave have that in common."

"They really do," she chuckled. "It's too bad Dave had to work today. Frank really misses seeing him."

She looked down and spoke softly. "I guess duty calls."

"Make sure you take a big plate of food home for the hard-working man."

Gina set the treats down and covered her mouth. She was fighting back the tears. Patty placed her hand on her shoulder and whispered to her. "Let's go into the house."

There were guests spread out over the yard, but the path to the house was clear. The last thing Gina wanted was to bring attention to herself. They made it into the bedroom without so much as a look from other guests. Mainly because everyone was watching Frank try to control the grill flames. Patty closed the door behind them. She directed Gina to a chair and had a seat in the other.

"How can I help Gina? If you just want to sit here in silence, then we will. If you want me to leave and you just want to sit here, then just let me know. You can take all the time you need."

Gina was fighting through the tears. She took a breath and let it out.

"I just don't know what to do anymore, Patty. Dave has gotten so distant. It's like I don't even know him."

Patty didn't say a word, she just placed her hand on Gina's. "He's not working today. He went up north to one of the guy's cabins to 'bond' with the fellas. That was our trip every year. He works so much more. He doesn't want to be home with me or the kids at all."

Patty handed her a tissue, and she took it. She wiped her eyes.

"Is there anything at all that Frank and I can do to help?"

"That's very sweet of you to ask. I wish there was." She paused. "Just maybe, please pray for us?"

"We can definitely do that."

They stood and hugged. Just then, the bedroom door opened, and Frank popped his head in. They both turned and looked at him.

"I'm sorry. I didn't mean to interrupt anything." He was pulling the door closed when he opened it again.

"Just so you know, someone already ate half a pan of your cereal treats."

He closed the door. They looked at each other and laughed.

"Yeah, someone," Patty remarked.

After a little more time passed, they left the room and walked back out into the yard to join the BBQ. Gina and the kids had a great time. She talked with a lot of her co-workers that day. Some she knew, and some she was meeting for the first time. The burgers and hotdogs were actually very good, despite all the smoke that filled the air around Frank and the grill. The fireworks were spectacular and the leftovers plentiful. As she and the kids were leaving, Patty gave her a hug and invited them to go to church with them on Sunday. Gina told her she would think about it and let her know. As she drove home that night, both teenagers slumped back in their seats with their eyes closed. She seriously thought about going for the first time. By the time she pulled into the driveway, she had decided. They were going to church on Sunday with the King's.

On July 6, 2008, Gina and her children walked into the Southridge Church of Christ. A deacon greeted them at the entrance with a warm handshake and a program. The adults sat somewhere in the middle, and they took the kids downstairs to attend a service that was catered for young adults. Patty smiled and looked at Gina.

"I'm so glad that all of you could join us today."

"Thanks for the invite."

"Of course. Frank and I hope that you and the kids will join us for lunch after the service. Every week we go to this all you can eat buffet. They have every kind of food."

"We don't want to intrude on your family time."

"Nonsense. It's no intrusion at all, and the kids, like Frank, will probably love the hot fudge Sunday bar."

"Okay, that sounds great." She smiled. "I'm looking forward to hearing your pastor speak today. You always talk about what great sermons he delivers."

"Gina, I completely forgot that Pastor Roberts and his ministry team are at a theological seminar in Dallas this weekend. We have some visiting pastor from across town. I'm sorry."

"No, that's okay. I'm still glad to be here."

The organist played and the music pastor took his place in front of the podium and asked the people to stand and turn to page 84 in their hymnal. The pianist played *How Great Thou Art*, and the congregation sang. Gina stood there, hymnal in hand, looking around the church. It was a beautifully built. Modern on the outside, with a more traditional cozy atmosphere on the inside. Something you might see in a Norman Rockwell painting. It was spotless and wonderfully decorated, and the choir that sang behind the pastor was in perfect harmony with the congregation. They sang two more songs before the visiting pastor walked over from his seat on the main platform and took the podium.

"Isn't it a great day to be here learning about the Lord?" He said with a big smile as he looked out at them.

"Amen," came the spirited response from those in attendance.

"For those of you who don't know me, I am Pastor William Dunkirk. Faith Bible Church is my home church, but it is my extreme pleasure to be here with you today. Now, you're probably asking yourselves, 'If he's preaching to us, then who is preaching to his congregation?' Well, let's just say that my associate pastor needs to earn his supper this week."

Laughter from the congregation.

"Of course, I'm just joking."

He tilted his head down and looked at them over his glasses. More laughter erupted.

"If you would please turn in your bibles to the book of John chapter ten verse twenty-eight." He paused and gave them a moment to find the verse. Gina didn't have a bible with her, so Patty placed her bible on Gina's lap and smiled at her.

"Frank and I will share his."

"Thanks," she mouthed.

She picked it up and looked at the verse as he read aloud.

"John 10:28 says, 'And I give them eternal life, and they shall never perish; neither shall anyone snatch them out of My hand.'"

He paused and looked out over them.

"Let that verse sink in for a minute."

He closed his eyes and waited a few seconds. "Let's pray." They bowed their heads.

"Father, we come before You today with open minds and open hearts, asking for Your grace and understanding in receiving this message. Teach us, oh Lord, that we might teach others. We ask this in the name of your one and only Son, Jesus. Amen."

"Amen," the congregation echoed.

Pastor Dunkirk broke down the three aspects of that one verse and spoke for forty minutes about its importance to the world. Gina found herself entranced by his words and couldn't believe that he could explain a single verse in such extreme detail, and with such passion. When the pastor finished speaking and the choir sang, she replayed the highlights of his sermon in her head over and over.

"The one true Son of God, Jesus, spoke these words. He said, 'And I give them eternal life.' He died and rose again for you and me. All we must do is accept this extreme gift of grace and He promises us eternal life. Continuing, He says, 'and they shall never perish.' He's telling us that with that acceptance, we will never, ever die. Our bodies on this earth will one day die, but our soul will live on in heaven with Him forever. And just when you didn't think it could get any better folks, he says, 'neither shall anyone snatch them out of My hand.'"

And he made an explosion noise that startled some of the congregation. They met it with laughter followed by him exclaiming, "Yeah, that's right. No one, and I mean no one, can take us away from Him. At that point, Satan has lost the battle and gone down in ultimate defeat. He cannot snatch us out of the Savior's hand."

As the singing concluded and just as the pianist was now playing, Pastor Dunkirk walked up to the podium.

"Please bow your heads."

Everyone bowed their head except Gina. She stared up at the pastor as he prayed.

"Lord in heaven above. We thank you for sending your Son, Jesus, to die on the cross for our salvation. But death did not have power over Him, and he rose on the third day, conquering death forever. He now sits at Your right hand as our advocate. All we have to do is believe in Him and accept Your gift of amazing grace. Father, please be with each member of this congregation today as they go out into the world. Guide them and give them Your grace this week. And we pray this in Jesus' precious name. Amen."

When the service was over, the pews emptied. Patty looked over at Gina.

"Are you ready to get some lunch?"

"Patty, can you go get the kids from downstairs? I'd like to go up and shake the pastor's hand and tell him how much I enjoyed the sermon."

"Absolutely. We'll meet you out by our car. Take your time, there's no rush."

Gina walked toward the front of the church. There was a short line to the left of the pastor. Each person was shaking his hand and saying some kind words about his sermon. She got into line. She did not know why her hands were sweating, and she was nervous. The lined moved quickly toward him, and she noticed she was the last one in line. Gina had second thoughts and took a half step toward her left to get out of line and walk toward the back of the church to go out the front doors. As she stepped, she heard a voice to her right.

"Thank you for coming today."

She looked to see the man in front of her gone and Pastor Dunkirk standing there with an outstretched hand. She took his hand.

"It was a very nice sermon, pastor."

She started to turn and walk away when he asked, "What did you like about it the most?"

She froze. At that moment, it felt like she was back in middle school, waiting to see the principal. She broke down and cried.

"I'm sorry. I didn't mean to put you on the spot..."

"It's okay, pastor...pastor..."

"Just call me Bill." He stated with a sympathetic tone.

He took her hand and guided her to the front row of pews. They sat down and he explained to her the path to salvation. She expressed to him she knew in her heart that she was a sinner saved by His grace. That day Gina Jackson accepted the Lord as her personal savior, and she knew that everything in her life would now be different. She was excited to tell her children, her family, and friends. But what about Dave? What would he think?

5

When Dave got back from his "boys' weekend" it was around eight in the evening. She gave him time to settle in and decompress and then asked to speak to him alone in their bedroom around ten. Marc was in his room playing video games and Melissa was in her room talking on the phone to a friend. They walked into the bedroom, and she closed the door behind them. He sat down on the corner of the bed and ran his hands through his hair, and yawned.

"What's on your mind, babe?"

She took a seat next to him, grabbed his hand, and smiled.

"The kids and I went to church with Patty and Frank today."

"I'll bet that was a real treat." He laughed.

"Dave, I accepted the Lord as my personal savior today."

He turned to look at her.

"You what?"

"I asked Jesus to come into my heart and forgive my sins."

"So, you drank the Kool-Aid. So, does this mean that the kids drank it too?"

"I talked to them about it and told them my decision, and why I made that decision. They asked me if they had to do it too. I told them it's a decision that we all make on our own."

"And they understood that?"

"They're thirteen Dave, not two. Of course, they understood. They both told me they had fun in church, and they would like to go back."

"What do I do now, Gina?"

"What do you mean?"

"You've joined the ranks of the King's, so now I can only assume that you're going to judge me and be on my case all the time to go to church."

"Dave, take a deep breath and look at me."

He let out a sigh. He then turned to face her. "What?"

"Dave, I'm not going to pressure you to do any of that. God gave us the free will to make our own decisions. I decided for my life to trust in Him as my Lord and Savior. I'm new at this and have a lot to learn about being a Christian, and what it entails reading His word daily and praying to strengthen my relationship with Him. But beyond that, I'll have to rely upon Him, the church, and other believers to nurture that relationship."

"Geez, you're already talking like the King's. Believers? Well, just so we're clear, I'm happy with my life and don't intend to change."

"Are you happy with your life, Dave? Because from where I'm sitting, our marriage has been slowly declining over the last two years. All you want to do is work, and when you're not working, all you want to do is hang out with your friends from work."

"Maybe that's because they're the only ones that understand me."

"Dave, I want to understand you. When we were dating and even in the first few years of our marriage, we were an open book for each other. We shared everything with each other, good or bad. Then one day you stopped sharing because you didn't want me to worry about you at work. I got news for you, Dave. When your husbands a cop, you worry every single time he walks out that door if it's the last time you're going to see him. Please trust me again."

"I never stopped trusting you."

She sat beside him and rested her head on his shoulder. He laid his head on hers.

"I love you. I need you. The kids need you. Please, just let me back in."

"I'll do better. I promise. But you're on your own with the Jesus stuff."

"Just let us back in."

He sounded sincere enough that night, so Gina went to sleep with hopes of a new beginning for them. Over time, that hope faded. He made her feel like he was trying at first, but then he fell right back into his old habits and started shutting her out again. Over the next two years, she would continue to build her relationship with the Lord. She would read her bible daily and pray. In every prayer, she would ask the Lord to be with Dave. To keep him safe and bring him back to her and the kids. Gina and the kids would go to church every Sunday with the King's. In the beginning, Dave made excuses why he couldn't go, but as time moved on, his reasons were cruder and colder. Through the church, Gina had made good friends who encouraged her and prayed for God's strength in her life. She joined a small group. Every Tuesday evening at seven, they would get together at someone's house to study the bible and pray together. They served dessert at the end of the meeting, so it gave them a chance to engage in small talk and learn more about each other. While Gina was learning more about God and expanding her friend's circle, Dave continued to stay distant and keep his circle limited. Their lives continued to grow in different directions.

Chapter 3

Dave continued to stare at the ceiling, willing his eyes to close so that he could get some sleep. He looked over at the clock. It was 9:30 a.m. Sleep was one area where he had never had a problem until now. He was normally off at 7:00 a.m., barring any last-minute accidents or runs, changed and in his car by 7:10, and in his bed looking at the inside of his eyelids with the lights out by 7:30. All of that was true today, except for staring at his eyelids. It was his weekend off, but he took overtime tonight and had to be back to work at 7:00 p.m., so he needed to get some sleep.

"I don't understand what's happening. Like clockwork, I'm out by 7:30, six solid hours of sleep, and I'm up at 1:30, ready to go."

Dave took a deep breath in and exhaled slowly. He shifted his position and laid on his side, propping an extra pillow between his legs. He shut his eyes. Ten minutes later, they opened. He clasped his fingers together and rested his head on them. He stared at the ceiling once again, this time focusing on what looked like a small blemish on the paint. That's the last thing he remembered before he fell into a deep sleep.

Dave came riding up in his squad car, lights shining and siren blaring. He slammed on the brakes and the vehicle skidded sideways and came to a stop, placing his tires at the opening of the large hole. Dave jumped out of the car and took in his surroundings. He was at the center of pure chaos. There were cars and houses on fire in every direction he looked. Vehicles were driving into trees, houses, and into other vehicles. People were running all over, some were screaming in pain from the accidents and fire, and others were viciously attacking other people. This was the very definition of chaos. He felt the ground beneath his feet move, and before he could act, his squad car was plummeting into the very hole that was now opening to swallow him. He fell and instinctually crawled away from the hole. As he moved, the ground under him disappeared, and he felt his body drop. He quickly reached out and grabbed onto the edge with both hands. As his body dangled above the hole, he struggled to pull himself up. He tried to fight the urge to look down to see what fate awaited him, but he lost that battle. He looked down, but all he could see was darkness. No light came from the pit. All he could hear was screams. Dave looked over his shoulder and saw person after person falling into the darkness, each one screaming as they fell. He closed his eyes and whispered, "How could this be?" Dave felt a sharp pain shoot through his fingers and hands as he struggled to hang on. He opened his eyes and looked up. There were two dark figures standing there, each standing on one of his hands. They were doing their best to get him to let go, and they were screaming in unison, "STOP FIGHTING, LET GO AND DIE."

"I don't want to die. Leave me alone."

The shouting grew louder, "STOP FIGHTING, LET GO AND DIE."

"No, I won't."

He could feel his fingers grow numb. Dave was slipping. He closed his eyes once again and he could see his wife and children. Dave thought about the last couple of years and the distance that had grown between them. He just wanted to hold them one last time and tell them he loved them. Tears fell from his eyes.

"STOP FIGHTING, LET GO AND DIE."

Just as he opened his eyes and looked up, he saw a third dark figure push the other two. They went falling past him into the darkness, continuing to shout at him. He watched as they disappeared, but he could still hear their far-off cry, "Let go and die." He looked up to see the third dark figure standing over him. Silence. No taunting or shouting. He tried to pull himself up, but he was just too weak. Both hands slipped, and he fell. Just as he lost hope, he felt a hand grab his arm just below the elbow. Instinctively, his hand clamped down on the stranger's forearm. Dangling above the pit, he looked up. The dark figure was lying on the edge, arm extended, holding onto him.

"Who are you?"

The figure did not answer him.

"Who are you I said?"

The figure spoke in a familiar voice.

"You don't need any help because you continue to destroy this life for yourself and others. You are more of an asset to us alive. Vinegar runs through your veins. The pit will consume you soon enough and you will leave a wake of destruction in your path on this earth."

He felt an overwhelming sadness creep into his heart. Was he so self-destructive that he hurt the ones he loved the most? He made a career out of fighting for others. He was the hero here.

"Who are you?" He shouted in anger.

The dark figure leaned forward, and his face was now illuminated. Dave's eyes widened and his heart jumped inside of his chest. "How can this be? It's not possible."

The face staring back at him was his own.

"We'll see you soon David."

As the figure released him and he fell toward the darkness, he tried to scream, but nothing came out. He could only hear the figure's ominous laugh echoing throughout the pit. He closed his eyes and pleaded for someone, anyone, to save him from this fate.

Dave awakened abruptly, sat up, and gasped for air. His breathing felt labored, and he was wet with sweat. He sat there for a moment, trying to get his barring's. Finally, after a while, his breathing returned to normal, and he slowly scanned the room. In through the nose and out through the mouth. His heart stopped racing, and he relaxed. He dropped back onto his pillow. He closed his eyes and exhaled loudly.

"It was only a dream," he whispered to himself. "I had a late coffee. No, that's not it. I've had plenty of those and slept just fine."

He could hear the birds singing louder than usual today outside of his window. He looked over at the clock. It was two thirty. Dave slowly sat up and swung his legs over the side of the bed. He threw on some shorts, a t-shirt, and a pair of red and blue Crocs that Gina got him two Christmas's ago. He laughed as he looked down at the weirdly comfortable foam shoes. As a nurse, Gina swore by them. She even bought him a little charm. It was a police hat. He bent down and ran his fingers over the top of the charm. She was right. These shoes were comfortable. Dave had worn them so much that the bottoms were becoming slick, and he probably needed a new pair. He put on a Detroit Redwings cap he grabbed off the table as he walked toward the door. He exited and jogged down the steps. Neither kid was outside playing, and Gina's car was in the driveway. He walked through the backdoor of the house and into the kitchen. Gina was making lunch, Marc was setting the table, and Melissa was at the fridge grabbing three cans of coke. All three looked up as he entered the kitchen, and he froze in his tracks. He smiled.

"I think I'm looking at a well-oiled late lunch assembly line."

"Dad!" Marc stated with excitement as he put down the bag of chips, walked over to his dad, and gave him a hug.

He put his arms around his son and squeezed.

"What are you, twenty now?"

"Nope. Fifteen."

"Fifteen! Say it isn't so. My little boy is already fifteen. Let me see your face." He held Marc at arms' length and scanned his face. "I think I'm going to have to teach you how to shave soon, son."

Marc rubbed his face and smiled.

"Yep. The beards coming in, dad."

He laughed and rubbed his son's head. Marc turned and grabbed the chips and resumed putting them on the plates.

"Would you like to join us for lunch? I can make another grilled cheese," Gina asked.

"No, I'm just going to have a cup of coffee for now, but thanks."

He looked over at Melissa, who was now standing in front of the fridge holding the cokes.

"Hey sweetheart?"

"Hey dad."

She hurried past him to the table and sat the cokes down.

"Any big plans today?"

"No."

She sat down and opened the can. He took the hint and moved toward the coffeemaker.

"Sit down, Dave. I'll get you some coffee. I already have it ready to go."

Before he could say anything, she pressed the button on the coffeemaker, and it made noises.

"Thanks Gina. No work today?"

"I work six to two now, Dave."

"Oh."

"How do you not know what time your wife works?" Melissa whispered in a cracked voice.

He looked over at her.

"Did you say something, sweetheart?"

She couldn't look up at him because if she did, the waterworks would start, and she wouldn't give him the satisfaction. She didn't answer.

He repeated, "Melissa. Did you say something?"

Keeping her head down and her voice low, she answered, "No, father."

He could feel himself getting angry. This was often his first response now.

"I have to go, Gina. I'll grab some coffee while I'm out."

"If you'll just wait about three minutes, it'll be ready."

He turned and left the kitchen. As he made his way to the back door, he heard Marc yell at his sister, "Nice going, idiot. You made him leave." Melissa retaliated quickly. "That's what he does best these days." He stopped in his tracks and thought about going back in. Dave waited a moment, but the yelling had stopped. He knew what had happened. Gina. She had become a master at putting out the fires he started. She was gentle and loving, and she had a wonderful way of calming the kids down when they got worked up. As he placed his hand on the door to open it and leave, a gust of wind came rushing through the screen door, and the book on the piano to his right caught his eye. The pages fluttered, and the sound they made reminded him of his father reading the newspaper at the kitchen table in the morning before he left for school. He stopped and smiled. It amazed him that something as simple as a sound could transport him back to a time that he would give anything to revisit. Just a couple of more minutes with his father. They didn't even have to talk. He just wanted to look at his father one more time and give him a big hug before he left for school. He closed his eyes and smiled. When he opened them, he realized that the wind had died down, and the pages had stopped shuffling. He pushed the door open but paused once again to look down at the book that was making so much noise. It had opened to a page that had sentences underlined. He picked it up. He recognized it was the bible that the Kings had given Gina as a birthday present last year. All the writing on this page was red, and she had underlined some in blue ink. He whispered them aloud as he read.

"'Ask and it will be given to you; seek and you will find; knock and the door will be opened to you. For everyone who asks receives; the one who seeks finds; and to the one who knocks, the door will be opened.'"

He stared at it for a moment. "Matthew 7:7-8."

Dave didn't know where she had it opened to originally, so he just closed it and sat it back down on the piano. He looked back at the kitchen and even thought about going back in to have that coffee, but decided against it. Dave walked out the backdoor and headed back to his room above the garage.

2

He climbed the stairs back up to the apartment. Once inside, he surveyed the room and located his cell phone charging on the kitchen counter. He walked over and took it off the charger and then had a seat at the kitchen table. He checked the phone to see if he had any missed calls. There was only one. He looked at the number and sighed. He pressed the message button and then held the phone up to his ear.

"Dave, this is Dr. Peyton. I need you to please call me so we can go over some treatments that might help you to..." There was a knock at the door. He exited out of the message.

"Yes."

Gina asked, "Dave, can I come in?"

"Absolutely, come on in."

She came into the room, and he noticed she was holding a cup of coffee.

"It seemed like a waste to throw out a good pot of coffee."

She walked over and handed him the cup. He accepted it with a smile. "Thank you, Gina."

He took a sip, closed his eyes, and hummed his praise. She almost laughed out loud, but she held it in. It might seem kind of silly to the average person, but these were the moments she missed.

"I don't think anyone enjoys coffee more than you, Dave."

They looked into each other's eyes and shared a laugh.

"You know, you're probably right."

She walked toward the door to leave. She opened it and then turned to look at him.

"Will you be joining us for dinner today? It's at six."

"Unfortunately, I picked up overtime tonight from 6:00 p.m. to 6:00 a.m."

"Okay. Be safe."

She closed the door behind her as she left. He placed the coffee on the table, hugged his stomach, and then doubled over in pain. He had been holding it in since she walked into the room. His eyes closed and his jaw clinched. He reframed from any sound because he wasn't sure if she was out of hearing distance yet. The pain lasted longer this time. His body finally relaxed.

Gina walked back into the kitchen and sat down at the table. She looked at Marc.

"What do you have planned for the day?"

"Not sure. I was just going to see where the day takes me."

She smiled. "That seems like a nice summer plan."

Melissa chimed in. "Are you and dad getting a divorce?"

She turned her attention to her daughter. "Why would you ask me that, Melissa?"

"Because we have a right to know."

Marc looked at his mom. An anxious expression appeared on his face.

"You're not, are you mom?"

"Nobody has talked about a divorce. Your dad and I are just going through a rough patch, that's all."

Melissa stood and looked at her mom. There were tears in her eyes and pain in her voice.

"A rough patch! A rough patch! He doesn't live in the house anymore. We never see you two together, and he couldn't care less about us."

Marc leaped up from the table and pointed an angry finger at his sister as he shouted.

"That's not true! He loves us! Take it back!"

"Marc, he barely even knows we exist."

Marc looked at his mother. She could see the look of desperation in his eyes. He needed her support.

"Melissa, that is enough!" She shouted at her daughter.

"Is everyone in this family blind but me!" she shouted back at Gina.

Gina just looked down at the floor. The tears were freely flowing from Melissa's eyes now. She threw her napkin down on her plate and turned to leave the room.

"Melissa honey please." Gina grabbed her daughter's hand. "Finish your lunch."

"I'm not hungry anymore. Can I go to my room, please?"

Gina knew her daughter needed to be alone. She needed a good cry to release all the feelings that were running through her. It was an emotion that she herself had experienced a lot. She released Melissa's hand.

"Yes, you can go to your room."

"Thank you." She placed her hand on her mom's shoulder. "They taught us that Jesus heals mom. Well, what about our family? Where's our healing?"

She looked up and smiled at her daughter.

"I don't know, sweetie. I wish I had some answers for you. Just please don't give up yet."

Melissa headed for her room.

Chapter 4

Pastor William Dunkirk stood at the podium, jotting down notes on the piece of paper in front of him. It's Friday, and he still isn't sure which message to deliver to the congregation on Sunday. His wife, Marsha, interrupts his thoughts.

"I'm going to take Brenda and Seth to get ice cream. Do you care to join us?"

"No, thank you, my love. I'm still trying to figure out what I'm doing for Sunday's service."

"It's not like you to have such a hard time deciding."

"I just can't seem to settle on what I want to talk about."

"Maybe you just need a break. Come and get some ice cream with us."

He smiled.

"I wish I could, but you know how I am. I need to figure this out now. If I go get ice cream, you know the only thing I'll be thinking about is this, and it's very unfair to the ice cream."

She threw her head back and belted out one of those infectious, wonderful heart-warming laughs. It was a great laugh. No matter what mood he was in, when he heard it, it always made him smile.

"Mom, come on."

He looked over to see his ten-year-old son, Seth, standing in front of the platform, arms crossed and a very impatient look on his face.

"Your father and I are talking, Seth. Now go run around and play or something and we'll leave in a few minutes."

"Okay, but Brenda's getting pretty impatient."

Brenda was sitting three rows behind him, completely submerged in reading a book. She didn't even look up when he mentioned her name.

"Yeah, I'm sure Brenda is the impatient one," Marsha shot back at him with a smile.

He rolled his eyes and plopped down in the first row. He crossed his arms and dropped his head to stare at the floor.

"Is there anything I can do to help?" She asked.

"Yeah, take Seth for ice cream, so I can think."

She gave him a playful shove and then a kiss. "Okay then, we are off."

He smiled at her and then turned his attention toward the kids. "Be good for your mom and don't give her any problems."

Seth jumped up from his seat.

"We won't dad."

Brenda still did not look up from her book.

He stared down at his daughter. "I think you could leave and come back, and she would never even know you were gone."

Marsha smiled. "Don't work that brain too hard. Whatever sermon you decide to give will be great."

"Thanks."

They kissed, and then she and the kids left. He took a seat in the pew on the platform. He bowed his head.

"Father in heaven, please give me clarity. Give me the wisdom to know how to serve You best. Guide me in my everyday walk with You and show me my path always. Thank you, Lord."

Bill stood and walked over to the podium. He was flipping through the pages of his bible when his cell phone chimed, so he took the phone out of his pocket and looked at the text. He had always had very good eyesight. Never a problem reading anything far or near. That is until February 28th of this year. His 45th birthday. He started noticing that his eyes were having problems adjusting when he read his bible, a restaurant menu, or anything where the font was twelve or below. His friends had told him that this would happen. Some said it happened to them once they turned forty, but he didn't believe them. They told him all he needed to get was a set of "Readers." He did just that. He found readers went from the number one to the number four. It was a minor consolation that he only needed number one, but how soon until he needed number four? He took his very stylish black wire-framed readers out of his front breast pocket and put them on.

"Pastor Dunkirk, this is Art. I knocked on your door, but no one answered, so I left the book you loaned me on the small table on the porch. Thank you, it was very inspiring. Again, I knocked, and no one answered. Have a good day."

He pressed buttons to reply to Art, but his fingers kept hitting two at once. It took him literally ten minutes to type the phrase, "You're welcome, Art, I'm glad you enjoyed ot." Send. He noticed the mistake after he hit the send button. "Ot." He laughed. Bill put the phone back in his pocket and stood in front of the podium once more. He hummed and then whispered the words to the song; *Jesus paid it all.*

"All to Him I owe. Sin had left a crimson stain. You washed it white as snow."

He Smiled from ear to ear at that very thought. The truest of love. The most amazing grace. He sat back down in the pew, removed his glasses, and put them back into his front pocket. Bill thought about Marsha and the kids, and about how grateful and blessed he was. He stared off into the distance and became lost in his thoughts.

The Dunkirk family lineage had a rich history of ministers and was a very interesting history altogether. William Dunkirk Jr. was a fifth-generation pastor, but the history in the family didn't start with a minister. It started with his Four-time Great Grandfather, Thomas Dunkirk, Sr. Thomas was born in March 1815 in the state of Virginia. His father was a blacksmith, so Thomas followed in his footsteps. In 1819, the family moved to the state of Illinois, which had just become a state on December 3, 1818. There, Thomas was homeschooled by his mother in the morning, and apprenticed under his father in the afternoon. By the time Thomas was twenty in 1835, he was married with a child on the way. He had taken over the family business after a man had killed his father in a drunken bar fight the year before. This was the reason Thomas swore to never let a drop of alcohol touch his lips. A promise he kept until his death at seventy-five in 1890. Thomas Dunkirk Sr was known for two important events. The first came on June 27, 1835, when his son, William's three-time great grandfather, Thomas Dunkirk Jr. was born, and the second came in the summer of 1845. Thomas Sr was working at his shop shoeing horses, when a tall, awkward looking man approached him. He needed the blacksmith's help in fixing the wheel for his wagon. The iron tire had broken, and he wanted to see if the blacksmith could weld it back together. Thomas Sr. told him he could, so they shook on a price and agreed that the tall man could pick it up in two days. The man returned two days later, but explained to him he no longer needed the wheel. The man still was prepared to honor the agreement and pay him for the work. Thomas was inspired by the man's integrity, and they made a deal that Thomas would keep the newly rebuilt wheel. Thomas, like all Dunkirk men, kept a journal that he faithfully wrote in daily. In his journal many years later, in 1865, Thomas wrote, April 15, 1865; "Today, a man that I admired and respected died. I want to understand the reasons, but I expect I never will. He was a kind soul. We spoke a few times over the years, and each encounter was a pleasant one. He loved three things dearly. Christ, his fellow man, and his country. I suspect Abraham is in the presence of our Lord now. God rest his soul." End entry. That wagon wheel hangs on the wall in William's home office. It's a little worse for the wear, but its significance is priceless.

On June 27, 1835, Thomas Dunkirk Jr was born to Thomas and Mary. He was the first of four children. In the summer of 1852, Thomas noticed that his then 17-year-old son was not interested in the family trade. Since the age of ten, Thomas Jr. would read his bible and pray faithfully, day and night. He wanted to encourage his son in his pursuit of more knowledge, so he raised enough money to send his son to stay with his brother in Clapham, London. His brother, John, was a businessman who did well for himself, but he was also a devout Christian. He felt John could guide him in the faith in ways that he could not. In London, Thomas Jr. started attending Binfield Chapel. He quickly befriended an up-and-coming pastor by the name of William Booth. For the next two years, Booth would mentor him. Thomas Jr. wrote in his journal, July 22, 1853; "William is one of the most dynamic speakers of the faith that I have ever heard. He truly loves God, and he has some radical ideas that might reach people in a whole new way. I know now what I must do in this life. Preach. Preach until my last breath." End entry. Thomas Jr. returned home in the fall of 1854. He started working at the local church, where he became the associate pastor. In the fall of 1855, Thomas Dunkirk Jr. became the first in a line of five generations of minsters.

On July 19, 1865, John Dunkirk was born to Thomas and Elizabeth. He was the first of two children; his sister Ann was born two years after him, but died from tuberculosis before she turned one. John was a journeyman of sorts for the first thirty-five years of his life. He tried many professions in looking for his calling. Being a pastor really didn't interest him. John worked at a printing company for a few months, but that didn't interest him either. He worked on a loading dock for a while. He quit that too. In finding who he was, he met Anna Frederick and fell in love. They were married in 1890 and moved to New York to look for a better life. Anna took odd jobs sewing and cooking to help them get by while he continued to look. John accepted Christ as his savior by the age of seven, but he often felt lost when he tried to read the bible, and even when he prayed. He knew his father wanted him to follow in his footsteps, but he never truly felt the calling to be a minister. A discouraged John wrote in his journal, February 10, 1880; "I do not know my purpose in this life. I hunger to find my path, but I have no one leading me there. My father is a great man of faith, and I cannot live up to his image. What am I to do?" End Entry. John was searching for something, but he didn't know what. In 1899, nine years after his marriage to Anna, the couple still did not have a child. They had been trying for some time now but were finding it difficult. John took to reading the bible again and praying daily. He found that this time, he understood it more clearly. He prayed for clarity. In February 1899, the country experienced one of its worst winters. John and Anna were enjoying some soup for supper one evening when there was a knock at the door. John opened the door to see New York's Governor Roosevelt standing there. He would write in his journal later, "He is a very jovial fellow. He spoke with complete authority in his voice, and merely asked if he could come in and get warm before he continued his journey home. His horse simply would not pull his carriage any longer and needed a rest. After putting the horse in the barn and giving him some hay, I returned to the kitchen to finish my meal. Anna had given Governor Roosevelt some soup as well. He was kind and respectful. He was passionate about his politics, and freely given with advice. When Anna went into the living room to sew, I confided to him I was a man lost. He simply looked at me and said, 'It doesn't matter how you serve God in this life. Pick something and serve him well.' He took a silver coin out of his pocket and placed it on the table. I tried to get him to take it back, but he would not. He thanked us and was on his way. It was an honor to have him in our home." After that interaction, John devoted his time to studying the word of God. In January 1900, John became the pastor of the local Baptist church, and in March of that same year, God blessed them with their first and only child, John Dunkirk Jr.

On March 16, 1900, John Dunkirk Jr was born to John and Anna. He was an only child. John Jr. knew what he wanted to do at a very early age. Growing up, he took his religious studies seriously, and he and his father would often have heated debates over the meaning of certain passages. This started when John Jr. was only fifteen years of age. John Sr. was very proud of his son, and he knew the debates helped to fuel his son's passion for the Lord. His faith only grew with each passing year, and he decided he would leave New York to go to Chicago to attend the Moody Bible Institute in the fall of 1919. He had already planned to live at the institute and work when he wasn't in class. The summer before he left, he worked at his father's church, doing odd jobs like cleaning and taking care of the landscaping. It was in July of that year that he had his brush with history. John usually made it to the church around 8:00 a.m. or so. His father was generous with his start times, but on one morning he was having trouble sleeping. He decided he would go in early so he could finish early. John made it to the church around 6:30 a.m. and grabbed his equipment. He needed to mow the lawn and trim some bushes out front. As he came around the corner with his equipment, he noticed a man sitting on the bench in front of the church. He also noticed that the sun was a beautiful red ball coming over the horizon, and that's what the man seemed to stare at. He walked over and sat on the bench next to him. They both sat there in silence for the next five minutes while the red ball completed its assent into the sky. Just before he could say anything, the man spoke.

"Only God could create something that beautiful."

John, Smiled. "I completely agree."

The man turned to him and offered his hand.

"George."

He took his hand, and they shook. George had a firm grip.

"John."

"It's nice to meet you, John. Do you work at the church?"

"Yes, sir. I'm working here until I leave for Moody in the fall. My father is the pastor here."

"Chicago. A great town. So, you're going to follow in your old man's footsteps, are you?"

"Yes, sir. I love the Lord with all my heart."

"Make sure you don't lose that love, son. He's the only one you'll ever be able to fully trust."

"I know, sir. Are you a pastor?"

George laughed. It was a gruff laugh.

"No son, I'm not. God had other plans for me."

He reached into the inside pocket of his suit coat and pulled out two cigars. He looked at John. "You want one?"

"No sir, I'm fine, thank you."

"You don't mind if I have one, do you?"

"No, sir."

He lit the cigar and took a big draw. He held it for what seemed like an eternity and then exhaled respectfully away from John. George then reached into the inside pocket on the other side of his coat and pulled out a book.

"You ever read this?"

He handed the book to John. *The Pilgrim's Progress by John Bunyan.*

"No, sir. I've been meaning to get around to it."

"Keep it. I have several copies."

"No sir, I wouldn't want to take your book."

"You're not taking it. I'm giving it to you."

"Thank you, sir."

He drew in another long puff and then exhaled.

"Well, I should go John. It was very nice to meet you." He smiled. "Read that book."

"I will, and it was nice meeting you."

George gave him a firm pat on the shoulder as he stood and walked away. John opened the front cover of the book. On the first page in black ink was G. Patton. He would write in his journal the exact conversation that they had, and even added, July 12, 1919; "George had a commanding presence about him I cannot explain. The sunrise was beautiful, and it was nice to see someone else enjoy it as much as I did." He read the book that summer before he left for Moody in the fall. It turned out to be one of his favorite books. He was hoping to run across George again before he left so that he could thank him, but he never did. He read the book many times over the years, and they found it on his nightstand under his journal when he passed away in 1985. After reading the journal entry and seeing the book, his son William kept the two together in a locked trunk for safekeeping. The book now sits in a nice display case on William Dunkirk Jr.'s hutch, which is located just below the wagon wheel.

On April 12, 1940, William Dunkirk was born to John and Mary. He was the fifth of five children, the only boy, and according to his mother, a surprising present from God. William grew up loving two things above all others. God and baseball. It was tough being a Cubs fan in the fifties as a young boy, but William didn't care. He watched them as often as he could, and his father scored tickets whenever he could, and they would make the trip to Wrigley to see them live. There was one game in William's life that he will never forget. It was July 19, 1954, and the Cubs were hosting the Brooklyn Dodgers. His father, John, had gotten good seats to the game that day, right behind the Cub's dugout. A 14-year-old William waved to the Cub's players every time they came off the field and shouted, "Good inning boys, good inning." After the fifth inning, a lot of the players smiled at him and waved back or gave him the thumbs up. When they got home that afternoon from the game, John would tell Mary that he had never in life seen William's smile so big. The game continued, and they watched as their Cub's beat the Dodgers, 9-4. At the end of the game, when the crowd filed out, William ran to the corner of the dugout and stood in the first row. As the players exited the field into the dugout, he shouted to each one, "Great game, boys, great game." It was then that a young Chicago player made his way over to where William was standing. He was holding a baseball in his hand and motioned for someone in the dugout to give him a pen. He stood in front of William with the ball in one hand and the pen in the other, writing and talking to the young fan. Later that day, William would pen in his journal, July 19,1954; "Mr. Banks came over to me and started talking to me. He told me that the entire team felt inspired by me cheering them on that day. He signed a baseball and gave it to me right there and then he shook my hand and told me to, 'Stay positive, kid.' I will keep this ball as long as I live. Even though Ernie didn't have a great day at the plate, 0 for 3, he shined in the field." End entry. That signed ball hadn't made its way to William Jr.'s house yet. William Sr. kept it in a glass case on his desk. William continued his love of baseball, but at 19 years of age, he registered at Moody and followed in his father's footsteps. Ironically enough, he met his future wife, Margaret, outside of Wrigley in 1958. She also loved the game. After he graduated from Moody, they got married and started a family. They moved to Wisconsin for a few years, but Chicago eventually called them back home in 1970, where William has been at the same church now for 40 years.

William Dunkirk Jr. has not had his brush with history yet. If someone in a family meets one famous person in their lifetime, it's talked about for generations, but his family has gone above and beyond that distinction. Two presidents, a famous evangelist, a beloved wartime hero, and a baseball legend.

Boom! A loud noise startled him. He looked around slowly, trying to catch his bearings. He realized he was still sitting in the pew near the podium, then something on the floor caught his eye. His bible, one of the larger and heavier ones in this world, had slipped off the podium and onto the floor. His first thought was, maybe it lay open on a particular page, and God was showing him what to teach on Sunday. He focused and looked down again. No such luck. It was completely closed. He laughed. He stood and walked over to the good book. Bill bent down, picked it up, and wiped off the cover. He was thinking about how his friend, Art, in his text, told him twice that he had knocked on his door and no one answered. Bill laughed and continued wiping it off before he sat it back on the podium. He stared at it for a few seconds, and then a smile ran all the way across his face. He had his message for Sunday.

"Thanks Art," he whispered as he opened the bible and got to work.

2

Dave sat on the row machine, looking down at his shoes. He had over an hour before his shift started. He hated lying to Gina, but after the scene with his daughter in the kitchen this morning, dinner with all of them was the last thing on his mind. Dave honestly didn't even know why he continued to work out. Did it really matter if he benched, or curled, or biked, or whatever? In his mind, it just did. When he worked out, he pushed everything else out of his mind and concentrated on the task at hand. But right now, he was finding it hard to get motivated. He kept replaying the scene in his mind, how he felt like a stranger in his own house. A house that he once called home.

"I need help to rebuild my house," he whispered under his breath.

He failed to see that another officer had come into the weight room to workout.

"What's that Dave?"

He looked up to see Officer Mike Shawnee standing there.

"What?" was his reply.

"I thought you said something to me. Something about rebuilding."

"Oh no, I'm sorry. I was just thinking out loud."

"What are you rebuilding?" Mike asked as he threw some weights on the barbell.

"Just something at home," he responded. Dave had become a master at changing conversations when he didn't want to talk about the subject at hand. He knew the key to doing it seamlessly was to put focus on the other person. "That charm around your neck. What does it mean?"

"That's Saint Michael. He's the guardian Angel of police officers."

"Says who?"

"Says, my mother. She's a devout catholic. Something about good over evil."

"Have you researched it?"

"What for? She told me that's what it is, and that's what it is. Are you calling my mother a liar, Dave?"

Mike was a 250-pound monster who lived in the gym. A meathead, some would say. His biceps were bigger than his brains, but he was a nice guy and Dave liked him.

"Easy big fella. I was just inquiring. So, are you catholic?"

"I guess. I got confirmed and everything when I was twelve."

"So, do you practice it?"

"I go to church on Christmas and Easter."

"Why those two days?"

"I don't know, because that's what you're supposed to do."

"Says who?"

"My mom."

"Does your mom only go to church on Christmas and Easter?"

"My mom goes to mass two to three times a week, maybe more, I don't know. What's with all the questions about my mom, Dave? You interested?"

"No, I'm married. I was just wondering about the charm you wear."

"It's Saint Michael, like I said, the protector of cops."

"Well, do you..."

Mike let out a sigh and turned to look at him.

"Can I just work out now? Please."

Dave laughed.

"Sorry, pal. Have at it."

Mike put his earphones in, turned his music on, and started benching a small bus. Dave rowed.

3

Javier Martinez was in the kitchen listening to Ray Charles, cooking dinner for his wife, Rita. At 28, he considered himself not just the world's best law enforcement officer, but also a culinary master. He held a wooden spoon to his lips like a microphone and serenaded his bride.

"Hit the road Jack, and don't you come back no more no more no more no more, hit the road Jack and don't you come back no more, what you say..."

"I get a meal and entertainment tonight. Did I win the lotto?"

He stopped singing, bent down, and gave her a kiss.

"Yes," he whispered in her ear.

She laughed. "What's got you in such a good mood this evening, my love?"

"It's my weekend off, and I get three solid days to spend with my beautiful wife, who is pregnant with our first little bundle of joy." He kissed her again. "Tonight, we are having chicken parmigiana with spaghetti, a Caesar salad, and a side of cheesy garlic bread. A homemade tiramisu cake will follow this meal."

She grabbed his face and pulled him in for a big kiss. As their faces separated, their noses touched.

"You really know the way to a pregnant girl's heart."

"I know what my baby likes." He glided over to the stove and checked on the food. "We have about twenty minutes left before your culinary journey begins."

"Did you make two of those tiramisus by chance?"

"I know you're hungry but, wow!"

She looked at him with one eyebrow raised and no smile. He laughed, and he threw up his hands in a show of surrender.

"I'm sorry. It was a poor attempt at humor. Yes, I made two of them. One for us," and he used air quotes as he said, us, "and one for the church bake sale."

"Good and thank you."

He walked back over to the stove and resumed cooking. *My Girl*, started playing, so he hummed along, occasionally mouthing the words. She smiled as he moved his hips to the beat and did a little twirl. He turned to see her staring.

"Are you digging my moves back there?"

"You know I am."

He turned and offered his hand to her. She accepted and stood. He pulled her in close and cradled her in his arms. The two of them slow danced to the music as he hummed. They separated briefly as he spun her away, but then reconnected as she twirled back in. They laughed. The song ended, and he gently kissed her cheek. He placed his hand on her stomach and his smile grew wider.

"How are you feeling today?"

"Today's a good day. No sickness or nausea."

"I'm glad."

She returned to her seat, and he opened the oven. The aroma of garlic bread permeated throughout the kitchen. It smelled amazing. He continued to cook, and she grabbed a magazine off the table and flipped through it. A few minutes of silence passed between before she asked, "How's Dave doing?"

He chuckled. "What made you think of Dave?"

"I'm looking at this article about mentoring, and I haven't heard you talk about him in a while."

"Dave is Dave."

She looked up at him.

"I don't know what that means."

"He's just spiraling deeper and deeper in his attitude. Do you know we went on a domestic together last night, and he told the man to get out of the marriage?"

"He didn't."

"He did. You could tell the wife still really cared about her husband. She was concerned about what he was going through, and Dave just looked past all of that and told him to end the marriage."

"Oh, my gosh. Poor Dave."

"I know, right...wait. Poor Dave?"

"He's obviously going through something right now."

"Yeah. A crisis where he gives out terrible advice."

"Javier, you know Dave better than that. I remember when you started at that department, and he was your training officer. He was always encouraging you when you needed it. Over the years, you two have become close. You partner together whenever you have the chance, and our families have had dinner together frequently."

"I've been there six years, babe. We did that for the first four. How many times have we had dinner with Gina and kids over the past two years?"

She thought for a moment.

"I guess maybe a hand full of times."

"Three times."

"See, you obviously care about him. What's happened over the years to distance your relationship?"

"He just stopped talking to me. It wasn't gradual. It just happened overnight."

"Have you tried to talk to him about it?"

"No. Men, especially cops, really don't deal with feelings that much."

"Javier Alberto Martinez, Jr."

Oh no. She used his full name.

"What?"

"You are not like that."

"I know."

"Can you pinpoint what changed?"

"Yeah, I have a pretty good idea. Two years ago, he started hanging around a certain group at the PD. All they do is party and work. They wrap their identity up in their job."

"Dave is a family man."

"He used to be. He just stopped. No rhythm, no reason. Just stopped one day."

"Is it some type of mid-life crisis?"

"I don't know, babe. He replaced talking about Gina and the kids, and every sentence started out, 'I drank too much on my days off.' Whenever I asked him about his family, he just changed the subject to one of his nights out with the gang stories."

"Did he lose someone close to him? Did something alter who he was?"

At that moment, he realized he hadn't been a loyal friend. He just accepted the fact that things were different now. He smiled at her.

"I don't know, but if he'll talk to me about it, I'll try to talk to him soon. Okay?"

"Okay. I'll go set the table."

"It's already set. Just go have a seat and I'll bring everything out."

"You're so good to me."

"You're my rock babe."

She left the kitchen and went into the dining room. He prepared the plates when he paused for a moment to reflect on the early years.

April 10, 2004, Javier walked into the roll call room, excited but nervous. He was just out of the academy and starting his first day at the PD. He found a table and put his gear on it. Dave walked up to him, smiled, and shook his hand as he introduced himself.

"I'm Dave, rook. I'll be your field training officer."

"Javier, sir."

He had never really seen himself as shy, but he felt intimidated and overwhelmed at that moment. Dave could tell how nervous he was when he shook his hand. Very sweaty and clammy.

"Relax Javier. My job here is to make sure that you succeed. You've already leaped the first hurdle by passing the academy."

"Thank you, sir."

"Call me Dave. We are going to get to know each other pretty well over the next several weeks."

"Okay. Thank you, Dave."

Dave was a great FTO. He taught him a lot. It wasn't all just police lingo, tactics, and safety, although Dave really helped him in these areas, but it was about a lot of other areas of life. He taught him how to be a better person. It's not just about the ticket or the arrest. These are real people they're dealing with who have actual problems, and sometimes it's okay to give them a break. He remembers one particular traffic stop they performed during his first month on the job. They were watching a traffic light at an intersection when a beat up, rusted out old Buick came through the light about a second too late. They pulled the car over a little way down the road, and Dave approached the driver's side of the car to speak with the driver. Javier approached on the passenger's side of the vehicle. He observed the driver was unkempt, whose clothes were dirty, torn in places, and a bit too small for his frame. The inside of his car suggested he was living in it, and even with the window up, he could smell the offensive odors emitting from within. Dave received the driver's information, and they walked back to the patrol vehicle. Dave handed him the information and told him to run the driver through the computer. Javier did as he was told and observed that the driver had just recently gotten his license back. He had a large history of tickets and arrests, but currently his license was valid, and he had no outstanding warrants. Javier showed Dave the computer screen. He remembers being completely shocked when Dave looked at him and stated, "Alright rook, let's go cut him loose."

"Cut him loose?"

"Yeah. Do you think he should get a ticket?"

"I do."

"Okay, make your case, counselor. You tell me why he should get a ticket, and then I'll tell you why he shouldn't, and then leave the decision up to you. Sound good?"

"Okay, where do I start? He ran the red light, and he has a crazy poor driving record. I rest my case."

"That's it?"

"That's enough, isn't it?"

"Ordinarily yes."

"What makes this case any different? They told us in the academy that you have to have your mind made up before you approach that car, if you're going to give someone a ticket or not."

"The academy teaches a lot of good stuff, but not everything that is said is what I deem as gospel."

"Where is the flaw in the logic?"

"People."

"People?"

"Yes, people. Sometimes we must take into consideration the human element. For example. This gentleman that we just stopped for running the red light. He apologized for his driving and owned up to the fact that his driving record in the past is atrocious."

"So that gets him out of a ticket?"

"Let me finish, rook. He also told me that to this point, his life has been one big screw up. For the last fifteen years, he has been through a divorce, the death of both his parents, a substance abuse problem, and terrible decisions in his friends. He told me he ran into a former friend and neighbor about a year ago, and they assisted him in getting his life together. For the last eight months, he has been clean. He sold everything he has to pay off his debt, which includes fines and fees to all courts, and he received his license back three weeks ago. Two weeks ago, he interviewed and got a job as a janitor. He's on the way to work now and stated that he knew the light would be close, but he didn't want to be late."

"What did this friend or neighbor do to help him out?"

"I asked the same question. He said that he got him into church. The church helped him get back on his feet, and even got him this job because one parishioner had a friend who needed a cleaning guy. When you showed me that his license was now valid, something inside me just said to give this guy a break. So, here we are. What say you, Officer Martinez?"

"I say give him his stuff back, so he isn't late."

Dave smiled at him. It wasn't a smirk or a fake smile, but a genuine smile that was warm and comforting. He can remember Dave walking back up to the car and giving the driver back his information. The driver shook Dave's hand. When Dave got back in the car, that same smile was still on his face.

"I've never seen someone so grateful."

"I hope things continue to get better for him."

"Rook, we all need a break sometime. Life is hard. You take the brief victories when you can get them. Who knows? Maybe he'll look back on this moment when he helps somebody and pays it forward. That would be nice if that could be contagious."

It was one of several traffic stops with Dave that he wouldn't forget. Dave was great at what he did. He knew the laws and traffic codes of Michigan front and back. Dave told him that a good cop knows these things, but an effective cop knows them inside and out. Javier had written a notebook full of Daveisms. For the next four years, they would become good friends and partners on the road whenever they had a chance. They used to do things outside of work together. Their families did too. But the last two years had been different. Javier noticed Dave distanced himself from him and his own family. He was worried about him.

"Javier, is the food ready?" Rita shouted from the dining room.

His thoughts shifted immediately back to the meal he was preparing, and that his young, beautiful pregnant wife was hungry.

"It is my love. I am on the way."

Javier gathered both plates and stacked them on his left arm like an experienced waiter. He grabbed the garlic bread with his right hand and headed into the dining room. He set everything down on the table. She smiled and took in a deep breath.

"Everything looks so good and smells so wonderful."

"I'm glad. I will say grace and..."

He stopped mid-sentence and focused on the wall behind Rita.

"Javier, are you okay?"

He smiled. "I am. I just have to straighten the sign behind you."

She turned to see the sign that his mother had bought them for the house. It was a tad crooked. She made fun of him daily for obsessing about the pictures, signs, or paintings that were hanging around the house. He saw everything as crooked, even when it was straight. She giggled.

"Why are you laughing? It's just a little crooked."

"I know it is."

He smirked as he walked by her. He tilted the sign to the right, then to the left, and then finally back a little to the right. Joshua 24:15 "...But as for me and my house, we will serve the Lord."

"There. Perfect." He stood back and admired his handy work. "I love that verse."

"I do too. Now come and eat."

He made double time toward the table. He walked up behind her and put his arms around her and squeezed. Javier kissed her on top of the head.

He let go and returned to his seat. They both bowed their heads and closed their eyes.

"Father, we thank you so much for Your love and grace, and for Your son Jesus, who died for our salvation. We thank you for the many blessings you have given us, and for the strength you give us each day. Please bless this food for our body. In Jesus' name, amen."

Chapter 5

Saturday—July 2, 2010

Dave looked at his watch. It was 3:13 a.m. He took the top off his coffee so that it could cool down a bit and took a sip. He looked at his watch again. Still 3:13 a.m. He pulled out his phone and looked at it. No calls, but the blue message light was still blinking at the top of the screen. He stared at it. He knew exactly what was in that message. Doctor Peyton spoke of treatment, but there was no treatment. The only thing he could do now was sit back and wait for death. It was coming for him. He thought about Pastor Dunkirk, and his invitation to attend church on Sunday. His parents never really talked about God or heaven. He caught bits and pieces from the TV or a stray friend here and there, but the only god that lived in their household was hard work. He picked up the carpentry trade from his father at an early age. Edward worked a lot of odd jobs until he opened his own business in 1972. The business lasted 31 years until his death in 2003. His dad preached about hard work, family, and respect for others. Edward modeled all three values until the day he died. His mother was a homemaker. She was a very loving stay at home mom. When he started going to school full time, she worked at the local daycare to make a little money and pass the time, but she was always home when he got home from school. She never spoke of God or religion either. She agreed with his father's principles, and that's what they lived by. Over the years, his mother went back to school and got an associate degree. She started working at the family business, doing secretarial duties, filling out invoices and attending to payroll. After Edward died in 2003, Sharon sold the business and lived off the nice little nest egg her husband left her. She eventually moved to Florida near her sister in 2007 and took a part-time job working for a local accounting firm. Just to pass the time. They talked on the phone from time to time, but she mentioned nothing about church, even though his aunt was very involved in the church. He expected her to call him one day and tell him about the same revelation Gina had two years ago. But to date, nothing. You live, you die, and that's it. Worm food. He took another sip of coffee. His phone rang. Dave looked at the number. He didn't recognize it. He pressed the green button to answer.

"Hello."

A recording.

"We show your automobile warranty is about to expire, if you would like to..."

He pressed the red button to hang up.

"Vultures," he whispered under his breath. "It's..." He looked at his watch again. 3:15 a.m. Two minutes had passed. Two lousy minutes. He tapped on the face of the watch. "We are in slow motion tonight." He put the phone back in his pocket and took another sip of coffee.

"Let's take a drive around and see what we can come up with."

He placed the lid back on his coffee and set it in the holder. He shifted into drive and pulled out onto the road. The radio had been busy earlier in the night. Domestic's, bar fights and a few other hot runs, but for the last forty minutes, nothing. He enjoyed down time like every other cop, but when it was busy, that's when the time flew by. He continued to drive, sip his coffee, and listen to his classic rock station. In his travels, he drove in front of Faith Bible Church. He did a lap through a nearby neighborhood, but then he did a U-turn and headed back toward the church. He pulled off the road and sat in front. The same spot he was sitting when he met Pastor Dunkirk last night. He surveyed the area. No lights on in the church, and no light on in the parsonage. He took his last sip of coffee. He shifted into drive to head back to DD for a refill when the pain hit. It was a searing pain that started in the upper abdomen area. He literally thought someone was driving a hot poker through him. He kept his foot firmly on the brake and gripped the steering wheel so tight he thought he was going to break it off.

"Please help me."

He didn't know who he was talking to or why he even said it, but after a few seconds, the pain finally subsided. Dave released his grip on the steering wheel and caught his breath. He placed his hand on his forehead and when he pulled it away, wet with sweat. He grabbed a napkin from the glove-box and wiped the sweat away. Soaked. He expected to see blood on the napkin, but it was just sweat. That was how intense the pain had been. He had to be bleeding from somewhere. The radio sprung to life.

"616 and 610."

He was still in a fog.

The dispatcher repeated, "616 and 610."

He grabbed the mic.

"616."

Officer Rogers responded, "610."

"Both units make 1412 Acacia Street. The homeowner reports seeing someone walking around in her backyard, and she lost sight of them when she grabbed her phone to call the police. She fears they may try to break into a window at the back of the house."

"616 copy," he responded.

"610 en route."

He was going to have to hustle to get there. The city was only twenty square miles, but the address was on the opposite end of town, and he was almost seven miles outside of his zone. Seventeen miles to get there and he figured that the straitlaced, never venture away from your zone, Rogers was three or four miles away from there. He slammed the shifter into drive and pressed the pedal. Dave sent Rogers a message from his computer and told him he was about ten minutes out. He sped toward the address. A short time later, he turned onto Acacia Street. He killed his headlights and went dark when he was a block away. He pulled up to Roger's squad car, who was sitting down the street with the lights off. Rogers looked over, gave him a nod, and let dispatch know the units were out.

"610 radio, you can show units out on Acacia."

"Copy 610."

They rolled down the street until they were a couple of houses away. They exited their cars and approached the house from different direction. Everything appeared normal in the front and on either side of the house. Dave rounded the corner on the west side of the home and observed a figure in dark-colored pants and a dark hoodie at the back window on the east side of the house. Rogers came around the corner at that same moment and the suspect saw him. He turned and ran toward the back of the yard. Dave ran after him and shouted.

"Stop. Police."

The figure disregarded his command. He got to the back fence, went over it like a deer, and kept running through the next yard. Dave leaped the fence and gave chase. They continued through the yards, hopping fences when needed, with Dave continuing to give the command for the suspect to stop. Three blocks over on Dover Street, as the suspect rounded a corner, he failed to see the tricycle in the residence's driveway. He hit it in stride and went down into the front yard. Dave came around the corner a short time later and grabbed the suspect as they tried to get up and continue running. He took them to the ground with a straight arm bar takedown, an academy favorite, and cuffed them up. As the suspect lay face down on the ground next to him, Dave sat there, trying to catch his breath. Throughout the pursuit, Rogers radioed dispatch that they were on foot pursuing a suspect. He gave out directions as best he could for being way behind them, and other patrol units came flooding into the area. Minutes later, Rogers came running around the corner and saw that Dave had the suspect in custody.

"610 radio. The suspect is in custody."

He stopped and placed his hands on his knees, trying to catch his breath.

"Copy 610. Your location?"

He looked over at Dave, and Dave was staring at him, smiling.

"You want to chime in here, Jackson?"

Dave turned, looked at the address on the house, and calmly responded to dispatch.

"616 radio. The location we're in front of is 28552 Dover."

"Copy 616. Status?"

He laughed as he watched Rogers, still trying to catch his breath.

"We're secure radio, maybe a little tired."

"Copy 616."

A squad car with its lights on came blaring up in front of the house. Dave got to his feet and helped up the hooded figure. He turned them around and took the hood off.

"You gotta be kidding me. Kurtis, what are you doing?"

"I was trying to see my girlfriend, Officer Jackson."

"Why did you run?"

"It just felt like the thing to do."

Rogers straightened up, looked over at Dave, and rolled his eyes.

"Come on, kid, we could have shot you."

"Judging from the way you're breathing, you couldn't even get your gun out of the holster without breaking a sweat."

Rogers walked toward him when Dave stepped in.

"I got him Jack."

Julie Stanwick had exited the cruiser and came running up.

"You guys, okay?"

Dave responded, "We're good, Julie. Can you give us a ride back to our vehicles?"

"My pleasure."

They loaded up in her car, Rogers in front, and Dave and Kurtis in the back.

Kurtis looked at Dave. "Who called you?"

"The homeowner, who is probably the mother of the girl you're stalking. She found it odd that someone was in her backyard trying to get into her house at three in the morning."

"I'm not stalking anyone. She's, my girlfriend."

"Who is your girlfriend?"

"Her name is Amy Howard. We go to school together. We started seeing each other a few weeks ago."

"Now I know you're lying. You don't go to school half the time."

"So, by your logic, half the time I do."

Dave laughed on the inside without showing him on the outside. He thought that was funny. Kurtis was a clever kid, despite his upbringing.

"Okay, funny man. We're going back to the house to see if mom wants to press charges."

"She won't."

"Oh, and whys that?"

"She likes me."

"If she likes you so much, then why didn't you just use the front door?"

"It's three in the morning. I didn't know if she liked me that much."

"Then you probably shouldn't be trying to see her daughter at 3:00 a.m. I'm sure your intentions were less than gentlemanly."

"Well, yeah."

They pulled up to the house and Rogers let them out. Dave escorted Kurtis to the front door and knocked. The door opened and a short, overweight woman in a bathrobe stood in front of them. She looked at Kurtis.

"Kurtis, what are you doing?"

"I wanted to see if Amy was home."

"She's in her room sleeping. Why are you poking around here at 3:00 a.m.?"

"I wanted to see Amy."

"Well, that's not going to happen tonight, and after this little stunt, maybe not at all again."

Dave chimed in.

"Do you want to press charges, Mrs. Howard?"

"Miss Howard, but you can call me Ashley."

Dave smiled. "Do you want to press charges, Ashley?"

She looked Kurtis up and down before answering.

"No, I guess not. But if it happens again, then I will."

Kurtis responded, "It won't."

"Okay then maim, I mean Ashley, have a good night."

"Thank you, Officer," She looked at his name tag, "Jackson."

He nodded at her, and she closed the door. He escorted Kurtis back to his squad car.

"You can take the cuffs off now, Officer Jackson."

"I haven't decided if I want to press charges yet."

"For what?"

"Obstructing a police investigation, or maybe disobeying a lawful order. Both are misdemeanors, but still applicable here. Not even to mention the curfew violation."

"Seriously Officer Jackson? Come on, man."

Dave laughed as he walked over to take the cuffs off. Even though Kurtis was only fifteen, they had already developed quit the professional relationship.

2

Their relationship started when Kurtis was ten. He got called to the Seven Eleven over on Proctor Street on a shop lifting complaint. When he got to the store, Kurtis was sitting in the backroom with one employee eating the honey bun that he had stolen. The store advised him they didn't want to press charges, but they couldn't get a hold of an adult to come pick him up. So, they called the police. He asked Kurtis where his parents were, and he told him that his mom was probably at home "Sleeping one off," and that he did not have a dad. Dave had him get in his patrol car and took him home. They pulled up to the house and Dave immediately noticed that the lawn hadn't been cut in a while. The bushes and trees remained overgrown, and they littered the front porch with debris. They made their way through all the mess and knocked on the door. There was no answer. He knocked harder. Still no answer. There was a place for the doorbell, but it was just an empty socket now. He looked down at Kurtis. Kurtis grabbed the knob and turned. It opened. They entered the house and Dave observed the inside was no better taken care of than the outside. Dave yelled, "Hello. Police." He waited a few moments for an answer. Kurtis's mom emerged from the kitchen.

"Why are you in my house?" she asked as she slurred.

"Is this your son?" He pointed to Kurtis.

"It is. What's the little peach done now?"

"Shoplifted."

She looked at her son.

"Didn't I teach you better, boy? You keep getting caught."

"Sorry momma."

She looked at Dave.

"Is he under arrest? What's the deal?"

Dave looked around the house and observed the absolute train wreck it was.

"No, he's not under arrest."

She swayed as she stood and her eyes were bloodshot, even though they were half open. She was high as a kite. He walked past her into the kitchen. She didn't respond. He looked in the cupboards and then in the refrigerator. There was enough food that CPS wouldn't take him from the home. Dave walked back by her and into the living room.

"You can't go through my house."

She reached over and grabbed one of the dining room's chairs so she wouldn't fall. She poured herself into the chair and tried to focus on Dave.

"I'm going to take your son to the station, but I'll have him back in about an hour."

"Fine."

She put her head on the table. He looked down at Kurtis. There were tears falling from his eyes, and he lowered his head.

"I was just hungry."

He placed his hand on Kurtis's shoulder.

"Come with me, son."

They walked out of the house, and he told Kurtis to get in the front seat of the car. They pulled out of the driveway and headed toward the main road. Kurtis looked at the floor as Dave drove. Ten minutes later he heard, "Welcome to McDonalds can I take your order?" He looked over at Dave.

"What do you want, kid?"

He didn't answer.

"Oaky. We'll have a two-cheeseburger meal, medium with a coke."

"No onions please."

He smiled at Kurtis.

"No onions on that, please. And we'll have a quarter pounder with cheese meal, medium with a coke, and no onions on that either, please." He looked over at Kurtis. "I guess we have something in common."

"Will that be all?"

"I think we'll have two hot fudge sundaes. That'll do it."

They pulled up to the window, Dave paid for the food, and they headed back out onto the road. A few minutes later, they were at a local park sitting at a picnic table, enjoying their food. Dave asked him about his home life. He told Dave that when his mom wasn't high or drunk, she was good to him. He never knew his father, who left before he was even born. His mom had countless relationships over the years with different men, and currently she was seeing the landlord of the house they were at now. He only came by once in a great while for the rent, which he didn't know how his mom paid because the only money they had was from welfare. Dave couldn't believe that a ten-year-old knew what welfare was. Kurtis told him he liked school, but he didn't get to go as much as he wanted because he had to take care of his mother most mornings. Kurtis scarfed down his meal like it was the first time he had ever eaten. Dave gave him the rest of his fries, and then they enjoyed their sundaes. The brain freezes kept Kurtis from eating the Sunday too fast, and they both laughed at the faces he made each time one hit him. When they finished eating, Dave took him back home and dropped him off.

"Kurtis, stealing is never okay. You're lucky they didn't want to prosecute you and put you in jail."

"I'm sorry. I won't do it again."

"Okay, be good."

Kurtis got out of the car and shut the door. He walked toward the front door and then turned.

"Thanks for the McDonalds, Officer Jackson."

"Your welcome Kurtis."

He watched as he disappeared behind the wall of junk and into the house. He pulled out of the driveway and headed back out on patrol. His heart went out to Kurtis. Before he could dwell on it too long, dispatch gave him another run. He never forgot about their first encounter. He really wouldn't have a chance to. For the next five years, he saw Kurtis a lot. From shoplifting, to fights, to welfare checks, to you name it. He watched as Kurtis fell deeper and deeper into the rabbit hole. He started hanging around other delinquents, some that were into more than petty crimes. The kind that incurred weapons and drug charges. He did his best to counsel Kurtis and remain somewhat of a positive presence in his life, but he feared that the darker side of life was winning.

3

Kurtis rubbed his wrists and watched as Dave put away his handcuffs.

"So, I take it you're not going to press charges?"

Dave smiled.

"Not this time, Kurtis. Stop running around at all hours of the night. How's your mom doing?"

"She's the same. The guy she's been going out with for the last two months is cool. He works and is nice to me. He's older though."

"Like how old?"

"I think he's like 65."

"Yeah, that's older." Dave scratched his chin and shook his head. Shannon was only 31, so he knew exactly what a 65-year-old man wanted from her. "Is there food in the fridge and cabinets?"

"Yeah," Kurtis smiled, "I'm not going hungry."

It was nice to see him smile. He smiled less and less these days. Life had beaten him down so badly at 15. Dave often spoke of Kurtis and his situation to Gina.

"That's good to hear. Get in and I'll give you a ride home."

"Can I just walk?"

"No, you're 15, it's," he looked at his watch, "It's almost four in the morning, and you're a good mile and a half from your house."

"So."

"Don't get smart with me, son. Get in the car."

Kurtis walked around to the back door, opened it, and got it. He slammed the door, crossed his arms, and pouted like a two-year-old. Dave opened his door and got in.

"Why did you get in the backseat?"

"If someone sees me in the front, I'll be labeled a snitch. Only snitches sit in the front seat."

"Who is going to see you at four in the morning?"

"Someone will. Someone always sees."

This was new. He didn't like this new attitude toward him. Even though their dealings had mostly been in a professional capacity, he saw Kurtis as a kid who still had a good chance to rebound, despite his circumstances.

"I was thinking about getting a coffee at DD. You want a donut and a milk or juice?"

"No. Take me home first."

"Okay."

Dave drove the mile and a half, searching for something else to talk about. Something that might give him some relief. Just before he pulled in front of the house, he gave it one last shot.

"So, how are you doing in school?"

"Fine," came the disgruntled quick response.

"What's your favorite sub..."

"Officer Jackson, please, can I go? I really don't want anyone to see me in this car."

Dave got out of the car and walked back to his door. He opened it and Kurtis quickly exited and headed for the front door without saying a word to him. Dave watched as he disappeared into the house. He noticed the car in the driveway. It wasn't new, but it looked to be in good shape, even taken care of. It must be the new boyfriend's ride. He noted the license plate. Dave scanned the neighborhood. He got back into the car and drove down the street. When he was roughly four hundred feet away, he parked along the curb, cut the lights, and faced the house. He sat there for maybe fifteen minutes when he saw Kurtis exit the front door, hit the sidewalk, and turn in his direction. He gave the overheads a quick flip, just enough to flash the red and blue lights for half a second. Kurtis stopped in his tracks. Threw his head back and looked at the sky and mouthed something that probably wasn't G rated. He turned around and walked back through the front yard. It was an angry walk. He only knew this because his kids had the same walk when they were mad at him and wanted him to know it. Kurtis disappeared back into the house. He laughed, waited five more minutes, and then shifted the car into drive. Hopefully that will keep him in for the night. He headed for double D. He pulled into the parking lot and noticed that the only other car there was a bright blue Ford escort wagon. Keith was working tonight. He got out of his car and walked to the front door. As he opened the door, he observed a bumper sticker on the front bumper that he had never noticed before. It read, "…It is finished! — John 19:30." He walked into the lobby and up to the counter. The smell was incredible. Keith came out of the back and flashed him a smile.

"Dave, what's up, my friend?"

Dave smiled back.

"Just living the dream, Keith, living the dream."

They both laughed and shook hands. Keith turned, grabbed a medium coffee cup, and filled it. He turned and gave it to Dave.

"Just this, or do you have a sweet tooth this morning?"

"Just the coffee is fine, Keith."

He took a sip, closed his eyes, and gave an approving hum. "That's good stuff."

Keith laughed, "You want to come work here when you retire?"

Dave smiled, "I just might."

"Are you going to sit in and hang for a bit, or do you have to get back out there?"

"I got to go back out, but before I do, can you tell me what 'It is finished' means?"

"It is finished?" Keith scratched his head. "Oh, you mean the bumper sticker? It's the final three words that Christ said on the cross before He died."

"So, what was finished?"

"You know, He died for our sins."

He turned and made another pot of coffee.

"What sins?"

"The sins of the world. Have you never been to church?"

He was a little embarrassed and decided that this was probably a good time to leave.

"Thanks for the coffee. I gotta run, Keith."

"No problem, Dave, have a good morning."

He walked out to his patrol car and got in. He looked at his watch. It was 4:50 a.m.

"Two hours to go."

He reached into his front pocket to pull out his notepad. As he pulled it out, a business card fell out and onto the floor under the gas pedal. He sighed as he placed his coffee in the holder and opened the door. Dave bent down and grabbed the card. He stood and looked at it. It was Pastor Dunkirk's business card. He sat back down and closed the door. He held the card up and studied it for a bit. Dave placed the card back into his pocket, removed the coffee from the holder, and took a sip. He reached down, grabbed his phone, and sent a text to an officer that works on his platoon, Brad Tucker.

"Brad, you still want that midnight overtime shift tonight? If you do, it's yours, and if not, no big deal." He went to push the send button, but stopped. He sat there for another few seconds, thinking about it. Finally, his thumb hit the send button. He probably wouldn't hear from Brad right away. It was 5:00 a.m. so he figured he would get his answer when he woke up. That would give him enough time to resend the offer if he needed to. His phone chimed. It was Brad. "I'll take it. Thanks Dave." And just like that, he was now free Saturday night, going into Sunday morning. He pulled Pastor Dunkirk's card from his pocket again and looked at it. Service started at 10:30 a.m.

Chapter 6

Dave's eyes popped open. He rolled onto his back and stretched. He looked up and saw the same ceiling he had been staring at for the last four months. Even though it was the apartment above the garage that he and Gina restored together, it was still a foreign ceiling to wake up to. It wasn't the ceiling of the bedroom that they had shared for the last sixteen years. He missed rolling over and putting his arms around her. Feeling her warm body against his, and the smell of her hair. She had used the same shampoo since they started dating, and he had gotten used to that wonderful, intoxicating scent. Her scent. He looked over at the clock. It was 1:30 p.m. At least that was back to normal. He rubbed his eyes. He froze for a moment to listen, and he could faintly hear a guitar playing. Dave stood up and got dressed. He opened the door and stopped in the doorway. He could hear the song more clearly now. It was one of his favorites. *Wish you were here*, by Pink Floyd. He smiled as he descended the steps. Dave walked through the backyard and around to the side of the house. He stopped and stood at the corner of the house and watched as Marc sat at the picnic table and strummed the song. Marc was looking down at the instrument and didn't notice his father standing there. He played it to perfection. The sound coming from that guitar wasn't the band playing; it was his son. He remembered when Marc asked to learn. He was only eight, but he was very persistent. Dave taught him a few chords and discovered he was natural. But, like anything, Marc eventually found other interests and the guitar just collected dust in the corner of his room. Dave himself hadn't played regularly in about two years, but the sounds took him back in time and put a smile on his face. Marc finally looked up and saw Dave standing there. He muted the strings with his palm and stopped strumming.

"Hey dad."

"Hey Marc."

"How long have you been standing there?"

"Long enough to hear that you've really been practicing."

He was holding Dave's acoustic guitar. The guitar had been a gift from his father on his 11th birthday. It was a beautifully crafted woodgrain,

Ibanez. Dave loved that guitar, and throughout the years, he took impeccable care of it. The last time he saw it was about six months ago.

"Sorry I used your guitar, dad. I broke the string on mine and haven't been to the store yet to get new ones. Mom said it was okay."

"It's fine Marc. You play it well."

He smiled, "Thanks. I've been practicing every day for at least two hours a day. I really like it."

"What changed? I haven't heard you play guitar since you were thirteen."

"One day I just picked it up again. I've been taking regular lessons for about six months now. Mom bought me a new electric guitar. It's a Fender, and I just bought a used acoustic maybe a month ago. With my allowance and some help from mom. I was playing it yesterday and the E string broke."

"It's always good to have an extra set on hand when those things happen. I'm surprised I didn't have a set lying around somewhere."

"We couldn't find any. Anyway, if I get a new set, maybe we can play together."

"Yeah, that would be great."

He walked over and sat down on the bench next to Marc. Marc handed him the guitar.

"Play something, dad."

"It's been a while. I'm a little rusty."

"That's okay. Take your time. Strum a little and get familiar with it again."

He laughed and then strummed. It wasn't quite like riding a bike, but with some work, he could get back to where he once was. He played for thirty minutes without realizing it and only stopped when Gina came outside to get Marc.

"Marc, come and get ready to go. We're meeting the Kings at the park in forty minutes."

He looked up, and she smiled at him.

Marc replied, "Okay mom. Just a few more minutes, please?"

She gave him a look he was all too familiar with. The look that all moms have mastered. It said, now. He looked at his dad and shrugged.

"See you dad."

"See you, buddy."

He gave his mom a hug as he passed her and then continued into the house. She walked over and sat next to Dave.

"It's been a bit since I've heard you play."

"Yeah. I almost forgot what it was like."

"Why did you stop playing?"

"I don't know. Work. Not enough time. Who knows?"

She knew. Work had a part in it, but it was more the fact that he just stopped coming into the house.

"You know, Dave, you can still have dinner with your family, or breakfast, or just come and hang out with us sometime."

He looked down at the ground. "I know."

There was an awkward silence between them for a few seconds. She changed the subject.

"You ought to come in and listen to Melissa play the piano sometime. She's gotten fantastic at it."

"She was good from the moment she started taking lessons. That girl is as smart as they come. I love the boy, but I think she has him in intelligence."

"Dave."

She playfully pushed his shoulder and laughed.

"I'm just saying. She got your brains and beauty, and that poor kid got saddled with my ugly mug and caveman mentality."

They shared a laugh together.

"You're very handsome, and even though you have caveman tendencies sometimes, you also have some good brain cells, too."

"You've got some work to do in the complement department."

"Sorry, I just couldn't resist. You gave me a softball, and well, you know?"

"Yeah," he chuckled, "I know."

She missed this. She prayed vigorously day and night for these moments to return, but to no avail. Gina pushed all the emotions that she was experiencing in that moment deep, because she knew she had to, or the tears would start flowing. She cleared her throat.

"I know you have to work overtime tonight, but we're going to the water park with the Kings if you want to join us."

"I have a few things to do, but I might meet you there later if that's okay?"

She didn't expect this. She was prepared for a solid, no. It caught her off guard.

"Yeah, that would be great."

"Okay. I think I'm just going to strum for a few more minutes."

"Okay Dave. Hopefully, we'll see you there."

He was strumming Layla when he stopped and looked at her.

"Maybe don't mention to the kids I might show up, because if I can't make it I..."

She cut him off because that was the initial answer she expected.

"I won't, but hopefully you can."

He just smiled at her and went back to playing. Dave strummed for a few more minutes until he heard the car doors slamming shut in the driveway. He stopped and listened to the car's engine humming as Gina backed up and then shifted into drive. He took a few more minutes to do some finger picking, and then he took the guitar back into the house and placed it on the stand in their bedroom. Well, her bedroom now. He walked out of the room and toward the back door. As he passed by the piano, he couldn't resist looking down at it to see if Gina's bible was open. He looked down to see that it was closed. He took a step toward the door, but stopped and looked back down. There was a piece of paper protruding out of the top of the pages with some handwriting on it. He opened it. The paper was resting in the book of John. He opened the piece of paper. Written at the top and underlined was the phrase, "Prayer Requests." He scanned down to see only one word written. "Dave." This made him angry. He slapped the bible off the piano, and it landed open on the bench.

"So now I'm a charity case? I need prayer?" He stated out loud.

At that moment, the pain in his stomach leaped up and grabbed him. His legs buckled, and he dropped to his knees, clutching his midsection. His eyes slammed shut, his jaw clinched, and a searing pain took over his body. He stayed kneeling on the floor for what seemed like an eternity, but was only a few minutes. The pain finally subsided, and he could open his eyes. Everything was a little blurry at first. He exhaled and wiped the sweat from his brow. As he kneeled there, he lifted his head to see that he was kneeling directly in front of the piano bench. He looked up to see the bible that he had thrown there opened to the book of John. He read the passage that was underlined. 'For God so loved the world that He gave His only begotten Son, that whoever believes in Him should not perish but have everlasting life.' He stood and picked the bible up off the bench. He looked around for the piece of paper and found it sitting in the middle of the room. Dave walked over, picked it up and placed it back into the bible. He set the book back in its original spot and then walked out the back door.

2

Dave was a runner. He knew that most people didn't understand why somebody would want to just run and run for no reason, but he didn't care. He loved to do it. The bulk of those who ran would tell you they do it because it's an excellent source of exercise, or because they're training for a 5K. Dave just loved to lace up the sneakers and run. He ran three to four times a week, and anywhere from two to four miles at a time, depending on how he felt. His favorite part of running was when he got that cramp in his side and his lungs felt so overwhelmed that they were going to burst, but they didn't. Something else happened. His lungs suddenly yielded to him. Instead of breaking down and stopping, they recharged and exploded. He felt as though he had unlimited oxygen, and he could run to the end of the world and back. That's why he ran. These days, though, he wondered how many more runs he had in him. He hadn't experienced any of those intense abdominal pains while running yet, but he knew it was only a matter of time. He headed out. Three miles in, and he looked at his watch. It was 3:00 p.m.

"I can go take a shower and still make it there for a couple hours," he whispered under his breath.

He ran another two miles before he found himself back at the house. He was bent over in the driveway, hands on his knees, catching his breath, when a nice-looking newer Cadillac pulled into the driveway. Dave straightened up, clasped his hands behind his head and started walking toward the Caddy. The door opened and Doctor Peyton emerged. He was tall and thin with a head full of silver hair, which really made his blue eyes pop, or so Dave was told by his mother. His smile was big and genuine, and he was flashing it at Dave as he walked toward him.

"David."

"Dr. Peyton," Dave responded as he shook the doctor's hand.

The kind doctor also had a very firm handshake.

"Dave, do you have a second to talk?"

"Sure, doc. Let's go into the house."

They turned and walked toward the main house. Once they settled in, Dave handed the doctor a cup of coffee and then sat down across from him.

"Thanks Dave." He took a sip. "Say, that's a good cup of Joe."

He smiled. "We take pride in our coffee around here."

"Dave, we need to talk about your..."

"Doc, I know what you're going to say, but nothing we do will make a difference. I am going to die."

"There have been advancements in medicine that..."

"Doc, please, let's not kid ourselves. You don't have to sugarcoat things for me just because you're a family friend."

The doctor dropped his head and looked at the floor as if it magically held the answer to this situation. It did not. He knew it, and Dave knew it. Dave was going to die.

"I brought you into this world, Dave."

The Doc and Dave's father were born in the same year, a month apart, and they grew up together in the same neighborhood. They graduated from high school together, and he was the best man at Edward and Sharon's wedding. He also gave the eulogy at Edward's funeral. It was one of the toughest days of his life watching them put his best friend in the ground in 2003 at the young age of 61. A car accident that should have never happened. He looked at Dave and tried to speak, but nothing came out. Dave leaned in and whispered.

"I know, doc. It's not your fault. It's nobody's fault."

"It's not fair."

"Since when is life fair? You know that, James. In our line of work, we see the worst. Sometimes there's an explanation, and sometimes there isn't. No one is exempt from the ails of the world. No one."

"We can make you more comfortable..."

"No! That's just a way of saying that I can be a vegetable for the time I have left." He sipped his coffee. "By the way, how much time is that, doc?"

"I wish I could tell you for sure, but I don't know."

"Do we have a ballpark?"

The doctor sipped his coffee and once again looked at the floor.

"The answers aren't down their doc. It's okay. I know it isn't a long time. I just need to know."

"6 months on the high end."

Dave smiled at the doctor.

"Well then, I hope it's the high end."

"Dave, have you and Gina talked about what..."

"No! Gina doesn't know, and I'll tell her in my time."

This revelation noticeably shocked doctor Peyton.

"You haven't told her? Dave, this is something..."

He held up his hand, and the doctor stopped.

"We have been going through some problems over the last few months and I didn't want to throw in there. Oh, and by the way, I'm dying. I will tell her soon, I promise. I also have a lot of loose ends to tie up. In the meantime, doc, is there anything at all you can give me for the pain?"

"How severe has the pain gotten, and how often is it occurring?"

"It feels like a mule kicked me in the stomach, and it happens every couple of days."

He pulled out a prescription pad from his coat and wrote on it, paused, and then put it back into his pocket.

"I'll call in the prescription to a pharmacy I use near my office. They know me well there and will fill it for you ASAP."

"Thanks, doc. What are you giving me?"

"It's a 30mg morphine extended-release capsule. It's used for severe cases where normal pain meds won't work. I'll give you a month-to-month supply to help you manage the pain. There might come a time when this doesn't even work, and when that time comes, Dave..."

"I know, I know, that's how I'll know my clock is running out."

The doc cleared his throat and got out, "yeah."

"Thanks, doc."

"Take them every twelve hours with food, or you'll get sick."

"Got it, every twelve with food."

"If you haven't told Gina, I'm assuming you haven't told your mother."

"I haven't, but I will. Just please keep this between us, doc."

Peyton managed a smile and slapped him on the knee.

"I don't have a choice. It's in the job description. But Dave, they deserve to know."

"I know, and they will. I promise."

The doctor took his last sip of coffee and placed the mug on his knee. Dave reached for the mug and the doctor handed it to him.

"Another cup doc?"

"No, I have to get going."

"Just let me put these in the kitchen and I'll walk you out."

Dave took the mugs and placed them in the kitchen sink. He met the doctor at the front door, and they walked out of the house together.

"I'm going to call that prescription in as soon as I leave here, David. You can pick it up around seven or eight tonight."

"Thanks doc, I really appreciate it."

"Say hello to the family for me."

He extended his hand, and Dave took it. The doctor pulled him in close and wrapped his left arm around him. Dave reciprocated. They stood like that for a few seconds; the doctor squeezing so hard Dave thought he was going to pop. They separated, and the doctor spun away from him and walked toward his car. He stood there watching until the doc's car was no longer in sight. Dave walked back into the house and locked everything up before he went to the apartment.

3

Dave stood in the shower and let the hot water run down his body. It usually helped with any muscle aches or pains that he was having. Not the deep stomach pains. Those were a different beast. He thought about the conversation he had just had with Dr. Peyton. "Six months on the high end," echoed through his head. In a weird way, Dave thought hearing it might give him some sense of peace. He was wrong. His clock now had a number. He was forty-two tears old, and he wouldn't live to see forty-three. Without warning, his knees buckled, and he had to catch himself by grabbing onto whatever he could to keep from falling. He steadied himself and took a deep breath in and then out. His grandfather died at 65. Massive heart attack. His father at 61. A drunk driver. He was only 42. Was his family lineage cursed? At that moment, he wasn't thinking about himself anymore. His thoughts shifted to Marc and Melissa. How old will they be? Younger than 42? Twenty something? He closed his eyes and shouted out loud.

"God no, please."

He opened his eyes. Where did that come from? Those words. That name. He turned off the shower and stood there for another second. He finally grabbed his towel and dried off. Dave wrapped the towel around his waist and walked into the kitchen. He filled a glass with water, and he took a seat at the table. His phone rang. He looked at the caller ID. It was Patterson. He answered.

"Patty, what's up, my brother?"

"I see you gave up the overtime shift tonight. You want to meet the rest of the shift at Joey's for a few rounds?"

Word traveled fast.

"What time?"

"9ish to whenever, which usually means two," he laughed.

"I should be able to meet you guys for a couple."

"Sweet. We'll see you there."

"Sounds good Patty. See you tonight."

He hung up the phone and placed it on the table. Patterson was a 30-year-old twice divorced hormone bomb that had no filter with women. He always wondered where it went wrong for Patterson. He was a good looking, well built, educated cop who just made terrible relationship decisions. It was all about the physical appearance. His former wives and girlfriends, and there were many, might have had a brain cell between them. He was a lost soul looking for a lifeboat. Dave threw on some shorts and a t-shirt, wrapped his swim shorts in a beach towel and slipped into his crocs as he headed out the door and to the water park.

4

He parked the car and made his way to the entrance. As he walked through the cars in the lot, he couldn't help but notice that people were very irresponsible. Maybe it was the cop in him, but he didn't think that it was smart to leave purses, GPS's, iPads, and a host of other larceny related items on the front seat. It was an invitation that said, "please damage my car by breaking into it and stealing my stuff." Maybe they kept their vehicle from getting damaged by leaving the door unlocked. Very smart of them. He finally got to the entrance, paid the fee, and walked in. Dave walked through the crowd looking for his family. Too many teens wore bathing suits that were extremely inappropriate for their age. He was hoping his daughter didn't fall into that category. That thought only crossed his mind for a second because he remembered who her mother was. He was just about to call Gina when he heard a familiar voice.

"Dave, you made it."

He turned to see Frank King standing there. Frank was wearing some blue swimming trunks that ended just above the knees and a white t-shirt with blue writing that read, "Jesus Saves."

"Hey Frank, how are you?"

"I'm good buddy. How have you been? I haven't seen you for a while."

They shook hands.

"I've been working a lot of overtime lately."

"Gina mentioned that. I'm glad you could make it out today. Follow me. We're right over here."

They walked for a couple of minutes until they made it to where the group was. Gina was talking to Patty when she looked up and saw them walking toward her. She stopped talking mid-sentence, got up from her chair, and walked up to Dave. She gave him a hug.

"The kids will be so excited to see you here."

"Well, Marc anyway."

"Dave, Melissa loves you. She's fifteen and going through a lot of changes, and our current situation is very confusing. She needs her dad to give her a hug and tell her he loves her."

"Where is she?"

"Her and Brenna went to the snack bar. It's right over there," she pointed at it.

"Okay, I guess I'll go say hi."

He handed her the beach towel. Dave made his way toward his daughter, and he felt nervous, like she wouldn't want him there. He didn't like this feeling. She was his little girl. He had always been there for her, well, not recently, but he didn't feel that two years should trump the previous thirteen. She had her back turned to him when he walked up. He breathed a sigh of relief; Gina had picked out an appropriate bathing suit. He tapped her on the shoulder. She turned.

"Hi sweetie, how are..."

She wrapped her arms around him and squeezed.

"Dad, you're here."

He wrapped his arms around her, closed his eyes, and placed his chin on her head. Anxiety relieved.

"Yeah, I thought I would come hang out for a bit."

"Well, I'm glad you did."

"What kind of snack are you getting? No, wait. Let me guess." He tapped his chin for a second before guessing, "Nachos."

"With?"

"Ground beef and jalapenos."

"Nailed it."

They shared a laugh. She was his spicy food buddy. Gina and Marc didn't care about the hot stuff, but he and Melissa loved the heat. Jalapenos and buffalo sauce on everything.

"Where's your brother?"

She pointed to the attraction across the park.

"He and Justin are over there somewhere."

"Maybe I'll wait for him to come back over this way." He looked up to see the kid in the booth making her nachos. The teen looked back at him, so he flashed the number two and added, "two of those please and heavy on the jalapenos." The teen nodded as if he understood. He looked over at Brenna. "Hi Brenna, can I get you something?"

"Hey Mr. Jackson. No thank you, I had a hotdog earlier."

"A Chicago dog with peppers and jalapenos?"

"Oh, no sir, I can't really handle spicy food. Just a plain dog with mustard."

He looked over at Melissa. They smiled. The nachos came out loaded with cheese, hamburger, and jalapenos. Dave paid and gave the kid a five-dollar tip for his generosity. They took their food back over to the group's table and sat down to eat.

"Should I get us some hot sauce?"

"Dad, I think it's spicy enough. I want to taste my food without my lips going numb."

They laughed. Gina watched from her chair as the two of them ate their nachos and talked. This was the old Dave. Marc came from nowhere and threw his arms around his dad's neck.

"You made it."

"I did."

Marc pulled back with a look of disgust on his face.

"What's that smell? What are you guys eating?"

"Nachos," Melissa replied. She extended hers toward him. "You want some?"

"Gross, NO!"

He covered his nose with his towel and took a step back.

Dave laughed, "What's wrong buddy?"

"That's nasty."

Melissa laughed as she stuffed another jalapeno loaded chip into her mouth. She looked at her dad.

"He eats boring."

Dave smiled, "Yes, he does."

They finished their nachos, and Melissa and Brenna were off to explore the rest of the park. Gina walked over and sat down next to him. He looked up to see Marc was nowhere in sight.

"Where's the boy?"

"He and Justin went to meet some friends."

"When did they get so big?"

"It happened overnight. One day they were clinging to my hip, and the next they were closing the door of their bedroom, asking for more privacy. Melissa more than Marc, he's still a momma's boy."

"Gina I..."

His voice cracked, and he stopped speaking. She didn't press him to continue. It was as if in her heart she knew he was feeling regret. She wasn't giving him a pass for the last two years, but this wasn't the time or place to discuss that. She grabbed his hand.

"You want to go ride the big slide?"

"Yes, that would be great."

They stood up and started toward the big slide.

"You guys going to ride the big slide?" Frank asked.

"We are," Gina responded. "You guys want to come?"

"Absolutely."

Patty grabbed Frank's arm.

"Can you give me about ten minutes dear, I need your help with something."

"Sure, babe. We'll catch up to you two soon."

Gina looked at Patty and smiled. Patty smiled back and mouthed, "go."

They turned and headed for the slide. On their walk, they encountered countless girls wearing suits that had less material than a washcloth. She laughed and grabbed a hold of his arm while they walked.

"What are you laughing at?"

"I can read you like a book, David Joshua Jackson."

"You think you can? Okay, Gina Maria Jackson, what am I thinking?"

"You feel like a giant perv walking in a sea of scantily clad, underaged girls whose parents need to buy more appropriate bathing suits for their daughters."

"Lucky guess."

They laughed the rest of the walk. They took their place in line. Dave looked at his watch. It was 5:13 p.m.

"You got a hot date?"

"No, but..."

"I forgot you took overtime tonight. We were going back to Frank and Patty's for some burgers and brats. Are you sure you can't get out of working?"

"It's a little late now."

Lying had become like second nature to him at this point. He justified it in his head because two-thirds of the lie was pure. He had to pick up the morphine pills, go hang at the bar, and he was planning to see Pastor Dunkirk's service tomorrow morning.

"Yeah, I guess."

What he didn't know was that Brad had called him back on the home phone and left a message to thank him for the extra shift. Gina listened to it and erased the message. She was hoping Dave would choose his family over whatever night of debauchery his shift had planned, but it didn't look like that was going to be the case. Her heart was even more fearful that he had found someone else. They stood in awkward silence, hoping that the line would move faster. It didn't. Finally, he spoke.

"I thought maybe tomorrow night we could all have dinner at that Italian restaurant we love."

"Carducci's."

"That's the one. It's been a while since we've been there, and I know how much you love their food."

"Yeah, okay. The kids would love," she stopped and corrected herself, "I would love that."

"Great. I made the reservations for six."

5

He sat in the corner booth of the little diner, waiting for his food. A Rueben on rye, extra kraut, and a side salad. It was a 50's style diner that was tucked away in the city next door. He did this to keep from being seen by anyone that he and Gina might know. He and Gina ate here a lot when they were dating. It was good food, the best milkshakes, and they still had those little jukeboxes on the wall in your booth. Otis Redding, *On the dock of the bay*, was playing on Dave's. He sat there staring at the little white bottle that he picked up from the pharmacy about twenty minutes ago. Hopefully, it would make the pain manageable enough so that he could function from day to day. When he received the diagnosis from Doctor Peyton, he didn't break down and cry, or pump his fist and yell at the sky. He simply sat there in silence. The doctor stood in silence until he was ready to speak. He eventually just put his clothes back on, and stood there in silence for another few moments before looking at the doctor and saying, "Thanks, doc." The only rational explanation for it was shock. The doctor tried to keep him longer so they could talk about treatment, or pain management, or whatever, but he didn't want to stay in that room any longer than he had to. He drove around for over an hour before he went back to the apartment above the garage. So many thoughts were running through his head. The only reason that he even went to see the doctor was because he had been having these uncomfortable pains in his stomach for a few weeks. He really couldn't even pinpoint when they started. They were mild at first, and then they increased in intensity. He looked up the symptoms on the internet and diagnosed himself with an ulcer. With all that was going on in his life, it seemed workable. He looked up to see the waitress standing there.

"Are you okay Hun?"

He cleared his own throat.

"Yes, I'm fine. Thank you."

"That must have been one good daydream. I've been standing here for about thirty seconds, trying to get your attention."

"I'm sorry. I was just thinking about how fast life goes by. You know, with kids and all."

She looked to be in her mid to late fifties, with a wedding ring on her finger. She was someone who probably understood what he was saying.

"Don't I know it? Just wait until you have grandbabies. The time really hits hyper-drive."

He smiled at her and looked down at the plate she had placed in front of him.

"That smells and looks great," he looked at her nametag, "Monica."

"It's one of our specialties. You need anything else?"

"I think I'm all set."

"Okay. I'll let you enjoy your meal. If you need anything, just look my way and give me a nod."

"Will do, thanks."

She winked and was off. He situated his napkin on his lap and covered his fries in ketchup. Gina always reminded him it looked like a battle from the Civil War. He picked up his sandwich and took a big bite. She wasn't lying. This was one of their specialties. He placed the sandwich back on the plate as he chewed. Dave looked over at the little white bottle again. He removed it from the table and put it in his jacket pocket. For the next twenty minutes, he just wanted it to be about that sandwich, those fries, and nothing else. The Temptations were singing, *my girl*, as he took his next bite with a big smile on his face.

When he finished his meal, he sat back in the booth and stretched. Monica walked over to the table.

"Someone ate his dinner like a big boy."

He laughed. "That was one of the best Reuben's I have ever had, Monica."

"Are you thinking about dessert tonight?"

He looked at his watch. It was 8:50 p.m.

"I am. What would you recommend?"

Without hesitating, she responded, "Our shakes are legendary."

He knew this to be true.

"Is there a particular flavor that you think stands out?"

"Our chocolate, peanut butter and banana shake is out of this world."

"I like chocolate. Check. I like peanut butter. Check. I like bananas. Check. Let's do it."

She chuckled, "What size?"

"A small doesn't seem like enough, but a large just seems like too much."

"So, a medium."

"Monica, that sounds perfect."

"One Elvis Presley coming up," she winked at him and he laughed.

She was gone five minutes before she returned with his shake. She placed it in front of him. The presentation was something off a magazine cover. It even came with the rest of the mixture in the metal cup. Classic.

"That looks awesome. Did you make it yourself?"

"I did. Enjoy sweetie, I'll stop back to check on you later."

"Thank you, Monica."

He placed the oversized straw in the shake. He took a drink. Delicious. He took another drink and sat back in his seat. This took him back to simpler times. He and Gina discussed many things in this place. Their hopes, their fears, and their future with each other. They talked about what they wanted to do in life, where they wanted to live, how many kids they wanted to have, and all the places around the world they wanted to visit. They had visited some of those places throughout their marriage, but there were many more on the list. He looked at the floor and sighed. She would visit those places without him now. He sat up in the booth and took another drink. He let that sink in for a moment.

"Can I get you anything else?" Monica asked.

"No Monica, I think I'm good. Thank you."

She placed the check on the end of the table.

"There's no rush. Take it up whenever you're ready."

"Thank you."

They exchanged smiles, and she was off to the next booth. He sat there for a while, enjoying his shake and contemplating his life. He was wondering if they were having a good time at the Kings. Dave wanted to go, but he wasn't ready to tell her about his condition just yet. He drank the last of his shake, stood, grabbed the check, and headed for the register. He made sure that he left Monica a very generous tip. She was a good waitress. He paid for his meal and then headed toward Joey's.

6

He walked into Joey's around 9:20 p.m. The crew was at their usual table in the back. Patty pointed at him and shouted as he walked up. "Jacksons in the house."

Dave smiled at them, and Patty came over and gave him the handshake bro hug. Patty handed him a beer from the bucket on the table, and Dave made his way around the room. He said hello to everyone on the crew and then found a seat against the wall. He took his jacket off and hung it on the back of the chair. His pills fell out onto the floor, and he quickly grabbed them. He stuffed them back in his jacket and zipped the pocket closed. He sat down, beer in hand, and surveyed the room. There were a lot of cheerful people there, laughing and smiling at each other. The bulk of the crowd was young, but the older patrons seemed to be the ones that stuck out to him. There were some in groups that were laughing and playing darts or pool, but he focused on the ones that were at a table by themselves or at the bar. He watched what he guessed to be a man in his late fifties, just sitting at a table in the corner, both hands wrapped around the bottle in the middle of the table. He was staring through the bottle, the world around him non-existent. People all around him were laughing and having a good time, but he noticed none of it. He just continued to stare off into the abyss, lost in his own thoughts. A feeling of sadness came over Dave. He shifted his eyes to the bar, where he observed another man, maybe in his late seventies, resting his chin on his beer bottle. His eyes half open, staring at the young bartender as she bent over to grab someone a beer from the cooler. Before he could find another depressing soul to look at, Lisa tapped him on the shoulder.

"Come on, Dave, it's me and you."

Lisa had been on the force for about three years now. She was twenty-five, beautiful, and had the attention of most every guy in that bar.

"How did I get so lucky?"

She smiled. "I figured you're the old guy. You got to be good at pool."

"Hey, I only have 17 years on you."

In a weird way, Dave didn't see what other guys saw. He was her FTO. He really got to know who she was throughout her training. She was very intelligent, and her cop sense was spot on for someone so young. It impressed him with how quick she could think on her feet. She reminded him of Melissa.

"I know dad, now grab a pool stick."

"Hey, don't talk to your father with that tone, young lady."

They laughed as he shouldered his way by her and grabbed a stick off the rack. He was chalking up his stick when Derrick, another young officer, walked up and whispered in his ear, "You two got something on the side?"

"It's not like that," he said with some annoyance.

"You guys have always been pretty chummy. I just thought it was going somewhere."

"No. She's young enough to be my daughter."

"Yeah, but she's not your daughter," he said with a wink as he walked away.

Dave was mad at himself in that moment because of what he should have said. The first words out of his mouth should have been that he was a married man who still was very much in love with his wife. But he didn't. He turned and walked toward the pool table, where Patty met him.

"You break old timer?" Lisa shouted at him from the other end of the table.

He smiled and took aim at the stack. He grabbed the end of the stick and threw it forward. The cue ball hit and sent balls flying everywhere. Two solids went in.

"I knew I picked the right partner. Nice break Dave." She smiled as she pointed at him.

He chalked the stick before his next shot, and Patty leaned in close to him.

"Hey, you two..."

He cut him off, "No," and walked around the table to eye his next shot.

The two of them dominated everyone throughout the night. Dave looked at his watch. It was already 12:30 a.m. He took the stick over to the rack and put it back in the same spot he got it from. He turned and Lisa was standing there.

"Don't tell me your bailing?"

"I'm tired and I have an early day tomorrow."

"You never bail this early. Are you okay?"

"Yeah, I feel great."

"You know you're leaving me in the lion's den?"

"I've seen you in action. You can take care of yourself."

She gave him a playful shove. "Thanks for helping me wipe the floor with these guys."

She wrapped her arms around him and gave him a hug. He squeezed back and whispered in her ear, "Remember our talks."

"I know, I know, make them respect you. Make no rash decisions. Always show them what a strong woman looks like and don't take crap from anyone.

He laughed as they pulled away. "Bingo."

He threw a hand up and waved to the rest of the crew. A chorus of boos followed, and he smiled. He looked back at Lisa and shouted, "Make sure all these idiots get home alright." She threw him a salute of understanding and turned to rejoin the group. As he walked toward the door, he observed four girls in the corner trying to comfort a friend who was crying and pointing toward a guy talking to another girl. Too much drama. He stepped through the door and out into the night air. He stopped and breathed it in. It was a beautiful summer night. He walked to his truck and got in. He started it up and sat there for a moment. Dave reached into his jacket pocket and pulled out the little white pill bottle. He would start taking them after breakfast in the morning, because he knew two important things about this medication. Take with food, and not with alcohol. He shoved the bottle back into his pocket and shifted into drive.

He parked two houses away from the house. Even though it was safe to assume that Gina was sleeping by now, pulling into the driveway would most likely wake her. Sunday school at their church started at 9:30 a.m., so she and the kids would be gone early in the morning. He gently closed the door of his truck and made his way toward the apartment. With cat like skill, he could make it in without so much as a creek on the steps. He softly closed the door and turned on the light. Dave washed his face, brushed his teeth, stripped down to his boxers, and hopped into bed. He grabbed his Stephen King book, *Thinner*, off the nightstand, put on his reading glasses and started chapter ten. Somewhere around chapter twelve he faded, and Billy Halleck's life was too interesting to miss, so he called it a night. He reached over and turned off the light. He still wasn't sure about tomorrow morning, so he would let fate decide for him, which meant that he wouldn't set an alarm. As he laid on his back, hands clasped behind his head, his mind replayed the day's events. The visit from the doc was a little stressful, but in the end rewarding. He smiled when he thought about spending time with the family at the water park and wondered if he should have just stayed with them the rest of the night. He closed his eyes and drifted off as he thought about shooting pool at Joey's with the gang. "For God so loved the world..." was the last thing he remembered.

Chapter 7

Sunday—July 3, 2010

His eyes popped open when he heard the car doors slam. He looked at the clock. It was 8:55 a.m. Gina and the kids were leaving for Sunday school. He stretched and then clasped his hands behind his head and stared at the ceiling. The sun was already out in full force. Despite the curtains that "guaranteed" to keep the room dark, its rays had already found their way into the room and engulfed it. He laid there for a few minutes, pondering what to do. Dave sat up, threw his feet over the bed, rubbed his eyes, and then headed for the shower. He stood under the head of the shower, letting the warm water run down his head, chest, back, and legs, while he thought about the day. The warm water felt great on his aching muscles. He laughed out loud as he remembered a conversation that he and his dad had about getting older.

He watched his father rub his lower back after simply getting up from a nap on the couch one day. Dave was sixteen and Edward was 42. Dave looked over at his father and laughed. Edward snapped back.

"What's so funny, boy?"

"You can't even take a nap without your old bones creaking. What are you, a 100?"

"I'm 42, smart guy. You wait until you get older, then we'll see how you feel."

"Not like that."

"Son, we come from a blue-collar family. We work hard for everything we get. We don't have the luxury of paying people to do our chores around the house or yard. As the years go by, that takes its toll on the body. A little creak here and there, a rubbing of the muscles, and some Ben-gay on the joints is every working man's rite of passage. I'm better than some, worse than others. You'll see."

"No, I won't. I'm not going to be blue collar."

Edward laughed.

"A titan of industry. Future CEO of a large corporation. That's where you're headed, ah boy?"

"Yes, sir."

"I've seen your grades. I'm sorry son, but you're going be a back rubbing, muscle aching, blue-collar worker just like your old man."

"No way, you'll see. White collar or bust."

He laughed out loud again as he scrubbed the scent of Joey's off his body from last night. Stale bar smell. Not appealing. He finished up, toweled off, threw on his robe, and walked into the kitchen. He grabbed a mug from the cabinet, poured himself a cup, and then set it on the counter. Scrambled eggs and toast sounded good this morning. He went to the fridge and opened it. There was a small casserole dish right in the front. It had a note on it. "This should give you a good start for a couple of days. I hope work wasn't too busy last night. G." He opened the dish. It was Gina's breakfast casserole. A layer of tater tots covered in eggs with fresh basil, cheese, and on top, crumbled up sausage. Delicious. She must have made it last night before she went to bed. He smiled as he took a nice, healthy slice and put it in the microwave for a minute. He took a sip of coffee and hummed, *On the dock of the Bay*. The microwave chimed, and he removed the slice. He took everything over to the kitchen table and sat down. The first bite was too hot, but he did it anyway. Third-degree burns in the mouth were nothing for him. Dave had a history of not being able to wait for good food or coffee. He walked over to his jacket and removed the little white pill bottle. He opened the bottle and took a pill out. Dave swallowed it.

"Do your job, little guy," he whispered to himself.

He sat there enjoying his breakfast, currently pain free now. He looked at the clock. It was 9:37 a.m. He had seriously considered attending Faith Bible Church at ten thirty this morning. He was having second thoughts now. Dave knew that his time was short on this earth, so did he really want to go to church now. What was the point? It wasn't going to change his circumstances. But he was curious. His talk with Pastor Dunkirk and Gina's transformation were two reasons to check it out. Still, it would not change his fate. The time was now 9:47 a.m. He took the last bite of his breakfast casserole. Dave thought about just going for a run, but a tiny pain had developed in the pit of his stomach. He froze and remained still for a few seconds, hoping the pain wouldn't materialize into something worse. It passed. He breathed a sigh of relief, got up, and started getting ready to go to church. He had given up his overtime to see what all the fuss was about, so why back out now? At 10:07 a.m. he was in his car and heading for the church. He pulled into the parking lot at ten twenty-seven. Three minutes to spare. He sat there for a couple of minutes, looking at the entrance. Nicely dressed men, women and children were going into the building. They had big smiles on their faces, and they were enthusiastically shaking hands with other people once they were inside. He looked at his watch. It was 10:31 a.m. He was so close and almost made it there. He couldn't go in late. That would be disrespectful. Dave put the car in reverse to back out from his spot. He got a magnificent spot up front, maybe the best parking spot he has ever had. He would never get a spot like this at the mall, or school, or a sporting event, or anywhere really. Dave shifted the car back into park.

"Stop making excuses. Just go in and get it over with." He said out loud.

He turned the car off and exited. Dave made his way toward the front door and hesitated for a moment before he opened it. He walked inside and was greeted by an older man in a nice blue suit.

"Welcome, friend." He extended his hand to Dave, and they shook. "Is this your first time here?"

"Yes, it is."

"That's great. The service is about to start. Go on inside and grab a seat."

"Thank you."

He walked toward the sanctuary and stopped just before he got to the large doors leading in. The large windows in the back allowed him to see in as the congregation stood and the choir sang. He scanned the back for a seat. He located a pew three rows from the back that was only half full, and the aisle seat was open. Dave opened the doors and went in. He could feel all the congregation's eyes watching him as he made his way to his seat. They knew he was an outsider. He should just turn and leave now. He didn't want to interrupt their little community. But he didn't. He took his place on the aisle in that third row and stood while the choir sang, *How Great thou Art*. When they finished, they had a seat. The man who was directing the choir approached the podium. Dave could see Pastor Dunkirk sitting by himself in a mini pew, one he would describe as a kind of loveseat for two, off to the right on the stage. The man at the podium introduced himself.

"Good morning, everyone. It's so good to see so many smiling faces this morning. I am the music pastor here at Faith, David Collins."

After introducing himself, he made announcements of upcoming events. He then reminded everyone that tonight at six thirty was the children's choir concert. "That's it for announcements." He turned to face the pastor. "Pastor Dunkirk." He then shook the pastor's hand as he exited the stage. Pastor Dunkirk stood in front of the podium and placed his bible on it.

"Thank you, Pastor Collins. Thant was some good singing this morning."

A few "Amens" were echoed by the congregation.

"Good morning, everyone."

The people responded in unison, "Good morning."

"Today I want to talk about Jesus."

He smiled and took his reading glasses out of his suit pocket. He put them on and then opened his bible. Dave crossed his legs and focused on the pastor.

"Who was Jesus Christ? If you went out onto the street and asked five different people that question, you might get five different answers. They could range from, he was a strong religious figure, or he was a gentle passivist, or a well-known preacher, or a man of deep conviction." He paused for a moment and then continued. "None of those answers would be wrong. But the answer that's most fitting is this. Jesus Christ is the Son of the living God. He is the King of kings and Lord of lords. He is the Messiah. The savior of a fallen and sin-stained world."

A few "Amens" rang out.

"Please don't just take my word for it." He then held up his bible. "Take His word for it." He then placed the bible back onto the podium. He smiled at them. "There's a reason His word has stood the test of time. It is the world's thickest instruction manual. It teaches us how we should live our lives, and how we should treat others.

Many think that Jesus didn't exist until His birth in the book of Matthew, but he was around before the world was ever spoken into existence."

This was an attention grabber. Multiple people in the congregation, including Dave, were now locked in fully.

"Genesis chapter one verse twenty-six says, 'Then God said, "Let Us make man in Our image, according to Our likeness; let them have dominion over the fish of the sea, over the birds of the air, and over the cattle, over all the earth and over every creeping thing that creeps on the earth." He smiled and paused for effect.

"'Let Us, Our image, Our likeness.' God did not say, I will make man, or My image, or My likeness. The father reveals himself to be plural here. God, Jesus, and the Holy Spirit are working together as one, because they are one. I'll give that a minute to sink in." He looked out over the congregation. He saw many faces that he recognized from his regular attenders, but a few visitors in the crowd.

"Jesus Christ has been around since before the beginning of the world." He put his hands beside his head and threw his fingers out "Poof!" He stated emphatically. A few of the congregations' drowsy members snapped to attention. "Blows your mind, doesn't it? So, the years' role on and the Old Testament lays the foundation of the world. We see life created, sins destructive nature, heroes and kings rise and fall and rise again, laws take root, and God's mercy and grace in all of it. He watched as mankind consistently disappointed Him and knew that sin was in their heart. Mankind's sinful nature was going to keep him from having an eternal relationship with God." He shook his head.

"Despite what many think. God loves you deeply. He created you out of love. He wants to have a deep, meaningful relationship with every one of us. So, the ultimate sacrifice had to be made. God wanted to show us that His love was so deep for us He was willing to give His only Son for our transgressions. Jesus' blood would sanctify us and allow us to accept the eternal gift of salvation. We could now live with Him eternally. John chapter three verse sixteen tells us that, 'For God so loved the world that He gave His only begotten Son, that whoever believes in Him should not perish but have everlasting life.'"

"Amen" was the response from the congregation.

"So, our message now focuses on the book of Matthew. Jesus comes down from heaven, giving up his celestial body to become flesh, and is born of the virgin Mary. We see in the book of Matthew chapter one verse twenty-one, that an angel appears to Joseph in a dream to outline that very plan. The angel tells him, 'And she will bring forth a Son, and you shall call His name Jesus, for He will save His people from their sins.' The angel didn't say he may save his people, the angel said, 'He Will...save His people from their sins.' So, Mary gives birth to God's only Son. He lives among us. Flesh and blood."

The pastor paused and took a moment to collect his thoughts. Dave could see the pure emotion on his face. This message was very personal to him.

"Jesus left paradise to come down and minister to us. Folks think about that. A king, living in all His glory, loved us so much that he left His throne to be among us. He grew up in a house like most. He had brothers and sisters, His earthly father Joseph worked as a carpenter to support the family, and His mother Mary tended to the home and the children. Jesus and His brothers learned from Joseph, and that's where we get those delightful bumper stickers that read, 'My boss is a Jewish Carpenter.'"

This got a few laughs out of the congregation.

"In the book of Luke, chapter two, we see that Mary and Joseph go up to Jerusalem for the Passover. It tells us they went every year for the feast of the Passover, and in this year in verse forty-two, we learn Jesus is twelve years old during this visit. When Passover has ended, the family starts the walk back home. It was a large group that made the trip, so when Mary and joseph didn't see Jesus, they assumed he was walking with friends. They walked for a day before they realized he wasn't with them. So, in a panic, they returned to Jerusalem to look for Him. Verse forty-six states, 'after three days they found Him in the temple.' I don't know about you, but I would go out of my mind if I couldn't find my son for three days."

Comments from the congregation echoed his sentiment.

"He was sitting amid the teachers listening to them and asking them questions. Folks, that's not like any twelve-year-old I know. But it gets better. We read in verse forty-seven that 'all who heard Him were astonished at His understanding and answers.' Mary went to Jesus and asked Him, 'Son, why have You done this to us? Look, your father and I have sought you anxiously.' That's code for, you had us worried sick. We thought we had lost you. We're glad you're ok, but you are in big trouble, mister." He looked over the top of his glasses at everyone and gave them a raised eyebrow.

They laughed, and he even got a few head nods.

"Jesus responds by saying, 'Why did you seek Me? Did you not know that I must be about My Father's business?' Folks, I'll say it again. He's twelve. So, they scoop Him up and take Him home. We then read in verse fifty-two, 'And Jesus increased in wisdom and stature, and in favor with God and man.' At twelve years of age, the bible says that Jesus amazed the scholars. After being your pastor for over fifteen years now, I feel I can share this personal tidbit with you. At twelve years old, I was not amazing to any scholars."

More laughter from the congregation.

"At twelve, all I was concerned with was baseball, bubblegum, and playing baseball outside with my friends while chewing bubblegum."

More laughter. He smiled as he took off his glasses and cleaned them again. This was more of a habit than a necessity.

"Let's fast forward a bit. We read about a prophet, John the Baptist. Now John was born to prepare the way for Jesus. Mark chapter one verse four and five tells us that, 'John came baptizing in the wilderness and preaching a baptism of repentance for the remission of sins. Then all the land of Judea, and those from Jerusalem, went out to him and were all baptized by him in the Jordan River, confessing their sins.' Folks, God sent John to prepare the way for His Son's ministry. I would implore you this week to read the first chapter of the book of Luke. It is the story of a priest, Zacharias, and his wife, Elizabeth. They were faithful, godly servants blessed by God with John. So, John is preaching and baptizing those who are repentant. His ministry is strong, and he has many followers. John is a no-nonsense kind of guy. He doesn't sugarcoat the gospel for the religious leaders or kings of his day. He preaches the truth, and the fire of God is in him. The other leaders preach to the people and leaders what they want to hear or what makes them feel superior. Not John. They were constantly looking for ways to get rid of John because of this, but they feared retribution from his followers, so they left him alone."

He smiled and shook his head.

"That's sounding all too familiar today, too. Ministers of God are afraid to teach the bible for fear of offending others. But that's a sermon for a different day. So, we see John is doing his thing, baptizing those who are repenting, and then John finds Jesus standing in front of him. John knows that this is the Messiah. This is the one that he is preparing the way for. I want to read to you Matthew chapter three verses thirteen through seventeen. 'Then Jesus came from Galilee to the Jordan to be baptized by John. But John tried to deter him, saying, "I need to be baptized by you, and do you come to me?" Jesus replied, "Let it be so now; it is proper for us to do this to fulfill all righteousness." Then John consented. As soon as Jesus was baptized, he went up out of the water. At that moment, heaven opened, and he saw the Spirit of God descending like a dove and alighting on him. And a voice from heaven said, "This is my Son, whom I love; with Him I am well pleased."

He paused again for effect and took the time to wipe his brow with a handkerchief.

"Can you imagine being John? The King of kings and Lord of lords is standing in front of you, asking you to baptize Him. John gave the appropriate response. 'Lord, it is You who should baptize me.' But Jesus explains to him it is to fulfill the prophesy, and kick-start His ministry. John doesn't hesitate. He does what he's been born to do. His Father then glorified Jesus in heaven, who proclaims Him as His Son."

He takes a moment to look up and smile. He then looks out at the congregation and smiles.

"What a moment to witness."

A healthy dose of "Amens" throughout the sanctuary. Dave cannot explain what he's feeling inside at this moment. His heart is racing, and his palms are sweating. It's not a bad feeling, it's a rush that he hasn't felt in a long time, or possibly ever.

"After His baptism we read in Luke chapter three verse twenty-three, 'Now Jesus Himself began His ministry at about thirty years of age.' It's now time for Jesus to go out into the world and do His Father's work." He stopped for a moment to address the congregation. "For those of you who are visitors or new to the gospel, you'll hear me jump around the first four books of the New Testament when telling the story of Jesus. It's because Matthew, Mark, Luke, and John were all written by men who spent a considerable amount of time with Jesus. They all have different details that they added when God breathed the gospel into them. Each is a remarkable book dedicated to the telling of the greatest story ever told. I just wanted to clear that up for those of you who were wondering why I skip around so much. Now, where was I?"

He took a moment to flip through his bible and then continued with the life of Jesus. Pastor Dunkirk explained how Satan tempted Christ and failed. He continued with all the miracles and teaching that Jesus did over the next three years.

"Christ knew what He had to endure for us. He had to shed His blood as an atonement for our sins. But before He went to the cross, He gave us a lifetime of teachings and assurances. In John chapter fourteen verse six, he tells us that, 'I am the way and the truth and the life. No one comes to the Father except through me.' But it can't be that easy? But it is. He also tells us in Matthew chapter seven verses seven and eight, 'Ask and it will be given to you; seek and you will find; knock and the door will be opened to you. For everyone who asks receives; the one who seeks finds; and to the one who knocks, the door will be opened.'"

Dave's thoughts reverted to the bible on the piano. The wind had blown the pages open to this exact chapter and verses. Gina underlined them. Was God talking to him? Did God still talk to people? He refocused his attention back to Pastor Dunkirk.

"Folks, today we have examined the life of Jesus, the Son of God, and His amazing ministry. The appointed religious leaders of that time still felt very threatened by His teachings. They were jealous and angry that so many followed Him and believed in Him. So, they decided that the only way to get rid of Him was to kill Him. They knew His followers would not have it, so they had to do it in secret. He was a gentle, loving and compassionate savior who taught love, kindness, forgiveness, mercy, and grace. They taught fear, vengeance, greed, and hypocrisy. He was a great threat to their power and wealth."

He again let that point sink in.

"So, we come to the part in the story where they arrest Jesus for His," he used air quotes "Crimes. We read in John chapter nineteen verses one through three, 'So then Pilate took Jesus and scourged *Him*. And the soldiers twisted a crown of thorns and put *it* on His head, and they put on Him a purple robe. Then they said, "Hail, King of the Jews!" And they struck Him with their hands.'" He took a moment to collect his thoughts before saying, "All for loving us so much. They beat him in the most brutal and barbaric fashion. The soldiers whipped His body until the flesh tore away from the skin. As the thick and pointy thorns from the crown pierced his head, blood ran down His face. A face filled with nothing but love. Finally, they made Him walk through the streets and carry the heavy cross He would ultimately end up nailed to."

Dave felt the lump in his throat growing and his eyes getting moist.

"They laid Him down and drove the spikes through His hands and His feet. They raised the cross, and He hung there, beaten and battered by the people He loved and was dying for. Did He curse them or ask His Father in heaven to rain down vengeance upon them for what they did?" He scanned the crowd. "We see in the book of Luke chapter twenty-three verse thirty-four that He simply says to God, 'Father, forgive them, for they do not know what they do.'" His voice cracked as he repeated the phrase, "'Father, forgive them, for they do not know what they do.' Would any of us do the same?"

Dave wiped a tear away from his eye.

"John chapter nineteen verse thirty tells us that Jesus exclaims, 'It is finished! And bowing His head, He gave up His spirit.' His human form was gone. He died and shed His blood right there on Calvary so that we could now have eternal life with Him. He paid the price for our sins. Salvation was purchased with His blood. Hallelujah!"

A hearty chorus of "Amens" filled the sanctuary.

"The last act was completed three days later when He conquered death. He had risen from the grave. Death was now defeated forever. Matthew chapter twenty-eight verses one through seven reads, 'Now after the Sabbath, as the first *day* of the week began to dawn, Mary Magdalene and the other Mary came to see the tomb. And behold, there was a great earthquake; for an angel of the Lord descended from heaven, and came and rolled back the stone from the door, and sat on it. His countenance was like lightning, and his clothing as white as snow. And the guards shook for fear of Him, and became like dead *men.* But the angel answered and said to the women, "Do not be afraid, for I know that you seek Jesus who was crucified. He is not here; for He is risen, as He said. Come, see the place where the Lord lay. And go quickly and tell His disciples that He is risen from the dead, and indeed He is going before you into Galilee; there you will see Him. Behold, I have told you.'"

Pastor Dunkirk smiled as he closed the bible. He removed his glasses.

"Our savior has risen and is alive today, sitting at the right hand of God. First John chapter two verse one tells us that, 'My little children, these things I write to you, so that you may not sin. And if anyone sins, we have an Advocate with the Father, Jesus Christ the righteous.' Jesus is our advocate for forgiveness of sins. He paid that price for us, so all we must do is confess and ask for forgiveness, and we are forgiven. Again, I say, Hallelujah!"

"Amen."

"For those out there who have never asked Christ into their heart, then I implore you to look inside yourselves and think about the lesson we learned today. And if you want to know Jesus as your Lord and personal Savior, then I ask you to please do so today. Let's all bow our heads in prayer."

Dave and the congregation bowed their heads and closed their eyes as the pastor continued.

"Please pray this prayer with me today if you want to make that decision. Lord Jesus, I know that I'm a sinner saved by your grace. I believe You are the Son of God, and that You died on the cross and shed Your blood for my salvation. You conquered death by rising on the third day, and You are sitting at the right hand of God today. Lord, please come into my life and save me. Make me whole. In Jesus' name. Amen."

With his head bowed and his eyes still closed, Dave added onto the pastor's prayer in his head. "Lord, please, I need you to guide me and show me what to do. I'm lost. I need you." Dave opened his eyes as a single tear dropped from his left eye. He wiped it quickly and looked around. No one was pointing or staring at him. His heart was light. In that moment, his heart felt extreme joy and happiness. Dave wanted to jump up and dance. He didn't. He just sat there, smiling from ear to ear. Where was this joy coming from? How could it be that one small prayer could be so exhilarating, so energetic, so...life changing? He looked up as Pastor Dunkirk continued speaking.

"If you prayed that life-changing prayer with me, hallelujah! You have invited Jesus into your heart to be Lord of your life. In the book of Romans, chapter ten verses nine and ten, we are told, 'that if you confess with your mouth the Lord Jesus and believe in your heart that God has raised Him from the dead, you will be saved. For with the heart one believes unto righteousness, and with the mouth confession is made unto salvation.'" His smile was warm and genuine. "Please, see me after the service so that we can get you started on your journey. We just want to give you some literature that will aid you in your walk with Jesus and get you on the road to experiencing His full love and grace in your life."

The energy was still coursing through Dave's veins. He didn't know how to describe the moment with anything more than amazing. He felt as if someone had lifted a giant weight off of his shoulders. In that moment, he truly knew that Jesus was his King. That He died for him, and that He conquered death so that he could live with Him eternally. He had been saved. Dave wanted to, no; he needed to tell everybody. Dave looked up as Pastor Dunkirk picked his bible up off the podium and walked toward the front of the stage. He stood in front of the congregation and scanned the sanctuary.

"For those of you who are visiting, we pray for your safe trip home. For those of you who are new to the area or to this church, we hope you will consider making this your church home. We would love to help you grow in the faith and grow with you. Just before Pastor Collins comes up and leads us in a final hymn, I want to share with you James chapter two verse twenty-six. It reminds us that, 'For as the body without the spirit is dead, so faith without works is dead also.' When you decide to let Christ come into your heart and change your life. You are making a commitment to serve Him fully. Not when it's convenient to you or to your life. It's a decision that can have a life-changing impact. It doesn't mean a life of only comfort now, free from pain, heartache, or tragedy. But it means that you now have a caring and loving savior who you can rely on to ease that pain in life's most challenging times. A life of faith doesn't make life easier; it makes it possible." He smiled. "I can't take credit for that one. I saw it on a bumper sticker and stole it."

The congregation laughed.

"Please go out this week and continue to wake the world up to Jesus. Don't forget that on Wednesday night we'll be continuing our talk on parables. Thank you and God bless."

Pastor Collins stepped up to the podium as Pastor Dunkirk walked down the aisle toward the back of the church. He smiled at each row as he passed, and when he got to Dave, his smile widened, and he threw out his hand. Dave smiled back and took it. The pastor pulled him in close as they shook and whispered, "So great to see you here, Dave."

"Thank you," Dave whispered.

The pastor continued to the back of the church, and Dave continued to smile. He was still feeling the high of giving his life to Jesus.

"Please open up your hymnals to page 395. *The Old Rugged Cross.*"

The pianist played, and the congregation sang. Dave held the hymnal and read the words. It was a beautiful song. It talked about how Jesus suffered the cross for all of us, and that one day our faith would lead us to life eternal with Him in heaven. Dave knew he had a lot to learn, and he was eager to get started. He couldn't wait to tell Gina tonight at dinner how he had given his life to the Lord. That he was sorry for the last two years, and that things would be different now. And then, out of nowhere, a shadow cast itself over his excitement. Doctor Peyton's words echoed in his head. "Inoperable. Terminal. Maybe six months." His heart was heavy again. It didn't seem right that after experiencing something so wonderful, so amazing, so revealing, that he should now feel so low. It wasn't Doctor Peyton's fault. He was only delivering the diagnosis; he didn't cause it. Nobody knew for sure what caused it, but it wasn't going anywhere. He could hear the people singing the song now, but it seemed distant. Like he wasn't in the room. It wasn't right. This beautiful song in the background. It should play from the roof for everyone to hear. And then the phrase that he would never forget for the rest of his life echoed in his head. "I'm so sorry Dave. You have stage four pancreatic cancer."

2

Across town, Gina and the kids sat in the pew listening to the pastor give his closing comments. Patty King sat on the other side of her, followed by Frank and the kids. They never let all the kids sit together during the service because it would be too chaotic. Too much talking and laughing would draw multiple looks from irritated listeners trying to hear the pastor's sermon. They experimented twice with letting the kids sit together, but it always ended in failure. So, it was easiest to separate them during the service and let them sit together for lunch afterward. The pastor finished his sermon and had them bow in a word of prayer. Gina blocked out everything and said her own prayer that morning.

"Lord, I need Your loving grace. I'm frustrated and hurt. I don't know what to do about Dave. I still love him so much, but if he isn't dedicated to this marriage or family...I need guidance. Show me Your path. Help me see clearly what I need to do to honor You and Your will. I trust You and know that you will lead me in the direction I need to go. Thank you, Father. In Jesus' precious name, I pray. Amen."

The service concluded, and they walked out into the lobby.

Frank asked, "Where's lunch at today? I'm starving."

Marc looked at his mom. "Can we do pizza today, mom? Please. It's been a while."

"I could do pizza," Frank and Justin stated together.

Everyone laughed.

"I'm okay with pizza if everyone else is," Gina responded.

"Pizza it is," Patty exclaimed.

Frank drove the boys in his truck, and the girls went with Gina. Once at the pizza place, they were seated relatively quickly, and the waitress came over and took their drink order. Cherry Coke all the way around. She left to get their drinks, and everyone grabbed their plate and headed for the buffet. Patty placed her hand on Gina's shoulder.

"You guys go ahead. We'll catch up."

As the rest of the group walked toward the buffet, Gina turned to Patty.

"Is everything okay?"

"That's what I was going to ask you. You seemed distant on the drive here. Are you okay?"

"Yeah, I'm fine."

"Are you sure? That line will keep them up there for at least ten minutes."

"It's just," she stopped and smiled, "Nothing."

"I'm not going to press you, but if you want to talk about it, then I'm here for you."

Gina smiled. "I might be overreacting, but I saw the light on in the apartment last night around 1:15 a.m."

"I thought Dave worked until seven?"

"He said he was working until seven, but..."

"Maybe he just forgot and left it on."

"It went off maybe a half hour later. I checked the driveway and his car wasn't there."

"Do you think someone broke in?"

"No. I walked out and looked to see if he parked it on the street, and I saw it parked a few houses down."

"Maybe he came home sick and didn't want to wake you or the kids."

She stared down at the floor.

"That's not it."

"What do you think it is?"

"I don't know Patty. He wants to have dinner and talk tonight. A piece of me thinks the worst. Maybe he's moving on to find someone else, or maybe he already has."

"Gina. From what I know about Dave, he's crazy about you. Of that, I'm sure. Is it just you and Dave tonight?"

"No, the kids will be there."

"I don't think he would have that type of serious discussion with you at a family dinner. That's a couple's talk, not a family one. At least not initially."

"Your right, I'm just letting my mind get the best of me. Thanks Patty, you're a good friend."

"Whatever happens, just know that I'm here for you."

They hugged.

"Thank you. Now let's go grab some food before Frank and the boys demolish that buffet."

They laughed and then headed toward the buffet.

3

Dave left his pew and walked toward the back, where Pastor Dunkirk was shaking hands and talking with others. Pastor Dunkirk looked up and saw Dave walking toward him. He smiled, and they shook.

"Dave, it's so good to see you here."

"Pastor, that was a great service."

"Thank you. I appreciate your kind words."

Dave couldn't contain his excitement. "I did it."

Dunkirk laughed. "Did what David?"

Still clasping the pastor's hand, Dave pulled him in close.

"I gave my life to Jesus."

Dunkirk pulled him all the way in and gave him a bear hug.

"That's awesome Dave. I'm so happy for you."

They separated.

"Thank you. I don't know what came over me. When I heard you tell the story, I just knew. I knew He died for me. That He rose to conquer death, and that He lives. I feel invincible right now. So much energy."

"I know what came over you. The Holy Spirit. Dave, come with me to my office."

He followed him to his office, and Dunkirk closed the door.

"Have a seat, Dave."

Dave sat down and the pastor took a seat across from him.

"Is this what it's always going to feel like now?"

The pastor laughed.

"No. The cynicism of people will continually try to knock you down off of that high. You'll have good days and bad days in your faith. The one underlying principle that you should always keep in your heart is that you now serve a loving God, full of mercy and grace."

"I'm a cop, Pastor Dunkirk. I know about the cynicism in the world."

"Yes, but as a believer, your eyes will be opened wider. When people find out about your faith, they will constantly put it to the test. They will try to tell you that a virgin birth is impossible. That God doesn't exist because science says so. That when life is over, it's over. We don't possess a soul that moves on, we just cease to exist. That's where you come in."

"How so?"

"Now that you have given your life to Christ, you can share with others His love and grace."

"How do I do that? I mean, how do I do that effectively? I'm new to this. I don't have any pull."

The pastor laughed.

"You have more pull than you think. The Holy Spirit now lives inside of you. You have a piece of God living in your heart, David, and He will guide you and give you the words to say. You can't just leave here today and expect your knowledge to increase just because you asked Him into your heart. Read His word and study it. Apply it to your life and show others your faith by the way you live your life every day. A big part of your growth will also come through attending church regularly. A church family will have a big impact on helping you through those tough times when you doubt your decision. We are here to build you up as the world tries to tear you down."

"I never really thought about it like that. I guess the way I came in here today to see what church was all about shows me that."

"The people in your life will have the greatest influence on you. A church family can really help through bible study groups. Plus, there are men's and family retreats. Just look at the people you hang out with the most. Your family, your friends, your co-workers all have an influence on who you are."

"I think deep down we all know that, pastor -."

"Bill."

Dave smiled, "Bill."

"1 Corinthians 15:33 tells us that, 'Bad company corrupts good character'. That's why it's important to surround ourselves with good people. Godly people. How is your family going to react to this?"

"My wife will be thrilled. She accepted the Lord as her Savior a couple of years back. I'm not sure if the kids did or not, but they'll be indifferent."

"Your kids study you every day. As kids, our values come from our parents. Both parents. Unfortunately, you have seen the hideous side of how disastrous some families can end up when the mom, dad, or both have a negative influence on their children. But now that both you and your wife are believers, they'll be able to see the love of Jesus in both of you and your marriage."

"I have some rebuilding to do there." He dropped his head in shame.

"Dave, if you ever want to or need to talk, you have my card. Call me and we'll get together."

"Thanks Bill."

"What kind of influence do you have at work?"

"I have friends who are Christians, and friends who aren't. They are all good people, but some are a little more positive than others. My co-workers might be a different story. They are hard-working men and women who believe in what they do and work hard to make a difference. The overwhelming majority are solid, but a few slip through the cracks once in a great while. Javier is the only one who has ever talked to me about the Lord."

"Do you like Javier?"

"I love him and his wife. They're great people."

"Dave, you work in a job where testosterone flows like the Nile. It wouldn't surprise me to find more than you think who are believers in Christ. Some have given their life to Him, and they believe He protects and loves them. But they don't really know the extent of His love because they've never really explored it. Unfortunately, fitting in is more important to them than standing firm for Him. I pray daily that those who are like this out in the world experience His true love and grace before they leave this world. There's nothing more exciting and fulfilling than that. Living a Christ centered life opens your eyes fully to how truly wonderful His love is."

Dave looked at his watch. It was a nervous tick that he did when he wanted to talk about something, but he didn't know how. On the surface, it seemed rude to all others except Gina, who knew her husband well. He wanted to talk to the pastor about his condition. He wanted to tell him he probably had less than six months to experience all of that wonderful love, but he was nervous.

"Am I keeping you Dave?"

"No. I'm sorry. It's just something I do when I'm nervous."

"That has to be a first for you." He laughed. "How can a pastor make a cop nervous?"

Dave laughed.

"There's just something I want to talk about, but I can't right now."

"That's okay David. When you want to, I'm here."

"Thanks. I actually have to get going. I've already taken up enough of your time."

"Dave, I have enjoyed our conversation, and I am so happy that you gave your life to the Lord."

He walked over to a filing cabinet and pulled out some literature and a new bible. He walked over and handed it to Dave.

"What's all this?"

"It'll get you started on your journey. Read through the literature and discover the path you just put yourself on. It will give you guidance on where to read the bible, and a study aid to help you understand. Don't let this be your only guide, though, David. Remember what we talked about? The importance of being involved with other believers who can help you grow."

"I won't. Thanks again Bill."

They shook, and the pastor walked him out and back through the building to the exit.

"I hope to see you here again."

"You will."

Dave left the church that day with a lot more than he came with. He expected to sit in the back, listen to the service, and then sneak out at the end to avoid talking to other people. His plan was to experience going to church without actually experiencing the church. What he found was that the people were inviting and warm. He discovered that despite his many flaws; God loved him unconditionally. That the God of the universe had mercy for a sinner like him, and that He sent His only Son to die for his salvation. Dave not only heard the truth that day, he believed it to be true and gave his life to the Lord. He couldn't wait to tell Gina and everyone else what he had done. He came out of curiosity and left with salvation.

Chapter 8

Dave was in the apartment looking at the literature Pastor Dunkirk gave him when he heard Gina's car pull into the driveway. He walked over to the window and looked out. He watched as the kids got out of the car and walked toward the front door. Gina exited and stood in the driveway for a moment. She looked beautiful. Gina looked up and their eyes met. She smiled and waved. He smiled and waved back. She turned and walked toward the front door when she stopped. She knew that curiosity killed the cat, but what the heck? Dave watched as she changed her course and moved toward the stairs to the apartment. He still had on his dress slacks, shirt, and tie from church. He Turned and watched as she stood in front of the door. It took her a few seconds before she finally knocked. He walked over and opened the door. She was about to speak when she stopped because she noticed he was wearing his dress clothes.

"There's no court on Sunday, Dave. I'm stumped. Where are you going?"

He laughed. "I'm not going anywhere. I've already been."

"Okay. Where have you been?"

Her tone was bordering on angry.

"Please come in and sit down. I need to talk to you about something."

"This feels like a trap."

"Please come in Gina. I have something wonderful to tell you."

"Wonderful? I'm all ears."

They went over to the table and sat down.

"Do you want something to drink? I was just about to make a pot of coffee."

"No, I'm fine, thanks."

He walked back over and sat down in front of her.

"You look beautiful." He smiled. "Gina, let me start by apologizing."

She didn't know what for, but she played along. "I'm listening"

"I've been a fool. For the last two years, I have done nothing but cause this family heartache and pain."

She interrupted. "Dave, no-"

"Please let me get this out. I've been going over it in my head since I got home from church."

"Wait...what? Got home from church."

He moved in closer and held both of her hands in his.

"We'll get to that in a minute. I've been a horrible husband and father and selfishly put my wants above yours and the kids. I've acted like a teenager and I cannot express how awful I feel." He looked down for a moment and his voice cracked, but he continued, "I'm so sorry, Gina."

She pulled her hands up and gently cupped his face. She lifted his chin until his eyes met hers. Gina could see that he was sincere. Something inside of her knew he was sorry. Instead of yelling at him and telling him all the ways he hurt this family over the past two years, she just wanted to hug him and tell him she forgave him. But it wasn't fair to let him off the hook that easily. Or was it? In that moment, a moment which seemed to freeze in time, she saw a man who was genuinely repentant. As a single tear fell from her eye, she looked at him with nothing but love in her eyes and told him. "I forgive you."

This was the very epitome of Christlike love. Dave couldn't contain the emotion that he was feeling. He fell to his knees and wrapped his arms around her waist. He cried, "Thank you." This was unfamiliar territory for Gina. He didn't cry like this when his father died. She assumed maybe he did it in private, but there was never a display of emotion like this. Never. She wrapped her arms around his head and held him.

"Talk to me Dave. Really talk to me and tell me what's going on in your life."

He didn't answer her at first. He just kept holding onto her, afraid that if he let go, she would float away, and he would never see her again. Finally, after a few minutes, he responded, "I love you so much and I've been such a fool." He pulled back from her and sat on his feet. Dave kept his head bowed because he didn't want to make eye contact. He felt weak. She was speechless now. He was being so real. She hadn't seen this side of him in a long time. "I'll be right back." He stood up and hurried to the bathroom. She walked over to the coffeemaker and poured two cups of coffee. She had a feeling she might need one now. Gina walked back over and placed the cups on the table as he was coming out of the bathroom. He sat down in front of her. He had thrown cold water on his face, but his eyes were still red and puffy.

"Did something happen at work last night?"

"I didn't go to work last night."

"Oh," she acted surprised, even though she already knew that.

"No, Gina, it's not like that. I had every intention of working the overtime last night, but I saw Keith's bumper sticker, then I dropped his card and when I picked it up, it got me to thinking, so I-"

She interrupted him. "Dave, you're not making any sense."

He stopped to collect his thoughts.

"I met a pastor, and we talked. He seemed like a good guy. I haven't been myself lately, and he made me feel comfortable. I'm not really a guy who believes in signs, but some things have happened recently that really got me curious about church. So, I gave up my overtime shift last night so that I could get some sleep and get up and go to church today."

"That's great. How did you like it? Where did you go? Did you-"

He placed his index finger over her lips and laughed.

"Take a breath. I'm getting to all of that. I pulled into the lot and tried to make every excuse in the world of why I shouldn't go in, and I almost left. But in the end, my curiosity got the best of me. I walked in the door and my heart felt peace. I took a seat in the sanctuary and listened to that pastor tell the story of Jesus. How He loved me so much that He died for me. It floored me that someone would do that for me." He was reliving the moment, and his voice portrayed the emotion in it of a man who knew this was true. "So, I gave my life to Jesus."

They kissed. It had been a long time since they had kissed, and even though it wasn't a passionate kiss, the feeling of their lips touching felt good.

"Dave, words can't describe the joy that I feel in my heart right now. What church did you go to? I must meet this pastor who could pique your interest."

"Faith Bible Church. I met Pastor Dunkirk when..."

"Pastor William Dunkirk?"

"Yeah, that's him. Do you know him?"

Gina told him the story of how she met Pastor Dunkirk. He was the visiting pastor on that day she first went to church with the Kings, almost two years ago to the date. He was the one who explained the path of salvation to her, and he was the one who led her to Christ. What were the odds? She smiled at him and took his hand in hers.

"You were the one who taught me not to believe in coincidences."

He smiled. "Can we go to his church together?"

"Yes. I would like that very much."

"I know we still have a lot to talk about. The last two years aren't going to erase themselves from our lives."

"It might take some time for us to get back to the intimacy we once shared. If you're serious about getting back into our lives, then you need to move back into the house to be with us. You need to put us first over work, over friends, and over any outside distraction to our marriage."

"I can do that." His voice softened. "How can you be so forgiving?"

"Dave, I love you. I never intended to give up on us. Christ is the ultimate example of love and forgiveness. Our goal is to be more like Him. He forgave those who hated Him, beat Him, and ultimately killed Him. It's in our human nature to rebuke that kind of love, but after reading the bible and praying for the last two years, He has changed my heart. I love you, so it was a lot easier for me."

They hugged, and he held her for as long as she would let him.

2

Carducci's seated them promptly at six thirty. They ordered the bruschetta, a Jackson family favorite, and each scanned the menu. Dave looked over at Marc.

"What are you thinking, champ?"

Gina interrupted.

"No pizza. You had that for lunch."

Marc sighed, "Come on, mom. A day of eating pizza is the dream."

Dave laughed.

"Yeah, come on, mom." He got the look. "I mean, your mom's right, buddy. That's too much pizza."

Marc responded, "What's the difference if I get pizza or manicotti? They both have red sauce, cheese and bread."

Gina smiled at him. "Manicotti is noodles, but you're right, no manicotti either, then. You like the chicken Alfredo here. Get that."

Marc sighed and lifted his menu to cover his face.

Dave covered his smile with his hand, and then asked his daughter, "What about you, Melissa? What are you thinking?"

"Cajun Shrimp Alfredo."

"That's a good choice. Maybe I'll follow your lead."

She continued to look down at her phone without responding.

Gina looked at her, "Put down the phone, we're at the dinner table."

"Since when does that matter?" She responded.

"Since right now. Put it down." Gina shot back.

Dave looked at her. "Listen to your mother Melissa."

She snapped back, "You make one dinner and now you're making the rules?"

This was a great start.

"Melissa, hand me the phone."

Melissa hesitated.

"Now," Gina asked firmly.

She handed her the phone and crossed her arms. Let the pouting begin. Dave leaned toward his daughter.

"Melissa." She didn't look up. "Melissa, look at me." She waited an extra second before finally looking at him. "Let's have a nice dinner together. Your mother and I want to talk to you two about something."

Her look changed from pouty to concerned. Dave looked over at Marc, and he had the same concerned look on his face. He panicked and blurted out the first thing that came to mind.

"I'm moving back into the house and we're going to go to church together every Sunday."

Their faces relaxed, and the relief was noticeable. He looked over at Gina.

"I thought we were going to ease into this," she casually responded.

"I'm sorry, but they both looked sick when I told them we wanted to talk to them. You guys thought it was the divorce talk, right?"

Both kids shook their heads, yes.

Gina smiled, "It's ok we were planning on telling them, anyway. Somewhere around dessert, but now is fine."

Both had a ton of questions. Dave took the time to explain to them he was wrong for moving out. That he never should have placed anything above Gina or them, and that unfortunately sometimes adults make poor decisions too. He apologized to them and promised that things would be different now. Dave also shared with them he gave his life to the Lord. He answered a flurry of questions from both kids throughout the meal and then listened to all the pain he had caused them over the last two years. His heart was heavy with what he had put them through, but he promised that moving forward things would be different.

"I love you guys very much, and I'm so sorry. I hope that over time, you both can forgive me."

Gina cleared her throat and spoke. "There's been a lot to digest tonight. Why don't we all have some dessert, a gigantic piece of whatever, and just decompress for the rest of the night?"

Dave smiled. "That sounds good to me. Marc? Melissa?"

They both smiled and nodded in agreement. They brought him up to speed on the current events in both of their lives, and by the end of dinner, things seemed better.

They went home that night and played board games together. It had been a long time since they enjoyed a family night like this. When they finished playing games, they watched some TV, and talked some more.

"So, what made you decide to accept Jesus, like mom?" Marc asked.

"When I heard Pastor Dunkirk tell His story, I knew in my heart that it was true. He died for me." He repeated with feeling, "for me. I didn't do anything to deserve His grace, but He gave it to me, anyway."

"Mom was pretty emotional about it, too."

"What about you, buddy? How do you feel about it?"

"I think it's great. I mean, who would do that? Someone that really and truly loved you."

Dave smiled. "Exactly."

"I'm tired, dad. I'm gonna go to bed."

Dave did not want to push the issue. Dave knew everyone had to discover the truth in their own time. He was just saddened because it took him so long to walk into a church and hear it. He thought about all the times he could have gone to church and didn't. Even in the last two years, his own wife knew, and he didn't want to hear it. He avoided religious conversation at all costs throughout his life, simply because he was always taught that it was a conversation killer. "Politics and religion are two topics to always avoid," his father would tell him. He realized he had gotten lost in his thoughts and looked over to see his son staring at him.

"You okay, dad?"

"I'm good. I just got lost in my thoughts for a moment there." He smiled and kissed Marc on the forehead. "Goodnight, son."

Marc hugged him. "Goodnight, dad."

He turned and walked toward the staircase. Dave looked over at Melissa. She was listening to her headphones and reading a magazine. She looked up to see him staring at her. Melissa removed her headphones.

"What? Do I have something on my face?"

He laughed.

"No. I'm just amazed at how much you've grown, and how beautiful you've gotten."

"Thanks." She pulled the headphones back over her ears. She waited a second and then looked up and noticed he was still staring. She removed the headphones again. "Anything else?"

"You look so much like your mother."

"I'm gonna hit the hay."

She stood and walked over to him and gave him a hug.

"I'm sorry you can stay and listen. I'll just watch TV."

"Dad, it's okay. I'm tired anyway."

He wrapped his arms around her and squeezed.

"Goodnight, sweetheart."

"Goodnight dad. I'm glad you're home."

"Me too."

She released and pulled away when he grabbed her and brought her back in. She laughed.

"Dad!"

"Okay...okay."

He let go, and she made her way upstairs to her room. A few minutes later, Gina walked into the room and sat next to him.

"That was a fun night."

"It was. I forgot how totally awesome you guys are."

They shared a laugh.

"Dave, I have to be honest with you right now. I am still struggling a bit with what has been going on for the past two years. I forgive you and I mean it, but I can't let go fully."

"I understand. My actions were the actions of a child, not a man. I was selfish and insensitive completely to this family's needs and regret it deeply."

"I know you do, but my human nature is dwelling on it, not my Christian one."

"It's because we're human. We strive to be Christlike, but our human nature still lives within us. And that's okay. We're not perfect. Trust me, you have been more forgiving and compassionate than most would ever be, including me. Thank you."

"You've learned a lot in a day."

"I talked to Pastor Dunkirk after the service, and when I got home, I read through the materials that he gave me. They explained a lot and guided me to scriptures about forgiveness, love, and grace. I know I still have a lot to learn, but I'm excited about the upcoming journey."

"I'm excited to walk it together, and hopefully one day with the kids."

She leaned into him and rested her head on his shoulder. He put his arm around her and rested his head on hers. His mind drifted once again to the dilemma of telling her about the cancer, or just enjoying the moment. He enjoyed the moment.

Chapter 9

Monday—July 4, 2010

Gina woke up to the smell of Bacon. She looked over at the clock. It was 9:30 a.m. She couldn't remember the last time she slept in that late. She threw the covers off and did a full body stretch. It felt great. She got up, slipped on her slippers and her robe, and headed downstairs. The smell of bacon and freshly brewed coffee was strong. She smiled as she walked into the kitchen to see Dave standing at the stove flipping pancakes. He turned and saw her.

"Good morning."

"Good morning," she responded.

"Have a seat. I'm making some pancakes, bacon, and home fries for breakfast."

He left the stove for a moment while he poured a fresh cup of coffee. He walked over and sat it down in front of her. Dave kissed her on top of the head and then retreated to the stove.

"Thank you," she said, smiling.

"You're most welcome."

"Do you want me to go grab the kids?"

"No, this breakfast is just for me and you. They won't up get until after eleven. I'll save them some bacon and they can eat it with their cereal."

She laughed, "I hope you made a ton of bacon because that's something you generally don't save."

He turned and smiled. "I promise I'll save them some."

"What's got you up cooking this morning?"

"A great night's sleep."

"Don't you have to work at seven tonight?"

"I do, but I'll take a nap later."

"What's your plan for the day?"

"That's what I was going to ask you."

"It's the fourth, so we made plans to go over to the Kings, but I can cancel."

"What time did you make plans to go over there?"

"Around six for dinner."

"We can hang out until then. I'll probably leave here for work around six anyway to get a quick workout in before I start."

"Why workout, aren't you dying from cancer, anyway?"

He froze where he stood. He slowly turned and looked at Gina. She was looking down at the paper and sipping her coffee.

"What did you say?"

She looked up at him. He had a deer in the headlights look about him.

"Are you okay? You look like you've seen a ghost."

"No, I just thought I heard you say something."

She smiled. "Nope, just waiting for my breakfast."

He stuttered, "coming right up."

Dave placed the pancakes, home fries, and bacon on the plate. He walked over and sat the plate in front of her.

"Bon appetite."

She folded the paper and sat it on the edge of the table.

"It looks and smells great."

"Hopefully it tastes that way."

She took a few bites as he walked over to the counter and retrieved his plate and coffee. He removed the pill bottle from his robe pocket and took one. He placed the bottle back into his pocket. So far, the pills had really helped with the pain, but for how long? He picked up his plate.

"You did a great job, Dave. You have six months left, right?"

He dropped the plate. It was only a few inches off the counter, so it didn't break, but it made a loud clanking sound as it hit. Some potatoes fell off the side onto the counter. The noise startled her, and she turned around.

"Sorry, butterfingers," he stated. "I didn't hear what you said."

"I said that you did a great job."

"I didn't hear the second part."

"There was no second part. I'm a little worried about you this morning. Are you sure you're alright?"

"Yeah, I'm fine. A little embarrassed about dropping the plate."

He picked it up along with the coffee and joined her at the table. She stared at him as he sat down.

"Thanks for breakfast."

"You're welcome. So, you do like it?"

"I do. It shouldn't surprise you. You're the breakfast man," she gave him a playful shove, "You used to cook breakfast on the weekends all the time. Most people look forward to the weekend to sleep in. I always looked forward to the French toast, or frittatas, or whatever you cooked."

"The twelves might derail that a bit, but I'll do my best to start that trend again."

She flashed him a smile. He wanted to tell her in that moment about the cancer. It wasn't fair not to tell her, but something inside of him still said, "It's not the time." Was there ever a great time to have this conversation? He knew it was going to happen. It had to. But after he told her, he knew things would change. He would see only pity and sorrow in her eyes when he looked at her.

"After breakfast, do you want to go sit in the swing?" She asked.

"That would be great. Can we take the bible and study it together?"

It surprised her to hear those words come from his mouth.

"Yes, of course."

"Great."

They finished their breakfast and met out back at the swing after he retrieved his new bible from the apartment. She brought hers and they sat next to each other, legs touching. They focused on the book of James. She told him it was one of her favorite books of the bible because it focused on living wisely. Although it is only five chapters, James really spoke to the heart of living a faithful life in Christ. They studied the first chapter together. She flipped to a particular verse.

"My favorite passage in James chapter one is verses nineteen and twenty. It says, 'So then, my beloved brethren, let every man be swift to hear, slow to speak, slow to wrath;for the wrath of man does not produce the righteousness of God.'"

"So, James is telling us to listen first, speak wisely, and not to let our anger get the best of us because anger does not show God's love to us."

"In a nutshell, yes, but he's not saying there isn't a time for wrath. He's just saying to be 'slow to wrath.' Take your job, for instance. You deal in a multitude of stressful situations that cause you to act and use physical force in those situations. But not all situations call for force quickly. Some allow you to get information and possibly find a peaceful solution without force. Just like everyday life, when we deal with one of those situations, He is telling us to take the time to listen. Choose your words wisely, and not to let your anger get the best of you. Anger has a way of muddying the waters and escalating a situation that can have a peaceful solution."

"That's good advice."

"It's godly advice. To end the chapter, he encourages those who are believers to share their knowledge with the rest of the world. In verse twenty-two, he tells us, 'But be doers of the word, and not hearers only, deceiving yourselves.' Once we know the truth. It is our obligation to share the joy of His grace with others."

"But what if they don't want to hear it?"

"Then we pray for them."

"That's it?"

"Dave, that's all we can do. You can't force anyone to believe. God gave us freewill to believe and live as we choose."

"It just seems like a straightforward decision."

"That's because you went into church yesterday with an open mind and an open heart. You heard the message and knew that it was the truth. It took you 42 year's Dave. Some make that decision a lot younger, some a lot older, and some never do."

"That's so sad. I want everyone to experience that feeling. The feeling of complete freedom. It was as if my soul leaped inside of my body."

"Mine too. It's a feeling like no other. But every man and woman must make that decision themselves. We can't make it for them."

"Freewill?"

"Freewill. You're going to understand a lot more after reading His word and going to church on Sundays. It's truly eye opening."

"I look forward to it." He grabbed her hand. "But what about the kids?"

"They have to make that decision as well."

"Can't we just make them accept Him? I mean, they're our kids."

"No. You must invite Him into your heart. They have their own heart. It's their decision to make, but with two parents living and modeling godly lives, their odds are much greater than most."

"I understand, but I thought that after you gave your life to Christ, and with the influence of the Kings, they would already have done the same."

"I was hoping, but neither has come to me with the news of their salvation yet."

"Maybe they just haven't told anyone."

"If that's the case, then I would have to question if they actually accepted Him into their lives. You remember how you felt?"

"Yeah, explosive."

"Exactly. I must imagine that's how all feel after making such a huge decision. If nothing else, I feel they would be excited to tell us."

"True, but they're thirteen. They're at a very confusing age. Maybe they're shy or embarrassed to talk about it in front of their peers."

"Maybe. We just must trust that they'll come to us when the time is right."

"Hopefully sooner than later."

"Hopefully."

"You know, in the information packet that Pastor Dunkirk handed me, there was a great quote from Saint Francis of Assisi. He said, 'Preach the gospel at all times; If necessary, use words.'"

She flashed him a big smile.

"I love that quote."

A slight pain in his abdomen jumped up and grabbed him. He flinched and gave her hand a firm squeeze. It passed as quickly as it had appeared, but he found her staring at him.

"Sorry," he chuckled, "Involuntary squeeze."

"And a good one." she pulled her hand back and massaged it. "What sparked that?"

"Life. I feel like a new man."

She smiled and nestled into his shoulder.

"I like this new man. He reminds me a lot of the old one I married...but with a twist."

He put his arm around her and rested his chin on the top of her head. They sat like that for a while. No words, just two people who truly loved each other enjoying a beautiful summer day.

2

At 6:00 p.m. Dave sat on the workout bench in the station weight room. He had his eyes closed, talking to God in his head. The voice of Mike Shawnee interrupted him.

"There's a couch in the locker room if you want to take a nap, old timer."

Dave opened his eyes and smiled.

"I'm like seven years older than you, Mike. What are you, like 35?"

Mike stopped and glared at him.

"I'm 27."

Dave laughed. "Sorry, you could pass for 35 easily."

"You wanna go, old man? Cause if you're itching to go a few rounds, I'll help you out with that."

"I try to make it a practice to never spare with giants."

"Ha, ha, ha, Dave the comedian. What do you want it to say on your headstone?"

Dave threw his hands up and laughed.

"You win. I'm not ready for a headstone just yet. How many days a week do you work out?"

"Two times a day, six days a week. My day of rest fluctuates."

"So, all you do is work and workout? Don't you have a fiancée?"

"Yeah, we workout together most days. She only does it once a day, though."

"What kind of work does she do?"

"She teaches fifth grade at Junction Elementary."

"Nice. Does she like it there?"

Mike stopped stacking weights and looked at him.

"Is this going to be a thing with you now?"

"What?"

"Talking instead of working out?"

"No, I was just making conversation."

"We got the next twelve hours to make conversation while we work. I'll write up a summary of my life and get it to you by the end of the week. That way, we'll really know each other."

Rude.

"Sorry Mike, I'll let you work out in peace."

"Thanks."

Mike walked over to the radio and popped in a CD. Heavy metal filled the airwaves as he cranked up the volume and returned to the bench. He looked over at Dave.

"This music is okay with you?"

As if Dave had a choice.

"It's fine," he shouted over the extended electric guitar solo.

Mike just nodded his way without saying a word. Before he could lie back and start benching, Dave added one more thing.

"St Michael is the angel who throws Satan out of heaven in the book of Revelation."

Mike walked over and turned down the volume.

"What?"

"Your charm. Saint Michael. He is the angel who casts Satan, and the fallen angels out of heaven."

"Okay."

"Remember the other day I asked you what it meant?"

"Oh, when you were trying to feel out my mom's situation?"

"No, I wasn't trying to feel out your mom's...I'm married. I'm just letting you know who Saint Michael is."

"I already told you, he's the protector of cops."

"I know, but he's much more than that. I just thought you should know the significance of the charm you're wearing around your neck."

His eyes looked upward as he sighed.

"Thanks. Are you a holy roller now, Dave?"

"A holy roller? What do you mean?"

"You know, someone who likes to preach at people and let them know how religious they are."

"I was just telling you about your charm, bro." He paused for a moment and then continued, "Sunday at church, I accepted the gift of salvation by placing my trust in Jesus. But I'm not someone who is going to flaunt how religious I am. I'm still figuring things out myself."

"Whatever, dude."

He walked over and turned the volume up louder. He laid down on the bench and started lifting. Dave sighed and walked over to the row machine. They worked out in silence until their shift started.

3

After roll call, Dave explained to his shift the decision that he made to accept the Lord. He knew they would find out over time if he just let things happen naturally, but he felt the need to share with them the life-changing decision that he had made. Most were indifferent to his decision. A couple cracked some bible thumper jokes, and a few shook his hand and wished him luck. No one shared they had made that decision in their own life, but he assumed some had based on their personalities over the years. Lisa walked up to him last. She smiled and gave him a hug.

"That's great Dave. I hope you find the peace you're looking for."

"I wasn't really looking for peace, but I was looking for something. I didn't know what until I walked into church that day. It would be great if you wanted to come to church with-"

She interrupted him before he could finish.

"I'm good right now, Dave. If I change my mind, I'll let you know."

He could take a hint.

"Okay. Meet up for coffee later?"

"You bet."

He collected the rest of his gear from the arms room and made his way out to his patrol car. He threw his bag on the passenger side seat and secured the shotgun in the stock. Remington 870. He was one of the last to carry a shotgun. Most carried the AR-15 or some other semi-automatic weapon, but Dave always preferred the good old comfort of the Remington. He walked around the car and completed his inspection. No new dings, scratches, or abnormalities to report. The emergency lights and siren worked, and the tire depth was acceptable. He sat in the driver's seat and fired up his computer. All seemed to work fine, so he opened a CAD number and logged his inspection results. He didn't love all the changes in law enforcement that had happened throughout the years, but he loved the digital logs instead of the handwritten one. Technology was at the forefront of his career, and they were all forced to accept the one thing that most of them hated. Change. He sighed and sat back in his seat. He was hoping to partner with Javier tonight. Dave knew Javier was a believer and wanted to share the good news with him, but he called in sick.

A couple of hours into the shift, he had pulled some stops and written a few tickets. He looked down at his phone. Nothing. Usually there was some chatter and texts would fly early in the night. Just goofy banter and silly pictures to lighten the mood. He looked at his watch. The time was 2215, or 10:15 p.m. according to the rest of the world. He finished filling out the notes on the tickets he had written and sat on the traffic light at Barton and Molar. Usually some of them grabbed a coffee at DD around 2100, but tonight the phone and radio were silent. He wondered if the rest of them were already cutting him out because of his declaration. Before he could overthink it, a white Cadillac Escalade drove through the red light almost three seconds after it had turned. Dave shifted into drive and went after it. He got behind the vehicle and ran the license plate. The registered owner came back to Darren Jefferson, living in their neighboring city, Harlan. The vehicle had no hits or wants on it and the registration was valid. Dave activated his lights.

"616 radio with traffic."

Dispatch replied, "Go ahead 616."

"Barton and Schubert with GLX139. That's, George Lincoln X-ray, one three nine."

"Barton and Schubert at 2221."

Dave angled his spotlight to shine through the back window into the rearview mirror. He could see people moving around in the vehicle. The owner of the vehicle came back with a valid driver's license and no warrants, but it showed that he had many tickets for multiple offenses. Dave exited the patrol vehicle and walked toward the driver's side. He kept his flashlight in his left hand, focused on the driver's side window, and his right hand resting on top of his holster. He scanned the vehicle as he approached and instructed the driver to roll down the back windows. The driver complied and as he approached the driver's side back window, he could see that it was children moving around in the vehicle. The little girl sitting behind the driver smiled and waved at him as he got to the window. He smiled and waved back. He stood just at the rear of the doorpost and observed that the driver was sitting with both hands on the steering wheel.

"Good evening, sir. Can I please see your license, registration, and proof of insurance?"

"What seems to be the problem, officer?"

"We'll talk about that after I get your information."

The driver pulled his wallet out of the center console, along with the registration and insurance certificate. He handed all three to Dave. It was the registered owner, Darren.

"Did I go through the yellow light?"

"It was red for a couple seconds before you drove through the intersection, Mr. Jefferson."

"Agree to disagree I guess officer, anyway, the kids were being rowdy and moving around and I looked down for, like, one second. Do you think you could cut me a break this one time?"

"That's another question I have for you. Why are the kids moving around in the vehicle?"

"They don't like to wear their seatbelts. They can't play with each other."

"You have three kids here all under the age of ten, I'm guessing, and none of them are wearing seatbelts."

"Good eye." He pointed to each kid and said their age. "Five, seven, and nine."

"You don't make them wear a seatbelt in a moving vehicle?"

"No. We let them make their own choices."

"Do you know how extremely dangerous that is? If you get into an accident, which is quite probable when running a red light, all three of them could be seriously injured or killed." He looked down to see the driver wearing his seatbelt. "You have yours on."

He looked at the kids, who were all sitting quietly in a seat. "That's because I make smart decisions." He then looked at Dave and winked.

"Do you think we're playing some kind of game here?"

"No officer, I was just trying to stress the importance of safety to them."

"You're the parent. You tell them to wear their seatbelt."

"That defeats the purpose of what me and their mother are trying to teach them. It's up to them to make the right decision."

Dave was getting frustrated.

"Well, let me tell you what the law is going to teach you today. It's going to teach you that a five-, seven-, and nine-year-old is required to wear a seatbelt in a moving vehicle in the state of Michigan. It's very irresponsible to expect children that young to do that on their own. You, as the adult, need to teach them that so they can be safe."

"We obviously have different parenting styles. You like to be a controlling parent who will teach their children not to think for themselves. You like them to rely on you their whole life so that you can control them and show them that following is the way to live. I will teach my children to be independent thinkers. They will make their own decisions, good or bad, and learn from their choices. In the end, they will function independently and live productive lives."

Dave felt his blood pressure rise as he stared at the smug look on Darren's face. He opened his mouth when he stopped. His mind went to the conversation that he and Gina had after breakfast today. 'The wrath of man does not produce the righteousness of God.' He looked at him and smiled.

"Mr. Jefferson, I agree with you on a couple of points that you made."

"Thank you, Officer Jackson, I see-"

Dave held up his hand and he stopped talking.

"Let me finish, sir. I agree that we have different parenting styles. As adults, we are tasked with the job of making sure that our children grow up feeling loved, safe, and responsible. To do that, we must enforce rules while their young. Rules that teach them how to be responsible, respectful, and reliable. Rules show people that there are boundaries. Boundaries keep your child from running out into traffic. From eating ice cream for dinner, or being disrespectful to others, or even jumping around the backseat of a moving car, just to name a few. Rules also are the difference between watching your children grow up to be productive members of society, or having a jobless 40-year-old living in your basement playing video games all hours of the night. I also agree with you that people will make their own decisions, good or bad, and live with those choices. So, the choice you have made today is to disregard a red light, and to let three minors not use their seatbelts. I see that your insurance certificate has expired, sir."

"The new one is on the table in the den."

"You realize you need to keep a current one in the vehicle at all times?"

"Yes. It's the same policy."

"So, you have consciously decided to not keep a current insurance certificate in the vehicle."

"I just forgot to put it in the car."

"But you opened the envelope from the insurance company, saw the new certificate, and thought it should go in the den instead of in the vehicle?"

Darren became frustrated now.

"No, I didn't think it should go in the den. I just forgot to put it in the car."

"Okay, Mr. Jefferson, sit tight. I'll be right back."

"Officer, can you give me a break this time?"

"I don't understand. You're the one who lectured me about decision making and consequences. How my ways are primitive and outdated. I don't understand what you're asking me to do, sir."

"You know what? It's fine. Do what you're going to do."

With that, he waved Dave away with his hand. Dave turned and walked back to his patrol vehicle. He returned a short time later with a ticket.

"Okay, Mr. Jefferson, here are your citations for disregarding a red light, no proof of insurance, and three seatbelt violations."

"Are you kidding me? You wrote me for every violation?"

"I did. You need to take care of them within 14 days. You can either pay them or call this number," he pointed to the phone number, "and make a court date to dispute the violations."

"I'll be making a court date, officer. You can count on that."

"I don't understand why you're so angry, sir."

"You don't understand why I would be angry about receiving five tickets?"

"You are the one who explained the rules to me. I was just going by your standards."

"You could have at least given me a break on one of them."

"I would have, but you let pride dictate the way this traffic stop progressed."

"I literally asked you for a break."

"Then I asked you to explain what you're asking me to do. You couldn't find it in yourself to apologize for any of the infractions. You didn't think about the wrongs, just the financial aspects, and even then, you couldn't humble yourself. When your kid breaks something at home, don't you want them to say they're sorry and feel remorse for what they did?"

"Are we through here? Can I go?"

"We're through. You can go when each one of these little ones is properly wearing a seatbelt."

Dave backed away. He jumped out of the vehicle. Dave stood at the rear of the vehicle and watched as he buckled each child into a seat. When he finished, he looked at Dave.

"Is that what you wanted? Can I go now?"

"You can go."

He got into his vehicle, shifted into drive, and left. Dave stared at the car until it was out of sight. He walked back to his patrol vehicle and got in. It was 2240, and he needed a coffee. He shifted into drive and headed for DD. He pulled into the lot and saw three other squad cars parked. He could see three officers sitting at a table in the corner. Lisa was one of them. He walked in and up to the counter. A young man he hadn't seen before approached the other side.

"What can I get you, sir?"

"Just a medium black coffee, please. Are you new?"

"Just started tonight."

"Welcome aboard."

"Thanks."

"Is Kevin back there?"

"Yeah, he's baking the donuts."

Before he could respond, Lisa appeared on his right.

"Hey Dave. I was just about to text you to meet us here."

He smiled at her.

"Oh yeah. I must have sensed it."

"Come on over and join us."

"Yeah. Give me a minute. I was just getting to know..."

He looked at the kid.

"Jake."

"I was just getting to know Jake."

"Okay, well, come on over when you're done."

He nodded, and she walked back over to the group.

"So, where are you from, Jake?"

"Home-grown sir."

"Yeah. You're going to enjoy working here. Good people."

"I hope so."

He smiled at him.

"You will." He leaned in and whispered. "How long have these schmucks been here?"

"About a half an hour, I guess."

Ouch.

"Thanks, buddy. Have a good night."

Dave walked out the door toward his car. He opened the door when he heard Lisa's voice.

"I thought you were going to join us?"

"Not tonight."

"Dave."

"It's okay. I get it."

Dave hopped into the vehicle and fired it up. He watched as Lisa turned and walked back into DD. He shifted into reverse and backed up. He shifted into drive and took one more look at the table in the corner.

She was staring out at him while the other two were talking and laughing. He left the parking lot and headed to somewhere he could dock, write his notes, and lick his wounds.

Chapter 10

Tuesday—July 5, 2010

Gina walked the cardiac floor, attending to her patients. Twenty years on the job and she still looked forward to going into work every day. She spent sixteen of those years in the ER, and loved every minute, but she really loved having the same patients to care for daily. Some were in and out in a matter of days, but others were there for weeks. She was a nurturer by nature, and after she accepted Christ into her heart, that nature kicked into overdrive. Her patients and their families loved her. She was standing at her station filling out a patient's chart when Patty walked up.

"Good morning, Gina."

She smiled, "Good morning, Pats."

"Frank and I were talking last night in bed, and we are still so excited about Dave."

"I know. He's like a different person, but somehow the same, if that makes sense."

"It does. Dave has always been a good guy, that's for sure, but when he trusted the Lord, he super-sized his life."

She laughed.

"Super-sized his life."

"Yeah. He took all the good qualities that he already had, the regular meal of life, and added the Holy Spirit. You know, super-sized."

"Do you want McDonalds for lunch Pats?"

"No. Well, maybe. I'm just saying he decided to supersize."

"I get it. What's your day look like?"

"Regular rounds. All my patients seem well today, knock on wood, so hopefully an uneventful day. You?"

"Same. Lord, willing it stays that way. Lunch at 1230 in the break room?"

"Sounds good. Your floor or mine?"

Patty worked on the cancer ward. Gina respected her for that choice, but she couldn't bring herself to do the same.

"Mine."

"Okay, I'll see you back here at 1230."

They hugged, and Patty headed back. Gina continued filling out the chart for Mr. Blake. Jonathon Blake was 34 years old. He had his first heart attack at 33 last year. He already had one stint put in and was back after his second heart attack two days ago for another. Jonathon was tall, with an athletic build, so he didn't look like your prototypical heart attack victim. Unfortunately, the men in his family, from his great grandfather on down, had heart issues. She finished writing and went into his room. He was watching the news.

"Good morning, Jonathon."

He turned to look at her.

"Good morning, Gina."

"Did you sleep okay?"

"I did."

"Good. How are you feeling today?"

"I feel good. Does that mean I don't need another stint?"

She smiled. "It just means that the medicine is working. Any pain or discomfort?"

"Not really. Just this small one in the center of my chest."

"Ha, ha, always the comedian." She stopped and stared at him. "Seriously?"

"No, I'm fine. When is my surgery again?"

"Two o'clock."

"So, by this time tomorrow, I will be on my own coach resting?"

"God willing, that's the plan."

"Why do people say that? God willing."

"If it's his will for you to be on that couch, you will be."

"And if it's not, I'll be right here, or in the ICU, or worse...Dead?"

Curveball thrown.

"I'm sure you will be on your own couch tomorrow."

"But you can't know for sure, can you?"

"No."

"I'm 34, in great shape, well outwardly, and I'm a good person. Why am I allowed to suffer the fate of this tragic ailment? Why not someone who is grossly obese with a dark attitude who makes no contribution to society?"

She sat down on the corner of his bed and looked at him.

"I can't fully answer that for you, Jonathon. I don't know for sure. All I know is that he allowed His Son to be beaten and put to death. So why would mankind get a pass from pain and suffering? We are all put through our own trials and tribulations, whether physical or mental. It's just how life on this earth is."

"But according to scripture, His son lived again."

"And so can we."

"But not in this life."

"No. Not in this life."

"Gina, I'm not a man of faith, so I'm not going to pretend to know about God or Jesus or any other religious aspect of life, but it just seems cruel to me."

"As humans on the outside looking in, that's how it seems. But His plan for your life can only be magnified and make sense if you trust and believe in Him. In the book of Isaiah chapter fifty-five verses eight and nine, He tells us, 'For My thoughts *are* not your thoughts, Nor *are* your ways My ways, says the Lord.For *as* the heavens are higher than the earth, So are My ways higher than your ways, And My thoughts than your thoughts.'"

"Maybe one day Gina. But right now, I can't force myself to believe in a God who refuses to give us answers."

"He gives us answers, Jonathon."

"The bible?"

"Yes."

"Those stories are so unbelievable. A great flood wipes out the earth except for a few chosen. An 80-year-old man leading people out of slavery against a mighty pharaoh. A young boy besting a giant with a stone. Men going to heaven without dying. Fish swallowing a man for three days and then spitting him out alive. A virgin birth. How can anyone believe these fairytales?"

"Faith. All these stories happened. They were recorded to show us that man has needed His guidance and love since creation. They serve as an inspiration to us and show us that our troubles are not new. That is when we call out His name and trust Him. As far as the belief factor goes, He tells us in Philippians chapter four verses six and seven, 'Be anxious for nothing, but in everything by prayer and supplication, with thanksgiving, let your requests be made known to God; and the peace of God, which surpasses all understanding, will guard your hearts and minds through Christ Jesus.' Those three words, 'surpasses all understanding,' explain God. As a believer we walk by faith. Not by sight."

"Gina, you're a wonderful nurse and a good person. I saw that in you when I was here last year, but I can't believe in someone I can't see."

"So, if you were born and your mother died giving birth, you wouldn't believe that she existed?"

"Well, obviously she existed or I wouldn't be here."

"But you have never seen her."

He smiled and scratched his chin.

"Okay, so there are exceptions to the rules."

"So, you believe we live for a short while and then we die? That's it?"

"I'm afraid so. I can't see it any other way."

She smiled and shook her head.

"If you don't mind Jonathon, I'll pray for your eyes to be opened."

"I don't mind at all."

"Okay then. Let's get those vitals."

She took his temperature, blood pressure, and logged his heart rate. She opened the door to leave the room.

"Gina."

She turned.

"Yes."

"Not that I believe in it, but can you pray that I'm sitting at home on my couch tomorrow?"

She smiled and responded, "I can do that."

"Thanks."

He smiled at her and then laid his head back on the pillow and resumed watching the news. She left the room and returned to her station to write more information on his chart. It was apparent that Jonathon read the stories of the bible, but he was having a hard time giving his life to God.

Something was holding him back from believing. She was grateful for the opportunity to share her faith with him. She closed her eyes and said a quick prayer for Jonathon. "Father, please watch over Jonathon today and help his surgery to go well. Open his eyes to Your love and grace. Thank you, Lord. Amen." She opened her eyes and moved down the hall toward the next patient's room.

2

Marc sat on the swing outside strumming his guitar. Dave had bought a few packs of strings in case Marc broke another one. Marc was lightly strumming because he knew Dave was sleeping and didn't want to wake him. He was playing one of their favorite songs, *Cat's in the Cradle*. Over the years, other artists like Johnny Cash and Ugly Kid Joe did a good job of remaking the song, but they both preferred the original by Harry Chapin to all others. He was strumming and whispering the words under his breath.

"My son turned ten just the other day, he said, thanks for the ball, dad, come on let's play, can you teach me to throw, I said-a, not today I got a lot to do, he said, that's okay, and he, he walked away, but his smile never dimmed It said, I'm gonna be like him, yeah You know I'm gonna be like him. And the cat's in the cradle and the silver spoon..."

He stopped. He took a moment to wipe the tears from his eyes and collect his thoughts. Too sad. He started strumming again. *Sweet Home Alabama* came to mind, and he started plucking those all too familiar opening chords. Marc was fully invested in the classic rock genre. Melissa had branched out a little over the years, but Marc truly believed that the 60's and s70's were the absolute best decades for music. He appreciated the hair band phase of the 80's and the grunge trend in the 90's. But nothing compared to bands like Pink Floyd, Led Zeppelin, Bad Company, and singers like Bob Seger, The Motor City Madman Ted Nugent, and Alice Cooper. From the moment they brought him home until now, classic rock never left the radio in the car or at home. Maybe he could be one of those musicians that inspired others. He really loved playing the guitar now, and he had gotten very good at it.

"Carry me home to my kin," He sang underneath his breath.

"What are you doing?"

He stopped and looked up to see Melissa standing in front of him.

"Writing an essay on the dumbest questions ever asked. Congratulations, you just made the top of the list."

"Oh, I thought you were trying to play Sweet Home Alabama."

"Not trying. Succeeding."

"Sure."

She knew exactly how to get under his skin. He fired back.

"Why don't you go try to play the piano?"

"What I do is music. What you make is noise."

"Right now, all you're making is noise. When you open your mouth, all I hear is blah blah blah."

"I knew you were tone deaf."

"You know..."

He was getting ready to yell at her when he caught himself and stopped. He stared at her for a moment. She was looking down at her phone, texting. He also knew what pressed her buttons. He was just trying to figure out the perfect comeback. Was it her clothes? Maybe her hair? She realized that he had stopped talking and looked up to see him staring at her. And there it was. A small red spot on the right side of her nose that looked like a developing pimple.

"What are you staring at, weirdo?"

"That disgusting giant red pimple on your nose...gross."

It was not giant or even that red, but he hit the mark. She immediately covered it with her hand.

"It's not that bad."

"I can see that thing from the moon."

"Stop it, Mark. Go back to trying to play music."

"I can't even hear what you're saying. I'm so memorized by that beast."

She was so flustered she couldn't even think of a comeback. He smiled and started strumming again.

"Why are you such a jerk?"

He stopped.

"Me? You started it. I was just out here playing my guitar and hanging out."

She thought for a moment before speaking.

"I came out here to talk about mom and dad."

"What about mom and dad?"

She sat down next to him on the swing.

"It's weird. Right?"

"What part?"

"The part where they were on the verge of divorce, and now he's back like nothing ever happened."

He stopped messing with the tuner on his guitar and looked at her.

"They were in a terrible place. I guess not really a terrible place, but like you said, a weird place. You could tell that they still loved each other, but they didn't spend a lot of time around each other. Sometimes they acted like nothing was different, like dad living in the garage, and other times they seemed like they didn't even know each other. I don't know how to explain it, Lis. It was just super weird."

"Yeah. It's like that show dad used to watch. The one where mysterious stuff happened and sometimes, they explained it and sometimes they didn't."

"The Twilight Zone."

"I think you're right."

"I am right. It's a show that ran from 1959 to 1964. Starring Rod Serling. It always..."

"You were born in the wrong decade. Your music, the shows you watch, the movies..."

"I just appreciate the past, that's all. Anyway, you're right. It has that feel to it."

"I know."

"Dad never stopped caring about us. I heard mom talking to Mrs. King once, and she thought he was going through something she called a mid-life crisis."

"Maybe, but it just felt like he didn't know who he was or what he wanted anymore."

"I think that's kind of the definition of a mid-life crisis."

"Oh, well, maybe he was. I enjoy having him back in the house. It makes me feel like an actual family again."

"Yeah. He really seems to have figured something out. He told us he accepted Jesus, like mom did. Maybe that's what he needed."

"Maybe. He looks happier. Do you think we should..."?

She stuttered a little and then paused. He looked up at her.

"Should what?"

"Accept Jesus too?"

He thought about this for a moment before answering.

"I'm learning a lot about Him in church, and about all the distinct characters of the bible, but I'm just not ready to make that decision yet. Are you?"

"No. I'm learning a lot too, but I don't feel ready either."

"It is nice to see mom and dad looking at each other the way they used to."

"It is nice. Hey, dad will be up soon. You want to go in and make some sandwiches and mac and cheese for lunch?"

"Sure."

He set his guitar on the swing, and they made their way into the house. Dave sat by the bedroom window and smiled. He had gotten up early today, and when he looked outside and saw them sitting on the swing in the backyard together, he cracked the window without them noticing. He came into the conversation somewhere around the Twilight Zone. It was nice to see them getting along. Dave walked over and picked his pants up off the floor. He rooted through the pockets until he found the little white pill bottle. He waited about ten minutes to give the kids a chance to make lunch and threw one down the hatch. They were effective in dealing with the pain. He put on his robe and slippers and headed down the stairs. He looked around the corner to see them hard at work. Dave walked into the kitchen with a big smile on his face.

"What's this?"

Startled, they both turned to face him.

"Lunch. Are you hungry?" Melissa asked.

"I am."

"I just made a fresh pot of coffee, dad. Want a cup?" Marc asked.

"You know I do. Thanks, guys."

He sat down at the table and seconds later Marc sat the cup in front of him. He picked it up and placed his nose in front of it. Big inhale and then a loud exhale. He smiled and took a sip. They looked at each other and laughed. They knew some things would never change.

"Mmmmm...now that's an excellent cup of coffee."

3

Across town, Kurtis was rummaging through the cabinets for something to eat. He was trying to be quiet because his mother's new boyfriend was passed out on the couch with a beer bottle still in his hand. Except for a few condiments, the cupboards were bare. There was beer in the refrigerator, but not much else. He walked into his mother's bedroom. She was lying on the bed, sound asleep. Her hair was back away from her face, revealing a new bruise just below her left eye. Last night's excitement. He sat on the edge of the bed for a moment, staring at her. The years of drinking and drugs had taken their toll on Shannon.

She was seventeen when she found out that she was pregnant with Kurtis. Eighteen when she had him. The father, whose name she refused to speak, left before he was born. Her parents pressured her to give the baby up for adoption, so she took what possessions she had and moved as far away from them as she could. Kurtis has never met his grandparents, or even heard their voices. They moved around a lot while he was young before finally settling down in Dargen City five years ago. They were supposed to be just passing through when she got a job as a secretary at a trucking company in Detroit. The money was good, so she stayed. Within a few weeks of starting, the late nights of drinking and partying with the many truckers who came through that door became her lifestyle. Kurtis took a backseat to the next revolving door of the love of her life, and she hasn't looked back since. The guy on the couch was the next loser in line who used and abused her, but they all paid the rent and picked up the tab for her lifestyle.

Kurtis pulled the covers over her and kissed her forehead. He looked around the room, hoping to see a dollar or two lying on the floor or on a table. Nothing. She mumbled.

"You okay, baby?"

"I'm okay, mom. Go back to sleep."

She rolled over and pulled the covers over her head. He walked out of the room and closed the door. He walked back into the living room and saw Rick sitting up on the couch. Rick turned to him and smiled.

"I'm hungry kid. Make me some eggs?"

"There are no eggs."

"Then what is there?"

"You've been staying here for a month now. There's nothing. Zip. Nada. There never is."

He jumped off the couch and moved toward Kurtis before he had time to react. Kurtis backed up and rested his back against the wall. Rick brought his forearm up and placed it against his neck and held him against the wall. Kurtis turned his head to the side and braced for a hit. Rick applied pressure to his neck and put his face inches away from Kurtis. The stench of alcohol filled his nostrils.

"Boy, don't you ever disrespect me again. You mind your tone when you talk to me. You understand?"

He clinched his teeth as he spoke through the pain.

"Yes."

"Yes, what?"

"Yes, sir."

"That's more like it."

He released the forearm and grabbed Kurtis by his hair. He pulled him into the living room and launched him forward onto the floor. Kurtis propped himself up and sat there staring up at him. A single tear fell from his left eye. He wasn't hurt. He was angry. Kurtis knew that if he tried to retaliate, Rick would just take it out on his mom when he wasn't home.

"What do you want Rick?"

Rick laughed as he dug into his pockets. He pulled out an old waded up five-dollar bill. He threw it at Kurtis.

"Go down to the burger place on the corner and get me something to eat. A burger and some fries."

Kurtis picked up the money and stood up.

"The usual?"

"The usual, and make sure I get all of my change."

There was no need to ask if he could buy something to eat for himself. The answer was always no. Without saying another word, he walked past him and out the door. He hopped on his bike and headed for the Burger joint on the corner. Over the years, Kurtis had gotten good at making friends in the right places. He had friends all over town that worked in restaurants, convenience stores, and department stores. He lived off their generosity. Occasionally, he had to steal, but it was rare. He got caught once or twice, but he could charm his way out of it. He met Officer Jackson on one of those occasions, and he doesn't regret it. Officer Jackson treated him with kindness and respect. Something he hadn't experienced much from other adult men. Even when Jackson was being tough on him, he didn't make him feel worthless. He knew Jackson thought he was into drugs, but he wasn't. Kurtis tried them a few times, but because of what he saw in his mother's life, he really tried to stay away from them. He had a couple of friends who were pot heads, and that's who Jackson usually saw him hanging around. A local dealer had approached him a few times to sell, but so far, he had resisted the urge. They promised him good money, and they sure could use it, but he knew what came with it. Trouble, jail, and maybe even death. Somewhere deep inside, this neglected, forgotten kid found the strength to say no. He parked his bike on the rack outside the burger joint and went in. He was relieved to see Alyssa working at the counter today. She smiled as he walked up.

"You the errand boy again today?"

He smiled back, "Yep."

"The usual?"

"Yep."

He handed her the five, and she gave him four singles, two quarters, four dimes, a nickel, and five pennies back. He would take two dimes and three pennies back to Rick as his change and pocket the rest. Alyssa made him two burgers, two large fries and a large coke. She handed him the bag. He opened it and ate a burger and some fries.

"When is your mom going to move on from this loser?"

"If history is any sign," he looked at his wrist, pretending there was a watch there, "about two weeks."

They both laughed.

"Good. So far, he's the worst."

He thought about that for a minute.

"I think Mason was the worst."

"Really?"

"Yeah. He was bigger and hit harder."

"Yeah, but he was only around for like a couple of weeks."

"True. But he did a lot of damage."

Alyssa grabbed his arm.

"Someday you'll be out of this place and be better off."

"Yeah."

"Whatever happened to Mason, anyway? Usually, guys stick around for longer than two weeks. I mean, your mom's young and pretty."

"I don't know. Maybe he moved or something."

What Kurtis would never find out is that Dave and three of the largest men on the planet to wear a uniform strongly encouraged Mason to stay away from their house. He found out that Mason had a violent history of abusing women and children. He knew what was going on in that household with Mason around, and he made it his mission to make sure that it stopped. Mason decided that there were plenty of fish in the sea and moved on.

"Yeah, maybe. Good riddance."

"I'll second that. Thanks a lot for the food, Alyssa. I should probably get going."

"No problem, Kurt. See you later."

He smiled and waved as he walked out the door and got back onto his bike. He got back to the house and when he walked through the front door, Rick was asleep on the couch again. A fresh bottle of beer half drank and on the floor by him. Kurtis placed the bag on the table by his head and laid the twenty-three cents next to it. He turned and walked back out the door. He hopped on his bike and headed for the park. It was a nice day to sit in the park and read.

4

Pastor Dunkirk sat in his office flipping through his notes for the Wednesday night believer's service. All four of his children were in the church either helping in some capacity or playing. Matthew and Sarah walked around the sanctuary, making sure that all the hymnals and bibles were neat and secure in the pocket on the back of the pews. Brenda was sitting in her dad's seat on the platform, reading. Seth was making sure that the choir section was clean, and that each chair had a song list on it for tomorrow night's service.

"Everybody else is working while you're just sitting there," Seth barked at Brenda.

Brenda said nothing. She just kept reading without even looking up.

"Did you hear what I said?" He yelled.

She continued reading with a smirk on her face.

"BRENDA!"

Matthew stopped straightening for a moment to address his sister.

"Brenda, you know that drives him nuts. Just answer him, please."

She held up her index finger to Matthew as if to say, one moment. He rolled his eyes and stood there, waiting for her response. She finished the chapter and put her bookmark in place.

"I'm not answering him Matthew (emphasis on the M) because I'm reading, not 'just sitting' as he so eloquently put it."

"You're no smarter than us, Brenda (Emphasis on the B)," Seth responded.

"That's enough arguing, you two," Matthew stated.

"You're not the boss of us," Brenda and Seth shouted together.

Sarah laughed as she straightened a bible.

"That's real mature Sarah," Matthew responded.

"They're not wrong. You're not the boss of them."

"I'm the older brother. It's my job to make sure they don't disturb dad while he's trying to prepare for tomorrow night's sermon."

"You just like bossing them around. Admit it."

"Stick a sock in it, Sarah."

"You think just because you're going to college this year, you're so much better than us?"

"Smarter, not better."

"Whatever Einstein."

She stopped talking, and they looked up on the platform when they heard the two youngest laughing. Brenda was watching Seth mimic Sarah.

Matthew shouted at them all, "Enough of this tomfoolery! Everyone needs to get back to work."

The three of them pointed and laughed at him.

"Tomfoolery? How old are you, Matthew?" Sarah asked.

"You sound like Dad," Seth stated.

"Yeah. Sorry, Pastor Dunkirk." Brenda joined in.

They laughed even harder.

Matthew shook his head and returned to work. Sarah continued to straighten, and both Seth and Brenda were now cleaning up the choir section as they continued to laugh. Matthew smirked as he cleaned because he knew something they didn't. He had given all three of them a common enemy to focus on. In doing so, they laughed at him but did their chores without thinking about it. Now, who is the smartest?

The pastor had decided that he was going Old Testament on Wednesday night. He would preach on the faith of Daniel. A man who refused to bow down to anyone other than the Lord. He spent a night in the lion's den without so much as a scratch from the beasts. Daniel was truly a man of great faith. Bill was writing some notes when Dave popped into his head. He was thankful that Dave gave his life to God. He put down his pen and prayed.

"Lord, thank you so much for Dave. Give him strength in the knowledge of Your love and grace. Guide him and protect him as he serves You by watching over all of us by night. Soften his heart to Your ways and help him see the full majesty of Your unconditional love for him. Help him be a light to others who are lost. Use him for Your glory, Father. I ask this in Jesus' name. Amen."

He opened his eyes, took his pen in hand, and continued making notes. There was a knock on his door.

"Come in," he responded.

The door opened and Matthew entered.

"Were all done cleaning, dad."

"Are you sure?"

"I'm sure. It looks great."

"Okay." He looked at his watch. "I've got roughly fifteen more minutes and then I'll come check. If you think it's good enough, then you all can go."

"Yes, sir."

He closed the door as he left. He walked back into the sanctuary and told them what the pastor had said. They walked down each aisle again before they left. When he finished writing all his notes for tomorrow's sermon, he put the pen down and turned off his desk light. He placed his glasses on the desk and rubbed his eyes. He left his office and walked out into the sanctuary. Everyone except for Brenda was gone. She continued to read her book. Without saying a word, he walked around the entire sanctuary, inspecting the rows. They had done a great job. He walked up onto the platform and stood in front of Brenda.

"You ready to go home, jellybean?"

She placed her bookmark to hold her spot and looked up at him and smiled.

"Ready daddy."

She stood, and he gave her a big hug.

"You guys did a great job in the sanctuary."

"They did okay. When they left, I had to go back through and make sure I did everything right. I only had to fix a few things that they missed."

He laughed.

"Well done."

"They mean well. I just have to check up on their work occasionally."

"Well, thank you for doing so."

He put his arm around her, and she put her arm around him as they walked out together.

Chapter 11

Dave sat on the bench in front of his locker, lacing up his boots. He was smiling as he thought about the kids making him lunch today. Dave could barely remember when he was changing their diapers and feeding them formula, and now they were making him lunch. He stood up to grab his vest when his phone rang. It was Gina. He smiled as he answered.

"Hello my love."

"Someone's in a good mood."

"Today was a great day."

"I know I told you before you left, but be careful tonight."

"I will. How are you feeling? I know you were concerned about Jonathon's surgery."

"The nurse who took over for me called about ten minutes ago. He's recovering nicely, and it looks like he will go home tomorrow morning."

"That's great babe. I hope he thinks about what you two talked about."

"Me too. He's a good person. Oh, if I forgot to mention that dinner was magnificent tonight, I'll do it now."

As he sat on the bench talking to Gina, Javier walked up and opened his locker. He looked over at Dave and nodded hello. Dave nodded back.

He laughed. "I think you mentioned it a time or two. It was my pleasure to cook for such a hard-working lady."

Javier was putting on his shirt, trying not to eavesdrop but failing.

"Steak, baked potato, and all the fixings. The summer months are my favorite time of the year for food, thanks to the grill master."

"I don't know about master...well, okay, you said it...so, master it is."

They both laugh.

"Do you have any overtime, Wednesday or Thursday?"

"No OT, my love. Just 48 straight hours of me after tonight."

"I'll take it."

"I thought that tomorrow night we could go to the service at Faith bible, if that's okay?"

Javier raised an eyebrow. Dave pretended not to notice.

"Yeah, absolutely. I think that would be nice."

"Great, I'm going to finish getting dressed, so have a great night. I love you."

"I love you too. Goodnight."

"Goodnight."

He hung up the phone, stood and placed it on a shelf in his locker. He grabbed his vest and put it on. Dave reached into the locker and grabbed his shirt, completely ignoring the fact that Javier was standing there staring at him the whole time.

"You are not ignoring me?"

Dave started laughing.

"Sorry. I could see you out of the corner of my eye, staring daggers at me. I was just waiting to see how long it took you to say something."

"Well, I'm saying something now. You're going to church now? When did this happen?"

"I have a lot to tell you, my friend. We'll have to get together for coffee the first chance we get."

"I saw the schedule. We have enough to ride double tonight."

"Chambers and Knight beat us to it."

"Last I checked, you were senior officer. Pull a little rank."

He smiled, "The sarge already blessed it. We'll talk. We have to get to roll call before we're late."

"Okay, but I want to hear about this sooner rather than later."

"You will." He closed his locker and finished adjusting the last snap on his belt. Just before he turned to head toward the door, he stopped and looked at Javier. "Just know that we are not only brothers in blue, but that we are brothers in Christ now as well."

Javier's threw his arms around his friend and gave him a bear hug.

"Dave, that's great. This is incredible news."

"Easy big fella, you're going to break my ribs." Javier relaxed his grip. "Thanks, buddy. I feel great for the first time in a long time."

"My brother in Christ. Exciting news indeed my friend. I can't wait to tell Rita."

He smiled, "Let's get to roll call before the sarge has us doing every rookie task in the book for being late."

They finished grabbing the rest of their gear and exited the locker room. They found a seat in the squad room with maybe thirty seconds to spare. The sergeant peered down his glasses at them as they took their seats near the front. He handed out their assignments, briefed them on BOL's, and assigned them to their sections for the night. Dave and Javier weren't paired up tonight, but they were assigned to the same section. Roll call ended, and they stood up to go grab their equipment from the arms room. The sarge looked at Dave.

"Jackson, come see me in my office before you go out."

"Yes, sir."

He looked over at Javier, and he shrugged. They gathered their equipment, loaded up their cruisers, inspected them, and then Dave came back inside to see the sergeant. He was sitting in his office drinking coffee and shuffling through some paperwork. Sergeant Kinard was strait laced. He told you how it was and expected you to do the same. He had a reputation for treating everyone respectfully. Dave walked up and knocked on the open door. Kinard looked up from his desk.

"Come on in, Jackson, and shut the door."

"Yes, sir."

He shut the door and stood in front of the desk.

"Have a seat man, don't just stand there."

He laughed then sat down.

"You wanted to see me, sir."

"I'll cut straight to the chase. The grapevine reports that you have found some type of religion. Is that true?"

"Not some type of religion, sir. I've given my life to Jesus Christ."

"That would count as some type of religion." Dave was getting ready to say something when Kinard continued.

"We're not going to mince words here, Dave. I think that's great. I have talked to the Lord off and on throughout my life."

"Yes, sir."

"The point I want to make is this. You can't make your co-workers, citizens, or anyone else feel you're preaching at them."

"If someone complained, sir, I'm sorry, but I don't know when I did this..."

"You didn't. As someone who has been around the block in the military and law enforcement, I have always felt that the best way to deal with anything if I can, is to be proactive, not reactive."

"So, when you heard about my salvation through the grapevine, you thought it best to address it with me right away instead of waiting for a complaint?"

"Affirmative."

"Sir, you don't have to worry about me pushing God on anyone who doesn't want to hear it. I'm saved now and proud of it, that's why I told my shift, and will tell anyone who will listen why I am who I am now. But I understand I represent this department and while I wear this uniform, my personal views are views I keep to myself unless someone wants to hear them. Christ commissioned me to do a job, this job, and that's what I'm going to do to serve Him best."

"So, no preaching on traffic stops, on runs, to your fellow officers, or anyone else unless they want to hear it, or you're on your own time."

"Yes, sir."

"Wonderful talk, Jackson. You can head out onto the road now."

"Thank you, sir."

He stood and took a step toward the door.

"On second thought Jackson, sit back down for a minute."

He sat back down.

"Yes, sir."

"You have ten minutes to go over your spiel with me. After seeing a different side of you the last two years, I'd like to understand why you sought God."

Dave sat there for the next ten minutes, explaining to him why he accepted the path of salvation. He reiterated what led him to the church service, and what he heard in that service that caused him to put his full trust in the Lord. When the ten minutes were over and he stopped talking, Kinard sat back in his chair, rubbed his chin, and then leaned forward to address Dave.

"You know I've asked people that question in the past and none of them could lay it out for me like you just did. It was always, 'Just because

I believe,' or, 'This is what my family believes,' or, 'I thought it was time to change it up.' Good for you, Dave."

"Thanks, sir. We would love it if you came with us on a Sunday."

"I'm not sure that me and the good Lord see eye to eye on a lot of things."

"Maybe that's the problem, sir."

"How's that?"

"We're not meant to see eye to eye with Him. Like the heavens are higher than the earth, so are His ways higher than our ways. We're meant to trust and obey Him."

"I guess that's a whole other problem for me then. Trusting Him. I trusted Him to heal my mother when I was ten. She had cancer. I watched as she endured a very agonizing six months before she finally died. I prayed every morning, noon, and night for Him to heal her. He didn't. That sticks with you. Trust me."

"I'm sorry you and your mother had to go through that. But let me ask you this. Would anything have satisfied you other than her complete recovery?"

He thought about the questions for a moment before finally answering. "No. I suppose not."

"After my father died, I thought a lot about the time we spent together. I was grateful, and I mourned the fact that I didn't have him here with me anymore, but his memories lived on in my heart. I can't tell you why your mother went through that sarge, but I can tell you He loves you unconditionally, and cares for you deeply."

"He didn't show it through those six months."

"It's an awful thing for a family to go through."

Kinard felt his emotions get the best of him. He reeled it in and looked up at Dave.

"Remember what we talked about, Jackson? Head on out."

"Yes, sir."

Dave closed the office door behind him as he left. He said a silent prayer for Kinard, "Father, please lift his spirits and give him strength. Let him see Your love. Amen."

2

Across town, in a back alley in the downtown area of Dargen City, Kurtis lifted the bottle of whiskey to his lips and took a sip. Seconds later, he was bent over at the waist, coughing, gagging, and trying to catch his breath. Ronnie Mann laughed hysterically at him and grabbed the whiskey bottle. He took a drink and smiled at Kurtis.

"Man, you are a lightweight."

Ronnie and Kurtis are the same age. He dropped out of school this year to explore a career in sales. Their home lives are similar, except that Ronnie has two younger siblings to care for. Ronnie is the friend and influence that Dave has been trying to keep him away from. They met five years ago when Ronnie was still going to school. Over the years, they have been mostly acquaintances, but in the last few months, they have been hanging out more and more. Ronnie has been working for the local dealer, Milo, for six months now. They have arrested him a few times for selling or possessing, but the money is too good to stop.

Fighting through the coughing fit, Kurtis says, "That stuff's awful."

"Maybe other substances are more your speed?"

"You mean like drugs?"

Ronnie laughed.

"Yeah, like drugs. Probably some Mary Jane to start."

"Mary Jane. What's that? A type of cigarette?"

Ronnie exploded with laughter. He took another sip.

"If you're going to work for Milo, you have to know and talk the lingo."

"I didn't say I was going to work for anyone. We're just hanging out."

"I know, but eventually you'll see all those Benjamins I'm pulling down and want a piece. There's no shame in making a little money for yourself. Especially with your home situation."

"It's fine at home."

"Please! Your mom's a train wreck, and her boyfriend is a user and abuser. You work for Milo, and he'll make sure he doesn't hit you or your mom again."

"I got things under control right now."

That was a lie.

"Whatever."

He held the bottle out for Kurtis.

"Nah, I'm good. That stuff ain't for me."

He saw what it did to his mother. He had no desire to go through life like her. A black Escalade with tinted windows pulled up and stopped at the end of the alley. It flashed the headlights at them.

"Hold this bottle Kurt, I'll be right back."

Kurtis took the bottle from him, and he jogged down the alley toward the car. Kurtis watched as the back window rolled down and Ronnie leaned into the car. The conversation lasted a few minutes before Ronnie left the window and walked back down the alley toward him. The Escalade drove away. As Ronnie approached him, he could see that he was counting a wad of money.

"Payday son," Ronnie shouted as he got to Kurtis.

"How much?"

Ronnie spread out the cash to show him it was hundred-dollar bills.

"Enough. Milo asked about you again. He asked me if you were ready to work for him."

"What'd you tell him?"

"I told him you were still thinking about it."

"What did he say?"

"He laughed and said you were being stubborn, but you'd eventually come around."

Kurtis stared back down at the wad of cash in Ronnie's hand.

"I gotta think about it."

"No problem. Let's go to Pop's and grab a pop and some goodies. On me."

Pops was a party store on the corner of the north end of the alley.

"Really? Thanks Ronnie."

Ronnie finished the rest of the pint and threw the bottle in an adjacent dumpster. They walked toward Pops, laughing and playfully shoving each other around. A squad car drove by just as they exited the alley and rounded the corner to go into the store. Ronnie ran through the door and looked out of the window through the rack of potato chips. Kurtis walked in after him.

"Was it that cop?"

"It was a cop, Captain Obvious." He laughed.

"No, not a cop. That cop? Officer Jackson?"

"No, it wasn't Officer Jackson. Why, what do you have against him?"

"He's busted me a few of times."

"Yeah, but you're not doing anything wrong right now."

"That doesn't matter. When you get on their radar, you're on their radar for life. Every time that dude sees me, he must stop and talk to me. 'Let me help you Ronnie,' and 'I can help you, Ronnie.' Unless he's going to pay my bills, he can't help me."

"He's arrested you before?"

"A few of times. He thinks he's better than us."

Kurtis had a different opinion of Dave, but he didn't want to share with his friend for fear that they would label him as a snitch. Plus, he really wanted a pop and some goodies. He was hungry. He changed the subject.

"What kind of pop are you getting?"

"Mountain Dew, son."

"Yeah, me too. Maybe a couple of slices to go with it?"

"Absolutely. Some chips and candy too. Come on Kurt, let's pig out."

Kurtis gave him a high five, and they headed toward the junk food.

3

Dave was heading toward Kurtis's hood when his phone went off. He pulled off to the side of the street and checked the phone. It was a text from Javier. "Coffee?" He smiled and text back, "DD?" Almost as soon as he sent his text, he got a response. "OTW." He set the phone back down and headed that way. Moments later, he got another text from Javier. "I'll grab two and meet you at the school." He sent back, "Sounds good." There was a middle school a couple of blocks from the coffee shop that they routinely met at throughout the night to talk and decompress. He sat at the back of the lot, waiting for Javier. A few minutes later, a set of headlights pulled into the west entrance. As soon as they got halfway through the lot, they went dark. Javier pulled up window to window and handed Dave his coffee.

"Medium two creams, two sugars, right?"

"Hilarious."

Javier laughed. "What I meant to say was, here is your medium black psychopath coffee."

"Psychopath. Where do you come up with this stuff?"

"It's common knowledge drinking black coffee reveals psychopathic tendencies."

"Says who?"

"Studies."

"Good grief. I just appreciate the flavor of the bean. I'm not someone who needs to pollute my coffee with sugar and cream."

He stared down his nose at Javier.

"Oh sure. You're a part of the one percent, but I'm messed up."

"Yeah, that's right."

They looked at each other and laughed. Javier held his coffee up.

"Agree to disagree my friend."

"Agreed."

They each took a sip.

"So, what did Kinard want to see you about?"

"You're going to love this, but first let me ask you a question. Did he or any other supervisor ever pull you into their office to speak to you about not sharing your faith while on duty?"

"He didn't?"

"Well, he didn't say that exactly. He just asked me to read the room. He didn't want me to make anyone uncomfortable while I was at work."

"Really?"

"I get it. I'm not a pastor. I'm a cop. My work and calling are different, but the same."

"I feel a deep thought heading my way."

Dave smiled.

"Were both servants of the Lord but have different callings. The pastor preaches while I enforce the law, but we're both tasked with living our lives holy and acceptable to Him. If we live by example, then it will open doors to minister to those who seek Him."

"Wow. A believer for less than a week and you're already talking like someone who has been one for years."

"Would you believe me if I told you that the Archangel Michael came to me in a dream?"

He choked as he took a sip of coffee.

"Are you serious?"

"Nah, I'm just yanking your chain."

"Not cool, Dave. I almost choked to death."

He laughed.

"I didn't know you were a drama major. I have really been reading the material Pastor Dunkirk gave me, and the bible. There are so many wonderful verses and stories."

"That's good. It appears you have a genuine passion to learn."

"I really do. The bible is like a great novel. I try to put it down, but I want to know what happens next. Before I know it, I've read chapters instead of verses."

"It can be like that. It's been a while since I've really read the word like I should. Sometimes you get so wrapped up in other things that you forget what's important. Like taking the time to read God's word and pray daily."

"I'm just sorry it took me this long to figure it out."

"You're only 42 buddy. You've got a lot of time left to serve Him."

Dave smiled at his friend.

"Yeah." He raised his coffee. "To time."

They took a sip.

"Now. Tell me about this transformation."

Dave told him about the initial conversation with Pastor Dunkirk and about all the circumstances that led him to church on Sunday morning. He filled him in on every detail, minus the whole pancreatic cancer diagnosis. When he finished telling him the story, Javier smiled and shook his head from side to side.

"That's a great story, Dave. I can't wait to tell Rita. She is going to be so excited."

"Thanks, buddy. Gina and I are reconnecting. It feels good."

Dispatch interrupted them. "616 and 612."

Dave responded.

"Go for both."

"23456 Acacia, the 7-11, there having trouble with a customer. A dispute over money exchanged."

Dave smiled.

"Both units on the way radio."

They shifted into drive and headed toward the 7-11.

4

It was 2:33 a.m. and Dave sat in the parking lot of Meyers Grocery, filling in some notes on the back of his tickets. As he wrote, he hummed, *This Little Light of Mine*. When he finished, he sat back in his seat and checked his watch. It was a relatively boring night. A couple of runs, a couple of traffic stops, some business checks, and a lot of downtime. He bowed his head for a quick prayer. "Lord, thank You for saving me. Please give me and my family strength to deal with the coming months. Watch over them and protect them. Thank you. I ask this in Your Son's name. Amen."

He lifted his head and opened his eyes. He shifted the car into drive and started toward DD. He and Javier were meeting there at three for another coffee. As he pulled out of the parking lot and onto the road, he headed north. He turned on the radio to classic rock and, *Old Time Rock and roll*, filled the airways. He smiled and sang along. Coming south in the through lane was a vehicle with one headlight or a motorcycle. As it passed him, it was indeed a one head lighter.

"I've got time for a quick stop before I meet Javier," he whispered under his breath.

He made the U-turn as the chorus blared and sped up to position himself behind the vehicle. He noticed the vehicle was picking up a little speed, so he flipped on the overheads. The speed limit on this road was 40 mph, and they were currently doing 53 and rising. He turned on the sirens. The vehicle continued to speed up. 53 turned into 62 quick and he grabbed the mic.

"616 radio. I'm south on Inkster approaching Sheridan with an older blue Ford Taurus, no license plate failing to stop."

"Copy 616 has priority. What's your conditions?"

"Were still south approaching Hill, speeds are 65 miles per hour, traffic is light, conditions are dry."

Hill was the road that separated Dargen City from the next city over Addison. It was a smaller town but carried a lot of crime. There were sections of Addison that officers stayed out of at night unless they absolutely had to go there.

"Copy 616, approaching Hill. Any units in the area respond."

"603 from Cliff and Burger."

Dispatch responded, "Copy 603 from Cliff and Burger."

The nearest unit was five minutes away. Dave knew it was down time, and most were in a parking lot having coffee and talking or resting their eyes.

"Were through Hill approaching Avon, speeds still 65, traffic light, conditions dry."

"Copy 616 still south approaching Avon."

Just before Avon, the vehicle slammed on the brakes and took a hard left onto the side street. Dave slammed on his brakes and made the turn, staying directly behind the suspect vehicle. The turns in the neighborhood were coming so fast now Dave couldn't keep up on the radio.

"616 radio. We turned east into the sub before we got to Avon."

Dave looked for the next cross street as they came to it, but the street signs were gone.

"616 status?"

Dave concentrated on his driving for the moment and put the mic down.

"616 status?"

They took two more quick turns in the sub, and the Taurus slowed down. He knew they were looking for a place to bale. He looked up to see a cross street as they passed it.

"Radio, we're at Daly and Eastern slowing down. It looks like he's trying to find a place to..."

Dave didn't get the words out of his mouth before the Taurus suddenly stopped and the driver was out running through the yards. He slammed the patrol car into park.

"He's on foot radio."

"616 in foot pursuit."

Dave hopped out of the patrol car and gave chase. He was maybe 25 feet behind the suspect as they ran through yards, jumping fences and avoiding obstacles.

"616 what's your status?"

"South through the yards." He responded, out of breath.

At least he hoped they were still south.

"Copy south through the yards."

Dave was closing ground fast on the offender. Those morning runs were paying off. They rounded the corner of a house and, without warning, the offender turned quickly on Dave, stopping him in his tracks. It was a young black male wearing jeans and a leather jacket. The male threw his hand into the right inside part of his jacket. Dave immediately drew his sidearm and pointed it at the offender.

"Police, let me see your hands." He shouted.

The young male took his hand out of the inside of his jacket, turned, and ran. Dave re-holstered his weapon and gave chase again. Just as they were about to turn the next corner, Dave was close enough to grab onto his coat. He grabbed the suspect's coat, slowing him down, and then grabbed onto his right arm. He took the suspect to the ground and could cuff his hands behind his back with no further resistance. Tired and out of breath, he radioed to dispatch.

"616 radio suspect in custody at." He looked at the address of the front yard he was in. "367 Eastern."

"Copy 616 one in custody at 367 Eastern. Units can slow down but continue."

"603 is almost their radio."

"612 is pulling up."

"603 and 612 out."

Dave got the young man to his feet and walked him back to his squad car. Both panting and out of breath. The young man spoke.

"Thank you so much, officer. Thank you."

"What are you thanking me for?"

"You didn't shoot me. You could have, and you didn't."

"Why did you do that? Why did you act like you had a gun? Did you want to get shot?"

"I don't know. I wasn't thinking straight. I don't know. I was just scared."

Dave shook his head and silently thanked the Lord that he didn't shoot this young man. As they walked out onto the street where they left their cars, Javier came running up.

"Dave. You alright?"

"I'm good buddy."

Javier grabbed ahold of the young man by the jacket and escorted him over to the squad car, where he put him over the car and searched him.

"You like to run from the police? You like to put officer's lives in danger?"

"No, sir."

"Shut up! That was rhetorical."

He finished patting him down and put him in the back of the cruiser. Dave was leaning against his squad car, still trying to catch his breath. Javier walked over.

"Are you sure you're alright man?"

"Yeah, I'm good. Kids got some good wheels. If he were wearing shorts and a t-shirt, I might not have caught him."

"But you did. My man. Up high."

Dave gave him the high five he was looking for and they smiled.

"Here comes the paper waterfall now."

"I'll get him to the station and start the booking process. Just catch your breath and take your time coming in to write."

"Thanks, buddy."

"That's what we do."

Dave smiled. "That's what we do."

Javier booked the kid while Dave wrote his report. Officer Dean, who was the third man in at the party, stayed for the tow and then brought everyone coffees to the station when he was done. Dave had learned that the young man simply ran because his driver's license had a suspension on it. He wasn't thinking properly due to fear. On the drive back to the station, Dave said another silent prayer, this time thanking his Lord for how the situation turned out. That everyone, including that young offender, was safe tonight. As he sat sipping on his coffee, Javier sat next to him.

"Nice job tonight, partner."

"Thanks."

"He wanted me to thank you again for what you did or didn't do to him out there. I made him explain it to me and he sang your praises like a full choir on Sunday morning."

Dave laughed.

"Yeah, he let me know over and over out there."

"Well, that's a heck of a thing you did. You would have been justified in shooting him. Most wouldn't have waited for him to bring his hand out of his coat because, as we all know; action is quicker than reaction. God was watching out for both of you tonight."

"I know he was. God is good Javier."

He raised his coffee cup. Javier reciprocated.

"God is good Dave."

Chapter 12

Pastor Dunkirk sat at his desk enjoying a nice, hot cup of coffee. He really enjoyed a dark roast that provided a rich, full-bodied taste with a bold, flavorful aroma. He pulled the freshly poured cup up to his nose, and took a deep breath in, and then slowly exhaled.

"Now that's coffee." He whispered under his breath.

Stella, the church secretary, popped her head into his office.

"Did you say something, pastor?"

Her desk was right outside of his door. Startled by the sudden intrusion, he flinched and almost spilled his coffee. He looked up at her and smiled.

"No, just whispering to myself."

"Do you need anything?"

"No Stella, I'm fine, thank you."

He brought the cup up to his lips.

"Are you sure it's no trouble?"

He pulled it away to respond.

"Everything good here."

"Okay then."

"Thank you."

He pulled the cup back up to his lips just as she poked her head back in.

"Are you sure I'm free as a bird right now?"

Almost another spill. He pulled it back away.

"I'm one thousand percent sure, Stella, thank you."

"Okay, then I'll go back to typing and printing the programs for tonight's service."

"Thank you, Stella."

She went back to her desk. He waited an extra second before trying to attempt another sip. The coast seemed clear. The cup was just about to touch his bottom lip when she poked her head around the corner again.

"Pastor do you..."

"Stella!" He shouted.

She froze where she was standing and didn't say another word. He placed the cup of coffee on the desk in front of him and took a deep breath. He looked up to see her standing there, face still frozen and body language that didn't quite know what to do. She finally spoke.

"I'm sorry, Pastor Dunkirk, I didn't mean to..."

He put his hand up to stop her.

"Stella, I apologize for raising my voice. You startled me."

"That's okay, pastor. I know I can be a bit much. I just wanted to make sure that you had everything you needed. It's only my second week here and I want to do a good job. I know Marilyn was your secretary for the last fifteen plus years, and she was awesome. I just wanted to make sure that I..."

He put his hand up again, and she stopped.

"Stella, you're doing a good job. Please come and sit for a moment."

She walked over and sat in the chair in front of the desk.

"Just like Marilyn, you will get to know me. My habits, my quirks and pattern of the way I do things. I usually get in somewhere between seven and seven thirty in the morning. I'm an early riser, and I always start the day with a nice fresh hot cup of coffee. You don't see this because you get in around nine, but that cup of coffee is important to me because it kick starts my day. I usually only have the one in the morning, but sometimes the day calls for a second cup, which usually happens somewhere between ten thirty and eleven. Like now." He pointed to his watch. She smiled and nodded. "That cup is equally important to me because, well, I love my coffee. I mean, out of all the things in this world that God created, coffee is my weakness. I have never met another soul who loves coffee the way I do."

He paused so it could sink in.

"I see."

"So, I truly apologize for being short with you, Stella. It's just that when I combine coffee with reading the word of God, I am in a zone that Larry Bird couldn't even touch on his greatest day."

There was nervous laughter. She didn't know who Larry Bird was.

"So, when I kept interrupting you, I was messing with the zone?"

"Yes. But that's no reason for me to take it out on you. I'm sorry."

"Apology accepted Pastor Dunkirk. Do you have enough coffee left? I can go get more."

"That's the other part of this story. I was drinking the last cup of this special blend I get from Chicago. I usually go back and visit my parents and grab a case, but I didn't realize I was out until today. I'll have to make a trip back home soon to grab some more."

"What will you drink in the meantime?"

"There's a nice breakfast blend from a company over in Novi called Black Rifle. It's good as well."

"I can run and grab some if you'd like?"

"That would be great."

He stood up and took a twenty-dollar bill from his pocket and handed it to her.

"Dark roast, right?"

"Yes, but they call it Freedom Fuel."

"Freedom Fuel. Got it. Do you need anything else?"

"Nope, that'll do it."

"Okay then, I'll go grab that and while I'm gone, you can enjoy that cup."

"Thank you, Stella."

"Your welcome sir."

She turned and walked toward the door. Just as she was about to exit, he stopped her.

"Oh, and Stella, make sure you get the full beans. I like to grind it myself here and experience the full aroma of the blend before I drink it."

"Got it. Freedom Fuel blend, full bean, not ground."

"That's it."

"Okie dokie."

She turned and walked out of the office. He looked down at his now lukewarm cup of coffee. He picked it up and took it over to the microwave and put it inside. Bill punched in a minute and a half and hit start.

"An abomination," he whispered.

He waited until it chimed and then he grabbed the cup out of the microwave. Bill walked back over to his desk and sat down. He once again placed the cup under his nose and inhaled. He smiled and brought the cup up to his lips.

"Owe!"

Bill heard the scream come from outside of his office window. He set the cup down and raced over to the window. He looked out to see Seth lying on the ground underneath the climbing tree. Bill ran out of his office around to the back door of the church and through it, down the steps and toward the tree where Seth was lying. He stopped when he was standing at the feet of his son. He looked down to see Seth holding his left arm.

"Seth, are you okay, son?"

"No. Owe, it hurts really, really, bad."

He kneeled by his son and gently put his hand on his son's right hand.

"Let me look, son."

"It hurts."

"I know, son, but I have to look at it."

Seth moved his right hand and Bill could plainly see that the arm was broken.

"Make it stop, dad."

"Let's get you up. We have to get you to the hospital, son."

"No hospital, please?"

Bill lifted him up off the ground as he resumed holding his arm. He walked him over to the car and buckled him in the front seat. He ran around to the driver's side and got in. Bill started the car, backed it out of the parking spot, and headed toward the hospital. The church was roughly 20 minutes from the hospital, but today the Lord parted the red sea, as Bill liked to say. Traffic was light, they made every green light, and there were no police cars in sight to witness him going a little faster than he should be going. They made it to the ER entrance 10 minutes after they left. The nurse at the desk handed Bill the paperwork to fill out and promised them it would be a brief wait before a doctor could see them.

"He's in a lot of pain. Is there any way we can get him in now?"

He knew the answer, but this was his little boy. He had to try.

"I'm sorry sir, but we're short staffed at the moment and doing the best we can."

Seth removed his hand and showed the nurse his arm.

"Dad says it's broken."

She looked down at it and without breaking stride replied, "And dad's right. We'll get you in ASAP buddy. I promise."

Bill looked up at her and smiled. He put his arm around Seth's shoulder and led him over to a section of seats.

"What's ASAP mean, dad?"

"It's an abbreviation for as soon as possible."

"Oh. Okay then."

"How's the arm, pal?"

"It doesn't hurt as bad as it did, but it still hurts pretty bad."

"Hang in their pal. Somebody will see you soon."

He turned his attention to the forms and started filling them out. He had always thought they gave people these forms to get them to just walk out. You answered the same question four different times, it was just worded four different ways. He wrote as fast as he could to get them in and get Seth on the list.

2

Gina was supposed to meet Patty for lunch, but an emergency on her floor at the last second kept that from happening. The cafeteria was huge, and at busiest, it's only half full. Today, it wasn't even a quarter of the way full. She had plenty of other friends in the hospital she could have eaten with, but she didn't see any of them at this moment. It seemed like a Cobb salad day, which was actually one of the better menu items in the cafeteria. She carried a small New Testament in her purse, but that was upstairs in her locker. Today was just a nice quiet day to eat salad and reflect.

"Gina, do you mind if I sit down?"

She turned to see Doctor Peyton standing behind her.

"Doctor Peyton. Of course not, please sit."

He walked around the table and sat down across from her.

"Long time no see," he said, smiling.

"It has been a long time. How are you?"

"I'm doing well, and you?"

"Can't complain."

Her bright smile led him to the conclusion that she was happy about something. He smiled back.

"I take it you really can't complain?"

"I can't. I know you're a man of science, doc, but Dave told me on Sunday that he accepted the Lord as his Savior."

"That's wonderful, Gina. Just because I'm a man of science, people automatically assume that makes me an atheist. The truth is Gina, it's because I am a man of science that makes me see even more that there is a benevolent, loving God who created the universe."

"I did not know that. That's great doc."

"Gina, please call me James."

"That's great, James," she laughed. "It floored me when Dave told me because I wasn't expecting it. In the course of a few days' things are different, but back where they used to be. He is so full of life and so hungry for knowledge. It's such an amazing transformation."

"That's nice to hear."

"I must tell you, though, the last few months have been scary. I didn't know which way we were going. In my head it was always going to work out, but in my heart, I had major doubts for a while there."

"Relationships can be tough, and we make them even tougher by hiding things from the ones we're supposed to love the most."

"I'm just glad Dave finally came to me and opened up."

Peyton put his fork down and looked across the table at her.

"That's good to hear, Gina. When I visited him on Saturday, I wasn't sure he was going to ..."

"You visited him this past Saturday?"

"Well, yes, he didn't tell you?"

"No."

"Well, when you talked about...

He stopped himself. He stared into her eyes and could see that she was lost. The good doctor felt a wave of nausea move over him. Of course, he hadn't told her about the cancer. She was way too casual in the way she was handling it. Had he lost his sense of reading people? He looked at his watch and then stood.

"I'm going to be late for my next appointment. I'm sorry to cut things short, Gina, but I must go."

"Why would you visit him on a Saturday, James? What was so important?"

"I misspoke Gina."

He took a step toward the trash to throw out his tray. She stood and positioned herself in front of him.

"No, you didn't. What's going on?"

"Gina, please, I have to get going."

She looked at him with that deer in the headlights look, searching for an answer. He stared back at her, his eyes telling a story she did not want to hear.

"James, please."

He took a step toward her and placed his hand on her shoulder.

"Gina, go home and talk to your husband."

With that, he walked by and deposited the rest of his tray into the trash. He sat the tray on the counter as he walked toward the exit and then turned to see if she had moved. She had not. She was still standing in the same position, staring out into the cafeteria. He turned and left. Gina eventually sat back down. She didn't take another bite of her food or even attempt to. Her mind drifted to a place of despair. Her only thoughts were of every combination of gloom and doom. After sitting there for a few moments enveloped in dark thoughts, a voice inside her spoke. She now remembered who her guiding light was. She bowed her head and prayed softly.

"Lord, please do not let my thoughts wander. Strengthen me in Your love and let me know that whatever we are about to face, You will be there."

She opened her eyes. She grabbed her tray, walked over to the trash can and disposed of the rest of her lunch. Gina walked toward the exit to go back to her floor and was seriously thinking about taking the rest of the day off to go home and speak with Dave. As she reached the elevator, her phone chimed. It was her supervisor asking her to stop over in the ER and grab some supplies that they needed. She put the phone back into her pocket and headed for the ER.

Bill had finished filling out the forms and returned them to the desk. The nurse looked them over and told him to have a seat, and they would call them in soon. He walked back over and sat down next to Seth.

"How are you holding up, champ?"

"It hurts dad, when can we see the doctor?"

"Soon buddy, soon."

"It feels like we've been here forever."

"I know. Hang in there."

Seth leaned into his father and placed his head on his arm. He looked at his watch. It was now 11:53 a.m. and he was growing impatient. Patience was supposed to be the trademark of a pastor, but this was his little boy and he was hurting. He felt himself drifting toward anger, so he closed his eyes. He heard a familiar voice.

"Pastor Dunkirk."

He opened them to see Gina standing in front of him.

"Gina. How are you?"

"I'm good. How are you?" She looked down to see the condition of Seth's arm. "Never mind. I know how you are. What happened?"

"He fell out of a tree while I was working at the church."

"I'll be right back."

He watched as she walked into a room next to where they were sitting. She came out of the room a few seconds later and sat on the other side of Seth. He sat up and looked at her.

"I'm Seth."

She smiled.

"Hi Seth, I'm Gina. Is it getting hard to hold that arm up?"

"Yeah."

"Let's see what we can do about that until the doctor sees you."

She opened the plastic bag and took out a sling.

"What's that?" He asked.

"It's going to hold your arm up for you, so you don't have to."

"Is it going to hurt?"

"For like 2 seconds and then you're going to feel better."

"Okay."

She pulled the sling over his neck. She gently maneuvered around the arm and then, without breaking stride, had the arm in the sling. He winced for a second when she had to touch the arm, but it was so quick that he didn't even have time to react to the pain. Once the arm was placed into the sling, it felt better, and he smiled.

"Is that better?" She asked.

"Much better. It still hurts, but I don't have to hold it up anymore."

"I'm glad it's better. I'll be back in two shakes."

She walked over to the counter and spoke with the nurse at the desk for a few minutes. She turned and walked back over to them. Gina handed Seth a grape sucker. His eyes lit up, and he sat up straight as he accepted it from her.

"Thanks."

"You're welcome." She looked over at Bill. "He should get in to see the doctor soon."

Bill smiled.

"Thank you so much, Gina."

"Your very welcome."

"I didn't know you worked here."

"Twenty years now."

"So, you and Dave hired in at the same time?"

"Yeah, like two months apart from each other."

"That's wonderful. You'll be able to retire around the same time."

"That was kind of the plan."

"Do you plan on staying here or is somewhere warmer calling your name?"

She smiled.

"We haven't thought that far ahead yet. Maybe..."

The lump that had been sitting in her throat since her conversation with Doctor Peyton wouldn't allow her to continue.

"Gina, are you alright?"

She took the seat on the other side of him. He turned to face her as Seth ate his sucker.

"It's just," she looked into his eyes, "Has Dave said anything to you about his health?"

"Nothing. Is he okay?"

"That's the problem. I don't know."

"Then why do you assume that something's wrong?"

"I was just in the cafeteria having lunch with Dave's doctor when he let it slip that he visited Dave at home on Saturday. When I asked him why, he made up an excuse that he had to leave and meet with a patient."

"And you think that it's something bad?"

"Has a doctor visiting a patient on the weekend ever been good?"

He scratched his chin.

"You got me there. Do they know each other outside of work?"

"Doc Peyton has been a friend of the family for a long time."

"Maybe he was just stopping by to say hello."

"The way he spoke about the conversation led me to believe otherwise. He was there for a reason. A reason that I don't know, and he won't tell me."

"I'm assuming he can't, just like I wouldn't be able to tell you if Dave confided in me."

"Did he tell you something?"

"No. So far, the extent of our relationship has been a friendly conversation. When I first met him as he was working nights, and when he accepted the Lord into his heart."

"There was something in Doctor Peyton's voice and demeanor that makes me think whatever Dave is hiding from me is very serious."

"I wouldn't say hiding just yet, Gina. Give him the benefit of the doubt."

"I want to, but right now I can't tell if it's anger or fear inside of me."

He placed his hand on her hand.

"I can tell you from where I'm sitting that it's definitely fear."

"I know it is. What do I do?"

"You are a child of God now. He loves you and is there for you. In Isaiah chapter forty-one verse ten, he reminds us to, 'Fear not, for I am with you;

Be not dismayed, for I am your God. I will strengthen you, yes, I will help you, I will uphold you with My righteous right hand.'"

"I do trust Him. But my mind can't suppress my fear when it's someone I love."

"He's not asking you to. He is simply telling you to cast your fear on Him and He will comfort you. Whatever you're going through or about to go through, He wants to be there with you." Bill smiled at her. "The whole point of faith is to trust Him, regardless of the circumstances or the outcome. His plan is much greater than ours, and we trust that we're a part of it."

He could see that his words right now were falling on deaf ears. She was hurting inside and nothing that he said was going to give her relief.

"I just don't know, pastor."

"I know. I guess the best place to start is talking to Dave."

"That's what Doctor Peyton said."

"It might not be as bad as you think. And if it is, then I know that you and Dave will weather the storm together."

"Thank you for the kind words."

"I am here for both of you, always. If there is anything we as a church family can do for you, then please don't hesitate to ask."

"Thank you, Pastor Dunkirk." She smiled at him. "We plan on attending your church tonight."

"I hope you do. It would be great to see you both, and the children, at the service."

A nurse came through the set of double doors off to their left. She looked over to see Gina. She smiled.

"Hey Gina, how are you?"

"I'm good Jess. How are you?"

"Good." She looked down to see Seth snuggled up to his father. "You must be Seth."

He nodded yes as he clutched Bill's arm. Bill smiled.

"I'm his father, Bill."

"Nice to meet you both. Are you ready to get that arm looked at Seth?"

He smiled and nodded yes.

"He's shy," Bill added.

"I can see that. If you'll both come with me, we can get him all fixed up. It's good to see you, Gina."

"You too. Take care."

She waved as she went over and stood by the double doors.

"I look forward to seeing you all tonight."

The three of them stood.

"Thanks pastor." She turned her attention to Seth. "Everything is going to be okay, Seth. You're in excellent hands. Jessica will fix you right up."

He smiled. "Thanks again for the sucker."

"You're very welcome."

She watched as they disappeared through the doors to go back into the room. She stood there for a moment, thinking about what he said. 'Fear not for I am with you.' She knew that as a Christian she should cast her fears on the Lord, but sometimes it was still so hard to do that, but she knew she had to. She was not alone in her struggles now. Gina had a loving Savior to carry her through the difficult times. She needed to talk to Dave, but first she needed to finish her shift with a clear head. The people she cared for depended on her, and they needed her best. She walked over to the supply closet and grabbed the supplies they sent her to get. She then walked over to the elevator and pushed the up button. Miraculously, the doors opened right away, and she stepped in. She closed her eyes and whispered under her breath, "Lord, please give me the strength to concentrate on my work. Thank you."

Chapter 13

Dave was out as soon as his head hit the pillow. Dreams usually weren't in the forecast, but lately, he seemed to have more of them, and today, he had something weighing heavily on his mind.

He was standing in the middle of a river. He didn't know where, but the scenery was breathtaking. There were mountains on every side of him, and all the colors were bright and vibrant. He was wearing hip waders that came up to his chest. Dave closed his eyes and breathed in the fresh air as a slight breeze came through. He smiled and exhaled.

"Amazing, isn't it?"

He opened his eyes and looked to his right. Standing there holding a rod and reel was his father.

"It is dad," He replied with a big smile on his face.

They continued to cast out and reel in. Fly-fishing had always been their thing. They took many trips over the years and caught their fair share of fish. But the goal was always to be one with nature and enjoy the beauty of the land, and each other's company. They had been to a lot of nice places over the years, but this place was all those places wrapped into one. Unparalleled beauty.

"What's bothering you, son?"

Edward asked as he cast out his line.

"I'm okay dad, why do you ask?"

"How many of these trips did we take together?"

He laughed.

"A lot."

"A lot. When something was bothering you, these trips helped you figure things out. If nothing else, it made you feel better to get things off your chest. Do you remember when Gina was pregnant with the twins, and we took a trip up north the week after you found out?"

"How could I forget? It scared me to death. I wasn't just going to be a father for the first time, I was going to be a father of two, immediately."

Edward laughed.

"Yep. We stood in that river casting and reeling, and it looked like you were about to throw up the whole time. I asked you early that morning if you were okay, and you said you were fine, even though you weren't. I didn't press, but finally a few hours later you opened up to me."

"Yeah."

"It scared you that you weren't going to be a good father."

"Terrified."

"Do you remember what I said to you that day?"

"You said, 'Son, as a father, you just have to know four things. Know when to hold em. Know when to fold em. Know when to walk away and know when to run.'"

They looked at each other and started laughing.

"That was sound advice."

"Yeah, from Kenny Rogers."

They laughed some more.

"I was never the greatest for advice, but I could at least make you laugh."

Still laughing, Dave responded, "That you could pop." He wiped his eyes and looked over at Edward. "But don't sell yourself short. Do you remember what you said to me when we you finished laughing then?"

He cupped his chin and searched his memory.

"I'm sorry to say that I don't son."

"You said, 'all you must do is love them.' That they're going to succeed and they're going to fail, but through it all, just love them. Love them by bringing them up right. By being there for them no matter what, and teaching them that failure is never final."

"I said all of that?"

Dave smiled.

"No. That day all you said was, 'all you must do is love them.' I put together our conversations over the years and came up with the rest."

"So, it's kind of my greatest hits album?"

"Exactly."

"Well, it sounds like I'm a wise fella. So, I ask again, what's bothering you, son?"

"I'm dying, dad. I don't know how to tell Gina."

Edward put his hand on his shoulder.

"*Gina loves you very much. She deserves the truth.*"

"*I know she does, but I don't have a plan.*"

"*A plan?*"

"*A financial plan to help her out when I'm gone.*"

"*You have life insurance. She'll eventually collect your pension. That, along with her income, will be plenty, Dave.*"

"*I don't think that it will. I worry she won't...*"

"*Dave, stop. You know she will be okay financially. What's really bothering you?*"

"*That is what's bothering me dad I...*"

"*Stop!*"

He turned and wrapped his arms around his son and held him. Dave placed his head on his father's shoulder and cried.

"*I'm scared about what's in store for me over the next few of months.*"

"*I know you are, son.*"

"*I don't know how not to be scared, dad.*"

"*It's a scary thing to go through. The only advice I can give you is to live every day to the fullest. Let them know how much they mean to you.*"

They separated, and Dave smiled at his dad.

"*Thanks dad.*"

"*Your welcome son.*"

"*I'm so sorry that I killed you.*"

"*Dave, you...*"

Before he could finish, from out of nowhere, an enormous wave crashed into them. Dave lost his balance and fell into the river. He looked up to see his father's hand reaching out to him, but it was just out of reach. His vision blurred from the water; he could only watch as his dad slowly faded from sight as the river took him rushing away. Dave could hear water crashing into rocks nearby, and just as he turned to see where the river was taking him, he saw the waterfall up ahead. He was rushing toward it with nothing to grab onto. He turned back to see his father standing in the same spot, waving in his direction.

"*Dad...dad...please help me.*"

Dave turned around just as he hit the top of the waterfall, and over he went.

He awakened abruptly and sat up. Dave looked around the room. He was in his bedroom. He looked at the clock. It was 1:10 p.m. He leaned over to his nightstand and turned on the light. He sat up in bed and rested his back on the headboard. He thought for a moment about the dream. 'All you must do is love them,' echoed in his head. It didn't just apply to his children. It applied to his wife as well. Just love her. In loving her, you trust her. In trusting her, you confide in her. He reached over onto the nightstand and picked up his reading glasses. He then picked up his bible and opened it to where the bookmark was holding his place. A couple of days ago, he and Gina were talking about the word, and she said something to him that made him think. She told him that her life's verse was Joshua, chapter one, verse nine. He asked her to explain to him the meaning behind the phrase, "My life verse." She told him in the simplest terms that it is a verse that people strive to live their life by. A verse that helps them focus when times are tough. It gives them perspective when they're feeling depressed or anxious. "Isn't the whole bible designed to do all of that?" he asked. She replied with a firm, "Yes." She followed it with a better explanation. "In times of strife or complete chaos, it's comforting to memorize a verse that explains to you perfectly who you are and who you serve." He smiled and then asked her what her life verse said to her. She told him that God commands us to, "Be strong and of good courage; do not be afraid, nor be dismayed, for the Lord your God is with you wherever you go." He told her it was a great verse. That he might adopt it as his own. She smiled, hugged him, and told him she would be glad to share it with him. Later that night, after their conversation, he was reading through the book of Isaiah and came to a passage that jumped off the page and grabbed him. He felt it was the true foundation of any successful Christian life. He read it repeatedly. It spoke to him and reinforced his new belief that the only way to be deal with this life was to fully trust in Him, His timing, and His ways. He read it again. Isaiah chapter forty verse thirty-one, "But those who wait on the Lord shall renew their strength; They shall mount up with wings like eagles, they shall run and not be weary, they shall walk and not faint."

He got out of bed and walked downstairs. The house was quiet. He walked into the kitchen and over to the coffeemaker. There was a note propped up against it. *Dad, we have gone over to the Kings. Be back around three. Love, Melissa. P.S. There's coffee in the maker, just turn it on.* He smiled as he tucked the note into his robe and turned on the coffeemaker. Dave walked over to the table and sat down, pulled his reading glasses out of his pocket, and opened the bible. He read as the coffee brewed. After a while, he got up and poured himself a cup. He sat at the table enjoying his coffee and reading. The time passed by quickly, and before he knew it, Marc and Melissa were walking through the door. They walked into the kitchen to see him sitting at the table.

"It's three fifteen and you're still in your robe. Life must be good on Dave Mountain."

He smiled and held his cup up.

"It sure is."

"How was work last night?" Melissa asked.

The question surprised Dave. It had been a long time since they asked.

"It was good."

"Good." She replied.

"Hey, you guys want to make dinner for mom tonight?"

"Sure," they replied.

"She's working until five today, so I figured we could start making dinner around then so it's ready by five thirty and then we could go to church together."

"Sounds cool," Marc replied, and Melissa nodded in agreement.

"Great. What about spaghetti and meatballs?"

They both gave him a thumbs up.

"Did you eat any lunch yet?" Marc asked.

"I am about to have a bowl of oatmeal and some fruit, then maybe a quick run before I hop in the shower."

"Can I come?" Melissa asked.

"When did you start running?"

"Last summer. My pace probably isn't as fast as yours, but I can hang."

"Alright. That would be great."

Some quality time with his little girl.

"I'm going to grab my guitar. I'll be out back," Marc responded.

"Great. Maybe after my shower, I'll join you."

"Cool," he responded, as he was texting on his phone.

Dave closed his bible and ate a nice hot bowl of oatmeal, a banana, and chased it with some orange juice. He walked back upstairs and put on some shorts and a t-shirt. He was sitting on the bench by the front door when Melissa came down the stairs. She was wearing a sports bra and some bike shorts.

"What's going on here?" He asked.

"What? It's what I run in. It's what every girl runs in."

"Today you run in shorts and a t-shirt."

"Dad!"

"Melissa, you're my daughter and I love you, but that is not appropriate running attire."

"It doesn't show anything."

"It shows everything. You go out there in that and you attract unwanted attention from every pervert within a ten-mile radius."

"So, I should have to suffer because men are perv's?"

"Short answer, yes. Melissa, I know you're at an age where you want to be noticed, but you should want people to notice you for who you are, not what you wear. People who wear that are only seeking the wrong attention. You're much more than that. Please, go change."

"Fine."

He rubbed his forehead as she stormed upstairs to change. Moments later, she came back downstairs with some regular shorts on and a t-shirt. She sat in silence as she laced up her running shoes.

"Thank you." He finally broke the silence.

"How far are we going today?" she asked.

"I thought maybe just fifteen miles today."

She looked at him, eyes as wide as saucers.

"Fifteen?"

He laughed.

"No, just three today. Is that okay?"

He got a smile out of her as she responded, "Three's good."

They walked out of the front door and took about ten minutes to fully stretch out. When they were done, he broke into a light jog going south. She followed. A few minutes in, they were side by side. He set his pace to hers so that they could stay side by side throughout the run. There was no talking, just concentration. He looked at her using his peripherals every so often, mainly because he was proud of her. When they were roughly a quarter mile away from home, he slowed down. She continued for a bit, but then noticed he was behind her. She slowed down and then noticed that he had stopped altogether. Melissa stopped and walked back to meet him.

"Are you alright?"

"Great."

"Then why did you stop?"

"Sometimes I walk the last quarter mile. Especially when it's a beautiful day."

"Oh, okay. Then I'll walk with you."

He pointed to a house as they were walking by it.

"See that house. There's a dog up against the fence in the corner. You see him."

They stopped, and she focused in.

"Yeah, I see him. It's almost like he's hiding." She looked closer.

"Yeah. I run by here often. He never barks at me or makes any kind of fuss that I'm running by. He just sits there, staring out at the world from his corner. Watching."

"That's sad."

Dave laughed.

"That's not funny."

"Look closer grasshopper."

She rolled her eyes.

"I'm going to assume that's some weird reference from your childhood." She stopped, concentrated, and really focused on the animal. "Is that a silhouette?"

He started laughing louder. She pushed him and started laughing.

"I had to almost run up to the fence before I figured it out. It's just part of the decorations, I guess."

"Why haven't we ever gotten a dog?"

"I don't know. We were always working, and nobody ever really asked for one."

"Yeah, I guess we never did." They walked a few more feet. "Dad, can I ask you a question?"

"Of course. You can ask me anything."

"Is God the reason you started loving us again?"

He stopped dead in his tracks. That felt like a punch in the gut.

"Baby girl, I never, ever stopped loving you guys. I'm so sorry that you felt this way all this time. I love all of you more than you can ever imagine. God is the reason I finally came to my senses. When I accepted His love and grace, the Holy Spirit came into my life and changed me. I could see clearly what I had done to the ones I loved the most, but there was never a time that I stopped loving you. I can't explain to you, or anybody, why I acted the way I did for the last two years. I was selfish beyond reason. But I love all of you very much."

He grabbed her and pulled her in close. He wrapped his arms around her and squeezed. She squeezed back.

"To tight, dad."

"Sorry."

He let go, and they separated. They started toward home again.

"I'm glad you're back, dad."

"Me too."

When they got back into the front yard, they stretched for another ten minutes. Melissa went upstairs to take a shower, and Dave grabbed his guitar and headed toward the backyard to play with Marc. He walked out of the back door and stopped before he rounded the corner. He could hear Marc strumming the guitar and singing along to Bob Dylan's, *Knocking on Heaven's door*. The kid was good. He waited while Marc finished and then rounded the corner. Dave went over and sat on the other corner of the picnic table, and he looked over at Marc. He smiled and started playing Bob Seger's, *Fire Lake*. Marc joined in without missing a beat.

2

On the drive home, Gina decided she would let Dave come to her when he was ready. Maybe it wasn't as bad as her mind was making it out to be, and that whatever it was, they would trust in God and get through it together. She pulled into the driveway and sat in her car for a few extra minutes. She shut off the car and gathered her things. As she walked around to the back door, she could hear music coming from inside the house. She opened the door and heard Dean Martin's, *That's Amore*, and the pleasant aroma of garlic bread filled her nostrils. She laid her things down on the piano bench and walked into the kitchen. Dave was standing at the stove with an apron on, singing along, and Marc and Melissa were setting the table, humming to the music. She laughed out loud, and when Dave turned to see her standing there, he walked over to her, grabbed her waist and hand, and started wheeling her around the dance floor. He sang to her while they danced, and the kids looked on.

"What has gotten into you, David?"

"Tonight Mrs. Jackson, we have prepared for you a fine Italian cuisine. Spaghetti with meatballs."

"Great, I'm starving."

The song ended, and they stopped. He gave her a hug and a kiss.

"Now go wash up, we're ready to eat."

She walked over to the sink and washed her hands. When she walked into the dining room, the food was ready. She took her seat. "Everything looks and smells amazing, you guys."

Dave smiled, reached over to his left, and grabbed Gina's hand.

"Let's thank the Lord for this wonderful meal," Dave stated as he prayed. "Father, we thank you for bringing us together tonight. We thank you for the laughter at this table, and for the love. Thank you for Your Son Jesus, who died for us and then rose again that we have salvation through Him. Please bless this food and the hands that have prepared it. In Jesus' name, amen."

"Amen," Gina added.

The conversation was light, with overtones of humor throughout the meal. While the kids were talking to each other, Dave looked over at Gina.

"Are we still planning on attending the service tonight?"

"Yes." She cleared her throat. "Anything interesting happen at work last night?"

"It did."

He started talking, and both kids turned their attention to him.

Gina smiled. "You have an audience, sir."

He told them about the one headlight traffic stop. He gave them every detail, leaving out nothing. No one interrupted his story, and when he finished, the table was silent. Finally, Marc spoke.

"That's scary, dad. If that guy had a gun, he could have killed you."

"It could have turned out differently, but it didn't."

"Were you scared?" Melissa asked.

"I didn't have time to be scared. My mind did what they trained it to do. Afterward, when I had time to think about it, I just thanked the Lord for watching over me and protecting me through the situation."

"How many times in your career have you almost died?" Marc asked.

"I've had a few close calls in the past."

"You just accepted the Lord, dad. What saved you before?" Melissa asked.

"I guess it just wasn't my time. When you get into a career, especially like mine or your moms, you train. A lot. And that training can be the difference maker in living and dying. I'm very fortunate to have lived long enough to see and accept the truth. Some haven't been as fortunate. They think they have more time because they are young, or in great health. There is no guarantee you will live a long life."

"So, what if you don't decide to accept Christ before you die?" Melissa asked.

"The bible tells us it's separation from God forever."

"So, you can't be a good person if you don't accept Him?" Marc asked.

"You can most definitely be a good person if you don't accept Him, but you won't live your best life, which means fulfilling His wonderful purpose for you."

"What do you mean?" Melissa asked.

He looked over at Gina. She smiled and took her cue.

"What dad means is that life is hard enough. You worry about things. Tests, what you're going to wear, if you'll make friends, grades, and so on. When you get older, it's, career, family, health, and whatever troubles can come your way. When you put your trust in the Lord, He has said He will carry your burdens for you. So, when your dad goes to work at night, he's trusting in the Lord to take care of him while he works, and his family while he is away from them."

"So, nothing bad will happen to him or his family?" Marc asked.

"So that he can have confidence that God will take care of us no matter what happens. Following Him doesn't shield you from tragedy in your life, but it gives you a loving savior to lean on in life's difficult times. Reading the bible and praying daily opens your eyes to His grace and mercy. It gives you the confidence to know that whatever happens, He is with you through it."

"So, why doesn't He just protect you from harm when you accept Him?" Marc Asked.

"Yeah. Why do those who become Christians experience any difficult times if He is on their side?" Melissa added.

"Because if that were the case, then freewill wouldn't exist. Everyone would do it just to become bullet proof, and they wouldn't do it out of love for Him. He wants you to make that decision based on a strong faith and love for Him, not out of obligation. If coming to faith in Him meant no tragedy ever, then the entire world would do it just to avoid pain and hurt. That defeats the principle of faith. Do you guys understand that?"

"I think so," Marc answered.

"Yeah," Melissa agreed.

"If you ever have questions, you guys know you can come to us," Gina stated.

They both nodded yes and continued eating dinner. Dave looked over at Gina.

"What about you? Anything interesting happen at work today?"

"I was coming back from lunch and ran into Pastor Dunkirk in the ER."

"Oh no, what happened?"

"It appears his youngest son, Seth, likes to climb trees. And today the tree wasn't so good to him. He fell out and broke his arm."

"Ouch!"

"Yeah. We talked for a bit, and I got Seth a sling and a sucker."

"That was nice. Did he have anything interesting to say?"

"Not really, but I told him we would probably be at the service tonight."

"I like to hear him speak."

"Me too."

"Other than that, a good day?"

"Yeah."

She wanted to tell him about running into Doctor Peyton, but she reframed. He told her about running with Melissa and playing guitar with Marc, and she enjoyed hearing that. They finished dinner, and she went upstairs to shower and change before they went to church. Dave and the kids cleared the table, rinsed the dishes, and loaded them into the dishwasher. When they finished, they all went upstairs to get ready.

3

They pulled into the parking lot with about ten minutes to spare. The crowd was lighter than Sunday, but still a decent turnout. Before they got out of the car, Dave took the kids' phones and put them in the center console. They groaned and promised that they wouldn't use them during the service, but he knew better. He told them that the best way to defeat temptation was to take it away. He got a dual set of eye rolls for his wisdom. Dave then took his phone and placed it in the center console as well, and Gina did the same. They walked toward the church, bibles in hand. The kids walked behind them, moping. Several people smiled and said hello, and when they reached the doors, an older gentleman held them open as they walked through. They shook some hands and said hello to a few people as they made their way to the sanctuary.

"Friendly church," Gina remarked.

"It is," Dave responded with a smile.

As they walked through the double doors and into the sanctuary, a familiar face handed them a program with tonight's message outlined in it. His freshly cast arm was being held in a sling up against his body. As he handed Gina the program, he smiled.

"Thanks again for the sucker."

"You're very welcome, again. How's the arm feeling?"

"It's good. A little itchy."

"Yeah, sometimes they get like that."

She gave him a wink, and he smiled as they continued to their seats. They found a section of four seats on the end of the pew midway down the aisle. They sat down and waited for the service to start. A few minutes later, Pastor Dunkirk took his seat in the small pew on the stage and the music pastor walked up to the podium.

"Good afternoon, everyone. It's good to see so many smiling faces looking back at me. I'm David Collins, the music pastor here at Faith. Please stand, grab your hymnals, and turn to page 237."

Everyone did as he asked, and he led them in song. They sang three songs before the music ministry concluded, then Pastor Dunkirk took the podium. He smiled as he took out his glasses from the front pocket of his shirt and put them on. He opened his bible and then looked out at the faces looking back at him.

"Man, you guys sounded great."

There was laughter from the congregation before a few members belted out a hardy, "Amen!"

Pastor Dunkirk smiled as he scanned.

"I mean it. You guys sounded awesome. Pastor Collins has worked a miracle."

More laughter from the congregation and a few more. "Amens."

"I say that because before he came to this church almost," He looked at his watch, "four years ago now?"

He looked over at Collins, who was sitting in the small pew.

"That's right, pastor. Four years and three days ago," Collins responded.

More laughter from the congregation.

"Looks like I forgot an anniversary."

Dave and Gina looked at each other and laughed along with everyone else.

"It's okay Pastor Dunkirk. I believe five years is the Shinola anniversary present."

A chorus of laughter and many "Amens" came from the congregation now. The pastor took his glasses off and cleaned them as he laughed along.

"I'll remember that Brother David." He finished cleaning his glasses and put them back on. "Who says you can't have fun in church?"

A few more "Amens" echoed the sanctuary.

"The church is blessed to have Pastor David and his family with us. When he came here, there wasn't a lot of participation. In four short years he has y'all singing along to every song and sounding great. If you haven't joined us here on a Wednesday night before, then welcome. It's a little more laid back, but we still preach the good news with passion."

"Amen."

Dave had noticed that the attire was mainly jeans and polos or t-shirts, which he was most comfortable in. Even the pastor was wearing jeans, which was a switch from the usual suits he had seen on Sunday.

"Tonight, we are going to be looking at the life of Daniel. Now the book of Daniel is known for its futuristic insights and prophesies. Daniel was a great interpreter of dreams and did so for the kings of his day. Folks, it's one way that God talks to us today."

Dave keyed in on this and he thought about the dreams he had lately. His dreams were vivid and real. He woke, remembering every detail. Was God talking to him?

"Please turn to Daniel, chapter six. Darius the Mede was the third king that Daniel served under. The first, Nebuchadnezzar, who came to love Daniel, and serve God after some initial resistance. His son, Belshazzar, was not so wise. He strayed from his father's ways. God's punishment can be seen here in chapter five verses thirty and thirty-one, '...Belshazzar, king of the Chaldeans, was slain. And Darius the Mede received the kingdom, being sixty-two years old.'"

He cleared his throat.

"A foreign king now ruled the land. The other kings knew and loved Daniel, but now he had to deal not only with a new king, but a foreign king who did not know who he was. Darius came in and verse one tells us he 'set over the kingdom one hundred and twenty satraps, to be over the whole kingdom.' Satraps were seers. They were magicians, people who prophesied. In a word. They were yes men. It made the king feel safe and powerful to have these," He used air quotes to continue, "Men of vision who could see the future."

He paused for a moment and a loud sneeze from someone in the congregation startled everyone. Pastor Dunkirk laughed.

"Bless you and thanks for waking some of them up."

Laughter throughout the sanctuary. Dave looked over at the kids and even saw some laughter from them.

"Things aren't much different today. There are still people out there claiming that they can talk to the dead, or see your future, or interpret your dreams. It's a scam as old as time. But Daniel was a man of God. A chosen prophet like those before him to advise God's people on godly matters. To guide them in His ways. Darius knew this because we read in verse three, 'Then this Daniel distinguished himself above the governors and satraps, because an excellent spirit was in him; and the king gave thought to setting him over the whole realm.' Let that sink in for a moment, folks."

He scanned the congregation.

"Folks that didn't go over so well with everyone else. From that point on, they plotted on a way to get rid of Daniel. They were jealous. He had something that they truly wanted. It should have been the favor of a loving God, but it wasn't. In their eyes, he had power. They knew the king trusted him more than anyone else, and that led to power and riches. Something they desired more than anything."

He took his glasses off and set them on his bible. He looked out at the congregation and smiled.

"Has there ever been a time in your life where you were filled with so much jealousy that you would kill someone to get what they had? Maybe you wouldn't physically do it, but you wouldn't lose sleep over it if it happened. They wanted Daniel dead. Out of the way. So, they set a plan in motion to do just that."

He turned and walked back to the podium. He put his glasses on and read.

"Verse five reads, 'Then these men said, "We shall not find any charge against this Daniel unless we find it against him concerning the law of his God.' Aha!"

The congregation jumped, and the pastor smiled.

"They found the loophole because they knew Daniel was faithful to God, and that he prayed every day. That he also prayed three times a day. They had there in, and they would appeal to the king's vain side. Oh, how their dark hearts must have rejoiced. This was it. The first thing they had to do was butter him up, so they went before him and verse six, it tells us they said to him, 'King Darius, live forever!'"

The pastor smiled.

"We've all been there, haven't we? Either we've been the one doing the buttering, or we've been the one receiving it. Dad, you're the best preacher I have ever heard. No one can bring the word like you do. You're working too hard right now. Let's go get you an ice cream sundae with extra hot fudge on it."

The congregation laughed.

"I think I've heard that one a time or two." He smiled. "That one is a little more on the mild side. How about this one? There's a job you've been eyeballing at work, but someone else has it. Maybe even someone that doesn't deserve it. They got their way there by being a yes man or a yes woman. They snuggled up to the boss real good, and fed his or her ego and now they have the job you should have gotten. Have you been there? Everyone please, close your eyes for a minute."

He scanned and saw that the vast majority had their eyes closed.

"Picture that situation. See the individual that has wronged you in the past. Make your way back to that point and time where you felt the most anger toward that person. Remember how you felt. Can you see them?"

Most nodded yes, but some verbalized it.

"I'm going to tell you exactly how you should handle that situation if it ever happens again. Listen closely." He paused. "Pray for them."

Most opened their eyes and stared at the podium. Some kept them closed.

"If you haven't already, you can open your eyes and look at me as I say again, pray for them. When you get home later this evening, read Matthew chapter five verse forty-four. It'll give you a little taste about this Sunday's sermon." He smiled. "Now, back to Daniel. These other men convinced King Darius to make an official decree throughout the land. After they buttered him up and stroked his ego, we read in verse seven they convinced the king to, 'establish a royal statute and to make a firm decree, that whoever petitions any god or man for thirty days, except you, O king, shall be cast into the den of lions.' Well, Darius was riding high on their praises still, so we read in verse nine that 'King Darius signed the written decree.'"

He paused and looked out at the congregation.

"Can you imagine having that bloated of an ego? Making a decree that every man, woman, or child can only pray to you for the next 30 days. If they don't adhere to that, then you can throw them into a den filled with lions, sealing their death warrant. Thank God times have changed, amen?"

"Amen," the people answered.

"So, knowing this new decree, what do you think Daniel did? Do you think he looked at God and said, sorry Lord, I have to take a break from praying for thirty days? But Lord, my life depends on it. I can't serve you if I'm dead."

The pastor slammed his hand down on the podium, startling some, but bringing every eye to him.

"God does not want servants who only worship Him when it's convenient! He doesn't want men and women who are afraid to express their love and dedication to Him when it's easy! He wants believers who will proclaim His name loud and proud, even when the consequence is death."

"Amen!"

"We see in verse ten what Daniel did. 'He knelt down on his knees three times that day, and prayed and gave thanks before his God, as was his custom since early days.' Amen."

He took a moment to wipe his brow with a handkerchief.

"Daniel answered the call."

"Amen." They responded.

"He did not cower in a corner and feel sorry for himself. He did not disrespect his God by conforming to the ways of man. Folks, he did not break stride. He continued to serve the Lord the way he always had...without fear of consequences." The pastor smiled. "It is no different today, except you won't get thrown into a den of lions. Society might label you an outcast. A weirdo. A Jesus freak. In the 21st century, that happens to believers who stand up for the Lord. I will proudly wear those labels if it means that they heard the word of God."

"Amen."

"Our nation is moving into the dangerous practice of cutting God out of the picture. They do not want prayer in schools. They do not even want the pledge of allegiance because of the phase, 'one nation under God.' If you express any opinion contrary to society, you're wrong. If you do not think the way they do, then you are a hater. Folks, we need to be more like Daniel."

"Amen."

"We need to raise our children to be more like Daniel."

"Amen."

"He did not start a war to protest the new decree. He was not in the center of town screaming at the top of his lungs that the king was unfair. Daniel simply did what he had been doing for years. He prayed to God. No violence, no anarchy, and no angry letters or speeches. He continued to honor God through worship and prayer."

The sanctuary was silent as he turned the page in his bible.

"In verses eleven through thirteen, it tells us that the men who sought to ruin Daniel went before the king and reminded him about his decree. When the king agreed it was so and not to be altered, they dropped the bomb. Daniel has broken your decree, O king. Verse fourteen tells us that, 'And the king, when he heard these words, was greatly displeased with himself.' The king was angry with himself because he let these men trick him. In that moment, he had clarity. He was not thinking clearly when he signed the decree, because if he was, he would have known that Daniel wouldn't follow it. That Daniel was faithful to his God. The rest of the verse tells us that the king tried everything he could think of to save Daniel from this fate. Finally, the men approached him at sunset. They reminded him in verse fifteen, 'it is the law of the Medes and Persians that no decree or statute which the king establishes may be changed.' Game over. It crushed the king in spirit because he had to throw his friend into the lion's den, and it would surely kill him. Think about that for a moment."

He paused as he reached under the podium and grabbed his water from the shelf. He took a drink.

"In verse sixteen, we read the king commanded Daniel to be thrown into the lion's den. But just before they sealed it, the king spoke to Daniel, saying, 'Your God, whom you serve continually, He will deliver you.' It sounds like Daniel's faith was rubbing off on the king."

"Amen."

"Verse eighteen and nineteen describes the king went to his palace and fasted. That he did not sleep that night. That early the next morning, the king, 'went in haste to the den of lions.' We read in verse twenty he yells, 'Daniel, servant of the living God, has your God, whom you serve continually, been able to deliver you from the lions?' Verse twenty-one and twenty-two Daniel answers, 'O king, live forever! My God sent his angel and shut the lion's mouths, so that they have not hurt me, because I was found innocent before Him; and also, O king, I have done no wrong before you.'"

The pastor smiled.

"The king was 'exceedingly glad' and had Daniel pulled out of the den. There was no injury to Daniel, 'because he believed in his God.' Folks, our God is an awesome God."

"Amen."

"The king realized the evil of the others. He saw them for what they really were. Imposters. They were so wicked that they manipulated him into signing a decree that almost took the life of a true prophet of God."

The pastor stared out at them. He shook his head and then looked down at his bible.

"Verse twenty-four reads, 'And the king gave the command, and they brought those men who had accused Daniel, and they cast *them* into the den of lions—them, their children, and their wives; and the lions overpowered them, and broke all their bones in pieces before they ever came to the bottom of the den.' We don't know why God allowed King Darius to cast the women and children into the den. We trust His ways are higher than our ways, and His thoughts than our thoughts. He knows the heart of mankind when He creates us. This act could have stamped out generations upon generations of evil. Do you trust Him?"

"Amen," came the enthusiastic reply.

"That's just the response I was looking for."

Laughter from the congregation.

"In verse twenty-five through twenty-seven we read, 'Then King Darius wrote: To all peoples, nations, and languages that dwell in all the earth: Peace be multiplied to you. I make a decree that in every dominion of my kingdom, *men must* tremble and fear before the God of Daniel. For He *is* the living God, And steadfast forever; His kingdom *is the one* which shall not be destroyed, And His dominion *shall endure* to the end. He delivers and rescues, And He works signs and wonders in heaven and on earth, Who has delivered Daniel from the power of the lions.' So did the warrior Daniel make his point?"

The congregation was silent. The pastor laughed.

"Don't go silent on me now. We're almost done. I said, did the warrior Daniel make his point?"

"Amen," came the loud response.

"There you go."

They laughed, and he smiled at them and passionately concluded his sermon.

"Daniel stood up for what he believed in. He stood up for the living God. He did not compromise his principles. Daniel did not cave to peer pressure. He did not turn his back on God. He knew that this world was temporary. That the things of this world are temporary, and he decided he was going to lie up for himself treasures in heaven. He was going to serve God, not man, and that he was going to walk by faith and not by sight."

"Amen."

He wiped the sweat from his brow and then closed his bible.

"If you want to put this life in perspective. Read Daniel chapter six repeatedly. It is the story of a man who refuses to abandon his faith. You look at me and you say, pastor, not all stories in the bible have such a happy ending. Although it's true that not all end with the servant of God walking away, the ending is still happy. The men and women of God, who preached and lived their lives as a testament to Him, influenced countless numbers of believers. Most ended in death on this earth, but life eternally with Him. It is a choice we all have to make. Do we please people and reap the benefits of this world for however long we're here, which is from the time we're born up to maybe 80, 90, or even a 100? Or do we choose to follow the one true God, serve Him, and show others that an eternal, glorious life in heaven awaits them? I am not great at math folks, but I believe that eternity is longer than 100 years. Will you bow your heads with me, please?"

Everyone bowed their heads.

"Father, please be with us as we brave this world for You. Give us Your strength to always do what is right. Help us see Your love and grace. You know our struggles. Our needs. Guide us Lord and help us always to remember the apostle Paul's words in Romans chapter eight, 'If God is for us, who can be against us?' Thank you, Father. We ask this in Jesus' precious name, and all God's people said?"

"Amen," echoed throughout the sanctuary.

"Amen. Thank you all for coming tonight."

As the service concluded and they left their pews to go home, Dave, Gina, and the kids made their way to the exit. They stopped, shook some hands, and met some of the congregation. They eventually made their way over to Pastor Dunkirk.

"Pastor, that was a great service."

"Thank you David. I appreciate you saying that."

"I agree," Gina added. "Daniel is a great story about faith and loyalty to God."

The pastor shook Gina's hand.

"It is indeed. I am thankful to see your family here tonight. And who are these two good looking youngsters?"

Marc stepped forward and shook the pastor's hand.

"Marc, sir. It is nice to meet you."

"It's nice to meet you, Marc." He responded.

Melissa then stepped forward and shook the pastor's hand as well.

"Melissa, sir. It is nice to meet you. The service was excellent."

"Thank you for saying that, Melissa. It is nice to meet you as well."

Gina smiled and asked, "How's Seth's pain? I saw him when we got here, and he seemed to be in good spirits."

"He loves the cast."

They all laughed.

"Good," she responded. "He's going to have it for a while."

"Thank you for being so kind at the ER today. Whenever he tells anyone the story of how he broke his arm, he never leaves out the part about the nice nurse who gave him a sucker."

She laughed. "It was my pleasure." She shook his hand once again. "Have a great night."

"You as well."

The kids respectfully said goodbye and Gina told Dave they would meet him at the car. The pastor looked at Dave. "You have a delightful family, Dave."

"Thank you. Gina told me about your son's arm at dinner. I am glad he is okay."

"Thanks Dave, it's just boys being boys. How is your walk with Christ going?"

"I have learned so much. I have read through all the material you gave me, and I constantly read the bible. I cannot put it down."

"I am so glad to hear you say that. Drop by my office, or house, anytime and I can give you countless study guides to the different chapters and characters."

"Thank you. I would like that."

"You know, Dave, we have a retreat coming up next month that I think you and your son might benefit from. It is a weekend of camping and bible study. It helps us get a little closer to God through nature. We have been doing it for almost ten years now."

"That sounds like fun."

"Let me grab you a flyer."

He walked over to a table a few feet away and returned with a flyer in his hand. He handed it to Dave. The flyer explained that between bible studies, they fished, hiked, kayaked, and had ample free time to explore the beauty of nature. Dave smiled.

"This looks nice. I will talk to my son about it and see what he thinks."

"Excellent. It is at the beginning of August, so you have a little time to decide."

"Thanks pastor. If I do not see you before, I will most likely see you on Sunday."

"Sounds good David. I hope the rest of your week is great."

They shook. "I hope yours is as well."

He exited the church and headed toward the car. As he opened the door and sat down, he handed the flyer to Gina.

"This sounds great. I think you and Marc would have a great time together."

He looked back at the kids. Both had headphones on and were in their own world.

"I think so too. I will pitch the idea to him sometime this week."

"I'm sure he'll jump at the chance to spend time with you."

As he looked into her eyes, he knew she deserved to know the truth about what was going on with his health. He did not know what possessed him to think about it right at this moment, but he did.

"Gina, do you think the kids could stay the night at a friend's house tomorrow night? I will make you a nice dinner, and I have something I want to discuss with you, but I do not think tonight is the time."

"A nice dinner. This must be serious."

He laughed. "What do you think?"

"I think that can be arranged. I will talk to Patty when we get home."

"Great, Thanks."

He started the car, and they headed home. She desperately wanted to drop the kids off over at the Kings tonight, but she didn't want to seem pushy.

Chapter 14

Thursday—July 7, 2010

Kurtis laid in bed staring up at the quarter sized dark spot on the ceiling directly above his head. It had been there now for over a year, and it started out the size of a dime. There were countless mornings and nights that he stared at that spot, losing himself in thought to dreams of a normal life. He looked over at the clock. It was 6:55 a.m. Most fifteen-year-olds were still fast asleep enjoying summer break, but not him. He endured another night of yelling, fighting, and then eventually crying. There was damaged drywall, furniture was broken, and finally, somewhere around 3:30 a.m., Shannon and Rick passed out. A few minutes later, he followed suit. A little over three short hours later, he was awakened by the rumbling in his stomach. Hunger was a pain that he had learned to live with, but today it seemed more intense, more pronounced. He felt weak and exhausted, but he could not sleep. He just stared at the magic spot. The spot that transported him into a world of loving parents, friends, and even a dog. He was so deep in thought that he hadn't even noticed the tears flowing from his eyes. He rolled onto his left side and faced the wall. Kurtis placed his hand under his pillow to prop it up and felt what appeared to be a waded-up piece of paper. He pulled it out and opened it up. It was a pamphlet from one of the local churches in the area. The title read; *God hears you*. The verse on the cover was, Psalm 50:15 'Call upon Me in the day of trouble; I will deliver you and you shall glorify Me.' He read the words out loud. He sat up in his bed and read the words again. He doesn't know how the pamphlet got there, but he does like reading that someone or something else hears him.

"I don't know if you're real, but if you are, can you please help my mom? She's had it rough, and she just needs to catch a break." He paused as the tears flowed again. "I love her. Please help her. I don't even care about me. Just help her."

He laid back down on his side, crumpled pamphlet in hand, tears flowing from his eyes, and fell asleep.

2

Across town, Dave's eyes popped open, and he sat up in bed when an intense, searing pain shot through his abdomen. He held it with both hands, clinched his eyes shut, gritted his teeth and winced in silence as it circled through his body. As it slowly passed, he forced his eyes open to look over at Gina. She was lying on her side, facing him. She was still asleep. He looked over at the clock on the nightstand. It was 6:55 a.m. As he closed his eyes and weathered the storm, another round of pain, he realized he had forgotten to take his pill last night. He sat there grasping his stomach, waiting for this wave to end. When it finally ended, he pulled the sheet away from his body and exited the bed quickly and quietly, doing everything in his power not to wake her. After successfully getting out of bed, he stood in front of his nightstand and stared down at his bible as another pain ripped through his body. After a few moments, it passed. He grabbed his bible and reading glasses from the nightstand. Dave quietly slipped out of the room without waking her and headed down the stairs toward the coat closet. He reached into his coat and grabbed the little white pill bottle. He opened it, took a pill out, and popped it into his mouth and swallowed it. Dave closed the bottle, placed it back into his coat, and shut the closet door.

"Oh, crap." He whispered under his breath.

He wasn't the type to swallow a pill without water. Dave knew that Murphy's law always held true for him. The pill had gotten stuck in the back of his throat and was releasing a very bitter taste that was making him gag, and his stomach contract. He hurried into the kitchen, placed his bible and glasses on the table as he passed by, and grabbed a glass from the cupboard. He turned to fill it with water but had to pause while his gagging intensified. When it passed, he filled the glass and drank. He drank the whole glass and then sat it down in the sink.

"So disgusting," He whispered as he walked over to the table and took a seat.

The bitterness of most pills was enough to make you gag, but the bitterness of a morphine pill seemed so much worse. He covered his mouth and chuckled as he thought about Gina. She would give it to him good right now if she could see him. "Big bad cop taken down by little white pill." He laughed some more. "You're so dramatic sometimes, Rambo," she would say. He loved everything about her. She was so devoted to caring for him and the kids, but she also had such a whimsical, sassy way about her. She was what truly defined the difference between loving and being in love. Another burst of pain shot through him and he quietly asked God for help.

"Father, please help me with this pain. Thank you."

After the pain passed, he put his reading glasses on and opened the Word. He paused. His mind shot to the time that he took Kurtis home and met his mom for the first time. It was just another eye-opening moment in his career. A young man being raised in a broken home. He has no father to look to for guidance or leadership. A mother who had lost her way and was desperately trying to find that one man who could love her like every woman wanted to be loved. She was looking in all the wrong places for that love and destroying the life of a young man who just wanted to be loved and cared for himself. Dave saw scenarios like it every day. Boys and girls left to raise themselves. He had taken a shine to Kurtis though, and wondered for a second if Marc would be okay with him inviting Kurtis to that camping retreat. He didn't know if he would go, but at the very least, it would give him a chance to experience a positive male role model and learn about the Lord. Dave scratched his chin and decided that he would talk about it with Marc when he got up today. The pain was still in his stomach, but not as intense. He opened his bible to the book of Daniel, chapter six and read.

3

It's 6:55 a.m. in Crystal City, Texas. Waylon Black stands on his front porch and sips his coffee, looking out at the pasture. The sun has been up since 6:45 a.m., he's been up since 5:30 a.m. He is drinking his second pot. He is a third-generation rancher. In 1895, his grandfather won the land in a poker game from a wealthy businessman and built the business from the ground up. It's his now, and at 61 he fears the ranch won't see a fourth generation holding onto it. He drinks his coffee on that front porch every morning for the last fifteen years, wondering if he'll ever see his daughter again. He regrets the way they handled her pregnancy news when she was eighteen. She walked out the door and never looked back. Shannon hasn't called or written a letter. She has completely disappeared from their lives. He didn't just inherit the land from his father, he also inherited generations of stubbornness. He has not lifted a finger to find her or his grandchild, and he has forbidden his wife to as well. Gail and Waylon have been married for forty years. She had Shannon when she was twenty-eight. It was a miracle because they were told that she couldn't conceive after going through three years of cancer treatments. She called Shannon their little blessing and made sure that they raised her with all the love and comforts she had never had. There were really no bumps in the road until Shannon turned thirteen. Her rebellious phase was more than they could handle. She was 'hell on wheels' as Waylon put it, and she consistently chose the wrong path with every decision she made. For over two years, she fought them tooth and nail on everything. She hung out with the wrong crowd, snuck out of the house daily, and reeked of alcohol and smoke when she came home. Waylon would often tell Gail that their little blessing came with horns. And then one day, as if someone had flipped a switch, poof, she was their little Shannon again. There was no rhythm or reason. She just returned to normal. Respectful, studious, and humble. She got good grades in high school, was popular, beautiful, and in her senior year was dating the starting quarterback for the football team. Shannon had applied to several colleges, and got accepted by her first choice, the University of Texas. She planned to go there in the fall. It was halfway through her senior year when she met Butch. He was twenty-five, tall, well built, with blonde hair and blue eyes. It was love at first sight. In an instant, everything changed. She couldn't see what Waylon saw from the beginning. Butch was a smooth-talking conman who drifted from town to town, taking what he could and then leaving without a trace. And that's exactly what he did. He led Shannon to believe that he was her knight and shining armor. He filled her head with dreams of a life together. Exotic travel, a big house, nice things, and a lifetime of love. For three months, he strung her along. Her parents and friends begging her to open her eyes. She never did. She allowed his rugged good looks, his charm, and his words laced with honey to blind her to the truth that everyone else could see. In the end he left her a note that simply read, *"Thanks for the good times baby, I gotta jet to my next adventure. It was fun."* It crushed her. He had left her with nothing, or so she thought. Two weeks later, she took her final exams, failing most of them because of her heartbreak. It was during that last week that she woke up in the morning feeling nauseous, sometimes vomiting. A week after graduation, she was walking through a drugstore with one of her friends when she saw the home pregnancy tests. On a whim, she bought one. That night in the upstairs bathroom of their house, she sat on the closed toilet, tears running down her face, eyes wide open as she stared at the plus sign on the test. She was seventeen, and her life was about to change forever. Now she had to go downstairs and tell her parents. She knew her father would be so disappointed in her. She decided not to delay it. Shannon walked downstairs and ripped the band aide off and told them.

Waylon sighed as he took a sip of coffee, closed his eyes, and replayed every detail of that day in his head.

"Pregnant! Pregnant! How did this happen?" He screamed at her.

"Well daddy, when two people get together..."

He cut her off mid-sentence.

"You shut your smart mouth, young lady...I mean, well, I don't know what I mean, but you're no lady."

Gail just sat at the table in complete silence. Stunned.

"I'm sorry this happened. I never meant for it to happen."

"Your seventeen Shannon!"

"Eighteen in a couple of months." She interjected.

"Fine. Eighteen in a couple of months! Sex should have never been on the table. EVER! You're way too young and, and...your way too young!"

"I know, daddy, it just happened."

"It just happened. It just happened. Car accidents just happen. Thunderstorms just happen. Sex doesn't just happen Shannon. It takes two people to be willing participants."

"I know. I'm so sorry, daddy."

"Sorry isn't going to fix the shame that you've brought on this family girl."

"So that's what it boils down to? Your precious reputation?"

"It boils down to the fact that a seventeen-year-old girl should never, ever have sex. I taught you better than that." He looked over at Gail. "You can chime in at any minute."

Gail just stared straight ahead, not knowing what to say.

"So what now, daddy? What do I do? Abortion?"

Before he even realized it, a flood of obscenities and very hurtful accusations came flooding out of his mouth. It was a rant that produced buckets of tears and a long-lasting resentment that she still held to this day. It was a knee jerk reaction, and one that he wished he could take back.

"We don't murder innocent babies because we made a mistake." He screamed.

"Well, what do we do now?" She yelled back.

He sat down in the chair and ran his hand through his hair. Waylon stared at the floor for a few seconds before he finally looked up at her. He wasn't crying, but his eyes were moist and on the brink. She had never seen him cry before. Ever. He looked directly at her and spoke in a somber tone.

"We'll look into finding a nice family to adopt the baby. Preferably one that is a few states away, so..."

"No," she interrupted.

"What do you mean, no?"

"I mean, no."

From there, the conversation only got worse. They didn't find a solution that night, and within a month, she was out the door and gone. In the middle of the night, she disappeared. Waylon's stubborn nature and pride impeded his duty as a father. He didn't look for her at all. He assumed one day she would show up on their doorstep begging for forgiveness. Days turned into weeks, and weeks into years. Without his knowledge, Gail hired a private eye to find her. He located her and her son living in Dargen City, Michigan. That was two years ago now. The PI supplied her with enough information that she knew it was her daughter. Gail created a new email to only contact her. It took Shannon a couple of months to respond to her mother's email, and when she did, she simply wrote, "Leave us alone." Gail enticed her with the promise of cash each month, and she finally broke down and agreed. Not to have a regular correspondence with her, but to send her an email on the first of every month that simply read, "We're okay." Gail accepted, and for the last year or so, has been depositing $500 a month into her bank account electronically. Since she handled the finances, Waylon never questioned the money that went out. For all he knew, it was a business expense each month to a creditor they owed. She hoped that one day he would come to his senses and realize they needed their daughter and grandson back, but it was looking bleak. One day, an old friend visited the ranch while Waylon was at the feed store. After a long conversation, he assured Gail that he would bring Shannon and her grandson home. She gave him Shannon's address in Dargen City and some cash for the journey. Gail was so blinded by hope that she failed to see the man standing in front of her.

Pride is a character trait that has destroyed many families. Waylon and his father were blind to that fact, and they often let its venomous poison affect their way of life. Waylon finished his last sip of coffee, sat his mug on the railing, cupped his hand around his eyes, and cried.

4

Pastor Bill Dunkirk sat in his office at the church, sipping coffee and flipping through the bible. It was 7:40 a.m. now, a little earlier than he usually got there, but he awakened out of a dead sleep at 6:55 a.m. He sat up in his bed, looked around, and then relaxed when everything appeared normal. Still, his spirit was restless, so he bowed his head and prayed.

"Lord. King of kings and Lord of lords. I thank you for giving me another day with the ones I love on this earth. Please help me serve Your purpose and give me the strength to leave my heart open to all of Your grace. Bless those who are hurting and comfort them in their time of pain. Thank you, Father. I ask this in the name of our savior and redeemer, Jesus, amen."

He knew there was no sense trying to go back to sleep, so he got out of bed, got ready, and went to the office early. He had an established a ritual that he went through every week to decide which sermon he would preach on Sunday and Wednesday. On Sunday, after the evening service, he prayed for God's clarity on what he should speak on Wednesday. On Wednesday night after the service, he bowed and prayed for God's clarity on what he should speak on Sunday. Ninety-nine percent of the time, it gave him clarity before he went to sleep that night, but every so often he wouldn't know until the day before. He already knew what this Sunday's message would be; dealing with hurt in our lives. There were several passages that stuck out in his head to help those who were dealing with pain. The thing about pain is that everyone experiences it. It doesn't discriminate between rich or poor, black or white, man or woman. Pain is the byproduct of original sin. Some experience abuse, some physical pain, and some mental anguish for decisions they, or someone else, made for them. There was so much pain in the world because of mankind's continual sin, but there was refuge in the Lord. The message would focus on the twenty-third Psalm, and David's declaration that, 'yea, though I walk through the valley of the shadow of death, I will fear no evil; For You are with me...' Pastor Dunkirk smiled as he read those words. He had two other passages bookmarked to give his flock hope and encouragement. He flipped to Psalm chapter one forty-seven verse three, 'He heals the brokenhearted and binds up their wounds.' Then the book of Matthew chapter five verse four, 'Blessed are those who mourn, for they shall be comforted.' It was just three passages out of many that God promised His children to comfort them in times of pain, but they were three powerful passages. He wanted to convey to the congregation that there was no formula for avoiding pain. There was no magic potion for dealing with loss. As a believer in Christ, we have the ultimate support system. That He understands our hurt and our sorrow, and He wants to comfort us and carry us through our pain, if we only let him. This concept was one that most everyone, believer or not, had trouble processing in life. He was no different. The simple truth of the matter was that God, in His ultimate wisdom, uses every part of your life for his purpose. There are things that happen in this lifetime that we will never understand, but there is nothing His hand doesn't touch. The book of Job is one of the greatest examples of this. Satan has to ask for God's permission to even touch a hair on Job's head. God see's everything, knows everything, and His hand is in every detail of our lives. Pastor Dunkirk flipped to the book of Jeremiah chapter one, verse five. "Before I formed you in the womb, I knew you..." He was speaking to the prophet Jeremiah, but it applies to every single one of His children since the dawn of time. Dunkirk writes the passage into his sermon and puts into parenthesis; God knows you intimately before you are ever formed in your mother's womb. He has a direct purpose for your life. You will achieve the ultimate fulfillment in this life if you decide to follow Him and commit yourself to achieving that purpose. He smiled as he finished the note and then took a sip of his coffee. He closed his eyes and felt compelled to pray again specifically for those hurting.

"Father, please help those who are hurting today. There is genuine pain in this world hurting good people. Your people. Comfort them, Lord. Thank you. In Jesus precious name. Amen."

Chapter 15

Dave made a traditional southern meal for Gina that night. Fried chicken, mashed potatoes, collard greens, cornbread, and for dessert, a peach cobbler with vanilla ice cream. This was the exact meal that he cooked for her on the first night they moved into their apartment. That was why he insisted that they have dinner above the garage tonight instead of in their house. He had recreated the moment precisely as she remembered it. Gina was lost in thought when Dave appeared to her right with a pitcher of sweet tea and poured it into the ridiculously oversized glass.

"Where did you find these glasses?" she covered her mouth and laughed.

"I tucked them away in the back of the closet," he laughed as he poured.

"Everything is exactly how I remember it was that night. Wow!"

He finished pouring his glass and placed the pitcher back into the refrigerator. He walked back over to the table, bent down, and kissed her on top of her head before he took his seat across from her.

"That was the plan. I remember that night in my head like it was yesterday, and you look just as beautiful today as you did then."

"Then why did you ever marry me if I looked that old then?"

He reached across the table and took hold of her hand. She looked into his eyes.

"You are the most beautiful woman in the entire world. Always have been and always will be. Looking into those big brown eyes gets me through my day and makes me look forward to the next day. You, my dear, are a natural beauty that only gets better with age."

"Thank you for those very kind words, for this wonderfully cooked meal, and for sparing no detail in recreating our early years." She smiled. "But I need to know. Are you okay?"

He smiled, "Always to the point, my dear."

"With the people I love, yes, I am, and you're at the top of that list."

"Can't we just enjoy the meal and each other's company for a moment?"

"I'm sorry David. Yes, we can. Let's eat."

He could see how anxious she was. She was scared. He dropped his head and stared at the floor. She tried to change the subject for the moment.

"The chicken looks..."

"There's nothing they can do for me, Gina."

She tried to speak, but nothing came out. The lump in her throat felt the size of a softball. In very broken English, she could finally say, "We...can...figure."

"It's stage four pancreatic cancer. Before I even realized what was going on, it was too late."

The tears now flowed freely, and she jumped up from the table and paced back and forth.

"No, no, no, no, no! There has to be a way to beat this!"

He rose to his feet and walked over to her. He threw his arms around her and held on tight.

"There is no way out of this. Doctor Peyton told me I had maybe six months to..."

She broke free from the hug, pushed him away and looked him in the face.

"Six months! Maybe! David...when were you going to tell me this?"

"I was trying to find the right time."

"If I didn't ask, when was that going to be? When you were lying in a hospital bed, unresponsive?"

"I don't know. It scared me, Gina. I didn't know what to do. I didn't know how to react."

"Bologna! You don't get scared."

"I do! I just hide it really well most of the time."

"Stage four? That's something you tell your wife, no matter how dysfunctional we are."

"I know. I'm so sorry. I only found out a week ago."

"Then you should have told me a week ago." She yelled. "How did I not see the symptoms before you started living in the garage? I could have..."

"Stop! You're looking for a way to blame yourself. Don't do that."

"It just doesn't seem fair. It's not right. David..."

Her words trailed off, and she cried harder. He moved in and wrapped her up in a big bear hug. She struggled to break free, but he wouldn't release her.

"Everything's going to be okay."

"Why are you saying that? No, it isn't David. You're dying!"

"I know. I'm sorry. "

She stopped struggling, started crying harder, and just laid her head on his chest. She eventually wrapped her arms around him and squeezed tight. He doesn't know how long that embrace lasted, but it lasted a while. She finally spoke.

"I don't want to lose you."

"And I don't want to leave you or the kids." He pulled back so that he could stare into her eyes. "But It's going to be okay. Until I accepted Christ, I had no clue what was going to happen. Now that I know the truth, I'm at peace with this life and with how He's going to take care of those I love."

"But I don't want you to go. I need you to stay here so we can grow old together."

He pulled her back in and they held on to each other tight. There was absolutely nothing he could say at this moment that would ease the pain she was feeling. He just held her. Time literally stood still in that moment. Everything around them was inconsequential. The only thing they could hear was the beating of each other's heart. Finally, he spoke.

"The chickens getting cold."

She dug her face into his shoulder to muffle a laugh. It didn't last long, but it was a laugh.

"Too soon," she whispered.

She closed her eyes and drifted back to a time where they had no kids, Dave wasn't dying, and a hug was the only thing they could afford. Her body melted into his. When they finally separated, he wiped the tears from her eyes and gave her a kiss on the forehead. They sat back down and he explained everything to her. She had many questions, which he answered. He warmed their food up and they ate, but the questions and the conversation continued. Even though she was devastated and her heart was broken, she pressed on.

"I just don't know why you didn't tell me right away, David. Even though we were not in a good place, you should have told me."

"I know. I was so ashamed of my behavior over the last couple of years that I kind of just shut down. It scared me you wouldn't care..."

"Why would you ever think that? David, I love you. I'm still very much in love with you. A rough patch doesn't change that. I prayed night and day that we would come back to where we once were." She paused and then choked out, "Be careful what you wish for."

"Gina, this isn't a result of your prayer. It's life. But it took this to show me the path to salvation. People suffer for Him in different ways. This disease is my cross to bear, and I only pray that I serve Him faithfully throughout it so others can see the love of Christ in me. And if it influences one person to decide to give their life to Him, then it was worth it."

"Dave, I'm speechless at how you're handling this. After I accepted Christ, it took me time to acclimate to a point of sharing my faith, and living my life visibly for Him. There are still times when I unconsciously hide my faith for fear of not fitting in, but you dove in with both feet."

"Part of it is because I don't have the luxury of time on my side. It takes time for some, or even most, to fully acclimate to the Christian lifestyle. Your heart has always been in the right place, and your faith is inspiring to me. It's just that when I did finally see the truth, I wanted to learn everything I could. I wanted to tell everyone I knew, because I knew I didn't have a lot of time to draw it out. It was no mistake that I was sitting on the road in front of Pastor Dunkirk's church the night I got the news. It was no coincidence that he couldn't sleep and went into his office to work. God gave me the chance to accept His perfect gift. He created the scenario, but it was my choice to make. I chose life."

He barely got the last word out before the tears started falling from his eyes.

"I love you," she smiled.

"I love you too," he smiled back.

She enjoyed seeing the softer side of him. One that wasn't afraid to show his emotions. She took a bite of mashed potatoes when a sobering thought entered her mind. She looked across at him with panic in her eyes.

"David, what about the kids? When should we tell them? What about your job? Quit work right away and..."

"I've thought about that it and prayed on it."

"And?"

"First, every decision we make about how to handle this is a joint decision. That being said, this is what I came up with for now. Doc Peyton told me that as the pain gets worse, that's the indicator that it is progressing. Right now, I take one pill in the morning and one in the evening to manage the pain. I want to hold off on telling the kids until the cancer progresses."

"David!"

"There's no sense in worrying them right now. If we tell them now the event," a word he used to keep emotions in check for the moment "might not be for another six months, and that's too much unnecessary worrying."

She thought about it for a moment and eventually agreed.

"So, how many pills do you have to take before you feel it's time to tell them?"

"I'll know when my body gets weaker, and one pill isn't enough to control the pain. Plus, I promise I'll keep regular doctor's appointments to monitor the progress. I'll update you every night on how I feel, and if I have any difficulties throughout the day."

"And work?"

"The same goes for work."

"David, I want to spend as much time with you as possible before you're gone. I can take a leave of absence and we can..."

"Gina, we can't. The insurance is what's paying the medical bills and the prescription coverage. Plus, we need the income. There isn't enough in savings for me to quit and you to take a leave of absence. It could be six to eight months before I'm gone."

As he finished his words, she collapsed in his arms and starting crying again.

"This doesn't seem real. It's like a movie of the week."

"I know. But right now, while I still have the strength in my body, I have to continue living as if nothing is wrong. I still feel strong. The only difference in my life right now is the stomach pain that I have to take the pills for. I'm still me."

He pulled away from her and gently kissed her lips. She held his face in her hands and smiled.

"Maybe God will give us a miracle."

"Maybe," he smiled.

She returned to his embrace.

"Are you scared?"

"I'm not terrified, but I am in fear."

"In fear of what?"

"It's not the pain or the dying part that I fear. It's having my family watch me slowly melt away into nothing. The thought of all of you looking at me day in and day out for God knows how long. Days, weeks, or even months. That's the part I fear the most. What it'll do to you and the kids long term. I just want it to be quick in the end. Not for me, but for those I love...well...maybe a little for me, too."

"Dave my emotions are going to be on a roller coaster for the next few months. They will range from devastated to angry and you can't get mad at me. The only possible reason for me being able to handle this right now is that God is carrying me. But just know, I am going to pray for a miracle."

"Thank you."

He held her close, and didn't feel the need to share with her what his gut was already telling him. It was stage four, and the writing was on the wall.

Chapter 16

Friday—July 8, 2010

It was 2:00 a.m. and Dave sat on the side of the road in front of Faith Bible Church. The same time and place he sat exactly one week ago. He didn't know how he was going to deal with the news he had gotten from Doctor Peyton. Hopelessness is the only word that could really describe it. What a difference a week makes. The prognosis for his health hasn't changed. He is still on track to leave this earth, most likely within the next six months, but he feels more alive than he's ever felt. Within a matter of days, his attitude and circumstances went from hopelessness to rejuvenation. He found something that was right in front of him the whole time. A caring and loving God, full of mercy, grace, compassion, and forgiveness. When he accepted the gift of salvation, everything changed. The constraints of this world no longer had a hold on him. This body that he was in on this earth would pass away, like all do, but he would live with his savior eternally in heaven. Hopelessness wasn't even in his vocabulary anymore. He was a new man in Christ. This allowed him to swallow his pride and reconcile with his family. It gave him the confidence to tell everyone he knew about the Lord. His faith was sincere. He looked up to see if the light was on in the pastor's office. It was not.

"Sleep well, my friend," he whispered under his breath as he took a sip of coffee.

He thought about the phrase, 'God works in mysterious ways,' and he smiled. He never really understood it before, but now it made perfect sense to him. His circumstances were going to be his no matter what, and he understood that now. God put him on a direct collision course with Pastor William Dunkirk. It's the adage that, 'you can lead a horse to water but you can't make him drink.' Dave was led there, but he went to church, and he accepted Christ into his heart. It was a straightforward decision when he heard the truth, because he knew in his heart that it was the truth. He put the coffee cup up to his lips to take another drink when dispatch came across the radio.

"616 and 612."

"616," Dave answered.

"612," Javier answered.

"28747 Lona. 28747 Lona. Neighbors are reporting a disturbance from the location."

Dave shook his head. It was Joe and Rachel again.

"616 en route."

"612 en route."

"Copy, both units on the way at 0212 hrs."

Less than ten minutes later, they found themselves in the living room of the couple's house, refereeing another pay-per-view special. Dave stayed with Joe in the living room, while Javier took Rachel into the kitchen to get her side of the story. He had Joe take a seat on the sofa while they talked. Dave started.

"What happened tonight?"

"Same old thing, Officer Jackson. She just started in on me again. You drink too much. Your priorities are all screwed up. I'm tired of it."

"Well, do you drink too much?"

"Come on man, not you too. What happened to, 'get out while you can.'"

"Well, why didn't you?"

"I have no place to go."

"And why is that?"

"No money in the bank."

"Why is there no money in the bank, Joe?"

"I don't know. I guess we spend more than we make."

"What about friends? What do they tell you to do?"

"Same thing you did. Get out. Leave."

"And which one of those friends offered you a place to crash for a while?"

He thought about the question and then dropped his head. "None."

"You two were obviously a happy couple at one time. What changed?"

"The constant nagging and accusations."

"About booze?"

"Yes."

"So just stop drinking and see what happens."

"Why should I?"

"Because it's destroying your marriage. Do you think you can stop?"

He ran his hand through his hair.

"I don't know."

Dave walked over and kneeled down in front of him to get to his eye level. Not the smartest tactic, but he felt comfortable doing it in this moment.

"Joe. If you don't know if you can stop. Then you have a problem."

"I don't know what to do or how to get help. Every time I think about getting help, she starts in on me and the cycle continues."

"That's because she loves you and wants her husband back. There will come a time when she goes numb to all that's happening, Joe. And then she'll just leave. No warning. She'll just walk out the door and not come back. I've seen it a hundred times in my career."

"I don't want to lose her. She's the only thing good in my life."

"Joe, life is a gift. Every day we breathe air into our lungs is a good day. A day we should appreciate that we have one more day with the ones we love. It's not meant to be taken for granted, because one day you wake up and you're in your golden years wondering where the time went. It sounds to me, Joe, that you still love your wife."

"I do. I really do."

He reached into his pocket and took out a business card. He handed it to Joe.

"That church is over on Rockdale Street. They have AA meetings every Wednesday night at 4:00 p.m. and Saturday morning at 11:00 a.m. If you're serious about saving your marriage, show her. Go to the meeting tomorrow and get a sponsor. Figure out a plan to kick the hooch from your life, and while you're there, check out some more brochures on marriage counseling. It's a wonderful church where people go to heal. I know the pastor there. He's a great guy. Someone who can steer you in the right direction if you need help."

"I'm not a really religious person."

"You don't have to be. You just have to accept help. In this life, Joe, there are two kinds of men. Talkers and doers. I really hope you're a doer for the sake of your marriage. At one time, you promised her a life of love and happiness. Be that man, Joe. Show her your committed to this marriage. To her."

He held the card in his hand and studied it. He looked up at Dave.

"I will. I want it to work. I want back what we had. I still love her very much."

"Then let's go tell her."

They left the living room and walked around and into the kitchen. Rachel was sitting in a chair at the kitchen table, dabbing her eyes with a tissue. Javier was leaning against the counter trying to assure her that everything was going to be alright. They entered the room and Dave spoke.

"Joe has something he wants to tell his wife."

"I know what you want to tell me, Joe. You're sick of my constant nagging and yapping. You just want peace around here, and you're going to work to sleep in your car..."

He interrupted her.

"I love you, Rachel. I'm sorry for falling apart on you when my mom died. I let booze control my life and ruin our marriage. I'm going to call in sick today and stay home so we can talk and figure some things out. Officer Jackson gave me this card to a church who has AA meetings on Wednesday nights and Saturday mornings. I want to go to a meeting, but I need your help to keep me focused."

She leaped up from the chair, ran across to him, and threw her arms around him. They embraced and cried together.

"Oh Joe. Yes. We can do this together."

"I can't do it without you."

"You don't have to."

Javier looked over at Dave and smiled. He mouthed the word "Nice" to his partner. Dave smiled and walked over to the couple, and put one hand on each of their shoulders.

"It sounds like you two have a lot to discuss. So, we'll get out of your hair."

They walked the officers to the front door. As Joe was closing the door behind them, Javier heard him tell Rachel about marriage counseling as well. They walked down the sidewalk toward their squad cars. Javier placed his arm around Dave's shoulder.

"That's a nice thing you did back their partner. It's a complete 180 from the last time we were here."

"He just needed a reminder of how he truly felt about his wife, not some disgruntled cop telling him to throw in the towel and abandon his marriage."

"You think he'll change?"

"The odds aren't in their favor. It depends on how serious he is about getting help, and how serious she is about sticking beside him. I hope they make it work. Regardless, I see us coming here a few more times throughout this healing process."

"Yeah. But you never know. If he's serious about going to the meetings, and trying counseling, then that church just might be their ticket to saving their marriage."

"I hope so, buddy."

"I'll clear us in a couple of minutes."

"Sounds good."

Dave went back to his cruiser and sat there, watching the house for a moment. He felt good about giving them an avenue to help their troubled marriage. He watched as Javier drove away and then followed suit. Javier cleared them.

"612 radio."

"612."

"You can show both units clear of the location. Verbal only. I'll be writing."

"Copy. Both units are clear."

2

It was 3:30 a.m. in the small town of Arley, Alabama. Butch McCabe sat in a hotel room with the blinds open, staring across the street at the small Savings and Loan that houses the town residents hard earned money. He takes a sip from the bottle of Jack that he's holding in his right hand. He doesn't have a team anymore, so all he can do is stare now instead of act. Butch is not a good man. He graduated from conman to hardcore felon when he hooked up with a girl in Juarez. She introduced him to her six brothers, who were firmly in the drug trade. They showed him a room filled with more cash than he had ever seen. They convinced him that if they could get into the states, they could all make so much money he wouldn't know what to do with it. He swallowed the bait. Hook, line, and sinker. Once he could get them across the border, their crime spree started. They picked up more recruits here and there, but after a couple of years, most were arrested or killed. He wasn't sitting on a mountain of cash, either. He barely had two nickels to rub together most of the time, but for now, he had his freedom. His rap sheet was a mile long, and he's wanted in several cities throughout Texas, New Mexico, and Oklahoma. The trail of crimes that he has left over the last ten years are many. Grand larceny, stolen cars, robbery, and felonious assault, just to name a few. When there was no team anymore and he was on his own again, he went further west to get away from the states that knew him best. He resumed the small cons again, but this time was different. He wasn't the young chiseled blonde hair blue eyed dream boat anymore that charmed you with his words. His way of living and time had taken away those tools. He mostly now just preyed on the elderly and took advantage of their trusting nature and weak disposition. He took another sip from the bottle and continued to stare at the bank. His thoughts shifted focus to information he had recently come across a couple of weeks ago. He was making his way back through Texas when he had an idea to stop by the city of Crystal City. Out of all the young girls he had conned in his life, he remembered Shannon as being the one who was head over hills in love with him. He thought it was a long shot, but it was a shot worth taking because he was down on his luck, broke, and desperate. Butch was happy that her dad wasn't home, and very surprised that her mom decided to not only talk to him, but share some very unexpected news. He was a father. He walked up to the house to inquire about Shannon. Gail came out of the house before he could walk up the steps and knock on the door.

"Can I help you?" She asked with her arms folded and cold stare.

"Yes maim. I don't know if you remember me, but..."

"Oh, I remember you. Time hasn't done you any favors, but I know who you are."

Pushing past her obvious dislike of him, he asked, "I was wondering, is Shannon home?"

"What's a matter? Did she finally see through all of your crap and kick you out?"

It stumped him.

"Maim?"

She studied his face for a moment.

"When's the last time you saw my daughter and grandson?"

This news almost floored him where he stood. His first instinct was to run onto the porch, grab her, and put his hands around her throat until she told him what he wanted to know. He didn't. This situation needed some finesse.

"A couple of years."

"Did you run out on both of them, or did she kick you out?"

"I guess it was mutual."

He didn't realize the totality of the situation between Shannon and her parents.

"You have the audacity to come back here and ask for our help in locating our daughter when you took her away from us and have never even let us see our grandchild? And you think I'm going to help you find her?"

He had all he needed to know.

"Your right. I'm so sorry that we've never even sent you a picture over the years. I was a lost man. I got caught up in the drinking and the gambling and took them for granted. I'm a changed man now. I've completely cleaned up my act and I just want to bring my family back home. Here, to Texas."

Bingo. That was the winning phrase.

"What are you doing for work? You don't look like you can afford a decent meal, let alone take care of a family."

"I got a good job lined up in Austin. It doesn't start for a couple of weeks, but it will be enough to provide all we need."

"What is it?"

"Car salesman."

"Figures. I can believe that."

She wasn't sure she believed it, but he seemed sincere in getting his family back.

"Please. I just need my family back." He mustered a few tears. "I can't be without them anymore."

Her thoughts were the same.

"Come inside. I'll make you some breakfast and we'll figure this out."

Twenty minutes later, he was enjoying some bacon, eggs, and potatoes. They sat at the kitchen table and she filled him in on what she knew.

"So, they moved to Michigan?" He got out between bites.

"Dargen City, according to the investigator I hired."

He smiled. "I'll bring them back. I promise. She just needs to see that I've truly changed."

She gave him the address.

"I really don't have much of a choice at this point. I haven't seen her in over fifteen years."

She broke down and cried.

"There, there." He reached across the table and patted her hand. "I promise I'll bring her home."

"Thank you." She looked up at the clock and noticed the time. Waylon would be home in less than twenty minutes. "Wait here. I'll get you some money for your journey."

"I'll pay you back when I get settled in at my new job."

"Don't worry about that. Just get my daughter and grandchild back here."

"That I can do, mom."

A chill ran down her spine. She left the table and walked toward the bedroom. He thought about following her, taking all the money in what he knew was a bedroom safe, and then choking the life out of her so that Waylon could come home and find her. This thought made him smile. But, the conman in him played the long game. She returned a few minutes later and sat back down.

"Here's two thousand. That should be enough to cover expenses. Do you have a cell phone to keep in touch with me?"

"No maim. Just got shut off because I didn't have enough to pay the bill."

She slid him a phone across the table.

"Waylon has a few of these lying around for emergency purposes. I have my number programmed in and it has two hundred and forty minutes on it. You can buy more minutes if you need to, but you shouldn't really have to. Please keep me updated on your progress."

"Yes maim."

"You have to go."

They got up from the table and she walked him out. He descended the steps, and she stood at the top, watching him walk away. He turned.

"I'll get them back. Don't you worry."

She looked beyond him to his vehicle.

"Is that ratty old truck going to make it to Michigan and back?"

"Yes maim. She doesn't look pretty, but she's solid."

"Okay then."

She waved, and he waved back. He hopped into his truck and sped off down the road. He kept in touch with her for about a week and a half, and got another fifteen hundred from her. After that, he tossed the phone she gave him in a garbage can somewhere around Savannah, Georgia. That was three weeks ago. He took another sip of Jack. Butch had three hundred dollars to his name now, which is why the bank across the street looked so good. He took another sip, and his thoughts drifted once again. This time to South Dakota, 2007. He was traveling down Interstate 90, through a small town named Montrose. It was two thirty in the morning and he had been driving for sixteen hours straight. They had just pulled a bank job in Albuquerque, and the cops were Johnny on the spot. Out of the six of them, Butch was the only one that could get away. He would learn later that four were shot and killed, and that one was taken into custody. He was tired and trying his best to get somewhere he considered safe. Butch did not know exactly where he was going, but Canada seemed the logical choice. One minute he was cruising along, and the next he remembers red and blue lights flashing behind him. He pulled over to the side of the road and waited. The spotlight from the police car shined directly into his driver's side mirror, blinding him as he tried to see when the officer was coming. Seconds later, the officer was at his window.

"Good evening, sir. Can I please see your license, vehicle registration, and insurance card?"

"This highway's deserted. I haven't seen another car for a while. You surprised me when I saw your lights flashing."

"At this time of morning, it's usually just me and the deer. Can I please see that information I asked for?"

"Of course. What seems to be the problem, officer?" He couldn't read the officer's nametag.

"It's actually Trooper. Trooper Post. You were having a problem keeping your vehicle steady for a few miles now."

"I'm sorry officer, I mean, Trooper Post. I'm just tired and have been driving for a while."

"Where are you coming from?"

He didn't want to tell him about Albuquerque, on the off chance that he heard about the robbery today, but he wasn't thinking straight. He was exhausted.

"New Mexico. Been driving for over fifteen hours now."

"That's a lot of driving. What's your destination?"

He took a little too long to answer, because he didn't want to say Canada, so the trooper stepped up his investigation. "Sir, have you been drinking?"

"Canada."

"What? I asked if you'd been...sir can you step out of the car, please?"

Butch reluctantly opened his door and stepped out of the vehicle. He stood in front of the trooper, approximately ten feet away. His mind was working quick. He had stolen this car only two hours ago from a nice, quiet little neighborhood. The third car he had stolen in the last sixteen hours. Since he wasn't face down on the roadway, he assumed it hadn't been reported stolen yet. He looked at the police cruiser and observed that Trooper Post was solo. Butch walked toward the trooper to close the gap. He threw in some exaggerated stumbles to sell the drunk angle. When he was within four feet, the trooper took a step back. He looked over at the squad car again.

"Who's your partner?"

Without thinking, the trooper instinctively turned to look over his right shoulder.

"I don't have a part..."

Butch had removed the screwdriver he found in the driver's side door from his back pocket, and moved forward quickly. Just as the trooper was turning back around to face him, he rammed it into the left side of his neck, almost certainly severing the carotid artery. He placed his other hand on top of Trooper Post's right hand, which was already on his gun. The trooper instinctively reached up with his left hand and tried to pull Butch's hand away from his neck while he struggled to get his gun out of his holster. Butch stared into his eyes as the lights went out and the trooper dropped lifelessly onto the roadway. He ran over to the squad car and turned off the lights. He did a quick scan of the area and saw a deer crossing the highway twenty-five yards up the road.

"He wasn't kidding," he chuckled as he whispered under his breath.

Butch grabbed the trooper under the arms and drug him to the driver's side door. He opened the door and sat the screwdriver on top of the dashboard. He hoisted him up into the car and sat him in the seat. Butch stopped for a moment to catch his breath when he looked over and spotted a picture taped just above the car's radio. It was a 5x7 photo of Trooper Post holding a baby, with an attractive brunette standing by his side. They were smiling at the camera. For one second, he felt something that he had never felt before. Regret. He didn't like it. He quickly switched gears and situated the trooper in the driver's seat and reclined it back a bit. Not that it mattered, because the trail of blood from the road to the police car was a dead give-away that something was wrong. He slammed the door and ran back to his car. He checked his rearview mirror again. No headlights coming. He shifted into drive and hit the gas. He was over ten miles down the road before he saw other car's headlights going the opposite way. Butch breathed a sigh of relief. He found a secluded spot in North Dakota and laid low for a few days. His clothes and the car ended up burned. He found a job as a ranch hand and worked there for maybe six months. Just long enough to buy an old truck and stay under the radar of law enforcement. He probably could have stayed there for the rest of his days and lived a good life, but old habits die hard, and the itch to make it big was the only god he knew.

A trucker's horn snapped him out of his trance, and he was back in Arley, staring at that bank. Yep. He had gotten away with murder. He smiled and then placed the bottle of Jack on the table and stood up and stretched. It was now 4:45 a.m. The bank could wait. There was an elderly widow in town he had his sights set on at the moment. If he could turn the charm on enough, he would be on easy street for a while. He scratched his chin and smiled at the thought of having a kid. He assumed he had several out there, nothing ever confirmed, but he knew he had one for sure with Shannon Black, or whatever her last name was now. Butch didn't have plans to head to Dargen City today, but it was definitely in his future. He walked over to the bed and laid down. He needed his beauty rest if he were going to run into the widow at the farmer's market today. She needed to see that million-dollar smile.

Chapter 17

Friday - August 6, 2010

It is 5:30 a.m. The whole family is still asleep, but Dave sits at the kitchen table sipping on his coffee, reading through the book of Matthew. The month of July was a blur. He paused for a moment to reflect on all that had happened last month. A diagnosis of an incurable disease. Salvation. He rediscovered the joy of family, and he was taking it day by day and truly appreciating the gift of life. He was still only taking one pill at a time for his pain, which told him that God still needed him in this world to continue to make a difference for Him, and that felt good. His co-workers had settled into the notion that he was still Dave, a solid cop who still does his job, but with a divine purpose now. He does it through his actions, and his words if asked. They have donned him with the nickname Divine Dave. He laughs when they call him that, and the shift still has coffee together at the beginning of each night, runs notwithstanding. He smiles and takes another sip. In a month's time, he has read through the bible, and is now going back through it to focus on the teachings of Jesus. He doesn't sleep much anymore, so reading has become a passion. He is reading one of his favorite passages. Matthew chapter eighteen verses twenty-one through twenty-two. 'Then Peter came to Him and said, "Lord, how often shall my brother sin against me, and I forgive him? Up to seven times?" Jesus said to him, "I do not say to you, up to seven times, but up to seventy times seven."' He smiled as he thought of Peter trying to do the math in his head.

"Forgive those who sin against you." He whispered under his breath.

It was a concept he tried to teach his children through example. He stressed the importance of forgiving those who wronged you. Even if they don't know you forgave them, God knows and will see your love for your fellow man. He told them it doesn't mean you have to keep going back to the well for more punishment. But your forgiveness of them leads to your peace of mind, and ultimately a more loving heart. He used the very painful example of how Gina, and both of them, forgave him for his behavior over the last two years.

"It's like for thirteen years of my life you were there. You were dad. Then the last two you were a stranger. An alien. You were sick of us or something," Marc stated in a somber tone.

"Yeah. We didn't even exist for some days. We actually went days without seeing you when you were working a lot of overtime, or hanging out with your work, friends." Melissa added.

"Exactly. I know that I'm dad and you love me, but even given all of our history together, how hard was it to forgive me?"

"It was hard," Melissa stated. *"But I have to believe it was harder for mom."*

"And she forgave me," he snapped his finger, *"Just like that. It didn't mean that she wasn't hurt, or that we didn't need to work some things out. When she looked me in the eye and told me 'I forgive you,' I saw the sincerity, and knew that she meant it. Her grace blew me away."*

"Yeah, mom was a pretty loving and gentle person before she found Jesus. After that, it multiplied times ten." Marc responded.

That conversation happened just the other day, and it's one he likes to reflect on. It's a great lesson in forgiveness. He took another sip of coffee and read the verses again. In a couple of hours, they will leave for the father and son camping trip with the church. When he asked Marc if he would like to go on the trip, Marc jumped at the chance to spend time with his father. He then asked him if it was okay to bring Kurtis. He explained to him the situation. That Kurtis has never really had a father figure in his life. He has no siblings, and his mother is "out of it" most of the time. Marc was very sympathetic to Kurtis's situation, which made him proud, and agreed that Kurtis should come. Now for the hard part. Getting Kurtis to want to come, and then getting his mother to agree. It turns out, it wasn't so hard. Kurtis wanted to get away from Rick, his mom's boyfriend, and Shannon wanted to get rid of him for the weekend. At 6:30 a.m. Marc came walking into the kitchen, rubbing his eyes. He sat down at the table. Dave looked over at him and smiled.

"You didn't have to get up for another hour and a half, son. We're not meeting at the church until nine."

"I know," he replied, and then yawned. "I'm just excited about the trip."

"Me too."

"What time are we picking up Kurtis?"

"I told him we would be by at about eight forty-five." He reached over and patted Marc's arm. "Thanks for agreeing to let him come, Marc."

Another yawn.

"No problem, dad. It sounds like he needs this, too."

Dave smiled. "Yeah, I think he does. You want me to make you some breakfast?"

"No. I'm just going to rest my head on the table while you read. Let me know when I need to take a shower and get ready."

He laughed.

"Can do, son."

He sat there and read some more, making notes in the margins and underlining passages. When he was gone, he hoped that one of them would pick up his bible one day and read it. It would be like he was right there with them, teaching them and helping them to understand things.

2

Dave pulled into Kurtis's driveway at 8:45 a.m. on the nose. Marc looked over at him.

"Do you want me to go get him?"

"Sit tight. I'll go grab him."

Dave did not know who would answer the door, or what condition they would be in. He no more stepped out of the truck when the door to the house swung open and Kurtis came running out. He had a duffle bag with him, and Rick was hot on his heels yelling at him.

"Get back here boy, I'm not through talking to you and..."

He stopped mid-sentence when he saw Dave standing by the truck, waiting for Kurtis. He stood at the opening of the door and watched as Kurtis got into the backseat. Rick fired up a cigarette and stared at Dave. Dave opened the backdoor and looked at Kurtis. He had a slight bruise on the right side of his face. It was maybe two or three days old, but it was definitely a bruise.

"Everything okay Kurt?"

"Fine. Can we just go, please?"

"Sure. I just need to talk to your mom for a minute."

"She's passed out in the bedroom."

"Okay then. I just need to talk to..."

"Rick."

"Rick for a second."

He closed the back door and walked up the sidewalk toward the front door. Marc looked back at Kurtis and smiled.

"We should have a pretty good time this weekend. You ever camped before?"

"No."

"It's easy. You sleep in a tent. You fish some. Do some looking at nature, and then at night make s'mores and tell some stories around the campfire. Usually scary, but since this is a church camping trip, probably tamer."

This made Kurtis smile a little.

"Yeah." He looked up at Marc. "I think I've seen you around school before."

"Yeah. We've had a couple of classes together."

"You have a sister named Melissa?"

"Yeah. Were twins. Not identical, but the other kind."

"Fraternal."

"Yep. That's the one. Did you bring an MP3 to listen to on the way up? It's like a four-hour drive."

"No. I brought a book."

"What's it about?"

"It's about a guy who hits and kills a gypsy lady by accident, but her husband puts a curse on him that no matter what he eats, he can't gain wait."

"My mom would call that a blessing."

They both laughed.

"He's pretty fat to begin with, but he loses so much weight that his skin is literally hanging off of him."

"So, the gypsy curses him to die a slow, painful death for killing his wife."

"Pretty much."

"Cool. What's it called?"

"Thinner, by Stephen King."

"My dad likes him. I bet he's read it."

"It's my favorite book. I've read it like ten times."

"Cool. Can I see it?"

Kurtis handed the book to him and he thumbed through it. On the back page, he looked at the name written in black marker.

"Who is Butch McCabe?"

"My mom told me she bought it at a yard sale a long time ago. The name was already on there from the kid who owned it before."

"Cool." he handed it back to Kurtis.

The boys continued to talk as Dave approached Rick.

"Is Shannon home?"

"She's in bed."

"Is she able to talk to me?"

"Whatever you have to say, you can say to me."

"That's good, because I was actually hoping to talk to you."

"Well then. Step up to the mic."

Dave stepped in so close that their noses were almost touching. Rick took a half step back and placed his back against the doorjamb. They were equal in height, but Dave clearly had spent more time working out and taking care of his body. His eyes locked on Rick's, and his voice dropped into Dirty Harry mode.

"I don't know who you are, and I don't care. Kurtis is a good kid. I don't know where that bruise on his face came from. But if I see another one," he leaned in to Rick. "I'm bringing my entire shift over here to talk to you personally. Now, my advice to you is this. If you really care for this kid and his mother, then do it better. But if you're here to take advantage of them and beat on them," switch to extreme Dirty Harry, "Then get out now. Nod if you understand."

Rick was not expecting this talk this early in the morning. He couldn't stop staring into Dave's eyes, because even after he had finished talking, his eyes were still driving the point home. "Nod," Dave repeated. Rick gave a nod, and Dave backed up. Without saying a word, he slowly backed through the door and into the house. He closed the door.

"Thank you, Lord, for giving me the patience to not beat the crap out of him," he whispered before he turned around and walked back toward the truck. The boys were only half paying attention to what he was doing, anyway. He walked back down the sidewalk and got into the truck. He slammed the door and looked up to see Rick peering at him through a crack in the curtains. Dave smiled and pointed a finger gun his way. The curtains closed immediately.

"Everything okay, dad?" Marc asked.

"Everything is great. Let's get to the church."

He shifted into reverse and backed out of the driveway. The boys continued to talk about this or that while he drove, but he was thinking about Shannon. Was this creep going to make her pay for his little speech? He didn't think about that before he delivered it. He hoped not. They pulled into the parking lot and there were already quite a few cars and a couple of RVs. He found a spot and parked.

"I'm gonna find Pastor Dunkirk. You boys can sit tight, or get out and mingle with the other boys."

He stepped out of the truck and stretched. He saw Pastor Dunkirk walking toward him, smiling and holding a cup of coffee.

"Dave, I'm so glad you guys are coming with us this year," they shook, and he continued. "Nice truck. Chevy Silverado 4x4, extended cab, metallic silver, and is it the 4.8-liter V8?"

"5.3-liter V8."

"Very nice. What year?"

"2008. You got one?"

"I wish. With four kids, we have two cars. A blue minivan and a white minivan."

Dave laughed. "How do you haul your boat?"

"You're killing me, Dave."

They both laughed.

"I see you brought Kurtis, the young man you were talking about."

"I did. He's a good kid pastor, in a really messed up situation."

"Well, we have a lot of good stuff planned. I'm sure he and your boy will have a great time."

"I'm sure." He smiled. "What's with the RVs?"

"Some dads are more glampers than campers,"

"They have hookups for them where we're going?"

"No. But they don't want to sleep in a tent on the ground."

"Okay."

He handed Dave a map of where they were going.

"It's about a four-to-four-and-a-half-hour drive depending on construction and how you drive." He pointed to the map. "Cheboygan, right here in the mitten's tip. We've got a magnificent spot we've been going to for a few years now."

"I've been to Cheboygan a few times over the years."

"Excellent. Well, let me give my quick safety speech and then we can be on our way. Say, can I use the bed of your truck to stand on?"

"Be my guest."

He walked around to the back of the truck and pulled down the tailgate. He hoisted himself up onto the edge of the bed and pulled out his megaphone. Once he captured the attention of everyone, they came over and listened while he explained to them the weekend's itinerary. He made sure everyone had a map, and then bid them safe travels. He told them his cell phone number was on the back of the map in case anyone needed help. When he finished, he stepped down, and the journey began.

"You boys ready for some fun?"

"Yep," Marc stated, and then put on his headphones.

"Yeah." Kurtis stated.

He actually had a smile on his face. Dave smiled back at him in the rearview mirror. It was great to see him smile. Before he shifted into drive,

Kurtis sat forward and tapped him on the shoulder. He turned around. "What's up buddy?"

"My mom gave me this to give to you to help with any expenses." He handed Dave a crumpled twenty-dollar bill.

"Don't need it, Kurt. Put it in your pocket and save it for something you want. We got a big tent, sleeping bags, fishing gear, and a giant cooler full of snacks and drinks."

Kurtis pulled the twenty back and smiled again. He buckled his seatbelt and opened his book. Dave shifted into drive and headed out. The drive wasn't bad at all. It took them four hours and fifteen minutes to get there, and they only stopped once to fill up with gas. Dave tapped along on the steering wheel to some classic rock. Marc listened to his headphones and slept some, and Kurtis read half his book and slept a little.

3

They pulled off of the main road onto a road that was once dirt, but now large gravel. There was a truck up ahead, and a man at the rear of the tailgate waving them forward. Dave pulled off to the side and parked his truck behind it.

"Wait here boys, I'll see what's going on."

As he exited the truck, the man was already walking toward him. He shook the stranger's hand.

"How was the ride up?"

"Peaceful. I'm Dave."

"I'm Pete."

Pete. Pete. Pete. Wasn't ringing a bell. He was probably mid to late fifties, a hulking man with a bushy salt and peppered beard, and a really firm handshake. Pete could see the confusion on his face.

"We've never met. My dad attends Pastor Dunkirk's church."

"My confusion was that obvious?"

"It's a good thing we aren't playing poker."

They both laughed.

"I hope you haven't been waiting for us."

"No. You're actually the first ones here. The pastor told me you all were leaving the church around nine, so I figured I'd get out here around one. We'll wait for the others to pile in behind us and when we're all here, we'll convoy to the site. Then I'll come back and escort the RVs and any stragglers."

"How far is it from here?"

"About five miles down the road. We have a large clearing where everyone can park, and then the sites about a half mile in."

"That sounds good. How long have you been hosting this?"

"It's been a few years now. The pastor expressed to my dad that he wanted to do a week-long retreat for fathers and sons in the great outdoors." He laughed. "It turned into a weekend after the second year. It was a pretty good idea he had, so we host them now for local churches and boy scout troops throughout the year."

"That's great. Do you own the land?"

"I do. One hundred acres."

"Are we truly roughing it this weekend? No toilets, showers, or outside amenities?"

Pete laughed.

"Well, we call it hybrid roughing it. There are no showers, but we have a beautiful creek that runs through the property about a tenth of a mile away, so you can take a bar of soap and bath there if you need to. It's deeper in parts, which is good for swimming and fishing. We put some port-a-potties in close to the site for number two goers. We figured it was more sanitary if we're going to have different groups up here throughout the year. Number one goers can choose any tree to duck behind. Last but not least, I built a giant brick grill to cook all the food on."

"I'm all for roughing it, but don't mess with a man's dinner."

"Amen to that, brother."

As they laughed, another car turned onto the road.

"Excuse me, Dave."

Dave turned and walked back to the truck as Pete directed the car in behind Dave. He got back in the driver's side and sat back down. Both boys were staring at him.

"Were waiting for the rest to get here and he'll take us to the site."

"That guy is huge, Dad," Marc responded.

"He's a big dude."

"No seriously. He could be bigfoot. He just shaved his body except the beard."

There was a laugh from the backseat. Dave smiled.

"He's a nice guy. He'll be doing the cooking for us."

"As long as we're not on the menu," Kurtis chimed in from the back.

All three of them started laughing.

When all the vehicles arrived and were ready to go, they followed Pete to the site. They parked their cars and grabbed the gear. Dave and the boys found their spot and set up camp. When everyone finished setting up, it looked like a hobo village of tents. Pete called everyone to the center of the campground and went over the layout and the rules. Pastor Dunkirk then told everyone to go explore for a couple of hours, and then meet back here at five for a bible study, and then dinner.

"You boys want to go find the creek and fish or swim?"

"Sound good," Marc responded.

"Sure," Kurtis responded.

They put on their swimsuits and grabbed their fishing poles. Dave grabbed the worms from the cooler. Marc looked at him.

"You kept the worms in the same cooler with our snacks and drinks?"

"I sealed the container up."

"That's still nasty."

He patted him on the shoulder. "This trip is going to be good for you, son."

Marc rolled his eyes and exited the tent. Dave stepped out and heard him talking to Kurtis.

"The worms were in the same cooler as the snacks."

"Are they in a container that's sealed?" Kurtis asked.

"Well, yeah, but that's still nasty."

"As long as there not spilled all over the food, I don't see the problem."

"You're a mini him. What if they spilled all over the food?"

"Is the food in sealed bags or containers?"

"Never mind."

Dave laughed as Marc walked away. He approached Kurtis and handed him a fishing pole.

"Let's go."

They walked along the creek and enjoyed the amazing scenery. You could see some smaller fish in the shallow water, and the water was so cold and refreshing. Dave bent down and drank right from the creek. He sat up and smiled.

"That's cold and good."

The boys bent down and did the same. They smiled at each other.

"Well, I guess we're mountain men now," Marc stated.

"Yep. Nothing to do but grow a beard and wear some flannel," Kurtis added.

Dave laughed.

"Come on, comedians, let's keep going until we find a bigger part of the creek."

They pressed on for another half mile or so until they came to a part in the creek that could pass for a small pond. They walked to the middle and decided this was the spot. No one else came down this far, so they had it to themselves. He showed Kurtis how to bait the hook. Marc already knew because they had been fishing plenty of times in the past. He had already cast his line into the water.

"I didn't know there was an art to baiting," Kurtis stated.

"There's an art to most things. Baiting is one of them. You want to make it as difficult as possible for the fish to take the bait and get away. There pretty crafty, and can pick your bait clean if you're not paying attention."

"So, if you bait it this way, they won't be able to?"

"It's not one hundred percent guaranteed, but the odds are sixty to forty in your favor."

"Cool."

All three of them cast their lines into the water and waited. Kurtis's bobber showed signs that something was interested in the bait. Dave watched it as it moved. He looked over at Kurtis, who was staring up into the trees and not paying attention.

"I think something is playing with your bait, Kurt."

He looked over at his bobber and noticed it moving.

"Do I reel it in?"

Dave whispered like an announcer calling a pro golf match. "No, just watch the bobber. When it goes down into the water fully, give the pole a powerful pull to your right. It'll set the hook and then you got him."

"Okay."

All three watched as the bobber disappeared under the water. Kurtis clutched the pole like he was getting ready to swing for the fences and then with a mighty pull, he hadn't noticed that the bobber had already come back to the surface. He yanked it to his right. The bobber, along with the hook and everything else, came flying out of the water. It got caught in the trees behind them and the hook set into a branch that was not giving it back. Kurtis stood there holding the end of the rod, staring up into the tree that now housed his hook, line, and bobber. He turned to look at Dave. He could feel the emotion swelling up inside of him. Kurtis told himself, don't cry. Please don't cry. He watched as Dave looked over at Marc, who was staring at him, too. They both laughed hysterically. Kurtis felt his emotions doing a one eighty. He smiled, and then he laughed.

"Wow! That was one heck of a yank there, Kurt." Dave stated.

"Yeah! Awesome bro," Marc responded.

Kurtis couldn't even talk. He was laughing so hard. They laughed so hard that it drew other campers to their location. Dave retold the story to them as only a fisherman could, and they joined in the laughter. When it was all said and done, Dave ended up cutting the line and replacing the bobber, hook, and sinker. But it was totally worth it, because the smile on Kurtis's face was priceless. They would talk and laugh about it for the rest of the trip. They fished for a little while longer, caught a couple of nice trout, but threw them back. Dave took a picture of Kurtis with a smile as big as Texas as he held up his first ever catch. A good-sized little bluegill that they also threw back. After fishing, they walked around the woods for a while, observing nature. Each boy had found a stick, and they used them to hit other trees or other things. At four thirty they headed back to camp so they wouldn't be late for the five o'clock bible study. They got back with about ten minutes to spare, and Dave opened the treasure chest of snacks.

"Who wants a little snack before dinner?"

Both boys walked over and looked into the super-sized Yeti cooler. Dave had changed the cooler to his liking, and built a divider to separate the two sides. One side was filled with pop and water. There was Mountain Dew, Cherry Pepsi, Orange Crush, and all kinds of sugary drinks. The other side had Slim Jim's, potato chips, candy bars, sour patch kids, licorice, and all kinds of sweet treats.

"I'll take some peanut butter cups and a Coke," Marc stated.

"That's too much sugar at once, Marc. How about peanut butter cups and water for now, and then a coke with dinner?" Dave countered.

"Deal," Marc responded.

"Kurtis," Dave asked.

"Payday and a water please."

"Agreed," Dave responded.

"Agreed?" He asked puzzled.

"When you say what you want, and I agree with the choice, I simply say, agreed. It means we agree and you can reach in and grab your choices." Dave smiled.

"He thinks that's clever," Marc added as he chomped down on a cup.

"It's brilliant," Dave responded as he looked over at Kurtis and winked.

"Agreed," Kurtis reiterated as he grabbed his snacks.

Dave reached into the cooler and grabbed a package of licorice and water before he closed it.

"Old people candy." Marc shook his head.

"Yeah. Old people candy," Kurtis repeated and smiled at Marc.

Dave laughed and shook his head. "Come on. Grab one of those chairs and let's head over to the study."

They each grabbed a chair and headed over to where the pastor was getting ready to speak. Dave grabbed his bible as well. Kurtis noticed that as they walked over, campers were carrying a chair in one hand, and a bible in the other, except for him and Marc. They got to the designated areas and set up their chairs. Dave set his in between the boys.

"I'll sit in the middle in case you boys want to look at my bible."

Neither said a word, they just sat their chair on either side of him. Pastor Dunkirk walked into the center of the circle and stood. Bible in hand. He started by introducing himself, and welcoming everyone. He talked about the ten years that they had been doing this and thanked their gracious hosts for the use of the property. The camp gave them a round of applause. He looked out at the campers and smiled.

"It does my heart good to see so many fathers and sons together this weekend."

Dave looked over at Kurtis, who dropped his head and was staring at the ground. He reached over and gave his knee a pat and whispered, "And friends." This made him smile.

"Tonight's message is simple. 'For God so loved the world that He gave His only begotten Son, that whoever believes in Him should not perish but have everlasting life.'" He smiled and looked out at the campers. "Now who said that?"

"Jesus," came the loud and unanimous reply.

"That's right. Jesus." He paused. "In John three sixteen, Jesus tells us this."

Dave tried not to be too obvious, but he watched as Kurtis, and Marc, listened to the pastor's message. He spoke of the sacrifice Christ made for mankind. How His love is so deep for us. He died and took the burden of all our sins, and His blood redeemed us. His resurrection conquered death for all eternity, and it gave mankind the hope to live with Him eternally when we pass away from this earth. After he finished the message, Pastor Dunkirk gave an invitation and prayed.

"For those of you who feel lost, who are in pain, or struggling with life's purpose, He has a plan for you. If you would like to give your life to Him and experience that plan. If you would like to experience His forgiveness, grace, mercy and love, then pray this prayer with me now. Lord. I am a sinner saved by Your grace. I believe that Jesus, Your Son, was born of the virgin Mary and came to earth as a man. That He lived among us, ministering and performing miracles to show us the power of Your kingdom. That He was crucified and shed His blood for our sins, and that He died on the cross. But the power of the grave could not hold Him, and He rose from the grave, conquering death and sin that we might live eternally with You. Come into my heart and save me. Thank you, Lord, for it's in Your precious name that we ask this. Amen."

They all raised their heads and looked up at the pastor. He smiled back at them.

"If you prayed that prayer with me, then hallelujah. Your journey is about to begin. Please either see me or one of our staff and let us celebrate the good news with you. We just want to give you some information to get you started on your journey so that you can experience the most out of your walk with the Lord. Now, I believe dinner is ready." he looked over toward Pete, who nodded yes. "Let's have at it."

The campers dispersed and walked over to where the picnic tables were. They sat down and each table went up as they were called and got a plate full of food. Dave and the boys chowed down and went back for seconds. When they finished, they went back over to where their chairs were and sat down. They had started a fire in the pit and a lot of the boys were roasting marshmallows around the fire. There was a table in the area that had all the ingredients for s'mores. Marc and Kurtis made their way to the table while Dave rubbed his stomach and motioned for them to carry on without him. He smiled as they stood next to each other roasting a marshmallow, talking and laughing.

4

The weekend went better than expected. Dave watched as the boys had a great time with all the activities. To anyone who didn't know them, they seemed like brothers. He did hope that they were paying attention to the camp's devotional talks. Still, Kurtis actually seemed like a kid this weekend, and that made him happy. Dave smiled as he packed their gear. It was around 1:00 p.m. and they had just finished lunch and the pastor had delivered his Sunday sermon. Dave was packing up, and the boys were saying their goodbyes to some friends they had made during the weekend.

The tent was the last thing to come down. He was getting ready to dismantle it when Marc and Kurtis came in.

"You boys done saying goodbye to your buddies?"

"Yeah," they both responded.

"Alright, everyone out so I can take this baby down."

"Officer Jackson. I have some questions."

Dave stopped what he was doing and sat down on the tent floor.

"Okay, Kurtis. Cop a squat and shoot."

Both boys took a seat.

"If Jesus is so loving and great, then why do we die?" Kurtis asked.

"It's the natural progression of life. At the end, is death. We can only stay in these human bodies for so long before they break down. God offers us a chance to trade these bodies in for a heavenly body. So that when we die on this earth, our soul enters a new body. A body that's perfect and free from any type of defects, pain, or ailments."

"If you're saved?" Kurtis asked.

"Yes. The pastor talked about Christ dying on the cross for our sins. It's through that faith that we accept Him and live a life according to His word."

"When you get saved, doesn't that protect from pain and sadness? Why do you have to endure the same pain as the rest of the world that isn't saved?" Kurtis asked.

"Because God didn't want people to see salvation as a magic pill. Get saved and all of your troubles melt away. It would defeat the purpose of coming to Him with a pure heart that is seeking His grace, mercy, love, and forgiveness. Some would take advantage of that grace by being deceitful and self-serving. He gives us free will in this world to choose who we follow. Him, or man."

"What's the incentive for salvation? It sure seems like people in the bible had a rougher life when they followed Him." Marc asked.

Dave laughed.

"Some did Marc. The bible teaches us a myriad of lessons. It shares with us the success and failures of those who served, or didn't serve Him. The lives of these men and women show us we have free will to choose our paths in life, and the consequences of our choices. But if there is one thing that stands out, it is that God is love. Salvation in Him doesn't keep us from having the same problems as everyone else. But it sure makes our problems a lot easier to cope with when you have a loving savior to rely on."

"So, what's keeping someone from getting saved and then living a life of crime or self-fulfillment?" Marc asked.

"God sees your heart and your sincerity. If you come to him with a sincere heart and accept Him, then he knows. If you do that, then your heart will truly change. Coming to Him with a false belief just because you think it will get you into heaven is a mistake. He sees your heart and knows that your belief is false."

"What if you come to Him and believe, but later in life you fall back into your old life of crime or other bad stuff? Are you still saved?" Kurtis asked.

"He knows that we're human. Most, if not all, of us will backslide in our lives. It might be days, weeks, months, or even years, but He will not abandon us. Ever. Finding our way back to Him can be part of our path that propels us to do great things in His name."

"Cool," Kurtis responded.

"Cool," Marc responded as well.

"If you boys have any more questions, I'm always available to answer them. If I can't then I'll get the answer for you."

They stood in silence for a moment, so Dave handed them some gear and asked them to take it to the truck while he broke down the tent. When everything was done and the truck loaded up, they started on the four-hour journey home. Marc took the backseat so he could lie down, so Kurtis sat up front with his book in hand. An hour into the trip, he looked into the rearview mirror to see that Marc was sound asleep. Kurtis was three quarters of the way through his book.

"That's one of my favorite books," he stated as he drove.

"Mine too," he responded.

"Do you read a lot?"

"I don't really have a lot of books. That's probably why I've read this one so many times."

"If you want to read more, I can give you some of my Stephen King books. I have a ton. I have books by other authors as well, if you..."

"No, I like Stephen King. He's an excellent writer. He captures the horror in life better than anyone."

"I agree. His detail is unrivaled." He smiled. "Reach under the seat and grab the book that's under there."

He reached under the seat and felt a hardcover book. He pulled it out and looked at it.

"The girl who loved Tom Gordon."

"That's a great read. It mixes baseball with suspense. Do you like baseball?"

"I don't know. I never played or really watched it."

This both surprised and saddened him. Fathers and sons bonded over sports, no matter if it was baseball or whatever. His body language and silence spoke to Kurtis.

"Are you okay, Officer Jackson?"

"I'm fine Kurtis." He softened his grip on the wheel. "Would you like to go to a game with me and Marc sometime?"

"Really? That sounds cool."

"We'll get a hot dog, some nachos, and a coke. We'll go early and watch them take batting practice. Sometimes they throw balls to the kids and..."

"So is Tom Gordon a ballplayer?"

"In the book, yes."

"Cool."

"Take that home with you and read it."

"I don't want to get it dirty or mess up any of the pages."

"Don't worry about it. I'm finished with it. You can have it."

"For real? Thanks."

Another smile. It was infectious and Dave had to smile himself.

"Can I ask you a question, Kurt?"

"Sure."

"Why do you hang out with Ronnie?"

He set the book in his lap and looked out the window.

"He's, my friend."

"Ronnie hangs out with some bad people. We think he might even sell for a dealer. You get yourself wrapped up in that stuff Kurt and sometimes it's hard to get out."

"I'm not selling for anyone. I'm just hanging out with another kid who has nothing to look forward to when he goes home at night."

"I know, but eventually..."

"I'm tired. I just want to sleep for a bit."

"Okay. Do you mind if I listen to the radio?"

"It's your car."

With that, he positioned himself to look out the window and laid his head on the headrest. Dave turned on the classic rock station and listened as Alice Cooper belted out *Schools out for summer*. He thought about the weekend and smiled, despite his error in judgement a few moments ago. The boys slept until he pulled into Kurtis's driveway.

Chapter 18

Saturday—August 14, 2010

Last weekend's camping trip was still fresh in Dave's mind as he sat in a parking lot, filling out some notes on the speeding ticket he had just written. Marc told him he and Kurtis had a great time, but he hadn't seen Kurtis yet this week. He had driven by his house a few times, and a couple of his hot spots, but no Kurtis. He wanted to see if he liked the book he gave him, or if he could answer any more questions that he had regarding the material at the campground. Dave checked the time. It was 1:45 a.m. He winced as a sharp pain in his stomach shot through. One pill every twelve hours was still doing the trick, but every once in a while, he got a tremor. He and Gina had just been to see Doctor Peyton that afternoon, and it appeared as if the cancer was standing its ground. No better. No worse. He was happy with the visit, but knew that everything could change in the blink of an eye, so he prayed about it daily. Dave finished his notes and took a sip of coffee. He closed his eyes briefly and said a quick prayer.

"Lord, thank you for Your Son, who died so we could live. Please give me and my wife strength to deal with this disease that will bring me home to You. Please take care of my family when I'm gone. Please forgive me for worrying about the pain I will endure and not trusting You. It scares me, Lord. I didn't think it would, but the suffering scares me, and for that I'm sorry. If there is any way to avoid the suffering, please help me. Thank you, Father. I ask this in Jesus' name. Amen."

Dave opened his eyes. He drew in a deep breath through his nose and then exhaled loudly through his mouth. He shifted the car into drive and headed for the downtown area. Traffic was light for a Friday night, but there were always plenty of people walking around downtown. He entered the district a little after two and drove slowly down the main street, checking each business carefully. There were a few people exiting the restaurants, bars, and businesses as they closed. Few cars lined the streets, and the city was shutting down for the night. He waved to a few citizens as he drove, and some actually waved back. He pulled off to the side and sat just down the street from Pop's, and shut off his headlights. Dave surveyed the alley entrance, or exit depending on how you looked at it, and observed a few people walk into the alley, and then emerge less than a minute later. He suspected they were buying. He grabbed the radio and called to Javier.

"616 to 612."

"612," came the quick response.

"Can you go to channel two please?"

"Copy."

Channel two was a semi-private channel they could speak freely on without tying up the main channel.

"I'm on two, Dave." Javier stated.

"Are you close to the downtown area?"

"I'm on Hodges near the Senate Coney."

Hodges was the next street over from Main, and he was almost perfectly in line with where Dave was sitting on Main.

"Perfect. Kill the lights and pull off there and don't go in front of the alley behind Pop's."

"Okay," he responded. A couple of seconds passed before he spoke again. "In position. Lights dead."

"Okay. I'm going to roll up to the alley entrance on this side and hit it with a spotlight. I think we have some activity going on based on the foot traffic I've observed going in and out of the alley."

"Copy that. Let me know when you're going to roll and I'll give you a five second head start before I block this side."

"Copy."

Dave crept that way when he saw a person in a hoodie enter the alley. He rolled up to the entrance, still dark, and hit the spotlight just as he entered the alley. The light hit the sweet spot and illuminated Ronnie handing the hooded figure a small plastic baggie with one hand, and taking cash in the other. He quickly hit the overheads and the red and blue lights lit up the alley. The hooded figure, without hesitation, turned and ran toward the cruiser. Dave slammed it into park, and the figure squeezed between the squad car and the wall and took off down Main Street. Ronnie stood there like a deer in headlights. Dave opened the door and ran at him before he finally snapped out of it and turned to run down the alley.

"Stop! Police!" Dave shouted as he gave chase.

Ronnie turned on the afterburners and was almost three quarters of the way down the alley before he saw Javier's squad car blocking his exit. He stopped. He turned to see Dave running toward him on one side, and Javier walking toward him on the other. Ronnie dropped to his knees and clasped his hands behind his head, interlacing his fingers. He kneeled and stared blankly into the brick building in front of him. Dave approached him and he could feel the handcuffs going on, but he didn't react.

"Ronnie," Dave stated as he snapped his fingers in front of his face.

Ronnie's looked at Dave.

"You alright little man? You zoned out on us for a bit," Javier asked.

"I'm good. I know the drill. Just take me to jail," he stated with defiance. "And oh yeah. I want a lawyer."

Dave and Javier looked at each other. Someone had taught well him, and with each arrest he became more and more familiar with the process. Dave escorted him to his squad car while Javier searched the alley for evidence. There was one small bag found where Dave had first seen Ronnie and hoody making the transaction. Dave and Ronnie stopped at the spot and he picked it up. He held it up to the lights in the alley.

"Look like little rocks to me. Javier?"

"Probably an illegal narcotic. That's a felony, right Dave?"

"Right, you are Javier. I would probably cooperate if I were in trouble for it."

"Lawyer," Ronnie repeated.

"Ronnie, you're fifteen years old..." Dave was saying when Ronnie interrupted him.

"Yeah. A juvenile. Slap on the wrist." He looked into Dave's eyes. "Lawyer." He then turned slightly to look into the police car's camera. "Lawyer."

Dave walked him over to the car and leaned him up against the front bumper. He searched him for contraband. In the left front pocket of his jeans, Dave found twelve more baggies with rocks in them. He held them up to the camera as he placed them on the front of the squad car.

"These aren't my pants, Dave (emphasis placed on the D)," Ronnie stated as he stared straight ahead.

"Whose pants are they, Ronnie?" Dave asked as he looked over at Javier.

"I found them in the alley before you got here."

"And they just happened to be your size?" Javier snapped back.

"There a little big, but there better than the sweatpants I had on."

They both laughed. The kid was really trying to sell them.

"And where are these sweatpants, Ronnie?" Dave asked.

"I threw them in the dumpster behind the Greek restaurant. I had jeans. I didn't need them anymore."

"So if I go through that dumpster, I'll find your sweatpants?" Javier asked.

"Yep. Dig deep."

Dave continued to search him as Javier made his way to the dumpster, which was about halfway down the alley. He opened it and the odors were overwhelming. Javier looked in to see a full dumpster of food that had been baking in the August heat for a couple of days. He closed it quickly. He walked back down to where they were standing.

"Only old food in that dumpster." Javier stated.

"How do you know, Officer," he looked over at his nametag, "Martinez? You didn't even go through it." Ronnie had a smile on his face.

"I didn't have to. There are no sweatpants in there."

"Come on Ronnie," Dave stated as he escorted him around to the back of the car and placed him inside. He went around to the trunk of his car and opened it. He reached in and pulled out a clear plastic evidence bag from a folder, and then walked back to the front of his car where Javier was standing. Dave placed the small baggies in the bag and smiled.

"What are you smiling at?" Javier asked.

"Hold on a second." He opened his door and shut off the lights. He walked back over to him. "I didn't want the camera to record this conversation. I'm smiling because either that kid was instructed well, or his street smarts are kicking in. We both know that, 'These aren't my pants,' is not really a viable defense, but just the mere fact that he went the extra mile with the story of throwing them in the dumpster." He shook his head. "Impressive."

"You don't think the prosecutor wouldn't charge because of that, do you?"

"No, they'll charge, but now they can plead it down to something they shouldn't."

"A misdemeanor parking ticket," Javier laughed.

"Bingo buddy," Dave laughed. "I'm going to take him in and process him."

"You want me to come in and help with the paperwork?"

"I'm good. There's no need to tie both of us up on this."

"Sounds good. When you're finished, we can grab some lunch at Coles."

"Sounds like a plan."

They bumped fists and Javier headed back down toward his squad car. He took out his flashlight and scanned the alley back and forth one more time as he walked. A little more than halfway down the alley, up against the wall of the business, his light reflected off of something shiny. He walked over and bent down to see what it was. He shined the light directly onto the source. It was a rather large pocketknife. He put on his black rubber gloves and picked it up. He unfolded it and laid the blade across his palm. It was roughly four inches. He folded it closed and looked down the alley, back toward Dave's car.

"616 radio." Dave stated.

"616," dispatch answered.

"I'll be 202 with one juvenile for PWID, starting mileage is 23,485. 612 will be clear."

"Copy 616 your 202 with a juvenile. 612 is clear."

Javier watched as Dave drove away. He couldn't see Ronnie's eyes, but he wondered if he had now graduated into the business of carrying a weapon for protection. Javier knew they couldn't charge him with it, and there's no way he would ever admit it was his. He stood up and put the knife into his pocket. He walked back toward his car and made a mental note to tell Dave about the knife at lunch.

As Dave drove Ronnie to jail, his mind was racing, trying to figure out what to say to this kid to get through to him. He looked in the rearview mirror and saw him leaning back against the seat, eyes closed. He started to speak to him when one of those paralyzing pains hit the pit of his stomach. Dave grimaced in pain as he clutched the steering wheel with a death grip. Just before his eyes clamped shut, he observed no cars in front of him as he continued on a straightaway. He let off the gas and kept the wheel straight, applying the brakes gradually. He could hear Ronnie talking, but he couldn't make out what he was saying. Everything was moving in slow motion and he desperately tried to force his eyes open, but they wouldn't cooperate. He heard Ronnie's voice again. It was a scream. There was no panic in it, so he assumed there was no pending danger in front of them. To be safe, he applied more pressure to the brakes and came to a complete stop. The muscles around his eyes relaxed, and they opened slowly. The moisture that had accumulated obscured colors. He reached up into the visor where he kept some napkins and wiped the water from his eyes, and a trace amount of blood from his lips. That was new. The pain in his stomach slowly subsided, and the fog was lifting. Ronnie spoke.

"Dude, what's wrong with you? Why are we stopped in the middle of the road? Are you mental..."

Dave put up his hand. "Stop talking Ronnie."

Dave looked around. They were stopped in the middle of the roadway fifty yards from a traffic light that was blinking yellow. There were no other cars behind them, or coming from the opposite direction. He looked in the rearview mirror to see Ronnie's eyes staring back at him.

"Seriously Officer Jackson. Are you alright? That was scary. You closed your eyes and coasted for like five minutes."

Dave knew it was actually more like a minute, possibly a minute and a half, but he concurred with Ronnie. It was scary. Ronnie was talking, but he was still trying to process what had just happened. Without warning, that pain shut him down in the blink of an eye. What happened? One pill was working fine. He hadn't experienced any tremors like this while driving before. This scared him.

"Earth to Officer Jackson, come in Officer Jackson."

He looked up at Ronnie.

"Sorry about that, kid. I must have dozed off for a second. Too much time on midnights," he smiled.

"Can we drive before a drunk eventually comes this way and hits us?" came his sarcastic reply.

Dave pressed the gas, and they were on their way.

"Why do you work for that guy, Ronnie? You seem like a smart kid. Why would you want to get mixed up in selling drugs?" He didn't answer, he just looked straight ahead. "This is not on the record. I'm just trying to understand why..."

"You didn't fall asleep."

"What?"

"I said you didn't fall asleep. I've been around enough old people to know when someone just zones out, and that wasn't what happened."

"What would you call it?"

"You got problems. Something ain't right inside of you."

"I don't know what that means."

"You had what my grandad calls 'an episode.'"

"Really. Why do you think that?"

"I don't think that. That happened. I've seen it before in my cousin. He has seizures, and that's what he does." He sat back in the seat and then leaned forward. "You need to go to a doctor."

Dave smiled.

"Are you worried about me, Ronnie?"

"No," came the quick response.

"I'll tell you something personal about me. Something that no one else knows if you do the same."

"What? I don't care about your personal business. Why are you always trying to get me to be a snitch? That ain't me."

"I'm not trying to get you to be a snitch. I'm trying to get you to do the right thing. You work for some bad people doing some bad things. You think drugs are the only thing he's into? He's a bad guy, Ronnie. He hurts people daily."

"It's easy for you to come up in here with your Jesus this and faith that. You ain't me. You don't live like I do, or even Kurtis. We do what we do to survive."

"Life is hard. Not just for you, Ronnie. For everyone. We all have our own problems to deal with. Faith doesn't make life easier either, but it makes it possible. Trusting in an all-powerful God to be there for you when..."

"When you're hungry. Or when you know you have a beating coming. Or how about when your dad decides he just doesn't want to be around anymore?"

He looked in the mirror at Ronnie and saw tears streaming down his cheeks.

"Exactly."

"No, not exactly Officer Jackson. I'm mocking you. I'm saying every cliché, every do-gooder pitched to kids like me over the years. God doesn't care about us. He left us to fend for ourselves."

"Did you ever think that maybe you're destined for greater things? That the life you live now is helping to prepare you for the future. That you are a leader who can influence others to become great. No, you didn't think about that, did you? You only want to wallow in your own self-pity and misfortune."

"Self-pity and misfortune! I'm a fifteen-year-old kid, you jerk. I should have fun and hang out with my friends, not selling drugs to support an ungrateful and abusive family. I got robbed, no I'm getting robbed of my childhood. Don't lecture me. I don't want to hear it."

Dave pulled off to the side of the road just before they got to the PD. He turned and looked at Ronnie.

"I'm sorry if it seems like I'm lecturing you about something I clearly don't understand, because I've never had to go through it. I just wanted you to know there was hope."

"Officer Jackson, hope is all I got."

Dave lowered his head and looked at the floor.

"Well then, I'll pray that your hope comes true." He smiled and looked at him in the mirror once again. "Until then, please be careful. People know you have a lot of cash on you when you're..." He searched for the right words, "working."

"I can take care of myself."

He leaned back in the seat and looked out the window. Dave pulled back out onto the road and headed to the PD. He made it to the prisoner receiving garage and dropped Ronnie off to be processed and booked. He parked and went into the report writing room to write, and then call Ronnie's mom to pick him up. That was a fat chance, but the law dictated that he called her, even though he would probably be the one taking him home.

2

It was 2:30 a.m. and Butch stared out of the window of his motel room. Nothing to see except the interstate. He had arrived in the Heights sometime around 5:00 p.m. the previous day, and settled in to one of those no tell motels. He had stuck to traveling only during the busy hours of the day now because he felt he had a better chance of avoiding the law that way. Driving at two in the morning with no one else on the road opened him up to bored cops trying to find something to do. The Heights bordered Dargen City to the east and to the south. After drifting for a few weeks, he felt it was finally time to get to know his son. He wanted to make the area first, get settled in, cleaned up, and develop a game plan. It would probably be wise to survey the situation before going in. If Shannon was single, then this was going to be easy. If not, then the first thing on the agenda would be to make that happen. Any way that he had to.

3

The smell of coffee and waffles filled the house. Dave smiled as he laid in bed, looking up at the ceiling. He looked over at the clock. It was 1:30 p.m. The door to the bedroom opened, and he looked up to see Gina standing in the doorway with a freshly brewed cup of coffee. He sat up and smiled.

"Good morning," she said as she walked toward him.

"Good morning. Am I that predictable?" He laughed.

"Yes. No matter what time you come home and go to bed, you are up like clockwork at one thirty."

"Do I smell waffles?"

"You do. We thought it would be nice to have a brunch type lunch today."

She sat on the bed next to him, handed him the coffee, bent down and kissed his forehead. He smiled and took a sip.

"I have a surprise for you guys." He smiled.

"What a coincidence. We love surprises."

He reached over and sat the coffee on the nightstand. He grabbed her hand, pulled it up to his lips, and kissed it.

"I love you."

"I love you too." She replied. "Now, come downstairs and enjoy a nice brunch with your family." She caressed the side of his face and then held her hand to it. "How are you feeling?"

"I feel great."

Her lip quivered, and she tried to speak, but no words would come out. He grabbed her hand and pressed it up against his face, and closed his eyes. "God has this, my love," he stated as he opened his eyes and looked into hers. "Let's go tear through some waffles."

"You go ahead. I'll be down in a minute. I just have to use the bathroom."

"Okay."

She stood up and went into the bathroom while he put his robe and slippers on. He grabbed the coffee and headed downstairs. When he walked into the kitchen, the kids were already sitting at the table. Marc looked up at him.

"Good morning, father."

Melissa then looked at him.

"Would you like some breakfast, father?"

He laughed.

"Oh my. The perfect breakfast and now the perfect children. What have I done to deserve this?"

They all laughed.

"Where's mom?" Melissa asked.

"She is on her way. She just had to go to the bathroom." He surveyed the table. "Belgian waffles with fresh fruit, crispy bacon, home fries, fresh coffee, milk, and juice. You guys have really outdone yourselves."

Gina entered the room.

"The kids did most of it. I was merely a spectator."

"Well, it looks amazing. Thank you everyone. Let's say a quick prayer and then dig in." They all held hands. "Lord. Thank you for this food and the hands that prepared it. Bless it to our bodies for nourishment and please bless our home. In Jesus' name, amen. Let's eat."

As they filled their plates with food, Gina called him out.

"So, what's this surprise, David?"

Both kids stopped what they were doing and looked at him. Dave smiled.

"Now that the cat's out of the bag, I have prepared a fun filled evening for us. First, I have taken a vacation day and will not be going into work tonight."

"Wow! That's a miracle." Marc responded.

"Ignoring your comment son," he looked at marc and winked, "I have purchased four seats, first row behind the Tigers dugout for the game this evening. But wait. Before you heap praises on your dear old dad, hear my full plan. I propose we get to Slows BBQ before and pig out on ribs, have some junk food during the game, and then back here for ice cream and rock band."

"Awesome!" Marc shouted.

"Yes," Melissa added.

"Slows...absolutely," Gina chimed in.

"All you focused on was the Slows."

"That's all I heard."

He laughed. "The weather is supposed to be beautiful, and they're playing the Red sox."

"Beantown is going down," Marc smiled.

Dave and Marc high-fived. Gina looked at Melissa.

"Testosterone." She smiled at Dave. "So, what's the plan?"

"Everybody be ready to go at 1630 hrs. That's," he pointed at Melissa.

"4:30 p.m."

"4:30 p.m., for all of you civilians."

As they continued to eat, they broke off into their own separate conversations. Marc and Melissa talked about their plans for tomorrow, so Dave leaned in and whispered to Gina.

"I arrested Kurtis's friend last night."

She whispered back. "Ronnie? The drug dealing kid he hangs out with?"

"Ronnie Mann?" Marc asked.

Dave looked over at him.

"Why do you two only hear what you want to and nothing else?"

"Did he run? I bet he ran when you tried to arrest him."

"Why would you say that? Do you know Ronnie?"

"Not well. We're the same age so we're in all the same classes together in school. Well, when he shows up, which last year was like, hardly ever."

"Does he try to sell drugs at school?"

"He's never tried to sell me any, or any, of my friends. He's actually pretty funny."

"I don't really want you hanging out with guys like Ronnie. Dealing drugs is never accept-"

"Dad, you don't have to worry about that. I know drugs are bad. We've sat at the same lunch table twice, but that's really the extent of our hanging out."

"Okay."

He looked over at Gina and sighed. She smiled and reached over and grabbed his arm.

"Our kids are smarter than you think."

He looked over at Melissa.

"Do you know Ronnie?"

"Nope," she answered as she grabbed a waffle. "I've heard his name, but I couldn't pick him out of a lineup or anything."

"Listen guys. Ronnie's in a dangerous situation. He's growing up in a household that doesn't take care of him or value him. He doesn't get the love and support you guys do, and he's trying to navigate this life the best he knows how, because he has no direction."

"So, how do kids like Ronnie ever find their way?" Melissa asked.

"Unfortunately, most don't sweetheart. We just have to pray for them and try to help them out anyway we can."

Dave steered the conversation in a different direction. He looked over at Gina and asked her about her week. They spent the rest of brunch talking about their week and what was happening next week.

4

Kurtis rubbed his eyes as he walked into the living room. His mom was sitting on the couch in her robe, staring at a TV that wasn't on. He walked over and sat down next to her. She looked over at him and smiled.

"Good morning, baby boy."

"Good morning mom. What's wrong?"

"I'm destined to be alone."

"Rick wasn't right for you. You're way too good for him."

Rick had left at the beginning of the week.

"He was an alright guy. Helped pay the bills."

"You mean helped keep you high or drunk..."

She reached over and grabbed his hair above his right ear, and pulled him toward her.

"Don't talk about him like that. He cared about us."

He reached up with both hands and grabbed her hand.

"Mom, please, you're hurting me."

She immediately let go and pulled her hand back. She stared at it like it had acted independently. Shannon then covered her mouth with it.

"I'm so sorry, baby. I didn't mean to hurt you. You know that."

She put her arm around him and pulled him in close to her, and kissed the top of his head.

"I know, mom. It's okay." He put his arms around her waist and hugged her. "Rick didn't care about us. He only cared about what he could get from us. He wasn't a good person."

She didn't say a word, she just ran her fingers through his hair and hummed. He was relieved that Rick was gone. He was just another loser in a long line that she had brought home. She was so beaten down by life that she couldn't see it. He knew it was only a matter of time before she would find someone else to bring home. Maybe another Rick. Maybe worse.

"You better get ready. You're going to be late for school."

"It's summer, mom. I don't have school right now."

He sat up and looked at her. Her hair was a mess, she had tear-soaked mascara running down her face, and her breath smelled like she had finished all the booze in the house.

"Mom. When I went on that camping trip with Officer Jackson, I learned about Jesus. Do you think He could help you...us...live a better life?"

"I doubt it, baby. He would just leave me, too."

"I learned that when you invite him into your heart. He never leaves you. He's there for you always. No matter what."

She shifted her eyes to his. It sent a chill down his spine. Her eyes seemed to look through him, and her tone was icy and stern.

"There isn't such a man. They all say they won't hurt you or leave you, but they do."

"I learned He isn't a man. He's...He's...God."

She stood and started walking toward the bedroom.

"I need to rest. I'll get up and make dinner later."

She left the room, and he heard her bedroom door slam shut. Kurtis walked out onto the front porch and sat down on the steps. He wanted to be there for her, but she wasn't making any sense half of the time. Kurtis didn't understand why he wasn't good enough for her. Why she needed to have another man in her life? He was so lost in his thoughts that he didn't see the car sitting down the block. The driver looking at him through binoculars, watching his every move. The sinister smile on his lips from reading that look of desperation and hopelessness on his face. He watched as Kurtis cried. "Bingo," he whispered under his breath. He put the binoculars away and shifted the truck into drive.

5

It was 4:15 p.m. and Dave shouted down the stairs to the kids.

"Fifteen minutes until we leave. This is your fifteen-minute warning."

There was no answer. He shrugged and went into the bedroom and closed the door. Gina was putting on her Alan Trammell jersey and finishing up her makeup.

"Do you think the kids heard me?"

"I think the entire neighborhood heard you."

He laughed. He laid back on the bed and watched her.

"Trammel never looked so good."

"Oh yes, he did." She laughed. "Twenty years ago, he looked younger and had no wrinkles or love handles."

He stood and walked over to her. He wrapped his arms around her and they looked in the mirror.

"He's just as beautiful today as he ever was."

"Wait. Are you talking about me, or are you actually talking about Tram?"

"You." He smiled. "Beauty has never aged so gracefully."

"Keep reading that bible. I like this guy."

He wrapped her up even tighter. He turned his back to the mirror and the name Whitaker reflected off the mirror.

"Do you remember when we bought these jerseys together?"

"I do. It was right after the kids were born in 1995. The same year, Sweet Lou retired. You said, 'You'll never see another duo like that. Ever. Well, except for us.' You said, and I quote, 'You are the Sweet Lou to my Tram.'"

"Man, they were great together." He stared off into the distance. She threw out an exaggerated throat clear. "But they got nothing on us, baby."

She laughed. "Are you ready to go? It's 4:26 p.m. drill sergeant."

He marched over and opened the door.

"Kids it's..."

"Time to go, we know," came the reply as Marc walked past him in the hallway.

"Good," Dave answered. "Is your sister..."

"Right behind him," Melissa responded as she walked by him.

"Very nice. Okay. Let me grab your mom and we'll be on our way."

She pushed by him as she exited the room.

"We're waiting for you."

Dave smiled. He ducked back into the room and grabbed his Tiger hat. He headed down the stairs.

They made it to Slows BBQ at 5:00 p.m. and got seated at a booth in the corner right away. The long line of people gave them plenty of dirty looks as they passed by, but no one said a word. The hostess seated them and gave them menus. Gina looked over at him.

"They don't take reservations here. How did you get us seated so fast?"

He smiled. "Connections, my dear, connections."

"I don't care how it happened. I'm just ready to mow down some ribs," Marc added.

The waitress brought them all a tall glass of water, and they ordered. They devoured ribs, brisket, mac n cheese, baked beans, and some homemade cornbread. They all sat back in the booth afterward and exhaled slowly. Dave paid the check, and they were out the door by 6:00 p.m. and on their way to the ballpark. They parked at gate D and made their way into the park. Right around the fifth inning, they got a big pretzel and some cokes. The Tigers were playing well and holding a 2-0 lead behind a strong outing from JV and a Miggy's 3rd inning two-run blast. Everybody was enjoying the game. The top of the sixth JV had struck out the first two batters and was trying to strike out the side. It was a three two count when he threw a tight slider that just painted the black on the inside corner of the plate. The crowd leaped to their feet and roared as the home plate umpire rung him up. Dave thew his hand up to give his son a high five when the pain in his stomach appeared. He fell back down into his seat and clutched his stomach. His eyes clamped shut, and he grabbed the front of his jersey and squeezed while the tremor went through him.

"Father please," he whispered.

He opened his eyes a short time later. When the pain hit, he lost all track of time. It must have only been a few seconds. The crowd was just sitting back down in their seats, and his son was still standing looking at JV run off the field and into the dugout. The pain was completely gone. He sat up straight in his seat, wiped the water from his eyes, and exhaled. His son hadn't seen. He looked to his right to see Gina staring at him. She had tears in her eyes. Marc turned to him.

"Dad, that was awesome. Did you see that slider?"

He smiled at him. "It was sweet to watch, buddy."

He turned, "Hey mom..." he stopped talking and sat down. "Mom, what's wrong? Are you alright?"

"I'm fine Marc. I just, I just..."

Dave leaned in close. "Hey Marc, stay here with your sister while me and mom go grab some ice cream."

Marc looked lost. Gina put her hand on his knee and smiled.

"I'm okay Marc. Really. I was just thinking about one of my patients at work."

She wiped her eyes with the napkin and stood up. Dave stood.

"What flavor you want, Marky Marc?"

"Chocolate," was the answer, but he was still looking at Gina.

"We'll be right back, buddy."

He made his way past Marc and asked Melissa what she wanted. She also wanted chocolate. He and Gina made their way to the aisle and then up the stairs to the concourse. They walked over to a vacant section and he gave her a hug.

"How bad is it, Dave?"

"I get these tremors once in a while. They hit me like a shockwave and then just leave."

"Dave...," she could barely speak.

"It's okay. It's just a side effect of the..."

He stopped before he said the word.

"Are you still only taking one pill?"

"Yes, I promise. I will definitely tell you when I have to go to two at a time."

"At that point, I don't care where we are financially. You're done and we'll figure it out."

Regardless of what was happening to him, he was still the man of the house and he would not let his family get into financial trouble, no matter what. She grabbed his face. "You promised."

"I know I did, but..."

"But nothing. You constantly preach that God will take care of us. Well, it's time to walk the walk."

"I know. You're right. And yes, God will take care of us. Walk by faith, not by sight."

He placed his forehead on hers.

"Walk by faith, not by sight," she reiterated.

They kissed.

"This episode is totally my fault. I was in such a hurry to have the perfect family night that I forgot my seven o'clock pill. If I don't take them regularly, then it's bad news."

"Oh, Dave, why didn't you say something?"

"I didn't realize it until we were at Slows. I didn't want to screw everything up by going back home. That would have thrown the entire night off."

She reached into her purse and pulled out a ChapStick sized tube. She opened one end and poured out a handful of pills. There was a morphine pill in the batch. She picked it out and handed it to him.

"You should have told me when you realized it."

He smiled. "I should have known. You are always prepared."

"Yes, you should have."

He swallowed the pill and took a swing of his water.

"Thanks babe. Let's grab that ice cream and get back to the kids. The boy was really worried about you."

"Because he saw the look of horror on my face. I hated lying to him, David."

"I know, but you probably think about some of your patients from time to time."

"Don't do that."

"Do what?"

"Lie to yourself so that you justify lying to others. It's not right."

"I know. But there really isn't any other way right now. I don't want to tell them, Gina. Not right now."

"You're going to have to, eventually."

"I know." He looked at the floor. "Not right now."

"Okay."

They kissed again and then walked over to the ice cream line. Marc sat back in his seat, staring at the back of the chair in front of him. The Tigers were getting ready to hit, so Melissa looked up from her phone and started cheering.

"Come on, Tigers!" She looked over at Marc. "What's wrong?"

"When I looked at mom, she looked like she had just witnessed a horrible event. She was crying, and she had this look on her face...I can't describe it."

"Do you think she got sick from something? We have eaten a lot of junk food today."

"No, it wasn't that. It was a distinct look. I haven't seen it before."

"Did she say anything?"

"She said she was thinking about a patient of hers, and then dad rushed her off to go get ice cream. She looked scared, like terrified Melissa."

"Maybe she was thinking about one of her patients. She gets pretty close to them."

"Maybe, I guess. We'll see how she acts when they come back."

He no more got the words out than they came walking down the row to get back in their seats. Dave handed him a chocolate ice cream cup, and they sat back down. He looked over at his mom. Her face was normal now, and she was talking to Melissa and laughing. Dave nudged his shoulder, and he turned to him.

"What did we miss?"

"Nothing. The Tigers went down one, two, three. JV's coming out for the seventh. Is mom, okay?"

"Yeah, she's fine."

He turned and Gina was looking at him.

"Are you okay, mom?"

"I'm good Marc. I just had an emotional moment there. Sometimes they just creep up on you out of the blue." She patted his knee. "It happens sometimes when you get older."

"Okay," he smiled.

He pushed it to the back of his mind, and they finished watching the game. JV got the win and went eight strong, giving up two runs on four hits. Miggy came through in the bottom of the eight with a two out double that scored the winning run, and the Tigers walked away with a 3-2 victory. On the car ride home, Marc watched as his mom and dad laughed and joked around, but saw no signs of distress in her face. He relaxed and sat back in his seat. Marc looked over at his sister, who was sitting back in her seat with her headphones on, mouthing the words to some song he was sure he didn't like. He smiled and leaned forward.

"Dad. Who do you think the greatest Tiger of all is?"

"That's a tough question. There have been many great Tigers over the years. Ty Cobb stands out as the most obvious choice. There's Al Kaline, Hank Greenberg, Charlie Gehringer, Miggy, and of course Sweet Lou and Tramm. They are the greatest double play combination in the game's history." He looked over at Gina and smiled.

"The greatest," she reiterated.

"My grandfather, your great grandfather, went on about some catcher in the 30's for the Tigers. He played literally one season in 1935, but they won the series that year. What was his name? Arthur...Arthur...Graham. Arthur Graham."

"One season. He can't be the greatest."

"I agree, but grandad didn't care. He must have really brought a lot to the table that year. I saw a lot of great Tigers in 84 when they won the series. Parrish, Morris, Gibson, Evans, Petry, Lopez..."

"Okay, I get it. Then let me ask you this. Who is the greatest player you've ever seen play in person?"

"Wow. I've seen a lot of great ballplayers over the years."

"Probably Babe Ruth, right dad?"

He looked over at Gina. She turned to look out the window and hide her face as she laughed.

"How old do you think I am?"

Marc smiled as he sat back in his seat.

"We still playing some rock band when we get home?"

"Absolutely." He answered with a nod.

"Cool."

Marc placed his headphones on his head and closed his eyes. He looked over at Gina.

"Just like that, the conversation is over," he laughed.

"Just like that," she responded and snapped her fingers.

Chapter 19

Sunday—August 15, 2010

Dave sat up in bed and rubbed his eyes. He looked over at the clock. It was 4:47 a.m. He looked to his left to see Gina sound asleep. He scanned the room. Everything looked normal. He exhaled and slowly lowered himself back down. He looked up at the ceiling as he massaged his temples. Dave smiled as he thought about last night. They rocked out until almost midnight. The four of them spending the whole day together brought back a flood of old memories. He almost laughed out loud as he thought about Marc mimicking Mick Jagger's moves as he sang, *dancing in the street.* Dave was feeling a peace and calm that he hadn't felt in a long time. He glanced over at Gina again and she was still sound asleep. He carefully sat up and threw his legs over the bed. Dave put on his robe, grabbed his bible and headed downstairs. It was Sunday morning, and the family wouldn't be up for another couple of hours. He walked into the kitchen, flipped the light on. He took his seat at the table and opened the Word. Dave had his place marked in the book of Hebrews. He whispered under his breath as he read Hebrews chapter twelve, verses one and two.

"Talk to me, Father. 'Therefore, we also, since we are surrounded by so great a cloud of witnesses, let us lay aside every weight, and the sin which so easily ensnares *us,* and let us run with endurance the race that is set before us, looking unto Jesus, the author and finisher of *our* faith, who for the joy that was set before Him endured the cross, despising the shame, and has sat down at the right hand of the throne of God.'" He smiled, "Thank you, Lord."

He read the verse again. He thought on it, and then he read it again. Dave wanted to commit it to memory. He read it again, and as he read it that third time, a voice inside of him spoke. He knew that the passage wasn't literally telling him to run, but he felt an energy that gave him the desire to run. Dave smiled. He got up and went into the laundry room. There, on top of the dryer, was a clean pair of jogging shorts and a t-shirt that read, Why Walk When You Can RUN. He changed and grabbed a clean pair of socks from the pile Gina had done the night before. Dave grabbed his running shoes from the pile near the door and went back into the kitchen and sat down. He read the passage once more. He then put on his shoes and walked out the back door. Dave did some stretches to loosen up his hamstrings and calves and then broke into a light jog out of the driveway and onto the street. He looked at his watch. It was 5:07 a.m. The sun wouldn't even be rising for another hour and a half. In the past, his first mile would dictate how long the run was going to be. If he felt good, he would usually go four to five miles. If he felt sluggish or that first mile seemed unenjoyable, then it was three or less. Right now, he felt good, so he concentrated on his breathing and enjoyed the cool morning breeze. He closed his eyes for a second and went over this morning's verse in his head again. "Got it," he whispered under his breath as he ran.

He observed his usual markers, and he was already a little over a mile into the run. He didn't feel good. Dave felt great. Amazing even. Right now, he was feeling no pain. He felt like he did fresh out of the academy. He would run seven to eight miles a day back then. Dave wondered just how far he could push it today. Eight, ten, maybe twelve miles. Maybe go downtown and back. He laughed out loud at that last thought. Downtown was at least fifteen miles away. He pushed the impossible out of his head and concentrated on more realistic goals.

"I'm gonna do ten," he said out loud as he smiled.

He knew exactly where the five-mile marker was, so he pressed on toward it. He thought about all the significant moments in his life as he ran. Ninety percent of them involved Gina and the kids. The day they first met, their wedding, and honeymoon, all the great times they had together and with friends over the years. He hit the marker and headed back toward home. He looked at his watch. Right now, he was running a six-and-a-half-minute mile. He thought about the day the twins were born. All of their firsts and everything in between until now. He smiled. Right now, there was no pain. There was no cancer. It felt good to feel normal again. Seven miles in, he was maintaining his pace when he thought about his childhood. His mother and his father. He loved them both dearly, and he missed his father deeply. He thought about the night Edward was taken from them.

It was spaghetti dinner night at his mom and dads. Dinner was at 6:30 p.m., so they arrived a little after six. His mother was in the kitchen frantically making sure that everything was perfect, and his father was setting the table. Gina placed the pumpkin cheesecake in the fridge, Edward's favorite dessert, and then started helping Sharon. Dave helped his dad set the table.

"How was work last night?" He asked Dave.

"Good. Monday nights aren't really that exciting." He replied. "Anything new at the shop?"

"No. Work is still steady. We're building an addition onto a house over on Jefferson."

"Bedroom?"

"Sunroom. We're almost done. Maybe another couple of days."

He smiled as he watched his dad set the table. Edward Jackson had been a hard worker his whole life. At 61 he didn't appear to be slowing down. He still loved to build things and create.

"Thinking about retiring soon?"

He stopped setting the table and looked up.

"What for?"

"So you and mom can go to Florida and enjoy the sun and fun."

"Why would I do that when I got everything I need right here? My family, four seasons, and the Tigers."

Dave laughed.

"At least you mentioned us before the Tigers."

"Well, I didn't put my reasons in any order."

He winked at Dave and continued setting the table.

"Funny guy," Dave responded.

"I think so," he stated as he looked over at his son.

"Shoot!" Dave stated as he looked at the table.

"What's the matter, son?"

"I forgot the real grated parmigiana cheese in the fridge."

"You know I can't eat spaghetti now unless I have it."

"I know." He shouted at his mother from the dining room. "Mom, how long until dinner's ready?"

"Five minutes," came the reply.

"Were about fifteen minutes away so I can..."

"Harvey's is three miles down the road. They have some."

"I was just about to say I'll go to Harvey's and get some."

"You finish setting the table and help your mother get the food on it. I'll run and grab the cheese."

"Dad, I forgot it. I'll go get it."

"Don't argue, just finish. I expect to see hot food sitting at this table when I get back. Maybe I'll grab your mother some flowers. She'd like that."

Dave smiled.

"Yes, she would."

Edward walked into the living room where both kids were watching TV.

"Either of you two want to go to the store with me to grab some cheese for dinner?"

Without looking up from the program they were watching, they both responded, "No."

"Watching an old program is more important than spending time with your grandpa, is it?"

Marc looked up from the TV.

"I'll go with you, grandpa." He then looked at his sister. "Let me know happened when I get back."

She didn't answer.

"Melissa," he pleaded.

"Okay, okay, fine, I will," she responded.

Edward laughed.

"It'll take me a couple of minutes. Finish your program."

"Are you sure, grandpa?" Marc asked.

"I'm sure."

He walked into the kitchen and explained to Sharon that he was going to Harvey's to get the cheese.

"Didn't Dave bring it from home?" Gina asked.

"He forgot," Edward responded.

"Make him go get it, dad."

"I told him to finish setting the table. I'll be back in a jiffy."

She smiled and kissed him on the cheek.

"Next time, I'll make sure he doesn't forget."

He smiled.

"I know you will."

He finished putting on his shoes and headed out. It didn't take him long to get to Harvey's and find what he was looking for. There were five lights in all from their house to the market, and he hit every one of them perfectly. He grabbed the cheese and a nice bouquet for Sharon. He was back in the truck and on the way home in a matter of minutes. On the way back, the first two lights were green, and he thought about playing the lotto. The third light was red, and as he pulled to a stop, the lotto thoughts left his mind. He was the first car in line. The radio was broken, so he sat there and hummed, *Love me tender,* by Elvis. He picked up his phone and sent Dave a text: *Be home in two minutes.* As he pressed send, the phone slipped from his hand and fell to the floorboard by his right foot. He unbuckled his seatbelt, bent down to grab the phone, and as he was coming up, the last thing that Edward saw was a car coming in the opposite direction, directly in line with his truck.

The horrible aftermath that followed is something Dave will never forget. When his father didn't make it home within a few minutes of the text, he worried. He was going out to get into his car to go look for his dad when he heard the sirens. An awful feeling came over him. He knew in his heart that those sirens were for his father. He jumped into his car and sped toward them. When he got to the scene, he immediately noticed the mangled hunk of metal that used to be Edward's truck. His heart sank. He ran to where his father's truck was and immediately noticed the massive amounts of blood throughout the interior. Everything else about that night is a blur. He would later learn from the reports that a drunk driver hit Edward head at roughly 63 MPH. If he had his seatbelt on, he might have survived. If Dave had remembered the cheese, he definitely would have survived. Dave had replayed the incident so many times in his head since that day. The forgetting of the cheese, the text to him that caused him to unbuckle his seatbelt, and that someone was that drunk at 6:37 p.m.

Dave stopped running and placed his hands on his hips. He clasped his hands behind his head and started walking. He was about a mile and a half from home. A few moments passed, and he caught his breath enough to drop his hands to his sides and walk normally. It had been seven years since the accident, but he still felt the weight of the guilt on his shoulders.

"I'm so sorry, dad," he whispered under his breath as he walked.

As he walked, he searched for comfort in the many bible passages he had learned and memorized. There were many that came to mind, but nothing was comforting him in this moment. He had screwed up. He had put his father in that situation. No one else. Just him. It was pointed out to him in the past that the other driver had driven drunk that day. That he was the one who took the life of a good man because his blood alcohol was a point 32. None of this made Dave feel any better. His dad was still gone. After accepting Christ, he found comfort in knowing that he now had a loving Savior to help him cope, but he still longed to see his dad again. He concentrated on the words of Jesus in Matthew chapter five verse four when he said, "Blessed are those who mourn, for they shall be comforted." He smiled as he thought about all the good times that he had with his father, and all the things that Edward taught him over the years. That was the way we honor those we love. Remembering them in life, not death. He walked that last mile with a smile on his face, replaying all the highlights from his youth. When he made it to the front porch, he sat down on the top step. It was now 6:41 a.m. and the son was just making an appearance. A few minutes later, the front door opened, and Gina walked toward him with a cup of coffee in each hand.

"Good morning," she said with a smile.

"Good morning," he responded with a smile of his own.

She handed him a cup.

"Did you go for a run?"

"I did. I woke up early and came downstairs to read, but the urge came over me to run."

"That is such a weird statement," she took a sip. "No one ever gets the urge to just run, David."

He laughed.

"I don't know what it is. I just love it."

"You have since I've known you."

She sat down next to him. They watched as the bright red sun continued to rise. He reached over and held her hand, and they watched the sun come up together.

"I love a good sunrise," he stated as he took another sip.

"They are incredible." She responded.

"What has gotten you up so early this morning?"

"I opened my eyes, and you weren't there. I walked downstairs, looked out the window and saw you walking up to the porch to sit down. I figured I would make some coffee and we could watch the sun come up together."

"I'm glad you did. It's been a while since we've watched a sunrise together."

"Too long," she agreed. "How are you feeling this morning?"

"I feel great. I just wanted to run while I felt this way." He smiled. "I thought about dad again toward the end of the run. That night."

"Dave, Edward would want you to stop blaming yourself for that night. It was a perfect storm of disaster. Are you okay?"

"Actually, I am. I started out feeling sad, but then my Savior comforted me by placing thoughts in my head of the great times we had together. I remembered some things I had forgotten. Things that made me smile. Things that really made me appreciate the time we had together on this earth."

At that moment, a cardinal landed on the porch railing to their right. It was a magnificent, vibrant shade of red. The early morning sun really brought out its beauty. They watched as the cardinal just sat there, staring at them. When he had enough, he took flight. Dave sighed.

"You know, they say that a cardinal is a sign that those we've lost will remain alive in our hearts forever."

Dave and Gina looked at each other and smiled. She dropped her head on his shoulder as they sat there and finished their morning coffee.

2

Pastor Dunkirk smiled as he shook Dave's hand in the church's foyer.

"I'm so glad you've chosen our church as your extended family, David."

"Gina and I agree that it's a great fit for us, pastor. We have concluded that it is a place of love and sincerity. It is truly a house, and people, who love the Lord and do His work."

"Amen, brother, I couldn't have said it better myself. And the preacher isn't too shabby." He smiled.

Dave laughed and then winked at him.

"The preacher is one of our favorite parts."

"Thank you, Dave. I appreciate that, and thanks for coming on the camping trip last weekend. I trust you and the boys had a good time."

"We had a great time. Kurtis could actually relax and enjoy himself."

"The misses and I pray every night for that young man. Hoping that his situation will get better. With faithful Christian brothers like you on his side, that's a strong possibility."

"He's a good kid pastor who is in an ugly situation. He needs all our prayers and help daily."

"Well, he has it. We look forward to seeing you and the boys camping with us for a long time. God willing, of course."

Dave hesitated for a moment and entertained the idea of telling the pastor about his diagnosis. That he wouldn't be a permanent fixture at the campground from year to year. But he didn't.

"God willing," he repeated.

"You know, Dave, we should get together one weekend and grill up some steaks. Our families seem to get along pretty good."

They turned to see Gina and Marsha talking to one another in one corner of the room. Melissa and Sarah talking in another corner, and Matthew and Marc talking near them. Marc didn't appear to be making eye contact with Matthew as he spoke, but seemed to stare at Sarah.

"That sounds like a plan, Bill. Is it Bill in church, or should it be Pastor Dunkirk?"

The pastor laughed.

"It's just Bill."

"Let's talk to the wives about it and reconvene on Wednesday." He snapped his fingers. "Shoot, I'm working this Wednesday."

"We have phones Dave."

Dave smiled. "I guess we do. I'll text you this week."

"Sounds great. Enjoy the rest of your Sunday, David."

"You too, pastor."

Dave rounded up the family, and they were on their way. On the way home, they were discussing where they should have lunch. Dave zoned out for a moment, thinking about whether he should tell Bill about the cancer. Maybe prayer from a distinguished man of God could bring about a miracle. But he knew in his heart that's not how it worked. God had put him on a path long before he was even born. Had he accepted the Lord earlier in his life, some things would have been different. He would have been able to serve God in different ways, possibly more effective ways. Maybe he would have been able to help more of his brethren in law enforcement find salvation. Maybe not, but he'll never know because that's not the life he chose for himself. But he knew one thing for sure. This diagnosis was his destiny from the beginning. Whether he was a police officer, pastor, or used cars salesman, at forty-two, he was going to be diagnosed with stage four pancreatic cancer, just as his dad was going to die in a car crash at sixty-one. God is omniscient. He knows the date of our birth and the date of our death before we are ever born, but we help navigate the dash in between. He knows the choices we will make, but he gives us the freedom to make them. The age-old question of, "would it better to know the date of your death or not?" has always been a hot topic of discussion. Before his transformation, he would have said, "Yes," because who wouldn't like to know how much time they had on this earth? He has a different perspective on it now. If one knew the date of their death, then serving the Lord with a selfless heart wouldn't be genuine. You could live selfishly and destructive, to yourself and others, and then decide to accept the gift of salvation with a day or two to spare. That's not what God's plan was about.

"David," Gina stated for the third time as she tapped his shoulder.

He cleared his throat and responded.

"Yes, dear."

Marc and Melissa laughed out loud from the backseat.

"Are you okay? I've been trying to get your attention for like thirty seconds."

"Sorry, I zoned out there for a minute."

"I'll say, space case Dave reporting for duty," Marc joked.

"Where do you want to go for lunch dad," Melissa asked.

"What does everyone else want?"

"That's' what we have been discussing since we left church. Are you sure you're, okay?"

"Yeah. All good. I say...The Ponderosa."

They all looked at each other and smiled.

"I believe we agree. The Ponderosa it is," Gina proclaimed.

3

Butch went over the plan in his head again. He would watch the house tomorrow until the boy left, then he would go knock on the door and surprise Shannon. He would gage by her reaction how much charm he needed to use, but if there was no man in the picture, and he suspected not, then he would be in. Butch thought of every scenario she could throw at him, and he was ready. He would lean ultra-hard on the sympathy card. He was a self-conceited jerk back then and that he didn't know what he had. If he knew she was pregnant with his child, then he never would have left town. He would have gotten a job right there in town and made an honest woman out of her. He would plead for one more chance, even drop to his knees if he had to.

"It has to work," he stated out loud.

Chapter 20

Monday—August 16, 2010

Butch was already sitting on the street to the east of the house at 7:30 a.m. He did not know what time Kurtis would leave, but he wanted to be ready when he did. He figured he needed at least a thirty-minute window. If he was still in the house with her after that time, then that meant that she was circling the worm and all he needed to do was set the hook. He watched all morning. People left for work, children came out and played, and some just came out and sat on the front porch to drink their coffee or enjoy the fresh air. Finally, at 11:15 a.m. there was movement at the house. Kurtis came out of the front door and stood at the top of the steps. He looked to his left and then to his right. He stretched and then an enormous yawn followed. Kurtis turned back around and looked at the house before he finally descended the steps and started walking west. He watched as Kurtis continued down two blocks and then turned to go north. He waited for another ten minutes before he started the car and headed for the house. Butch pulled into the driveway and killed the engine. He sat there staring at the house for another five minutes before he finally exited the car and made his way up the front steps. He cleared his throat and knocked. No answer. He knocked again, harder. No answer. Maybe she was staying at a boyfriend's house. Maybe he had read the situation all wrong. He pounded on the door one more time. He was turning around to leave when he heard Shannon's voice yell from inside the house.

"Keep your pants on. I'm coming."

He waited. She opened the door and saw him standing there with a smile on his face. He was wearing black slacks and a polo shirt. He was clean shaven and his hair, what was left of it, was combed to the side. Butch had put on some weight over the years, but she recognized him right away.

"Hello Shannon," he said with an air of confidence. "I missed you."

Before she could slam the door in his face, he wedged his foot in between the door and the jam.

"I have nothing to say to you, Butch."

"Just give me five minutes of your time. Please."

"Why should I?"

"Because I've missed you. You were the only girl I ever truly loved."

She tried to kick his foot out of the doorjamb.

"Still using those stupid one liner's I see. Well, I'm not that same naïve small-town girl anymore."

"I know you aren't. Shannon, please just give me a few minutes of your time to explain what happened, and if you want me to leave, I will. No argument. We can even talk out here if it makes you feel more comfortable."

She relaxed her grip on the door.

"Five minutes?"

"Five minutes. I swear."

She opened the door and stood to the side. He walked past her and into the house.

"Take a seat on the sofa."

He walked over to the couch and sat down. She walked over to an adjacent chair and sat.

"Thanks for hearing me out."

"Five minutes."

"Where to begin. First off, you're still as beautiful as the day I first saw you…"

"That's it. Get out of here."

She stood and pointed to the front door when he changed gears.

"Okay…okay…I'm sorry. Here goes. I was a complete idiot back then. I was young and stupid. I lived life in the fast lane all the time. I didn't care who I hurt, how much I hurt them. I was selfish and arrogant."

She sat back down.

"Go on."

"You didn't know much about me back then, but I came from a broken home. My parents divorced when I was real young. My dad raised me, not my mom. She ran out on us and never really looked back. My old man taught me that if you wanted anything in life, you had to take it. He told me that women were put on this earth to torture us. He now knew that they were only here for our pleasure. 'Love em and leave em quick' is what he always said. I didn't know what a family was. I didn't really even learn the concept until about three years ago."

He paused and looked at the floor.

"What happened three years ago?"

"I fell in love with a girl down in Mexico. Anna. She was pretty and nice and made me feel special all the time. The problem was that her father didn't like me. He told her she would not marry a gringo and move off to the United States. I told him I would move there."

"To Mexico? It must have been love."

"It was." He paused for effect, looking off into the distance and smiling. "She made me realize I felt like that a few other times in my life. I was just too stupid to see it. Shannon, when I came through Crystal City, I wasn't looking for love. I had conditioned myself to feel dead inside. The words of my old man kept ringing in my head, 'Love em and leave em.'"

"So, I suppose you're going to tell me I was the only other true love of your life."

Time to reel her in.

"No, not at all. There have been a couple over the years that when I look back, I can definitely see myself settling down with and raising a family. You were one of those. When I met you, I saw the same things in you I saw in Maria."

"I thought her name was Anna?"

"Anna Maria. Sometimes I called her Anna, and sometimes Maria. The point is, when I look at you, I still see that young, beautiful, smart girl I couldn't get enough of while I was in Crystal City."

"So, you can see yourself settling down with me and having a family?"

"Absolutely."

"How did you even find me, Butch? I moved fifteen hundred miles away."

"When I realized the mistake I had made, I went to see your folks."

"You went to the ranch to see daddy?"

"Yep."

"I'm surprised you're here talking to me right now and not buried on the property somewhere."

"I needed to see you. If we had a chance. I didn't know if you were married or moved away, but I had to find out."

"I haven't talked to my father in years. I don't even think he knows where I am, and if he does, he hasn't reached out. So, you must have talked to my mother."

"I did. She told me you were here. That you had a son. She actually thought that I was here with you. That we were together."

"She told you about Kurtis?"

"She did. I don't care whose boy he is Shannon, I'll..."

"He's yours Butch."

He placed his hand on his heart and sighed, for effect, of course.

"He is?"

"Yes. It's the present you left me with before you went gallivanting around to find your next conquest."

"Shannon, I did not know. I never would have left."

"Yes, you would have. You just explained to me your entire theory about women in a nutshell." He went to speak, but she stopped him and continued. "You seem to have grown up a bit."

"I have changed a lot. I can't believe I have a son."

He once again played the part of the forlorn father. She was buying it hook, line and sinker. Maybe he had truly changed. Maybe they could make it work. She had no one currently, and every relationship in her past turned into a dead end.

"Kurtis is a good kid."

"You're his mother, so I know."

She smiled.

"Listen Butch. I might give you another chance. If you're serious about trying to make it work with both of us."

"I am, I am."

"What do you do for a living? How would you support us?"

"Rob banks, of course."

She laughed out loud.

"No...seriously."

He smiled. "It's good to hear you laugh, Shannon. Honestly, I'm in between jobs right now because I had to quit to come up here and try to get you back."

"What kind of work have you been doing?"

"I'm a handyman. A Jack of all trades type of guy."

"That's helpful to have around the house, but does it pay the bills?"

He could feel his blood pressure rising.

"It does."

The front door opened, and Kurtis came walking into the house. He stopped dead in his tracks when he saw Butch sitting on the couch, talking to his mother.

"Mom. Who is this?"

He stood up and smiled at Kurtis.

"The name's Jack Post, young man, and you are?"

"Kurtis."

"Nice to meet you, Kurtis."

"Who are you?" Kurtis asked with hesitation.

"He's just a salesman, baby. Did you forget something?" Shannon asked him.

"What's he selling?"

"Cable," Butch interjected.

"What kind of cable?"

"We're a new cable service provider and I am going door to door to see if people in this area are happy with their current service."

"What's the name of your cable..."

Shannon cut him off. "What did you forget, Kurt?"

"My book."

"Where were you going?"

"Just down to the park to sit under the big oak tree and read."

"Oh. Well, grab your book so, Mr. Post, was it?" She looked at Butch and he nodded yes. "Mr. Post and I can talk more."

Kurtis went to his room and grabbed his book. He was walking back through the living room toward the door to leave when Butch noticed he was carrying *Thinner*.

"Do you like that book, Kurtis? It's one of my favorites."

Without answering, he walked by the two of them and went out of the door when he turned and looked at his mom.

"I'll be in the park if you need me."

"Okay baby, have fun."

He closed the door behind him as he left.

Butch sat back down.

"You came up with that lie really quick, Butch."

"I've always been able to think fast on my feet. You know that."

"Yeah. Too fast. Some say it's a second nature, but for you it's definitely first."

"Come on Shannon. You're mad at me because I'm a quick thinker?"

"I'm not mad at you." She studied him for a second before she continued. "Do you have a phone number where I can reach you?"

He already had the number written out on a piece of paper in his pocket. He stood and gave it to her.

"Anytime day or night."

"I'll call you. Maybe we can have dinner and ease into this."

"That's great Shannon, that's just great." He started toward the front door and then turned. "So, I'll hear from you soon?"

"I'll call you."

Before he left, he peeked out to see if Kurtis was still hanging around. The coast was clear, so he walked out and stood at the top of the steps. In his mind, he was in. She watched from inside the house as he walked down the steps and to his truck. He hadn't changed a bit. Even in her everyday fog, she could see that he was still the conman that left her high and dry over fifteen years ago, and she came close to falling for it again. She walked back over to the chair and sat down. Maybe it was time to go home.

2

Butch sat in his truck and watched as Kurtis read his book under the big oak tree. He felt good when he left Shannon's, but as he sat in his truck, another plan developed in his head. Instead of playing the long game and waiting for her to come around, he would just tell Kurtis that he was his father. The boy was probably starving for the attention of a male role model. He would win Kurtis over and then it would be two against one. She would eventually submit and they could bilk her parents for thousands. Yes, this was the way to go. He got out of his truck when he saw Ronnie approach Kurtis. He stopped. The two of them were obviously friends. They talked and laughed, and then they started walking north through the park together. He watched them make their way to the sidewalk and then continue walking east. He thought about following them, but he didn't want to take the chance of being spotted. Butch shifted into drive and headed back toward the motel. He would wait a few days to see if Shannon called him, and if she didn't, then he would put Plan B into effect.

Kurtis and Ronnie walked toward the fast-food place where Kurtis had his connection. He was hungry, and he wanted to talk about Ronnie's job some more. Kurtis didn't know how he and his mom were going to survive with no income coming in. He needed to be the man now and step up. They walked into the restaurant and up to the counter. Leslie was working. She smiled when she saw him.

"What's up scrub?" She asked.

"Nothing maggot." He shot back.

"You want the usual?"

"Yes please. Can I have two? One for me and one for my friend?"

"You sure can."

"What's the usual?" Ronnie asked.

"A burger, some fries, and a large coke." He answered.

"Cool, that sounds good to me."

Leslie gave them the food, and they went and sat down.

"You work last night?" Kurtis asked.

"Nah, Sundays are a little slower. The scrubs work those nights. They want me out there on the busy nights because I'm a 'go-to guy.'"

"Still making bank?"

"You know it. You ready to come to work?"

"Still thinking about it. How's the home life?"

"Same. You?"

"Rick is gone."

"That's good. Why?"

"I don't know, but he's gone." He went to take a bite of his burger and then stopped. "Something weird happened today."

"What?"

"As I was on the way to the park to meet you, I decided I would go back home, grab my book and read before you got here. So, I went back home and when I walked into the house, there was a guy sitting on the couch talking to my mom."

"Have you seen him before?"

"Never. He jumped up and made some excuse about being a cable guy. He wanted to make sure that everyone in the neighborhood was 'satisfied' with their cable."

"Weird." He thought about it for a minute and then said, "He's probably trying to date your mom."

"That's exactly my thought." He shook his head. "Rick's barely out the door and another loser is ready to take his place."

"Your mom is pretty hot."

Kurtis stopped eating and cocked his head. Ronnie could feel his stare and started laughing.

"Not cool man. Not cool."

"I almost forgot to tell you. Remember that cop that I told you is always trying to," He used air quotes, "Reform me?"

"Officer Jackson?"

"Yeah, that's the one. He busted me on Saturday night."

"What? For selling?"

"Nah, busted me for jaywalking. Of course, he busted me selling."

"Your gonna eventually go to prison. That's like the third time you've been busted."

"Fourth actually. Twice by Officer Friendly. I need to set that dude up. Have someone take him out."

Kurtis stopped chewing and stared at him.

"You're kidding. Right? You would never do..."

"Relax Kurt, I'm just playing. Besides, I'm 15 years old. I would have to be much higher up to have something like that done."

Kurtis got out a nervous laugh.

"Yeah. Crazy."

"Although if he keeps costing Milo money, he might have someone take care of the problem." He looked at Kurtis and smiled, "Lighten up dude, I'm still playing with you. It's a drop in the bucket when we get popped. You like this cop or something?"

"No!"

"He might not be around much longer, anyway."

He took a bite of his burger.

"What do you mean?"

"We were driving back to the jail, and the dude had an episode."

"What the heck is an episode?"

"He started wigging out. We stopped in the middle of the street and his eyes rolled back into his head and he started making noises like he was turning into a zombie. He tried to play like he dozed off or something, but I've seen that happen to my cousin a few times. It was definitely a seizure. Dudes got problems."

Kurtis studied the ground for a moment. He liked Officer Jackson. He could feel Ronnie looking at him, so he spoke up.

"Maybe they'll force him to retire and you won't have to worry about him anymore."

Ronnie smiled at the thought of this.

"Yeah. Yeah. Thanks Kurt. You just made my day."

"Glad I could help. You got any plans for this weekend?"

"Friday and Saturday, I'll be back making that green."

"You just got busted, and he's going to have you right back at it?"

"In his words, 'The reward is greater than the risk.' He said being a juvenile has its perks. The courts aren't really interested in doing anything to me, so he might as well exploit it as long as he can."

"What happens when you're not a juvenile anymore?"

"He said we'll cross that bridge when we come to it."

"I guess he just has all the answers, doesn't he?"

"Why don't you come out with me this weekend? I can show you how easy it is and maybe change your mind. Trust me, bro, it's so easy."

"Maybe. I'll have to see what's going on at home." He laughed as he said it.

Chapter 21

Friday—August 20, 2010

It was 4:20 a.m. and Dave sat at the corner table in Dunkin' Donuts with his shift, drinking a cup of coffee. Lisa, Patty, and Shawnee were listening to Dave tell stories of his twenty-year career. He had more years on the job than all three combined. He had some grand stories of law enforcement in the early nineties. They loved the stories that revolved around his time with Phil Woosnam, a dinosaur who retired in 1995 after forty years on the job.

"Tell us the story of July 30, 1975 again, Dave." Patty asked as he sipped his coffee.

"Okay, okay. It was about two months into my career, so early 1990."

"Wow! I was born in 1985," Lisa added. "So, I was five. Shawnee?"

"I was born in 1983, Lisa. So, I was seven. Patty?"

"I have a bit more wisdom than you two. I was born in 1980. So, I was ten."

Dave smiled.

"You know what? Forget about it. I gotta go," Dave stated as he got up.

Shawnee put one of his big mitts on his shoulder and pushed him back down into his seat.

"You're losing your sense of humor in your old age. Please tell the story again, pops?" Patty pleaded.

Dave shook his head and took a sip of coffee.

"Okay, okay. It was July 30, 1975. Phil was working a dayshift on that day. He was driving around town, when he saw this 'green Pontiac Grand Ville' run the red light on Sylvester at Chedister. He says that he stopped the car and walked up to talk to the driver. The guy was 'acting all squirely.' He said when the guy finally looked up, he was like, 'your Jimmy Hoffa,' and the guy said, 'yeah, and your Officer Woosnam, let's get on with this, I got some place to be.'"

"What time was it?" Lisa asked.

"Phil said that it was around ten in the morning."

"Wasn't he supposed to meet people at the restaurant at 2:00 p.m.?" Patty asked

"You guys know the holes in the story, so can I please just tell it?" Dave asked.

"Our apologies, sir. Please continue," Shawnee stated.

"Okay, where was I? Oh yeah. So, he questions Mr. Hoffa about why he ran the light. He states that 'Jimmy was trying to make it to a meeting and didn't want to be late. When you're late, guys get the drop on you.' So, then Phil decides he doesn't care who this schmuck is, he's getting a ticket for running that light. He turns to walk back to his car when 'Jimmy says, hey fella, you make me late and I'm telling them who was responsible.'" Dave laughed as he told the story. "Phil walks back to the car and says, 'You tell em fella that big Phil Woosnam is waiting for them anytime they want to come calling.'"

All four of them started laughing so hard tears were coming out of their eyes. Dave powered through and finished the story.

"He says that he walked back to his car. Wrote the ticket and walked back up and threw it into the car. He turned to walk away, looked back at Hoffa, and stated, 'Don't let me see you in my town again.'"

They were falling out of their chairs they were laughing so hard.

"Wasn't Phil like Five and a half feet tall, and maybe a hundred and sixty pounds?" Shawnee asked.

"If he was soaking wet," Dave answered.

"Big Phil Woosnam, I love that part," Patty stated between laughs.

"So, did anyone ever tell him that his times are totally off?" Lisa asked.

"I think over the years people tried to get him to change the times of his story to be more accurate. He would just laugh and say, 'What, you never go out for milk at ten in the morning. So that meeting was later, I guess.' He always stuck to his guns about the times, and tickets were hand written back then. Sometimes they just disappeared."

"You believe his story, Dave?" Patty asked.

"I don't know. I'm not discounting it all together."

"You know people lie, Divine Dave," Shawnee added.

"I know they do, but it's just kind of fun to believe."

They finally laughed themselves out and resumed regular conversation. Two minutes later, Shawnee and Patty got called out to an alarm run at the business across town, and that left Dave and Lisa sitting there together.

"Dave, I've been meaning to ask you something." She started.

"I'm an open book. Shoot," he responded.

"When you told us you 'Accepted Jesus' as your savior, didn't you feel like it was a very rushed decision?"

"I would describe it as a decision of urgency, but not rushed."

"It's just...you changed overnight when you became a Christian,"

He smiled as he explained to her the circumstances that led him to attend Pastor Dunkirk's church. It was a story he has retold frequently. He told her they had a pleasant conversation, and it piqued his interest. Again, he left out the part about the cancer diagnosis. He went to the pastor's church, heard the message of salvation, and knew that it was true. Something in his heart changed that day. He wanted to experience that true unconditional love that only a heavenly Father could give. So, he gave the rest of his life to Jesus. It's a decision that he hasn't regretted.

"When I gave it all to Him, I felt someone had lifted a great weight off of my shoulders. No matter what, He would always be there for me."

"How can you know this for sure? It's impossible. You're basing everything you stand for on faith now. You can't see faith, Dave?"

"Exactly. In the book of Hebrews, he tells us, 'Faith is the substance of things hoped for, the evidence of things not seen.' We have to walk by faith, Lisa, not by sight."

"I don't know if I can do that."

"I didn't think I could either, but here I am. Is there anything else holding you back from believing, besides the principle of faith?"

"I guess the concept that all you need to do is trust in Him, and your heaven bound. Really? Just believe that He died for you and you're going to heaven. That's way too easy."

"Your trust and faith have to be true. You can't just repeat a prayer and rely on that to get you to heaven. He truly sees your heart and its sincerity. Anyone can say that they believe it doesn't make them a believer. You have to truly believe, and when you do, your heart will change and your life will reflect that."

"So, you think it's that easy?"

"It's easy to accept the gift of salvation. The hard part is giving it all to Him and living for Him. As human beings, we struggle with giving away our control."

"I have heard the story growing up a million times, but I could never wrap my mind around a god that has that much grace. It seriously can't be that easy."

"Can I read to you a passage from the book of Luke that might aid you in your struggle to believe? It's only a few verses, but it completely sums up the whole of Christianity."

"Yes, please do."

He pulled out his phone and went to his bible app.

"The book of Luke chapter twenty-three verses thirty-nine through forty-three, 'Then one of the criminals who were hanged blasphemed Him, saying, "If You are the Christ, save Yourself and us." But the other, answering, rebuked him, saying, "Do you not even fear God, seeing you are under the same condemnation? And we indeed justly, for we receive the due reward of our deeds; but this man has done nothing wrong." Then he said to Jesus, "Lord, remember me when You come into Your kingdom." And Jesus said to him, "Assuredly, I say to you, today you will be with Me in Paradise."' He looked up from his phone and into her eyes. "All he did was believe in the name of Jesus, and it saved him."

She sat there speechless for a moment. He could see that she was thinking about what he had just read to her.

"So, it's that easy?"

"It's that easy. He will forgive us all our sins if we just place our trust and faith in Him. Even after we do, we will slip and fall many times, but He will always be there to help pick us up."

"That's pretty powerful stuff, Dave."

"The most powerful. They don't call it amazing grace for nothing."

She laughed, "Like the song?"

"Yep." he took a sip.

"I am so thrilled for you, Dave. You seem so happy."

"I am. Lisa, I am always here for you. If you ever need someone to just listen, or you need advice, I'm here."

"Thank you. That means a lot." She looked at her watch. "I better get back out there. I have a few business checks to do before the end of shift."

He smiled, "Me too."

They finished the last sip, tossed their cups, and headed back out onto the road. Dave got into his cruiser and looked at his watch. It was 4:53 a.m. He backed out of his spot and headed for Kurtis's house.

2

Dave drove down the street slowly with his head on a swivel. He didn't see anyone walking around the neighborhood this morning, only the usual early birds who were getting ready for work. As he passed the house, he observed no lights on and no cars in the driveway. This made him smile. Someone got the hint. He stopped in front briefly, but then continued on down the street. He was so focused on the house that he failed to see the old pickup truck he passed sitting down the block. When Butch saw the headlights from the car, he ducked down and stayed low as the cruiser passed him. He watched as the police car briefly stopped in front of Shannon's house and then continued on. When the cruiser was gone, he sat back up in the seat. She hadn't called him since his visit on Monday, so now he wondered if she had a suitor. The kind that wears blue and arrests degenerates like him. This was not good. If she was dating a cop, then he was in danger of being exposed. He did not intend to spend the rest of his days in a cell, or worse, get the needle for what he did in South Dakota. Maybe he was overreacting, or maybe it was just a coincidence that the cop car stopped there. Maybe his boy was just like him and the local cops were making sure that he was staying home at night. His mind was racing with possibilities. He would have to do some more digging, and the only way to do that would be to revisit the house when the boy wasn't there. He would sit and wait for Kurtis to leave today and then go back.

3

It was a beautiful night for a ballgame. The Tigers were hosting the Cleveland Indians, and although they were under five hundred, any day you could spend at the ballpark to watch a game was a good day. Dave had never watched the game from a suite before. The suite was compliments of the son of one of Gina's regular patients. He was an executive at GM who often used the company suite for games. Today, he was out of town on business and decided that this very caring and compassionate nurse should have it. She had been taking care of his father for a couple of years now, and she had always been so very good to them in her care and attitude. The suite was spacious and accommodated up to 25 people. Joining the Jackson's were the Kings, the Dunkirk family, a few friends from the hospital, and finally, Kurtis. Dave had talked to him on Wednesday and his mother agreed to let him go. It was thirty minutes before game time. Everyone was walking around the suite talking and feasting off of the generous buffet that was provided for them. Dave found a seat in the front corner and sat down. He was eating some shrimp and taking in the park's view when Kurtis sat next to him.

"Thanks for bringing me Officer Jackson?"

Dave looked over at him and smiled.

"Glad to have you Kurt, and you can call me Dave if you'd like."

Kurtis smiled.

"Why are you being so nice to me?"

"Because I like you, Kurt. You seem like a good kid. I want you to have some fun while you're young."

"You don't think I have fun?"

"No...I didn't mean anything by it, I was just..."

Kurtis laughed.

"I'm messing with you, Dave. I know you look at me as a charity case. You see someone who is poor. Who doesn't have a father of his own to teach him stuff?"

"Kurt, I never intended to offend you."

"You didn't. It's all true. The kids at school make fun of me for wearing the same clothes all the time. I'm not the smelly kid, though. I shower every day."

He took a drink of his pop, and Dave covered his mouth and laughed into his hand.

"Well, that's good. You can come back from a lot of things, but being the smelly kid isn't one of them."

Kurt nodded his head in agreement. "Yep. Anyway, I just wanted to say thanks."

"Your welcome. I wanted to invite Ronnie today, but I couldn't find him."

"I'm sure he was hiding from you. Whenever he sees a cop car, he hides."

"That's too bad. I think he would have had a good time."

"He would have, especially with all of this great food. He's a good guy too, but he's also alone, like me."

"I believe he is, but he's playing a dangerous game working for his employer right now. I can't help him if he won't let me."

"He'll figure it out, eventually." Kurtis started chomping on a nacho. "He said you arrested him last weekend."

"I did. Did he tell you why?"

"He didn't really have to. I'm assuming because he was dealing. He said you had an 'episode.'"

Dave took a moment to choose his words wisely.

"Yeah, he told me I had an episode, too. I didn't really understand what he meant."

"He said he thinks you had some sort of seizure."

Dave turned and looked around the room, making sure no one was in earshot.

"I didn't have a seizure, Kurtis; I promise you that."

"Okay, I believe you if you say you didn't. I like Marc."

There's that teen ADD kicking in again. Perfect.

"Yeah, he's pretty cool. You know where he gets that from, right?"

Without missing a beat, "I'm assuming his mom." He continued to eat his nachos and then smiled as he observed Dave staring at him out of the corner of his eye. He laughed. "Seriously though, can you cut Ronnie a break sometimes? I don't want to see him go to Juvy. He's just trying to make money to support his family."

"I get it Kurt, but I can't turn my back on someone dealing drugs in my town."

"So you wouldn't cut me a break either?"

Dave turned in his seat to look at Kurtis.

"Your, not thinking about joining him are you, Kurtis? If you are..."

"No, I was just saying..."

"Well, don't just say. You're way too bright of a kid to..."

Kurtis got up from his seat.

"You want me to be bright. I'm not smart. Stop treating me like I have this hidden intelligence inside of me."

"I'm just concerned about your wellbeing, Kurt. I didn't mean too..."

"I'm going to get more nachos. I just wanted to come over and say thanks."

He turned and walked back toward the buffet. Pastor Dunkirk came over and sat next to Dave.

"Are you alright, Dave?"

"I'm good pastor. He's just...why do kids have to suffer for their inept, crappy parents?"

"Part of the whole free will package, I guess. It's heartbreaking to see a child suffer for the choices made by the parents, or in this case, by the parent."

"I'm sorry, I'm just..." he was looking for the right words.

"Human. You're human, Dave, with human feelings. There are way worst things in this world than having a compassionate heart. What you're doing for that boy is an act of love. You want him to grow up seeing that the world, and people, can be kind."

"Does it matter if that's only a five percent influence in his life?"

"Absolutely. It would matter if it were only one percent. First John three eighteen tells us to, 'let us not love in word or in tongue, but in deed and in truth.' Kurtis will look back on these days with fondness and remember the kindness that you showed him. You're making memories for that boy that he will never forget. I promise you that."

"I just want him to see what I see."

"Perhaps in time he will."

"But it's not guaranteed?"

"No, it's not. But you're giving him a chance to experience it. You're creating a spark that could lead to something bigger. It's the same with our own kids. You have a bigger influence because you're around them a lot more, but we can't predict how they will turn out either. We just hope that our influence carries more weight than the worlds."

"I know. We just have to hope that in their life they wake up to the truth of His salvation. It took me forty-two years."

"It did, and you were a good person before that. You and Gina influenced your kids to do the right things before you accepted Christ, but after your transformation, what changed?"

"I found a loving Savior full of mercy and grace. One that I can take comfort in, no matter what. One that enables me to live my very best life because I choose to follow his path for my life and trust in His will."

"Wow, brilliant answer. Just remember Dave, this life is tough. Kurtis is trying to figure things out as he goes along, just like the rest of us. Although you say that your influence is only five percent, it is influence, and that can make an enormous difference."

Dave looked down to see his plate was empty.

"Thanks for the encouragement, Bill. I'm going back to grab some more food. Can I get you anything while I'm up?"

"Another coke please."

"You got it."

"Thanks for inviting us, David. I've never been in a suite before."

"Me either. It's super cool, right?"

"Super cool," he reiterated. "Hurry back, it's almost time for the first pitch."

The Tigers were electric in every aspect of the game that night. They beat the Cleveland Indians 6-0. On the drive home, Dave and Gina held hands while all three of the kids passed out from a food coma in the backseat.

"I think everyone had a good time," Gina laughed.

"I'd say a great time. That was a gracious thing your patient's son did."

"It was. I'll have to make sure I thank him again. Did you enjoy yourself?"

"So much," he smiled.

"Did you talk to Kurtis much?"

"I talked to him a little before the game started. He came over to say thanks. Then he scurried off and hung out with Marc and Matthew the rest of the night."

"I saw you talking to the pastor."

"Yeah. He's a good dude. I got to catch up with Frank, too."

"It's a shame Javier and Rita couldn't make it."

"Yeah. The one night the guy takes OT. He was pretty bummed."

"I know he's a big Tiger fan. I talked to Rita last week. She told me that everything is going great with her pregnancy."

"Yeah, Javier says most days she feels pretty good."

"What do you want to do when we get home?"

"I figured that me and you could cuddle up on the couch and watch a movie."

"That sounds nice."

They pulled into Kurtis's driveway a few minutes after eleven. He looked in the rearview mirror to see him sound asleep. Dave got out of the car and walked over to the passenger's side rear door and opened it. He tapped on his shoulder.

"Hey Kurt. Wake up."

His eyes fluttered and then opened. It took him a few seconds to realize what was going on, and then he slowly climbed out of the car. Dave held onto his arm for a moment to steady him.

"Thanks again for inviting me to go to the game, Officer Jackson."

"Your very welcome Kurtis. Maybe we can do it again."

"That would be great." He turned and looked at Gina, who had her window rolled down. "Goodbye, Mrs. Jackson."

"Goodbye Kurtis, and thanks for coming."

He turned and headed toward the front door. Dave walked with him halfway up the sidewalk.

"It's okay. You don't have to walk me to the door."

"Okay. Have a great night, Kurt."

He smiled and continued down the sidewalk and then through the front door. Dave turned and walked back to the car. He pulled out of the driveway and drove toward home. Butch watched as Dave dropped Kurtis off at the door and left. This was a new wrinkle that he wasn't expecting. Who was this family dropping off his son at such a late hour? He watched as the car turned north down a street. He shifted into drive but kept his headlights off and followed the car until they hit the main road. Dave was too engaged in conversation with Gina to notice.

"What do you want to watch?"

"We haven't seen a good Bogie flick in a while. How about Casablanca or the Maltese Falcon?"

"I could go for some Casablanca."

"Casablanca it is. Maybe a little popcorn and something sour and gummy?"

"Didn't you get enough junk food at the park?"

"Oh my dear, you can never have enough junk food."

"I think I can help you with the popcorn, but you might be on your own with the sour gummy whatever."

He smiled and looked in the rearview mirror. The kids were still sleeping.

"We might have to carry them into the house."

"Maybe if they were five, but not at fifteen. They can walk."

He laughed. "Agreed."

They turned down their street. Butch pulled off onto the side of the road and killed the lights, hopefully giving the illusion that he was parking. He didn't know that Dave was a cop, but he assumed that most people didn't drive around paranoid that they were being followed. He still wanted to air on the side of caution. Butch watched as Dave pulled into a driveway and the family got out and went into the house. He waited ten minutes and then drove by. He wrote the address down, 16701 Dolphin Street. Butch thought about sitting outside the house to watch it for a bit, but this looked like a neighborhood that paid attention to cars that didn't belong. He didn't want the cops called. He left and drove back to the hotel.

4

Dave's phone awakened him out of a dead sleep. He reached over instinctively and grabbed it off of his nightstand. Half asleep, he placed it to his ear and cleared his throat.

"Hello."

"Dave, sorry to wake you, buddy. This is Javier."

He sat up in bed and looked at the clock. It was 2:23 a.m.

"Javier, is everything alright?"

Gina stirred but didn't wake up.

"I'm downtown in the alley by Pops."

"What happened?"

"The guy working at Pops went out back to throw a bag of garbage in the dumpster. He found a body. It's Ronnie Mann."

There was silence on the other end while Dave tried to process this information.

"He's fifteen years old."

"I didn't know if you wanted to come down here, but I know you've been trying to help Kurtis out, and they were friends."

"This is going to crush him. Ronnie was the only real friend he had."

"I know. I didn't want to wake you, but I thought you might want to know before you woke up and saw it on the news."

"I appreciate the call, Javier." He rubbed his eyes. "Drug deal gone bad I take it?"

"The detectives are out here now. We probably won't know for sure for a few days, but if I had to guess, I would say yes."

"How did he die?"

"There's a knife sticking out of his chest. With any luck, there will be fingerprints on it."

"Thanks for calling me, Javier. I have some things to figure out."

He hung up the phone and sat in bed, thinking. He was wide awake now. Dave slipped out of bed and went downstairs to think. He sat in the

Lazy-boy, turned on the overhead lamp, and opened his bible. Somewhere in the book of Romans, he closed his eyes and fell asleep.

Dave was back in the squad car, transporting Ronnie to the jail. He checked the rearview mirror and observed him lying in the seat with his head back, eyes closed.

"Ronnie. You doing all right back there?"

"I'm in handcuffs going to jail. Would you be all right?"

"Your choice Ronnie, not mine."

"If you're giving me a choice, then I choose to be let go."

"That's not how it works. This is the consequence of your actions."

"Just let me go. I'm not hurting anyone."

"You don't know how many people have overdosed on what you sell them."

"You can't OD on crack, Dave, or didn't you learn that in police school?"

"What? Yes, you can."

"Whatever. That's the consequence of their actions. They don't have to buy it."

"But they do because they get dependent on it. It ruins lives and families, Ronnie."

"Not my problem, Dave (emphasis on D). What does it matter? You're gonna die soon, anyway. You won't be around to lecture me anymore."

He came to a stop at a red light and looked up in the mirror at Ronnie.

"What did you just say?"

"You heard me. The episodes are going to get worse, if there not already."

"There fine. Stop talking."

Dave dropped his head and sighed. He then covered his eyes with the palms of his hands.

"Dave, I need help," Ronnie sounded panicked.

He looked up, and he wasn't sitting in his cruiser anymore. Ronnie was standing in front of him in the alley by Pops. Ronnie's eyes were like saucers as he gripped the knife sticking out of the center of his chest. Dave reached forward to help him and noticed the blood on his hand. He looked down into the palms of his hands and they were covered in blood. Dave felt weak, and he stumbled.

He felt two hands grab him and steady him. He raised his head to see how Ronnie was doing. Standing in front of him, holding him up was Kurtis. He looked around the alley and Ronnie was nowhere to be seen.

"Where's Ronnie, and how did you get here?"

"It's okay. It wasn't your fault."

He frantically looked around the alley now.

"I know. I didn't stab him."

"And you weren't driving the car, Dave."

He looked up to see his father standing in front of him now.

"Dad." Tears fell from his eyes. "What's happening?"

"Let go son."

"Let go of what? Dad...Kurtis...Ronnie..."

His eyes popped open. He scanned the room. He was still leaning back in his recliner, and the sun was just coming through and lighting up the room. His body relaxed, and he exhaled. It was just a dream. He looked down to see his bible closed on his stomach, and his reading glasses on top of it. Dave set the bible on the table next to him and got up and went into the kitchen. He leaned up against the counter. He knew he had to go over and tell Kurtis about Ronnie early this morning. Dave looked over at the clock. It was a little before seven. He bowed his head.

"Lord, please comfort Ronnie's family and be with them, and please be with Kurtis. He lost his friend. Guide them into Your loving arms. In Christ's name, I ask this. Amen."

He grabbed a mug from the cabinet and filled it. He walked back into the living room and took a seat in the recliner, this time keeping it upright. Dave sipped his coffee and read his bible, waiting for Gina to get up so he could tell her he needed to go over to Kurtis's and give him the bad news.

5

It was a little before nine when he pulled into the driveway. Kurtis was actually sitting on the front porch. Dave had stopped and bought McDonald's breakfast for him and his mother. Kurtis stared over at him. He didn't wave or stand when Dave got out of the car and started toward the house. He just looked down at the steps that he was sitting on. Dave sat down across from him. He placed the bag of food in between them.

"I brought you and your mom some breakfast."

He could see the tears forming in Kurtis' eyes.

"As soon as I saw you, I knew something was wrong."

"Kurt I..."

"Is he dead?"

Dave dropped his head.

"Yes."

Kurtis put his hands over his eyes and cried. Dave moved over and sat next to him, putting his arm around his shoulder.

"I should have been with him last night."

"Kurtis, there's nothing you could have done to help him."

"You don't understand. I was supposed to be with him last night. He asked me to hang out with him and I went to the game with you instead. I blew off my friend and now he's dead."

He knew that now was not the time. Kurtis needed someone to be there for him.

"The detectives will do everything they can to find the person responsible for this."

"That won't bring my friend back."

"Your right Kurt, it won't." He pulled Kurtis in closer and placed his chin on top of his head. "I'm so sorry this happened to Ronnie."

Kurtis cried harder.

"I liked Ronnie. He understood me. He was my friend."

"I know, buddy."

"He didn't matter to any of you. He was just another messed up kid. A 'Drain on society' according to one of your partners."

"He mattered to me, Kurt. I'm sorry someone said that. It's not true. Ronnie just needed some help..."

Kurtis broke away from him and looked at him.

"Some help. Like me. I'm just a charity case. You don't want to help me. You just want to do something for me so you can feel good about yourself."

"Kurtis, that isn't true and you know it. I see..."

"You see what? Potential? Ronnie and I are the same."

"Your situation is similar, but you're not the same. You've stayed away from dealing drugs for a reason. Because you're a good kid and you know it's wrong."

"For your information, I was supposed to go with him last night and learn what to do. I was going to sell and start making money."

"I don't believe that for a second. You can lie..."

"It's the truth. Believe what you want. Please get out of here."

Kurtis ran up the steps and into the house. He slammed the door behind him. Dave didn't try to stop him. He knew Kurtis needed time. He stood and started walking toward the car. Dave got in and waited for a few minutes before he left. He finally backed out of the driveway and headed home. He whispered a prayer as he drove.

"Father, please be with Kurt. He's angry and hurting inside. Comfort him and guide him. Thank you, Lord. Amen."

They had Ronnie's funeral four days later at a large cemetery just outside of town. The family had no church affiliation, and his mother, like Shannon, was in a fog ninety-nine percent of the time. She had no friends or family to rely on, so when Dave came to her and asked if he could take care of all the arrangements, she jumped at the offer. Dave immediately went to Pastor Dunkirk and his church family, seeking their help. There was a mortician in the congregation. He gave them a very generous rate on a casket and his services. He spoke to the cemetery's caretaker, who also reciprocated in kind. Dave and Gina, along with very generous donations from the church congregation and other private donors, paid for the casket and burial plot. Pastor Dunkirk performed the services. It was a small gathering which comprised Ronnie's mom and two siblings, Kurtis and Shannon, and the Jackson family. There were a few others, and maybe ten other people, who loosely knew Ronnie and just wanted to pay their respects to the family. After the service, as everyone else started walking away from the gravesite, Kurtis stood in front of his friend's casket. Gina and the kids walked with Shannon toward the car, and Dave walked over and stood next to Kurtis. They just stood there silent for a few minutes, when Kurtis finally spoke.

"Thank you for arranging all of this," He stated through broken speech and tears.

"It's the least I could do for a young man who left this earth way before his time."

Kurtis leaned into Dave and started crying. Dave put his arm around him.

"I wish I could have helped him."

"You were trying to figure your own life out." Dave squeezed his shoulders and he cried harder. "Take your time Kurt."

Gina and Shannon stood by the car and watched from a distance as Dave comforted him. Shannon wiped the tears from her eyes.

"I'm thankful for your husband. He has meant a lot to Kurtis."

"Dave has a big heart. Kurtis helped bring that out of him."

"You're lucky too. I haven't been able to find a man worth a dime. Kurtis has never known his father, and every man that I go out with ends up being worthless."

"Well, where are you looking?"

"I don't really look. They just find me." She laughed.

"Where is his father?"

"You're going to love this. I haven't seen that smug, self-absorbed jerk since he got me pregnant, but the other day he found his way to my doorstep."

"Really. So, Kurtis has bever actually met his real father?"

"He doesn't even know his name."

Shannon didn't have any real friends to confide in. It had been a long time since she actually felt comfortable enough to share any part of their lives with someone, but Gina had a way about her that really made her feel that level of comfort. She told her the whole story. How she ended up in Dargen City, that she ran to get away from everyone, and that her mother had recently found her and was giving her money each month.

"So, Kurtis has never met his grandparents either?"

"No. I have shielded him his whole life from their influence."

"Don't you miss your family?"

"They abandoned us."

"They made a bad judgement call sixteen years ago. I bet they miss you and miss knowing their grandson."

"You don't know my father. The most stubborn man on the planet, and my mother won't change. She won't go against him. Not even to see her own grandson."

"It seems like she has. She paid someone to track you down. She gives you money each month, and she even enlisted the help of the father of your child, who she thought you kept in contact with, to bring you home. Your dad probably knows none of this."

Shannon thought for a moment.

"Maybe. I don't know."

"How did Kurtis's father seem? Changed? The same?"

"The same. He tried to tell me he missed me. That I was the one that got away. His true love."

"You didn't buy it?"

"I did for a couple of minutes, and then when Kurtis came in to get something he forgot, Butch lied about who he was without even missing a beat. I should have known that a leopard doesn't change its spots."

"So, Kurtis met his dad..."

She interrupted her, "Biological donor."

"Right. And he doesn't know it?"

"No. I've given serious thought lately to going back home to Texas. Maybe it is time to bury the hatchet with my parents and give Kurtis a better life. I don't want him to end up like this."

More tears flowed from her eyes. Gina handed her a tissue.

"Shannon, we're here for you and Kurt anytime you need us."

"I appreciate that."

"If you're not doing anything for dinner tonight, we would love to have you and Kurtis join us."

"That's very kind of you. I'll talk to Kurtis and see how he's feeling."

They both got into the van to wait for Dave and Kurtis. The Kings were kind enough to loan them the van so that they could drive Shannon and Kurtis to and from the services. Twenty minutes later, Dave and Kurtis entered the van, and they were on their way home.

Chapter 22

Butch had waited long enough for Shannon to reach out to him. Today, he was going to meet his son and get some answers. It was 9:30 a.m. when he knocked on the front door. The door opened and Kurtis was standing in front of him. A few seconds passed between them before anyone spoke.

"My mom's not up yet, Mr. Post, right? I'm also pretty sure we're happy with our cable, because we don't have any."

"I came to see you, Kurtis."

"Why would I want to talk about cable..."

"I don't sell cable. I need to tell you something important. Can we just have a seat on the porch and talk for a second?" He looked into Kurtis's eyes. "Please."

"Sure." He shrugged.

Butch walked over and sat down on the top step. Kurtis closed the door to the house and walked over and sat on the other side.

"How have you been?"

"You said you had to tell me something important. I'm not out here for small talk."

"Please, just humor me for a few minutes. I'm curious what kind of life you've lived."

"Well, we sold the mansion in Beverly Hills to move here, and the Maserati is currently in the shop, so we're forced to drive the Porsche...what kind of life I've lived? Why do you care? I've never seen you before in my life. You show up here to sell my mom cable and..."

"I'm your father."

He just blurted it out without warning. Kurtis stopped talking and leaned back against the post in shock. Butch waited for him to speak.

"You're lying." He finally got out.

"I'm not. I'm telling the truth, I swear."

"You're lying. How?"

He didn't know what to say. This had truly blindsided him. Could it be true? After all these years. No. This had to be a sick joke by a desperate man.

"Kurtis, I know this is coming out of left field, but I finally found you."

Kurtis stood and backed toward the door.

"Get out of here. I'll call the police. You'll get arrested."

"Surely your mom had talked about me over the years."

"She's never so much as mentioned my dad's name. She said he was a loser and a conman, and that we were better off without him around. You're sick, mister. You need help."

He grabbed the handle to the door.

"My name is Butch. Butch McCabe."

He froze in his tracks. He took his hand off of the doorknob and turned to face him.

"Butch McCabe."

His face showed signs of recognition. The kid had heard that name somewhere before, and he couldn't hide the fact that he did.

"Yes. Butch McCabe. I never even knew you existed until recently. She's been hiding you from me your whole life. I just want a chance to talk to you, Kurt. Maybe get to know you."

Kurtis walked back over to the steps and sat down. He didn't speak at first, just looked off into the distance.

"Thinner." He finally stated.

"Thinner?" Butch repeated as he stared at him with a puzzled look.

"The book."

"Oh...yeah...Stephen King," He smiled. "My absolute favorite book of all time. I must have read it at least twenty times before I lost it."

"Where have you been?"

"I told you. I did not know you existed."

"I need to know why my mom ran away from you. Why she thought it was better to live a life without you around, and why it took you so long to find us. How you found us. What you..."

"That's why I'm here now, son. To answer all of those questions and see if I can become a part of you and your mother's lives."

"Start from the beginning."

Butch had been working on this story in the motel ever since he had rolled into town. He told it masterfully. He told him they were together and in love. That he traveled a lot those days for his job, and that while he was doing his job, she cheated on him with someone else. He still loved her and forgave her, and desperately wanted to work things out. Butch stated she agreed, but that while he was on a week-long trip to California, she ran away with this other guy. He looked for her for months, but eventually gave up hope. He couldn't make her love him like he loved her, and he was unaware that she was pregnant with his child. During the story, Kurtis interrupted him.

"So, she just left you for this other guy,"

"Yes. In her defense, I was on the road a lot. I didn't spend enough time at home with her, and I allowed her to fall in love with someone else."

He continued his story and told him that after fifteen years, he finally went back to where she grew up to see if she had returned. She hadn't, but her mother, his grandmother, had given him the information that she was living with her son, their son, here in Dargen City, Michigan.

"You've met my grandmother?"

"Yes. She was excited to see me and hoped that I could convince your mom to come home."

"Is my grandfather still alive?"

"Yes."

"What are their names? Where do they live?"

"Waylon and Gail Black. They live in Crystal City, Texas. Your grandfather is a rancher. Your mom really hasn't told you any of this, has she?"

"Mom refuses to talk about anything in her past. She doesn't want me poisoned by all of those 'bad people.' She told me she knows eventually I'll try to find them, but it's her job to protect me from all of you right now."

Butch noticeably took his time and scanned the house and yard.

"And this is where you two ended up? Do you like the life she's provided so far? The men she's dated? The people she has brought into your life?"

"No. They haven't been nice to her or me. They're not good people."

"So maybe her judgement has been a little off all these years."

"Maybe."

He had Kurtis really doubting his mom now. Maybe she was the one who needed help. Maybe she was the one who took him from a life of comfort and love, and they were suffering because of it.

"Kurt, I just want to be a part of your life. You need a positive male role model."

"I like Officer Jackson. He's been good to me, and recently they've been helping mom too."

"Officer Jackson?"

"Yeah, he's this cop who has been trying to help me for a few years now. We've gone camping, to baseball games..."

"And you like this cop?"

"Yeah. He's cool. He's got a really nice family, too."

"But he's not your dad. I am." His tone made Kurtis feel a little uneasy, and he picked up on it. "Sorry Kurt. I'm just angry that someone else has been doing the job that was meant for me. I could have taken you camping and to ballgames."

Kurtis sat silent for a moment.

"Maybe now you can start?"

He smiled, "I would like that, Kurt."

"What did mom say last week when you were here? I'm assuming you guys talked about things."

"Shannon said she had to think about it. I gave her my number, but she hasn't called me."

"I'll talk to her."

"Maybe we should keep this meeting between us for now."

"Why?"

"If she knew I talked to you behind her back, she might never forgive me."

"So why did you?"

"Because I couldn't sit back any longer and not have a relationship with my son. I've lost way too much time as it is already."

"Okay, so what should I do?"

"Just because she's not ready doesn't mean we can't get to know each other. While she's deciding, maybe we can hang out a bit?"

He gave this some thought.

"Okay. What did you have in mind?"

"I'm staying at a motel on the edge of town. Maybe you could swing by and we could just talk some more and get to know each other. Have lunch or dinner and just hang out."

Kurtis smiled. "I would like that."

"That's great Kurt." He looked at his watch. "I should get going before your mom gets up and sees us out here together." He had already written his phone number on a piece of paper, and he handed it to Kurtis. "Call me. I'm staying at the Torres Inn on Berkshire."

"I will."

He folded it up and put it into his pocket. They both stood, and Butch took a step toward him. Kurtis extended his hand and Butch took it.

"Baby steps. I like it."

After they shook, Butch walked down the sidewalk and then east. Kurtis watched him get into an old pickup truck. He waved as he drove away and Kurtis waved back. He stared at the truck for a long moment. Kurtis had seen it before. He wasn't sure where, but he had. He sat back down on the step and processed all the information that he had just learned. It was a lot. Twenty minutes later, the front door opened and Shannon peaked her head out.

"What are you doing?"

"Just thinking."

"You want some pancakes and bacon for breakfast?"

"I'll never say no to bacon."

She laughed.

"Okay. Come in and help me."

"Okay mom."

She closed the door and went to the kitchen. He stood and stared off into the distance. Who was telling the truth, his mom or Butch?

2

She picked up on the third ring.

"Hello."

"Mom?"

"Is that my baby boy?"

"It is."

"I missed hearing your voice. How are you, Gina, and the kids doing?"

"Good. We're doing good. How are you doing?"

"It's summer in south Florida. I'm sweating buckets daily."

They both laughed.

"Other than the bucket sweat, are things good?"

"They are. I bet those grandkids of mine are growing like weeds."

"They sure are. Both are going to be sophomores this year. I can't believe how time flies. It seems like just yesterday I was taking them to kindergarten."

"It seems like yesterday I was taking you to kindergarten." She laughed. "How's the fighting crime going these days? I tell everyone around here my son is Batman."

He laughed, "It's going well. Job security is not a problem."

"That's a shame."

"I agree. I would happily find a new career if the world didn't need me."

"You're a little long in the tooth to be changing careers."

He laughed, "Mom. Are you saying that your son is old?"

"Your 42 now. You're no spring chicken."

"Says the 61-year-old."

"Hey, I have a 21-year-old spirit."

"I know you do."

There was silence for a few seconds.

"Davie, are you okay? Is this just a 'how are you doing' call, or is something up?"

"Everything is wonderful. Why do you ask?"

"Because it's 2:30 p.m. and you never call me before seven thirty. You usually like to catch up after dinner time to wind down a bit."

"It's just been a minute since we talked and I wanted to see how my mother was doing. Is that allowed?"

"Red flag number two. You never get short with your mother."

He laughed. It was a nervous laugh because he wasn't looking forward to having this conversation with her. Gina was at work and the kids were hanging out over their friends, so it was the perfect time. How do you just blurt out something like this? "Everything's fine, mom. I'll be dead, most likely by Christmas. If you were thinking about visiting, now is the time." He remembered the pain and grief she went through when she lost his dad. He didn't want to be that source again. Telling her over the phone seemed cruel. Maybe he would just write her a long letter, and they could talk about it at her convenience.

"Hello...earth to Dave...you still there?"

"Sorry, I zoned out for a second. I didn't mean to be short with you, mom. I called early because I have to work tonight."

A lie.

"Oh. That's okay. You probably got a big case on your mind or something. There is something I need to tell you, Davie."

"Okay."

"About a month ago, I met someone."

Gut punch.

"Okay."

"He's a really nice man and we get along well. I don't know if this has the possibility to go anywhere, but I needed to tell you. Are you okay with this?"

"Is he good to you?"

"Yes. He is very kind and respectful, and has a gentle way about him, like your father."

"He sounds great, mom."

"I haven't called because I was afraid to tell you. I didn't know if it was too soon after your father died.

"Dad died seven years ago, mom. You're still a young woman. You shouldn't feel bad because of what I might think. I'm okay with it."

It hurt him to think about her being with someone other than his dad, but under the circumstances, it just might end up being the best result.

"What you think means everything to me. You're my favorite guy in the entire world. I miss seeing you every day, but I just couldn't live there anymore after I lost your father. That's why I moved here with my sister."

"I know. How is Aunt Lorraine, by the way?"

"She's good. Same ornery cuss she's always been."

They both laughed at that.

"Tell her we miss and love her."

"Will do. But Davie, are you sure you're okay with this? I don't want any secrets between us."

Ouch.

"I'm sure, mom. What's his name?"

"Alvin."

"Like the chipmunk?"

She laughed, "And you're going to love this. He has a son named Theodore."

"You're lying."

"Hand to God," she responded.

He couldn't tell her he was dying, but he could tell her about his decision to accept Christ.

"Mom. I gave my life to Christ a couple of months back."

There was silence.

"Good for you Davie." She finally replied.

"Really?"

"Yeah. It's a huge decision. Your father and I did that once. A long time ago, before we even got married. We went to this tent revival in Kentucky and the pastor there was so fiery for God. He was cute too."

"Mom."

"Alright...alright. He really made us see the grace of God that weekend."

"What happened?"

"Life happened. Over time, life beat us down so badly that we lost focus of everything."

"But that's when you need Him. That's when His grace wraps its arms around you and squeezes."

"We both knew that, but we didn't let that stop us from drifting away. Each day it became easier and easier because we put our bible down and stopped going to church. He became a fond memory at some point, and then when I lost your father, that was it. He had abandoned me completely."

"But he didn't. That's when you, we, needed to rely on him the most."

"What happens when you don't practice things, Davie?"

"You eventually forget how to do them. But what about the saying about the bike? 'It's like riding a bike.' You just have to get back on and it will come back to you."

"Maybe. But for now, that bike's staying in the garage."

"It's never too late to come back to him, mom. In the book of Matthew chapter eighteen verses ten through fourteen, He reminds us that the shepherd will leave the ninety-nine to go out and find the one that is lost. We are His sheep and He is our shepherd. When we decide to accept Him, then we are His children forever. We will stray and get lost at points in our life, but we can always find our way back to Him. He loves us and died for us."

"Wow! My son is quoting the bible to me by memory. You must be all in."

"I am."

"I'm surprised you didn't call me when it happened. Gina did."

"I know I should have. I'm sorry I didn't, but you need to know that He loves you always."

"Maybe one day I will find that road back."

"Life is fleeting. Tomorrow isn't a guarantee. I just wish that I had learned the truth sooner. I would have spent more time in His word and seeking His will for my life."

"A little dark, but I understand your logic. I'm so glad you found your purpose in life, and that you're passionate about it. I just...I need more time to figure things out."

"You know that Gina and I are always here for you mom. No matter what."

"I know. I'm sorry to cut our call short, but I have a hair appointment."

He laughed.

"It was great talking to you, mom."

"You too Davie. Kiss Gina and the kids for me."

"I will. We love and miss you. Take care, mom."

"You to Davie. I love you, and let's not go so long in between calls."

"I agree. Tag. You're it."

She laughed.

"Goodbye, smart guy. I love you."

He hung up the phone and sat there for a moment. He couldn't get the words out. It was selfish, and he knew it, but he didn't want to hear her cry. She sounded happy. It had been a while since he heard that it her voice. If he told her, he knew that for the rest of his days on this earth, he would never hear that again.

3

Kurtis sat at the kitchen table picking at his food. He was still thinking about the encounter that he had with Butch, his dad, this morning on the porch. Did his mom take him away from a loving home? Is she the reason they've struggled, bringing countless degenerates into their lives that did nothing but abuse them and take advantage of her? He had been so deep in thought that he didn't hear her calling his name from the other side of the table.

"Kurtis!" she stated with more inflection in her voice.

"What?" He answered as he looked up at her.

"Where are you right now? What are you thinking about?"

Now was not the time to address his issue, even though he desperately wanted to.

"I'm right here, mom."

"No, you aren't. You're a million miles away."

"I'm still thinking about Ronnie. I miss him and his sense of humor. He was funny and nice. He didn't deserve to die like that."

"Your right. He didn't. I really didn't know him, but he made you happy and I'm so sorry that he's gone."

"Thanks."

"Did anything else interesting happen today?"

"No. I was here all day. How could it?"

She put her silverware down, rested her elbows on the table and propped her chin upon her folded hands. She stared at him, and her eyes told him she knew.

"Kurtis. Please don't lie to me."

"Is it true? Is Butch my father?" He asked through clinched teeth.

"Yes."

He didn't know whether to yell, cry, or storm out of the room. His breathing was noticeably loud and exaggerated. Finally, she stood up and walked over to him and put her arms around him. This surprised him, but he didn't resist. He cried.

"Why didn't you tell me?"

"I told you. We are far better off without him in our lives, Kurt."

"He told me a different story. He said that you were the one that broke up our family. That you just got up and ran off in the middle of the night. He looked for you for months, and he didn't even know about me."

She squeezed him tight.

"Let's go into the living room and sit down. I'll tell you whatever you want to know, and I want to hear about everything he told you this morning."

He pulled away from her and looked at her.

"How did you know about this morning?"

"I woke up and came out into the kitchen to get a drink." He looked down at the floor. "A drink of water. My throat was dry. I saw you both sitting on the porch, and I didn't know how long you two had been sitting there, and I didn't really know what he told you to that point. I gave you the whole day to tell me about your conversation, and when you didn't bring it up, I assumed he told you who he was. I couldn't let you go to bed tonight thinking about whatever lies he told you. Let's go sit down and discuss everything. Go grab the box of pizza. This could take a while."

He grabbed the box and took it into the living room and sat down on the couch where she was already siting.

"Where do we start?"

"From the beginning. I'll tell you exactly what got us to this point, and then we can address what you two talked about this morning. Is that okay?"

He smiled, "Yes."

He had longed to have this exact conversation with her for so long. Kurtis wanted to know where he came from and why they had no family, especially a dad, in their lives. She had lived her life like a reckless teen on a lifelong bender. Giving no consideration to the fact that she had a son who needed her. Living only for her and no one else. Sure, she loved him, but treated him as an afterthought. Shannon felt responsible for him, but she couldn't see the selfish, self-absorbed person she was. Despite her ability to tell herself that everything she was doing was for his own good. She took a deep breath and then told him everything. She confessed she wasn't the ideal youth growing up. That she didn't respect her parents the way she should have. That she did well enough in school to get accepted to the University of Texas. But that she threw it all away because she met a handsome young man who swept her off of her feet and promised her the world. That he left in the blink of an eye, without so much as a thought of their love, and she was pregnant and scared. She told him about the awful conversation with his grandparents, so she just picked up and left in the middle of the night. She was alone and scared. Jumping from state to state, trying to find a fit for them.

"They never tried to find you? In all these years?"

"Your grandfather is as stubborn as the day is long. He knew where I was for the first few years of your life because I was still on his insurance. But I finally found a job in Iowa that gave us insurance through the company and could go off the grid."

"How many states have we lived in? What state was I actually born in?"

"Nebraska."

"Nebraska?" he scratched his head. "And grandpa never looked for you? Ever?"

"Nope. I guess he just didn't care enough about us."

"I thought maybe you were from the south. You have an accent."

"I have an accent?"

"Yeah. It's not strong, but it's there."

She laughed.

"Your funny, like your grandma. She is also very warm and kind. Not a stubborn old goat like your grandpa."

"So...my dad, Butch, never knew I existed?"

"No."

"How do you know he hasn't changed? If he knew about me then, he might have changed."

"I'm sorry Kurtis, but he is who he is. A snake oil salesman who only thinks about his wants and needs."

Kurtis looked down at the floor and bit his lip. She cried. "I just described who I've become. I'm so sorry Kurt. I'm so very sorry."

He stood and walked over to her. She put her arms around his waist and hugged him.

"It's okay, mom. I love you."

This made her cry even harder.

"Please forgive me. I promise things will be different."

"You've said that before."

"I know I have, but this time it'll be different. I won't drink anymore. No more wayward men who just want to take advantage of us. Just you and me and no one else."

They hugged, and she cried for a bit, and then he walked over to the table and grabbed the box of tissue. He handed it to her and walked back over and took his seat.

"We need real help, mom."

"I know."

"Officer Jackson's church offers counseling and help to families who are in need. Maybe we could check that out?"

"Yes. Gina invited us to attend church with them whenever we wanted. Maybe we could go there on Sunday and see if we can get some of that help."

He smiled. Progress.

"Thanks. I still have a few questions, though."

"Of course, baby. I told you I would answer questions you had."

"Butch said that he wanted to be a part of our lives now. Maybe he's changed. Do you think we could give him another chance?"

"I didn't get the sense that he changed when I talked to him. I got a vibe that told me to stay away. He's running from something, or someone."

"He seemed sincere to me. Can we give him just one more chance? Please."

"Okay. We'll have him over for dinner. I'll call and ask him if he wants to join us tomorrow night."

He smiled.

"Thanks. Are we going to talk to Grandma and Grandpa again?"

"Maybe. One step at a time, though."

"Okay mom." He went to take a bite of pizza and paused. "Butch said that grandma sent him here to get you back. He said that she was really excited to see him."

"Did he now?"

"Yeah. That's what he said."

Definite snack oil salesman. She just smiled at him.

"You want to watch a movie while we finish eating?"

"Yeah. Can we watch the Incredibles?"

"You and that movie. Fine. Put it in."

He placed the DVD in and they started watching. She was looking at the screen, but she was trying to figure out what she was going to do about Butch. She thought about telling Dave, because she was sure he had something criminal in his past he needed to answer for, but then that would be betraying her son's trust. A trust that she wanted back.

Chapter 23

It had been a week since Butch had come over for dinner. He played the part of the reformed man beautifully in the eyes of Shannon, but her instincts were still the same. He said what he had to and did what he had to, to get what he wanted. Shannon didn't question him in front of Kurtis about his ridiculous version of her leaving him in the middle of the night. It was nothing more than a, he said, she said right now. Shannon didn't try to influence Kurtis's view of him. She hoped that in time, sooner rather than later, he would see it for himself. But last week, Butch had all the right answers. Kurtis wanted to know where he had been all these years. He had been working at a ranch in Oklahoma for a few years, and while there, he fell in love with one of the rancher's daughters.

"What was the name of the ranch?" Shannon asked.

"Thompsons I believe."

"What was the girl's name?"

"Katie," he said as he stared at her.

"Let him finish the story mom," Kurtis interrupted.

Butch continued. He told them she was killed in a car accident and that he had to leave the ranch because he couldn't continue to work there. Everything reminded him of her. So, he left the ranch and went back to Texas. He worked at another ranch there for about a year before he realized he had love right in front of him the whole time.

"What was the name of that ranch?" Shannon asked.

"Fredericks." He sarcastically responded.

"Mom!" Kurtis pleaded.

"Sorry. Please continue."

Butch then told them that's what led him back to Crystal City. He was searching for the "One that got away." He once again stated that her mom was really glad to see him, and that she missed having him around. She gave him the details about where they were, and here he was. Shannon could barely hold her food down, but Kurtis was eating up every word. When he finished, she smiled and simply asked him a few questions.

"What happened to Anna, or Maria, or Anna Maria down in Mexico?"

"That was a different time, darling." Butch responded with a smile.

"Was it before or after Miss Oklahoma?"

"I'm just trying to get to know my son Shannon. Is that okay with you?"

"Yeah mom. Can we just get to know each other?"

That's when it hit her. He wasn't angling to get back into her life as much as he was Kurtis's. She felt sick to her stomach, but she didn't show it.

"I'm sorry. Please continue."

Dinner continued on, with Butch and Kurtis acting like they had been best friends for years. She watched and took notes of everything that was said so that she could address it later. When it was all said and done, Butch went back to the motel that night, confident that he had done exactly what he came to do. He had also told Kurtis that he was staying at the motel for as long as it took to win them back. He had enough money in his savings to stay for a year if he had to. After he had gone, Kurtis sang his praises to Shannon about what a great guy he was. Way better than any of the men that she had ever brought home. She just smiled and hoped the true Butch would make an appearance soon. Shannon knew it would be hard for him to accept the truth, but once he did, they could move forward together. She invited him back to dinner tonight.

2

Dave was at the grocery store buying the burgers and brats for a BBQ tonight with the Martinez's, Kings, and Dunkirk's. Kurtis and Shannon were also invited, but she called and canceled at the last minute. They had attended church with them and gone to lunch with them the past two Sundays. Shannon seemed like a completely different person than the one Dave had met a few years back. He could tell that she was really trying for Kurtis's sake. He and Gina had informed her they would watch Kurtis whenever she needed them, too, and Gina talked to her on the phone regularly to see how she was doing. She had informed Gina that she was seriously considering contacting her parents and possibly making the move back to Texas. Gina encouraged her to talk to her parents, but she didn't push. Since Ronnie's death, Marc had been an enormous influence on Kurtis. The two of them got together and Marc introduced him to video games and the guitar, both of which Kurtis fell in love with immediately. Dave finished at the meat counter and was making his way toward the produce for some ears of corn when he saw Kurtis walk in through the double doors. Kurt noticed him at the same time and walked over to him.

"Kurtis, what's shaking today, buddy?"

"Just here to grab a pop."

"Gene's closed today?"

It was a party store a few blocks away from Kurtis's house, and much closer than the grocery store, which was almost ten miles from him.

Kurtis stuttered as he answered. "Yes."

"What kind of pop you getting?"

"Code red."

"A little of the dew. I like it." He smiled. "Everything okay at home?"

"Yeah. Mom's good. Things are good. How's Marc?"

"Hanging in there. You guy's still busy tonight or have you changed your mind about coming over?"

"Still busy."

"That's too bad." He was dying to ask him what they had going on, but he didn't want to pry. "Maybe next time."

"Yeah...for sure." He flashed a nervous smile. "Well. I should probably get the pop and then get back home."

"Okay then. Tell your mom we said hi and we'll miss you both tonight."

"I will. See you later, Officer Jackson."

"Take care Kurt."

Dave watched as he walked away and then disappeared around a corner. He stood there for a moment, wondering if he should have Gina call Shannon and see if everything was alright. He decided against it and walked over to where the corn was. Dave quickly snatched up what he needed and made his way to the register. He was standing in line when he watched Kurtis get on his bike through the glass windows at the front of the store. The person in front of him filled the conveyer belt and had a lot more in their cart, so he had time to hop out of line and exit the store. He told the person behind him he would be back in time to load his groceries on the belt, and he stepped out of line and made his way to the exit. Dave walked out of the door and into the parking lot just in time to see Kurtis ride his bike west on Derby Street, in the opposite direction from where he lived. He thought about jumping into his car and following him, but it seemed too much like the stalker thing to do, so he went back into the store to pay for his groceries.

He sat in the grocery store parking lot trying to convince himself that Kurtis was there simply to purchase a code red. It just didn't make sense. Drugs entered his mind, but this wasn't a usual spot. His head told him to go home, to talk to Kurtis about it at a later date, but his gut told him otherwise. Dave shifted into drive and headed west on Derby Street. He might get lucky and see the bike, he might not, but he had to try. He drove down Derby Street slowly, looking for the bike or Kurtis. Dave saw neither. He eventually came out onto Berkshire, a major street that separated Dargen City from the Heights. He sat at the light, looking in all directions. Nothing. He didn't even realize that the light had turned green. The car behind him honked the horn. He waved and then turned left to head back toward home. He hoped that his gut was wrong about this situation, but he wasn't optimistic. Dave passed the Torres Motel on his way home.

3

Kurtis slipped his bike into the bike rack and walked into the office. Butch had told him which motel he was staying at, but failed to give him the room number. He walked up to the front desk and rang the bell. A few seconds later, an older lady emerged from the back and smiled at him.

"What can I do for you, Hun?"

"My dad is staying here and I don't have his room number."

"Okay sweetie, what's his name and we'll look him up?"

"Butch. Butch McCabe."

She grabbed the book and flipped through it.

"I don't recall seeing anyone with that name checked in, but I'll look."

"Thank you."

She flipped through a few pages of the book, stopped and went back to the beginning, and then flipped through the same pages again.

"I don't see anyone with that name, Hun. You're welcome to walk through the complex to see if you can find his vehicle."

"Okay, thank you."

He walked out of the office and back over to his bike. He jumped on and slowly rode through the lot, looking for the truck that butch was driving. Kurtis spotted it around the corner at one of the back units. He rode that way and found a hallway off to the side of the room. He leaned his bike up against the wall, grabbed the code red and started to walk around the corner when he heard a door slam, and then Butch's voice. Kurtis stopped and listened.

"This is Mitch. Yeah, I'm selling the engagement ring. No. The price is $1500 firm. No, there's no payment plan. Cash only. It's a beautiful ring that I'm selling for a heck of a deal. If you don't want it fine, I'll just move on to the next buyer." There was a long pause. "Good. Yeah, I can meet you there at three. Okay. See you then."

He heard another door open and then slam shut. A female voice spoke.

"Hey Mitch."

"Hey Erica. Can I bum one of those off ya?"

"Sure."

He could smell the smoke from a cigarette.

"What have you got planned today?" He asked.

"My schedule is wide open. Why? You wanna keep me company?"

He laughed.

"I got dinner with my kid tonight."

"So. It's not even noon."

"Do you take credit?"

She laughed.

"Not on your life."

They both laughed together.

"Sorry. I'm flat broke."

"Where does your kid live?"

"Next city over with his mother."

"You in from out of town to visit or hoping to reconcile with the ex?"

"I'm hoping to reconcile, at least for a little while, until I get back on my feet."

"Oh yeah, and then what?"

"I don't know. I'm just winging it right now. I figured I could live off the ex's parents for a bit until I know exactly what I want to do. If a relationship develops between me and the kid, great. Maybe he can support his old man to make up for lost time."

"Well, you know where I'll be if you need me."

"Okay Erica. Take care, sweetheart, and thanks for the cig."

He waited until he heard both doors slam shut. He peeked around the corner and saw no one there. Kurtis jumped on his bike and rode it back toward the office. He stopped in the office and the nice older lady was sitting at the desk.

"Well, hello again, kiddo."

"Hello. Do you have a Mitch that's staying here?"

"Let me check." She opened the enormous book again and thumbed through the pages. She placed her finger on a spot. "Mitch Arnold. Room 165."

"He drives the pickup truck that's parked in the back corner?"

"Yeah, that's him."

"Okay. Thank you."

"Your welcome."

She closed the book and sat back down. He walked out of the office and jumped onto his bike. He rode toward home, tears in his eyes. Kurtis was going there to hang out with the man that he thought wanted to start a new life with him and his mother. Shannon was right. He was nothing more than a two-bit conman. A criminal. He was hurting inside and didn't know what to do, but he knew one thing for sure. He didn't want to see Butch tonight, or possibly ever again. Kurtis dumped his bike in the front yard and walked into the house. He passed the bathroom on the way to his bedroom and heard the shower running. He went into his room and closed the door. Kurtis laid down on his bed and stared up at the ceiling. A few minutes later, his door opened and Shannon walked in.

"I thought I heard you come in. What do you want for dinner tonight?"

"Can we go to the BBQ at Marc's house?"

His request surprised her.

"What's wrong?"

"Nothing. I just really want to go to the BBQ."

"Butch is supposed to come over. Did something happen that I'm missing?"

"No. Can we just go to the BBQ? I want to hang out with my friend Marc."

"Okay sweetie, sure. I'll call Butch and let him know we can't do it tonight. We'll reschedule."

"Thanks mom."

He rolled over onto his side and she left the room. She closed the door behind her. She walked out into the living room and sat down on the couch. Shannon didn't know what happened, but she was sure that Butch did something really stupid. She dialed his number. He picked up on the second ring.

"Hello."

"Butch, this is Shannon."

"I was just wondering what I should bring tonight."

"Nothing. We have to cancel."

"What? Why? What did you do?"

"I didn't do anything. I'm assuming you did."

"What's that supposed to mean?"

"Kurtis just suddenly came home and said that he didn't want you to come over tonight."

"What? That doesn't make any sense. I haven't seen the kid since our dinner last week. He has no reason to be mad at me. It has to be something you said. What are you poisoning his mind with?"

"I haven't said a thing. Maybe he just figured it out a lot sooner than I thought he would."

"And what did he figure out, Shannon?"

"That your soul is black and you only ever think about yourself and no one else."

"After one dinner. I don't think so. You had to have said or done something."

"Well, regardless, tonight is off."

"I'm coming by, anyway. I want to talk to my son."

"Fine. Officer Jackson will be here to referee."

"If you think I fear the cops, think again. No one is going to keep me from my son."

"Then come on by. Around six sound good."

He hung up the phone, spun around and whipped it against the wall. It hit the wall and exploded into pieces. He screamed at the top of his lungs some very unkind words about Shannon and then sat down on the bed. It took him a moment to realize that he had just destroyed his only means of communication. His anger was at a new level.

4

The grill sizzled as Dave flipped the burgers and the brats. All the guests had arrived and were mingling with each other. Javier, Frank and Pastor Bill were talking about the upcoming hockey season. The ladies were talking to Rita about her pregnancy, and the kids were in the yard talking or playing. Dave was just getting ready to close the top and join the guys when Kurtis walked up.

"Thanks for letting us join you, Officer Jackson."

"Of course, Kurtis. You and your mother are always welcome here."

"I know that when we talked earlier today, I said we weren't coming, but our plans kind of fell through, and so here we are," nervous laughter followed.

"Not a problem. Can I ask you a question, though?"

"Sure."

"What were you doing all the way over at Jacobs today? Genes is only a couple of blocks away from you."

"If it's okay, I'd rather not say?"

"You don't have to say, but are you in some kind of trouble, or is there anything I can help you with?"

"No, nothing like that. It's just personal."

"Okay. You know if you need help with anything Kurt, you can come to me. No matter what it is. Okay?"

"Okay." He smiled. "I have something on my mind, and would like to ask the pastor a question, but I don't want to do it in front of anyone else."

"No problem." He looked over to where the boys were sitting. "Pastor Bill," He shouted. The three of them stopped talking and looked his way. "Can I have a second of your time please?" he asked. The pastor smiled as he stood and walked over to Dave.

"Need some tips on the grill?"

Dave laughed.

"No sir, that's one area where I need no help. This young man right here has a question he would like to ask you." He looked over at Kurtis and nodded. "I'll be over there talking hockey."

The pastor smiled at Kurtis. "What can I help you with, Kurtis?"

"I just. I was wondering if God ever gave people a break? I mean, in church you talked a lot about trials and tribu...tribul..."

"Tribulations," he finished for him.

"Yeah, tribulations. That even when someone gives their life to God, he lets them experience those, and it helps them to grow. Develop patience and other stuff like that."

"That's correct Kurtis." He smiled. "You paid close attention."

"I haven't done the prayer yet, but I was just wondering, is there a time When God says enough is enough? Because if our whole life is nothing but trials, that's just...bad."

"A life devoted to living by God's standards is tough. Sometimes ultra-tough to where you think you just can't do it anymore, but then something wonderful happens. You read His word and talk to Him, and suddenly it isn't so bad. He is the ultimate hope to bring you out of whatever you're going through. You feel His love and mercy inside of your heart, and you just know that everything is going to be okay."

"Do people ever stop disappointing you?"

"No. People constantly will disappoint you because they're unpredictable. The people that really love you will do it less than most, but the fact is that they are human. They decide and choose what's best for them ninety-nine percent of the time. That's just human nature, Kurtis. The bible tells us in Hebrews chapter thirteen verse eight that Jesus is the 'same yesterday, today, and forever.' He never changes Kurtis. He loves unconditionally."

"How?"

"Because we are His creation. He only wants to see us prosper, but he knows we will stumble and fall. It's a condition of having free will. He wants us to Love Him on our own. He won't force us to do it."

Before Kurtis could speak, Marc shouted from the deck, "Kurt, come on! We're gonna play some wiffle ball."

He smiled at the pastor. "Thanks pastor. See you on Sunday."

"See you on Sunday Kurtis, but just know I'm always available to you." He handed him a business card.

"Pastors have business cards. Cool, and thanks."

He shoved the card into his pocket and jogged over to where Marc was standing. Dave walked up and opened the grill cover.

"Is he okay?"

"Yeah. He's starting to ask questions, which is very good. He's a good egg."

"I know he is." He looked down at the grill. "Were minutes away from full gorge mode."

"Thank God. I'm starving. Hey while we have a few minutes, I wanted to ask you something. Well, it's more of a, if you feel comfortable doing it type thing."

"Sure. Shoot."

"I was wondering if you would like to give your testimony in front of the congregation next Wednesday?"

This rendered Dave speechless for a moment. The request surprised him.

"Share my testimony?" he finally asked.

"Yes. If you're not ready now, you could do it at a future date, or if it makes you completely uncomfortable, you don't have to. I just thought it would be a great way to let people see the way the Lord changed your life. The hope that it gives you."

"No, that's totally cool...um...can I think about it?"

"Of course. I don't want you to do anything you're not comfortable doing."

"I want to do it...eventually...I'm just not sure I'm ready for next week."

"Not a problem, David. Think about it and let me know toward the end of this week."

"I will."

The pastor smiled, patted him on the back, and then walked back over and sat down at the table. Gina walked over and gave him a hug.

"That food about ready grill master? It smells heavenly."

"Yeah. The pastor." He stopped and smiled. "You know I love it when you call me that."

"I know."

"Pastor Bill just asked me if I would give my testimony at next Wednesday night's service."

"Really. That's great. What did you tell him?"

"I told him I would think about it and let him know."

She smiled.

"I would like to see that. You have a passion for talking about the Lord now, and telling your story might help persuade others to give their life to Christ." She kissed him on the check. "Whatever you decide, I'm with you."

"Thanks babe." He smiled, kissed her, and then looked down. "This food's ready now."

Everyone had a great time at the BBQ, and they all left with plenty of leftovers

5

On Wednesday night, Dave had to work, so Gina picked up Shannon and Kurtis for church. After the service, one member approached Shannon and told her to come by and interview for the vacant receptionist's job at his car dealership. It was full time, dayshift, and provided a benefits package. When Gina drove them home, she and Shannon talked about the opportunity. The excitement in her voice was a nice change of pace. Gina pulled into the driveway and watched them get into the house safely before she drove away. As she drove down the street, a man from out of nowhere appeared in front of her. She slammed on the brakes and the car came to a stop. He walked around to the driver's side of the vehicle and motioned for her to roll the window down. He looked normal. Nothing about his appearance alarmed her, so she rolled her window down a quarter of the way.

"I'm so sorry to bother you, miss, but I seem to be lost. I was wondering if you might help me find my way to Newberry Street?"

Everything about him seemed normal, but she saw something in his eyes. They told her a different story. One that frightened her.

"I don't really live around this area. I was just dropping a friend off. But I think I saw a sign for Newberry Street two blocks north of here."

"Well. I'm sorry to have bothered you. You and your kids have a good night."

He slowly backed away from the vehicle, but never broke eye contact with her. It sent chills down her spine. She rolled the window up, gave him a nervous wave, and drove away. She watched him slowly disappear in her rearview mirror as she headed down the road, almost striking a parked car. He just stood in the middle of the road and watched them drive away. Her heart was racing.

"That dude was weird," Marc stated from the back.

She cleared her throat. "He was strange."

The rest of the drive home, she couldn't get his image out of her head. She almost called Shannon to warn her about the stranger, but decided that it would just make her look paranoid. He just needed directions, after all. He wasn't hurting anyone. They pulled into the driveway of their home, and she breathed a sigh of relief.

6

Dave walked in the door at 7:10 a.m. Marc was just coming out of the kitchen, so he gave his dad a hug before ascending up the staircase.

"Morning dad."

"Morning son."

He walked into the kitchen to see Gina take her last sip of coffee and then put the mug into the sink.

"Good morning," she said with a smile.

"Good morning," he smiled back and then gave her a kiss. "Where's Melissa?"

"Running around upstairs like a chicken with its head cut off, I'm sure. The first two to three weeks of school are very intense around here."

"Ah. I can take them if you need to get to work."

"Nope. You hit the hay. I've got this with time to spare. How was work last night?"

"Boring."

She smiled and held his face in her hands.

"Boring is good."

He laughed.

"How was church?"

"Very good. The pastor went Old Testament. He spoke about Samson."

"Great story. I'm sorry I missed it. I talked to Javier for a bit about giving my testimony next Wednesday night."

"And?"

"I'm going to do it. It's not like preparing a sermon. I just have to get up there and tell people about my decision to give my life to the Lord. There's maybe fifty to sixty people there on Wednesday nights, so the crowd isn't too big."

"Are you nervous about talking in front of people? I don't think that I've ever seen you nervous before."

"Not nervous, just...okay, maybe a little."

"But why David? You're an excellent speaker, and this is on a subject you love talking about. Just keep it real. Talk from the heart and you'll do great."

"Thanks."

"Are you going to invite anyone from work?"

"I hadn't really thought about it."

"You should. Maybe seeing you up there will inspire others to give serious thought to giving their life to Christ. You always talk about how much you love your brothers and sister in blue, and that your hope was for them to see the love of Jesus in you. That they would grab onto that hope themselves, or their eyes would be opened to a loving and gracious savior who died for them."

"It is my hope. Thank you for keeping me focused on His will and not mine."

He wrapped his arms around her and held her.

"How are you feeling?"

"I feel good." Before she could ask it, he said it. "I promise."

"Good. I hate to leave this warm embrace, but I've got to get these delinquents to school."

He laughed as they separated.

"Drive safe."

"You know it." Just before she left the kitchen, she stopped and turned around. "Something weird happened last night after I dropped Shannon and Kurtis off at home."

"What happened?"

"I was driving down their street, and this guy came out of nowhere. I almost hit him. He just needed directions."

"That doesn't seem too odd. What made it weird?"

"I don't know, I just, there was something about him. His eyes were so chilling."

"Other than his eyes, did he appear normal?"

"Yeah. I can't explain it. He just seemed off."

"I'll drive around that area tonight to see if I see anyone. What did he look like?"

"He was over six-foot, blonde thinning hair, well built with a belly, blue eyes."

"Was his clothing odd?"

"No. Jeans and a t-shirt."

"Where did he ask directions to?"

"Newberry Street. I told him I thought it was two blocks to the north."

"It's actually the next block over. Huh."

"Huh, what?"

"I'm sure he drove around the area first, and it's not like it's a few blocks away. It's the next block over."

"See, something weird."

"Mom, we need to go. I don't want to be late," Melissa called from the living room.

"Good morning, honey," Dave yelled from the kitchen.

"Good morning dad, sleep tight. Mom!" she yelled back.

"I'm coming. Go get in the car. Geez. Anyway, have a good sleep and we'll see you later."

She kissed him and disappeared. He sat down at the kitchen table and scratched his chin, thinking about the stranger she encountered. Dave eventually concluded that he needed to go to bed and think about this later, after he got some sleep. He said a quick prayer for his family, thanked God for bringing his crew home safely, and then went upstairs to bed.

Chapter 24

Thursday—September 9, 2010

It was a beautiful September morning. Shannon sat in a rocker on the front porch enjoying a cup of Earl Grey tea. She smiled as she thought about Kurtis getting on the bus earlier this morning for school. He actually seemed excited to go. This made her feel good. The last few weeks since she started putting him first, they talked more. They laughed more, and they bonded like a mother and son should. That's why last night when they got home from church, he told her everything that had happened at the motel the day before. That Butch was using a fake name to rent a room, and that he was pawning a ring that probably wasn't his. He said he was planning to live off of her parents at least until he figured things out. Shannon just wrapped him up in her arms and held him. She didn't tell him what they were going to do. She asked him what he wanted to do. He told her it would probably be a good idea if they didn't have Butch in their lives right now. They needed to work on their relationship, and bringing somebody in like Butch would only complicate that. She was proud of him for making that decision. She took another sip of her tea and watched as Butch came walking up the driveway. He looked disheveled and angry. He sat down on the top step and pulled his flask from his pocket and took a sip.

"Good morning, Shannon."

"What do you want, Butch?"

"What happened with dinner the other night?"

"You happened."

"And just what is that supposed to mean?"

"The boy sees you haven't changed. That you're no good. A taker. You don't want to be a father to him. You're looking for your next con, like always."

"I came here to reconcile with you and be a father to my son," He shouted.

An old man two doors down was raking his lawn. He stopped and looked their way. She smiled and waved at him.

"Good morning Mr. Riggs."

He didn't wave back. He turned and started raking again. Butch laughed.

"I see he doesn't much like you either. Listen and pay attention. I'm not going anywhere. Do you understand me?"

"He doesn't want you around, Butch. He told me so last night."

"After church?"

"Are you following us?"

"It's the only way I can keep tabs on you. You're not sneaking out in the middle of the night on me."

"You're crazy."

"Like a fox darling," he laughed. "I want to come back over for dinner."

"No. We don't want you here."

"I want to hear it from his lips."

"No."

A sinister smile came across his face.

"You know that lady and her kids, the one that dropped you off at home last night? We had a friendly chat when she left. She looked scared. The kids looked a little scared. But she knew the Christian thing to do was to roll down the window and help me out. Maybe I'll need directions some other time from her, at her house on Dolphin Street."

A look of concern came over her face, and his smile widened.

"You leave them alone. They've done nothing to you. They're good people."

"I don't like the way he's trying to parent my boy. I'm the one who should take him to baseball games and to, to, other stuff."

She laughed.

"You don't even know where to take him. How about church?"

"Let's not get crazy darling." He smiled. "The only church he needs to know about is the church of money."

"Please, just leave all of us alone. How much money would it take to help you move along?"

"Are you trying to deprive me of a relationship with my boy?"

"Save it for someone who doesn't know who you are. Money is the only language you've ever known. How much?"

"Ten million dollars."

She laughed so hard she almost spilled her tea.

"Okay. Let me just drive down to the bank and get that for you."

"There is no amount of money that you can give me to keep me from my boy. I will see him again, with or without your help, so you better get on board."

She held the cup to her lips for a long while as she thought. She took a drink.

"Okay. We can do dinner again, but I have to talk to him first."

"Okay. That's more like it." He reached into his pocket and took out a piece of paper and handed it to her. "That's my new phone number. Call me and let me know when to come over."

"What happened to your old phone? Did it find a wall or a sidewalk?"

"You just call me. Soon. And don't try anything funny. I'll be watching."

"What if Kurtis doesn't want you to come over?"

"Just make it happen."

"Okay. Give me a couple of days and I'll call you."

"Soon!"

"Soon."

He stood and walked over to her. She didn't acknowledge his presence or say a word. She just held her tea up high and stared straight ahead. He bent down and kissed her on top of the head. She didn't flinch. He stood, turned, and walked down the steps toward the driveway. There was something different about her. He didn't like it. Butch looked back over his shoulder to see a smirk on her face. He turned and headed toward his truck.

2

Kurtis, Marc, and Justin sat in the cafeteria eating their lunch. Over the summer, the three of them became close, even though Justin had his reservations at first. The three of them were going over to the King's house after school to hang out. Justin had saved up enough allowance and bought the new MLB 11 video game, and they were going to play. Justin looked at his watch.

"Oh crap, I gotta go."

"What's the rush? We still have plenty of time for lunch." Kurtis stated.

"He's got a band thing," Marc added.

"Yeah. I told Mr. Gilliam that I'd be in there during my lunch hour to practice."

"What do you play?" Kurtis asked.

"The saxophone," Justin responded.

"Cool. You any good?" Kurtis asked.

"I don't know, am I?" Justin responded as he looked at Marc.

"He's okay," Marc smiled.

Justin shoved him as he got up off of the bench.

"Better than anyone else, you know."

"That's because you are the only dork I know that plays the saxophone," Marc laughed.

"Shut up, dweeb," he responded. "Catch you guys later."

"Later," Kurtis responded.

"Later," Marc responded. He looked behind him to make sure Justin was gone. "He's actually fantastic."

"You guys play together?"

"Sometimes. We mainly play video games when we hang out."

"Yeah, video games are cool." He took a bite of his sandwich. "Can I tell you something, Marc?"

"Sure."

"If I tell you, can you keep it between us? Tell no one else, not even Justin?"

Marc stopped what he was doing and turned toward his friend.

"My attention is yours."

"You gotta promise not to tell anyone."

"I promise."

"I met my real dad."

"No way! That's awesome."

"That's what I thought at first."

"Oh man, what happened?"

He told him everything. About the meeting on the front porch, verified by the book with his dad's name it, and then further verified by his mother. He then told him they had dinner together, and that everything seemed great, even though his mom tried to warn him about Butch. He then told him about the motel. Butch was not a good man. He was a liar and a user.

"I don't know what to do?"

"That's tough. Your dad sounds like a bad guy."

"He's not my dad. Let's call him Butch."

"Got it. Maybe Butch just doesn't know what family is, and he's the way he is because of his family."

"Maybe, but that's no excuse. Eventually, you grow up and figure it out."

"You sound like my dad."

"Maybe I do, but he isn't wrong."

"So, what are you going to do? We could tell my dad."

"No. I think me and my mom just have to tell him it isn't going to work until he can get his act together. We don't want him around."

"What if he doesn't accept that?"

"Then we get your dad involved."

"It sounds like he won't accept that. We should just skip to the, get my dad involved part."

"I think I want to try it this way first."

"Okay. Keep me posted."

"I will. You gonna eat both twinkies?"

He smiled and handed Kurtis one. "Nope."

Marc felt bad for his friend. He had been without a father his whole life, and this is the jerk that rolls into town. He was fortunate to have Dave in his life.

3

The week flew by and Friday was upon them. Shannon interviewed for that job at the dealership in the morning. They had a few more interviews to do, and she was told that they would call her on Monday with the results. Dave had the weekend off, so they had dinner at the Martinez's house on Friday night, and the adults surprised the kids with a trip to Cedar Point on Saturday. Frank's work gave him ten passes to use, so the Jacksons, Kings, Shannon and Kurtis headed to Sandusky. Pastor Dunkirk graciously allowed Dave to use the church van so that they could all drive together. Dave drove while Frank was his co-pilot, and everyone else just fell into place. The boys sat in the front row, the two girls in the middle, and the three women sat in the back row. Patty told the ladies she was sorry, but she had gotten up early that morning and was beat. If she was going to be any fun at Cedar Point, she needed a nap. She put some headphones on and laid her head back. Within minutes, she was out. Shannon sat in between Gina and Patty, and she opened up about Butch. She spoke quietly so she wouldn't disturb Patty, and Kurtis wouldn't hear her.

"Gina, I think I need help," Shannon looked at her.

"What's wrong?"

She explained her current dilemma and gave Gina a full history lesson on Butch. Gina was both amazed and sympathetic to her situation.

"I am so sorry to drop all of this on you, Gina. I just don't have anyone else to talk to, and I feel that we've gotten close, so I..."

"Shannon, don't be sorry. That is a lot for one person to carry around for so long. We are friends. And if I can help you, I want to."

"I also felt the need to tell you this because of what he said to me before he left yesterday."

"What did he say?"

"He told me he spoke with you after church on Wednesday night."

"I don't remember speaking with..." She stopped mid-sentence, as if she had an epiphany. "The guy in the middle of the street."

"Asking for directions, yes."

"He made me feel very uncomfortable."

"That's what he does. He plays psychological games. If he can see the fear in your eyes, he knows he's accomplished something."

"Well then, he knows he did that night."

"Gina, he knows where you live, and that Dave's a cop."

"How? Why would he..."

"Because he does that too. He's a scam artist. Those types of people do their homework. He said he wouldn't bother you or your family if I cooperated with him. I'll keep cooperating so you guys don't get hurt."

"No. You and Kurtis can't live like this. Dave will know what to do. You know I have to tell him. Right?"

"I know. I'm so sorry that I brought this drama into your family's lives."

Gina could see that she was trying to hold back the tears.

"Shannon, you were young. Manipulated by a predator who saw that, and now he's coming back around because he has nothing left and he wants to take some more from you. Well, we won't let him." She grabbed Shannon's hand. "By the time Dave's done with him, he'll wish he would have just left you two alone."

"Thank you."

"Let's worry about this problem tomorrow. Today we're here to have some fun and ride some roller coasters."

"Okay. That sounds good."

The drive was only a couple of hours, and they made it to the park at 9:45 a.m. Ten minutes before it opened. They exited the van. Dave addressed them.

"Okay. We have ten fun filled hours waiting for us just on the other side of those gates. Let's eat junk, ride some rides, and go home exhausted."

Everyone cheered. They were some of the first patrons admitted into the park that day. They did things as a group, as families, and as friends. At one o'clock they ate lunch as a group. They met at a pizza place in the center of the park. As everyone sat there enjoying their food, Dave could feel an uncomfortable pain developing in the pit of his stomach. He excused himself to the bathroom. Instead of going to the men's room, he decided it might be best to use the family bathroom. It was private, and he did not know what he was about to go through. He didn't want someone running out of the men's room for help if the pain caused him to scream. The family bathroom was free, so he went in and locked the door. The pain was steadily getting worse and sharper. He went into a corner of the room and sat down. He removed his shirt and pressed it hard up against his face as a wave of pain flooded over him. The shirt muffled his screams. He asked God for help in thwarting the pain, praying in his head over and over for relief. Another burst shot through his body and he was sure that this was it. He was going to die on the bathroom floor in an amusement park. He lunged toward the toilet and just got his head over the bowl when the vomiting started. It was fast and furious. When he finally felt well enough to sit back on his feet, he took several deep breaths and exhaled loudly. He forced his clinched eyes open and peered into the bowl. Blood. All over the wall around the bowl, the back of the bowl, and a sea of red in the bowl. He waited a few minutes until he could find the strength to rise. The waded-up shirt in his hands had blood all over it. He soaked the shirt completely and used it to clean the walls and the rim of the toilet. He flushed the toilet several times to clean it out. Dave reached into his pocket and pulled out the pill he was saving for tonight, and took it. He waited a few more minutes and then walked over to the sink. He looked into the mirror and witnessed the pale, sweaty man standing in front of him. Dave placed the shirt into the trash can under all the discarded paper towels. He threw water on his face and checked his watch. It had been twenty-five minutes. He pulled his phone from his pocket and saw that he had two missed texts from Gina.

"*Are you still in the bathroom?*" and ten minutes later, "*Are you alright?*" The last one was three minutes ago. He texted back. "*I'm good. Must have been all of this junk food. Be back in two.*" Send. He waited a few more minutes, and the color returned to his face. The bathroom was attached to a clothing shop, so he exited, praying that people wouldn't stare. There were only a couple of people in the area, and they were too preoccupied with screaming kids to notice him. He hurried around the building to the shop, garnering only a few odd looks, and into the store. Within two minutes, he had picked out a shirt, put it on and paid for it. He headed back to the table. When he got there, he saw Gina sitting at the table alone. He smiled as he walked up.

"Did everyone tire of waiting for me?"

"Dave, have you been in the bathroom this whole time?" She asked, concerned.

"I'm good. Just a little indigestion, I think. Oh, and sorry. I saw this shirt in the shop earlier and had to have it."

A lie. His stomach was maintaining a lower level of pain, but it was constant.

"Really? You had to have a shirt that says simply says, 'Cedar Point Amusement Park,'?"

"I like the color." He smiled.

"Indigestion? David, did you forget to take your pill again?"

He would tell her when they got home about the episode, as Ronnie called it, but he would not ruin this day of fun.

"You know I'm sorry, I did. Do you have one on you?"

"You know I do."

She reached into her purse and pulled out her portable pill tube. She dumped the contents in her hand and produced one pill. He took it and swallowed it down with a sip of pop.

"Thank you."

"Dave, you would tell me if the pain was getting more frequent, and worse, wouldn't you?"

"I would. I just need you to help me keep the junk food to a minimum the rest of the day."

"I really haven't seen you eat much junk."

"I have." He raised his eyebrows. "Slipped a box of Nerds into my pocket before we left home."

"I don't think one box of Ner..."

Frank interrupted them.

"There you are, buddy. Come on kids, let's hit some coasters."

"Lead the way," Dave said with enthusiasm.

Gina hugged his arm and leaned in to whisper in his ear, "We'll talk about this more later."

He kissed her forehead and smiled.

"Okay my love."

He broke free and joined Frank. Patty slowed to a walk next to Gina.

"The men have definitely become boys today."

"Yes, they have." She looked around. "Where's Shannon?"

"She went off with Kurtis for a little mother and son time."

"That's nice. It's good to see them having such a good time."

"I know. I don't think Kurtis has stopped smiling since we got here."

"Neither has Dave nor Frank."

They both laughed at that.

When the day was over, they piled into the van and headed back home. Ten minutes after leaving the park, Dave stopped to gas up the van and grab a very large black coffee. He stopped, got out of the van, put gas in it, and then got back into the van and drove away with no one waking up. They were all exhausted from ten straight hours of riding, walking, and eating. He looked over at Frank, who was sleeping with his head tilted back and his mouth wide open. Dave thought he saw a fly disappear into it. He laughed. He looked into the rearview mirror to see everyone leaning and sleeping on everyone else.

"Thank you, Lord." He whispered and then took a sip of coffee.

The pain in his stomach was gone for now, but he knew it would return. One pill had been enough for the last couple of months, but he feared it wasn't going to be enough anymore. He looked into the rearview mirror again. This time focusing on Gina, Marc, and Melissa separately. He loved them all so much. Dave knew that the time was drawing near to tell the kids. He took another sip and focused on the road ahead.

4

Dave rolled by and picked up Shannon and Kurtis for church on Sunday morning. The pastor had advised Dave that he could just return the van when he came to church that morning, so he wouldn't have to make the switch late at night. Dave told him it was a clever way to get him to church on Sunday, and the pastor laughed, but didn't disagree. He pulled into Shannon's driveway at 10:00 a.m. Gina paid close attention when they entered the area, looking for Butch sitting in his truck or walking around. She didn't see him. Shannon and Kurtis came out of the house when they saw Dave pull up. Kurtis ran and got in the van. Shannon stood on the porch for an extra minute, scanning the area. She saw nothing. She then walked to the van and got in.

"Good morning," Dave said with a smile.

"Good morning," she responded.

"Did you guys sleep good?" Gina asked.

"Like the dead," she answered as she laughed.

"Ditto," Gina shot back.

Dave pulled out of the driveway and headed for the church, with both Gina and Shannon keeping their head on a swivel. He made it to the church and pulled up in the circle drive to let all of them off at the door. The kids piled out, but Gina and Shannon remained in the van because they told him they needed to talk to him. He drove the van and parked it next to the truck. He shut it off and then turned to look at them.

"Okay, what gives? Both of you almost got whiplash whipping your heads back and forth at the house, and now you both need to talk to me."

Gina looked at Shannon. "Tell him."

"Maybe we should do this after church. It starts in ten minutes, and I have a feeling this is going to take a lot longer."

"Maybe you're right," Gina agreed.

"No. I'm not going to concentrate on the sermon. If you were going to tell me after the service, then you should have waited to tell me anything."

"Your right, but this is going to take some time, and I'm sure you'll have questions." Gina responded.

He sat there for a minute and just looked straight ahead.

"Fine. After church."

He got out of the van and slammed the door. Dave started walking toward the entrance, both of them still sitting in the van.

"He's not happy," Shannon stated.

"He's not, but he'll get over it. Come on, we don't want to be late for the service."

"Are we even going to be allowed to sit with him?"

Gina laughed.

"I don't know. I guess we'll see when we get in there."

They both laughed.

Pastor Dunkirk spoke about the world and mans need to be accepted by it. That there are still believers who seek man's approval over God's. His message was simple. When you accept Christ as your savior, you have made a commitment to live your life for Him and not the world. The world is a temporary place where man stores up temporary treasures while here. When we live for Christ, we store up treasures for ourselves in heaven that moths can't destroy. Gina had given Shannon a bible of her own. She took it to and from church when she went, but other than that, she didn't really open it. But today she made it a point to underline the passage that the pastor referenced. Matthew chapter six verses nineteen through twenty-one, "Do not lay up for yourselves treasures on earth, where moth and rust destroy and where thieves break in and steal; but lay up for yourselves treasures in heaven, where neither moth nor rust destroys and where thieves do not break in and steal. For where your treasure is, there your heart will be also." Somehow, that passage resonated in her. When church was over, they chatted with the pastor for a bit, thanked him for the use of the van, and then headed off to lunch. Dave suggested they pick up subs and head back to their house, to which everyone agreed. He tried to listen to the service today, but all he could think about was what they wanted to talk to him about. When they got home, the kids ate outside at the picnic table in the backyard, and the three of them remained inside. Dave sat down at the kitchen table and got right to the point.

"So, what did you two want to talk to me about?"

Gina looked over at Shannon. "Tell him everything you told me."

Shannon did. The story took a while to tell, mainly because the kids kept coming in periodically to interrupt them, but she eventually got it all out. Dave listened to every detail carefully. When she finished, it was his turn to ask some questions. Marc and Kurtis came in for the umpteenth time to ask if they could go upstairs and play video games.

"Yeah, have fun," Dave answered. He looked over at Shannon. "I don't think you've ever seen our little apartment above the garage, have you?"

"No, I haven't," she responded.

"Follow us," Gina added.

The three of them headed up to the apartment for a little privacy. They passed Melissa, who was sitting at the table with her headphones on, listening to her music. She looked up to see them walking by and removed the headphones.

"Can Matty come over and hang out?" She asked.

"Sure," Gina answered as they continued toward the apartment.

"Where are you guys going?"

"Shannon hasn't seen the apartment. We're going to show it to her," Dave answered.

"She moving in?"

"No, she just wants to see it," he responded.

"Cool. I'm gonna call Matty."

They made it up the steps and into the apartment. They all took a seat at the kitchen table.

"So...Butch, is it?" he asked.

"Yes. Butch McCabe."

He thought for a moment.

"I've heard that name before. He's not local?"

"No. He's from all over. I don't know exactly where he's been for the last fifteen years, so I can't say for sure he hasn't stayed in Michigan before. He acts like he's only been here for a couple of weeks."

"Okay. Right now, we don't have much to go on. It's kind of he said she said situation."

"He's staying at the motel under a false name. Mitch Arnold. Is there anything you can do about that?"

"I'll check in to it when I go in tomorrow. If he has stolen the name and fraudulently used a credit card or other piece of identity, we'll try to hold him on that for the detectives."

"He's expecting a dinner invite this week."

"Push it off as long as you can. Maybe we can figure something else out."

"Okay."

"I'll see if he has any outstanding warrants or maybe a suspended license. Maybe we can catch him driving. Just try to stay alert and if you see him sitting outside of your house, then call me and I'll call the station. We'll try to get a car over to at least make him aware that we know he's there."

"Thanks, Dave. As far as I know, he isn't a violent man, but like I said, I knew him a long time ago when he was a small-time con artist going from town to town pulling scams to get by."

"If he's graduated to something more, his record will show it."

"If you need us, we're here for you," Gina added.

"I appreciate all the help and all that you've done for me and Kurt. He really looks up to you, Dave. I know I haven't been there for him...ever. I love him so much. I want to show him what an actual mother should be like. In time, I hope he can forgive me. Both of you have really been a big help, and for that, I'm truly grateful."

Gina walked over and gave her a hug.

"Were happy to help."

Dave drove Shannon home a short time later, and the truck was nowhere to be seen. He walked through the house to make sure that it was empty. In the backyard, he spotted her 1991 Saturn SL1.

"Does it run?"

"No. It tries to start, but then doesn't."

"How long has it been sitting?"

"Probably at least five years. I stopped driving it because my boyfriend's usually drove everywhere. I know I need to get a car so people will have to stop taking time out of their day to drive me around, but I just don't have the cash to buy one right now."

"Do you have the keys?"

She went into the kitchen junk drawer and pulled a set out. She handed them to him.

"Do you think you can get it started?"

"Let's go have a look."

They walked out the back door and over to the car. He opened the door and got in. He turned the key. Nothing. It didn't even try to turn over. He popped the hood and walked around to the front of the car. He opened it and looked at the engine.

"What do you think?"

"You definitely need a new battery, and possibly a new alternator. I got a friend in town who's an excellent mechanic. Maybe he can look at it."

"Hopefully he will defer the payment until I get a job and can pay him."

"Don't worry about that. He'll work with you."

"I really appreciate that, Dave."

"It's not a problem. What time do you want Kurt home today?"

"By five. We have some homework to go over."

"By five it is."

He handed the car keys back to her and headed home. After he left, she called Butch. She didn't want him to get too anise about dinner. He picked up on the first ring.

"Hello."

"Hello Butch."

"Shannon. What time's dinner?"

"Friday at 6:30 p.m. if you can make it."

"Friday? That's like five days away. Why not tonight, or tomorrow?"

"Because it's Friday."

"So cold. Fine. Friday it is. Maybe a nice lemon chicken with some rice and green beans, and good old apple pie for dessert. What do you think?"

"That's fine."

"And since it's a weekend night, and the boy doesn't have school the next day, maybe a movie?"

"We'll see."

"I'll bring the movie. Something child appropriate, of course."

There was silence on the other end for a few seconds.

"Fine."

"Good. It's a date then. See you and Kurtis Friday at 6:30 for dinner and a movie, and then who knows what?"

Before she responded, he hung up. She really hoped Dave could find something on him, and that Friday would never happen.

Chapter 25

Monday—September 13, 2010

It was 11:43 p.m. and Dave sat in the high school parking lot writing an accident that he took earlier in the shift. It was a quiet night so far (knock on wood) and he hoped it would stay that way. After dinner, Shannon had called Gina and advised her she got the receptionist's job at the dealership. She would start next Monday. He had called his mechanic friend, Paul, when he got up this morning, and they went to her house and towed the car to his shop, at no cost to her, for which Dave was grateful. Later in the day, Paul called him and advised that the car needed a new battery, alternator, spark plugs and wires, and an oil change. Dave asked what the damage was going to be, and Paul told him he could do everything for $275. Dave knew that this was the ultimate friend's discount and told him to do the work. Paul told him he could throw in a complete car detailing for an extra fifty bucks. His kid was trying to get his business started, and this would be a significant challenge for him. Fifty bucks for a complete detail was another big steal. Dave gave him the go ahead. He told Dave that they could pick the car up on Wednesday after 11:00 a.m. Paul wasn't one to beat around the bush with questions, so during the call he was blunt with Dave.

"Are you and this chick a side item?"

"You know I'm married to Gina."

"I know, but this seems like an awful lot of trouble for someone you're not involved with."

"Shannon and her son Kurtis have had a rough road. God has placed it on my heart to help them and love them as Christ loves us."

There was a pause.

"I'm just saying that I've never seen a guy go above and beyond like this for a lady unless there was something else going on."

Dave laughed. "Well, now you have."

"You're a good person Dave."

"So are you. You're doing this work at a fifty percent discount minimum."

"It's not that much, but you have always been a good friend to me and my family, and if this gal is important to your family, then she's important to me."

"Thanks Paul, and I haven't always been a good person, but Christ changed my life. He made me want to be better."

"Rock on brother. Anyway, I'll see you Wednesday after eleven."

"Thanks again buddy.

Dave never would have thought about glorifying God in the past. He would have taken the credit and run, but Christ changed his heart. He never used bullying techniques to ram God down anyone's throat, but he never shied away from introducing the Lord into a conversation. Dave now lived his life as a testament to his savior. Paul didn't inquire about his newfound faith, but it had placed a spark. Dave knew what a spark could do. As he finished his report, he now focused on the Butch problem. He got all the information he needed from Shannon and typed it into the database. Nothing. He placed a call to dispatch.

"Dargen City PD, how can I help you?" the friendly voice on the other end asked.

"Diane, it's Dave."

"Hey Dave. What can I do for you?"

"Is LEIN down?"

"It is. We got a message last night that it was going to be down for maintenance from midnight to seven in the morning."

"Okay. Great timing, as usual."

"Always is. Can I do anything else for you?"

"No, I was just wondering."

"Okay Dave. Be safe."

"Thanks Diane."

He hung up the phone and stared at his notepad for a moment. "Butch McCabe. Well, I guess you'll have to wait until tomorrow night." He put his pad away and looked at his watch. 12:02 a.m. He shifted into drive and decided that a nice hot cup of coffee was the answer. Dave grabbed his coffee from DD, chatted it up with the worker, and then found a booth in the corner. He pulled his notepad back out of his pocket and flipped to the last page. He agreed to share his testimony with the church on Wednesday night, so he had been writing some notes on what to say. The pastor told him not to worry about trying to deliver a sermon. Just tell us about your life and what led you to your salvation. But Dave wanted to make more of an impact. He needed to quote a lot of scripture and really drive home the point. He was deep in thought about it when dispatch called him. She sent him to one of the local liquor stores on a beer run report. He closed up his notebook and placed it in his pocket. To be continued.

His night was ending, and he pulled into the back of the PD around 6:50 a.m. Just before he shut the computer down, it started dinging like crazy, sending back every query that he had made during his shift. Driving records came back, criminal hits, warrants, and all the other information on a person entered into the law enforcement database. He had already hit the power button, and the system was shutting down. Butch McCabe was the last thing he saw at the top of the screen before it went black. He sighed. Does he boot it back up and read the information over the in-car computer? Or does he wait until he is in tonight so he can get out of here on time and go home and get some sleep? The later, besides, he isn't supposed to go over for dinner until Friday, anyway. If there's anything on him, he'll see it tomorrow and they can pick him up beforehand if they need to. He hopped out of the car, grabbed his gear, and headed for the locker room. Once downstairs, he and Javier talked while they changed. Javier was excited about going to see him share his testimony on Wednesday. He stated he had shared it with the shift and a few officers in other departments. Dave thought to himself, "Now I really have to bring it."

2

Dave woke up Tuesday around 11:30 a.m. with another paralyzing pain in his abdomen. He curled up into the fetal position, clamped his eyes shut, and braced himself. There was no blood this time, and he doesn't remember screaming in pain, but when he looked at the clock again, it read 11:53 a.m. Maybe he passed out. Whatever the case, he's glad that his wife was at work and the kids were at school. He slowly stretched out of his position, carefully taking his time so that he wouldn't unintendedly trigger another episode. He put his feet over the bed and planted them on the floor, and stood up. The remanence of pain was still there, but it was now a one, maybe a two, instead of a ten plus. He reached into the nightstand drawer and took another pill and swallowed it. He took his time in putting on his robe and going downstairs. There was a note on the counter.

I hope you slept well. Have a great day. I love you. — Gina.

Dave smiled. He sat down at the kitchen table with his bible. He opened it to a passage that he marked the very first time that he started reading the scriptures. It was in his first meeting with Pastor Dunkirk that he heard about, 1 Thessalonians 5:16-18, "Rejoice always, pray without ceasing, in everything give thanks; for this is the will of God in Christ Jesus for you." He ran his fingers over the passage. He bowed his head.

"Lord. I thank you for Your amazing grace in giving Your Son Jesus to die for me. You have given me so much. Please give me the strength to go through what's about to happen to me. I'm ashamed to admit it, but I'm still scared. I love my family so much and I don't want them to see me go through this. Guide us through this tough time that's about to come upon us. Take care of them, Lord. I ask this in the name of Your Son, my Savior, amen."

He wiped the tears from his eyes and ran his fingers over the passage one more time. He smiled. Today felt like a sick day. He wanted to spend more time with them while he had the chance.

3

Wednesday night was upon him. Gina drove to church while he went over his note cards in the car. Shannon and Kurtis would meet them at the service. She had gotten her vehicle back earlier that day and it ran and looked amazing. Paul told her she could pay him when she got settled into her new job and started receiving paychecks. Gina looked over at him. The man that she had been married to for eighteen years now never showed signs of stress. Right now, he looked like a 1950's movie portrayal of an expectant father in the waiting room.

"Dave, you're going to do great," she said, trying to reassure him.

"This is just a weird feeling. I've spoken in a room to hundreds of people and never been this nervous."

"That's because you knew the subject you were talking about well. This is no different. You know your own story better than anyone. It's a great story."

"Then why do I feel so...so...anxious?"

"You're afraid you're going to say something that doesn't represent the Lord in the proper light."

"What if that's exactly what I do?"

"You won't."

"How can you be so sure?"

"Matthew 10:20."

He closed his eyes and recited the verse from memory.

"For it is not you who speak, but the spirit of your Father who speaks in you."

"That's how I know."

She smiled and grabbed his hand. He smiled back.

"You always know what to say. You're right. This opportunity to share my testimony came from God. He will be with me and guide me."

They pulled into the church parking lot twenty minutes before the service. They went inside the church and found Pastor Dunkirk standing in the lobby talking to the deacon. He looked up, saw them, and smiled. He walked over to them.

"Good evening, Jackson family."

"Good evening, pastor," Dave responded.

He shook all of their hands.

"We're excited to hear you give your testimony this evening."

"Thank you, I'm a little nervous."

"It's only natural to be nervous, but I know you're going to do great."

"I hope so."

"Did you invite anyone from work?"

"Javier, my partner, and I think he invited some of my shift mates."

"Wonderful. Javier is a pleasant fellow. I enjoyed talking to him at your BBQ."

"He's a solid guy."

Pastor Dunkirk spotted a deacon across the room waving him over.

"I have to go take care of a few things before the service. Meet me at the front of the sanctuary just before the service starts."

"Okay," he responded with nervous energy.

"Dave, just relax. Give us some history about your life before Jesus, and then after Jesus."

"Okay, thanks."

The pastor walked away. Gina grabbed his hand and held it. It was sweaty and clammy. While they were in the lobby, some of their friends walked in. Javier and Rita, the Kings, and Shannon and Kurtis. They all encouraged him and wished him luck. The organ played, and that was their cue to go into the sanctuary. They all sat in the second pew from the front, and Dave took his seat on the stage next to Pastor Dunkirk. He looked out over the crowd. All the regulars were there, his family and friends, and there were a lot of faces from officers he knew in surrounding police departments. A lot. The sanctuary was at least fifty percent fuller on this Wednesday night. But he didn't see the faces of his co-workers.

"Nice crowd, Dave," the pastor whispered.

Dave just smiled. The pit of his stomach was aching. He was sure that when he stepped up to the podium. He was going to vomit blood everywhere and curl up into the fetal position. Dave prayed to the Lord.

"Please, not now Father. Take this pain from me until after the service." He then realized it was an unfamiliar pain. It wasn't the cancer acting up. He had taken two pills before they left home to be safe. It was anxiety. "Talk through me, Lord. I need Your strength." The music pastor led the church in a couple of hymns, and then Pastor Dunkirk stepped up to the podium to introduce Dave.

"We have a special treat for you all tonight. One of our newest members, David Jackson, is a going to share his testimony with us." The pastor said some nice things about him and his family and then introduced him. Dave walked up to the podium, shook the pastor's hand, and then took his place in front of it. The pastor walked down the steps and had a seat in the front row. Dave looked out over the sanctuary. He looked down at his family and smiled. As he stared into Gina's eyes, a calm came over him. He was about to speak when the door to the sanctuary opened. Lisa, Patty, and Shawnee scurried in and took a seat in the back row. He smiled at them and then addressed the congregation.

"Good afternoon, everyone."

"Good afternoon," came an off-key mixture of voices.

"I hope everyone is having a wonderful week so far. My name is Dave Jackson. Born and raised right her in Dargen City. I have been married to the love of my life, Gina, for eighteen years now, and we have two fifteen-year-old twins. Marc and Melissa. I have been an officer for the Dargen City police department for twenty years now."

He paused while there was light applause from the congregation.

"Thank you to the four people that support their police department."

There was laughter throughout the sanctuary. He smiled.

"For forty-two years I lived my life not knowing, or possibly ignoring, that there was a God who loved me so much that He sent his one and only Son to die for my salvation."

"Amen," came the response from some of the congregation.

He talked about life before Christ. Growing up in a good household with a mother and father who cared deeply for him, and raised him to be an honest, hard-working man. He talked about meeting Gina, and the friendship that turned into a lifelong love affair. He talked about the joy in his heart after watching the birth of his children, and what a true blessing that it's been watching them grow. His voice cracked as he talked about the death of his father and the anguish that he experienced carting around the guilt of that death for the last seven years. The church was silent, and tears were shed. He talked about the last couple of years, and the inner struggles he was battling because, at 42 years of age, he felt empty. Like he was missing something, but couldn't pinpoint what it was. He had a family that he loved dearly. A career that he loved. Life was good, but something was missing. He admitted to abandoning his family and searching for that filler by working more and hanging out more with his friends. His family life suffered. Now he came to the part in his life where he met Pastor Dunkirk.

"I was working one night. July 1, 2010, to be exact, sitting in front of a local church at 2:00 a.m. Pondering life when there was a knock on the window of my squad car. I looked to my left and a bright light surrounded an angel, and I had no fear." He smiled. "I was just trying to add some drama to the story. It was actually a floodlight from the church illuminating Pastor Dunkirk and he scared the crap out of me."

There were smiles and laughter throughout the church. He looked down to see Pastor Dunkirk laughing in the front row. He stood and faced the congregation.

"I think the angelic part was the correct telling of the story."

He sat back down as more laughter echoed throughout. Dave smiled.

"He simply asked me if I was okay. I wasn't." He smiled and reflected for a second before continuing. "I was completely lost. This man who had never met me, who did not know who I was, came out to check on me. I didn't want to admit it to myself that night, but that really touched my heart. We chatted for a while, until I got called out on a run, and he planted a seed that night. I didn't realize that he had. You can ask anyone that knows me and they'll tell you I am a man who does not believe in coincidence or luck. I was exactly where I needed to be that night."

"Amen," a few voices rang out.

"Now God gives us the freewill to choose as we please, and I sat in that spot at that hour of the night. Your move God." He smiled. "God placed one of his servants at the church that night. I don't know why he couldn't sleep that night. Maybe he ate something that didn't agree with him. Maybe he had a cup of coffee before bed. Regardless of the reason, he was in the church that night looking down from that window, noticing that I was just sitting there for over an hour, not moving. The compassion in his heart moved him to check on me." He paused. "Your move Dave." He smiled. "From that encounter, it intrigued me. I left to go on that run, but the rest of the night I dwelled on our conversation. I went home in the morning and couldn't go right to sleep. I had a disturbing dream of mortality, and then when I awakened that day, and continued to think about this church. The seed grew."

"Amen," more voices shouted.

"My wife Gina, who accepted the Lord two years ago, has shown nothing but love and patience for me over the last two years of our marriage. When she told me about her salvation, I was angry. My first thought was, not you too. If she hadn't made that decision, I don't know if our marriage would have lasted. Without knowing it, she has shown me nothing but the love and grace of God over the past two years."

He looked down and wiped the tears from his eyes. He looked over at her and mouthed the words, "I love you." She was wiping her eyes with a tissue, but then she smiled at him and mouthed them back. People all over the sanctuary were sniffing and clearing the frog from their throat.

"So, on July 3, 2010, I walked into this church for the very first time. I heard the story of a loving God who gave His only Son so that I could live. I gave my life to Jesus that day."

A very loud and hearty chorus of "Amen" rang throughout the sanctuary.

"Since then, I haven't looked back. My only regret is that it took 42 years to find that joy. Folks, it's never too late to accept His grace. Whether you're five or a hundred and five, He will welcome you in to His flock. His grace is real, and it's free. It costs you nothing. I've heard people say, 'Yeah. You don't have the freedom to do what you want anymore.' That couldn't be furthest from the truth. You absolutely have the freedom to do what you want. It's just that when you decide to truly accept Him and follow His path, you want to live a better life, one that glorifies Him. Free from the shackles of seeking fortune and fame. Free from being someone who lives to please others, and free from a life of worry and regret."

"Amen."

"My marriage is stronger, my relationships with others are more meaningful, and my work is more fulfilling. It doesn't mean that life is going to be perfect. I still have my good and bad days. There is still chaos in my life from time to time. The only difference now is that I have a loving Savior to carry the burden for me. He opens His arms and I rest on His mercy. Since my transformation, I have also watched a lot of documentaries on Christian men and women from the past. Missionaries who suffered and were martyred for bringing the gospel to others. One quote always sticks out in my mind. The martyred missionary, Jim Elliot, said, 'He is no fool who gives what he cannot keep, to gain what he cannot lose.'" Dave scanned the sanctuary and made eye contact with members of the congregation as he continued. "This life only lasts for a moment. You blink your eyes and you're married with kids, and then grandkids. You can't keep it. It's a fact that the result for life on this earth is always death. Jesus gave us the key to eternal life with him. He shed His blood for us. In John chapter fourteen verse six, He tells us that, 'I am the way, the truth, and the life. No one comes to the Father except through Me.' There is no guarantee you'll live to be old in this life. Death knows no age. Won't you please accept Him before it's too late? I did."

He smiled and looked over at the pastor. The pastor smiled back and nodded his head. He had told Dave before the service started that he could say the closing prayer if he wished. Dave wished to.

"Please bow your heads and close your eyes. Father in heaven. Thank you for sending Your Son Jesus to die for us. For shedding His blood for our salvation. Your grace has no end. Bless this congregation and convict our hearts to always do what is right. I ask this in Jesus' precious name. Amen."

Everyone lifted their heads and opened their eyes.

"Thank you all for coming out tonight and listening to my story. Pastor."

Pastor Dunkirk walked up onto the stage and shook Dave's hand. He then turned to the congregation.

"The church would like to thank Dave for being brave enough to stand in front of us tonight and share his story of faith with us. It takes a brave soul to do such a thing. Dave had graciously agreed, just now as I'm talking, to stand down in front and meet whoever would like to come up and shake his hand. If anyone here tonight would like to learn more about God's graceful gift of salvation, then please see me or one of my many wonderful staff members. If you just need us to pray for you, then let us know. God bless you and please drive home safely."

Dave stood at the front of the church, shaking hands with smiling people who thanked him for speaking, and encouraged him in his faith. There were quite a few police officers from other agencies who came up and shook his hand as well. Each gave him a business card, lending their support if he ever needed it. He turned to his right to address the next person in line, and was pleasantly surprised to see Patty, Shawnee, and then Lisa.

"Great talk you, old son of a...gun," Patty shook his hand.

He laughed, "Thanks Patty."

"When you told us you found religion, I just assumed it would be a passing fancy. But you're really into this. I'm glad you're happy, Dave, but we miss you when we go out now. Anyway, good talk buddy."

"It's a true-life changer. You guys are still very important to me, and it doesn't mean we can't hang out once in a while, but this is who I am now. A man of God who seeks to do his will. You know I'm always here for you, Patty."

"I know. See you at work, buddy."

The next person in line was Mike Shawnee. Shawnee extended his bear paw out and engulfed Dave's hand.

"Nice job David."

"Thank you, sir."

"You looked good up there. Natural. You should think about doing this when you retire."

He laughed. "Maybe. I'm really glad you came."

"I am too. Maybe I'll make this more of a habit. Like once a month or something."

"We'd love to have you sit with us if you're serious."

"I said maybe. We'll see."

"I'll buy you lunch afterward."

"Hey, now I can get behind that. See you at the shop, Davie."

"See you, Mike."

Before he moved on, Shawnee wrapped him up and gave him a bear hug.

"Devine Dave the preacher. That has a nice ring to it."

He smiled and moved on. Lisa was next. She came in and gave him a hug.

"Great job Dave."

"Thanks, but I was just telling a story that's familiar to me. I didn't prepare or deliver some big sermon."

"Yeah, but that's how it came off. You look very comfortable on that stage." She leaned in and whispered in his ear, "And very handsome, I might add."

"Shucks miss. You're going to make me blush." They shared a laugh. "I'm so glad you came. Glad that all of you came."

"It's okay, they can't hear you. I know I'm your favorite." She smiled. "You have been a big help to me over my career. Thank you so much Dave. Seeing you up there today, hearing the passion in your voice, it took me back to when you were training me. I could see the pure love in your eyes for law enforcement. I saw that today too. Really, every time you talk about God. I have to admit that you have me really intrigued."

"Anytime you want to talk, I'm there. It's the best decision you'll ever make."

"I heard Mike. Maybe I'll tag along with him once a month if he makes this a habit."

"I would love that."

She gave him another hug and then moved on. He shook a few more hands before the line was done and then walked over to where his group was hanging out.

"Anybody want to go grab some coffee and dessert?"

Rita spoke up quickly, "Absolutely." She walked over and gave him a hug and a kiss on the cheek. "Great job Dave."

"Thanks Rita."

Javier came over and hugged his partner.

"I'm proud of you, Dave. It takes guts to get up in front of people and tell your story. Man, when God entered your life, you didn't look back. Pure passion. You're an inspiration buddy." He looked over at his wife and then back at Dave. "Yeah, we gotta go get that dessert now. You put it in my wife's head and started a countdown."

Dave laughed. "Let's go."

The Kings congratulated him but took a raincheck on dessert. Pastor Dunkirk and the family took a raincheck as well. Gina went with Shannon so they could talk on the way, and Kurtis hopped in with Dave and the kids. On the ride there, Kurtis asked to sit up front with Dave.

"Was it tough standing in front of all of those people?" he asked.

"At first it was, but I prayed God would give me strength and speak through me, and he did."

He thought about that for a moment.

"Cool. I thought you did a good job. You made eye contact, spoke well, and even through in some humor."

Dave smiled, "All positive. Do you have questions for me about anything I said?"

"It must have been tough for you when your dad died. You seemed very close. But it wasn't your fault."

"I didn't see it that way for a long time."

"If it's one thing I've learned in my fifteen years on this earth, it's that life just happens."

Dave smiled.

"That's a wise observation, Kurtis. Life does just happen to all of us. But it's a lot easier to live when we have Jesus in it."

"I'm getting that. Do they have ice cream at this place?"

"They do. The best ice cream in the world."

"Awesome."

Marc chimed in from the back.

"It's the same ice cream everyone else has."

Dave looked at him in the rearview mirror.

"Buzzkill."

"Yeah. Buzzkill," Kurtis repeated with a smile.

4

Farrells was a mega dessert place that had anything and everything you could want. The conversation was sparse when the dessert was in front of them. The kids finished first, of course, and went to the giant attached arcade on the other side of the restaurant. Shannon asked Dave about Butch.

"Did you find anything on him?"

"Oh shoot. I was checking on Monday when LEIN went down. I knew I would be back on Tuesday night, so I figured I would just check it then. I called in sick. I'm sorry, Shannon."

"It's okay. One more dinner with him isn't going to hurt."

Gina was talking to Rita, so Javier was listening to Dave and Shannon. He stared at both of them with a lost look on his face. Dave looked at Shannon and she gave him a nod. He explained the situation to Javier, but more of a reader's digest version.

"So, Butch is actually Kurtis's dad?"

"He is. From a terrible decision I made many years ago."

"He sounds like a piece of work. All he does is take."

"That's exactly who he is."

"Does Kurtis know you're supposed to have dinner with him on Friday night?"

"No. I haven't told him yet. I suppose I'll talk to him about it when we get home. He's not going to be happy, but hopefully he will understand."

"I don't work tomorrow, but I'm going in while Gina is at work and the kids are at school to check his LEIN work." Dave stated.

"It's okay Dave. He'll do something stupid eventually and probably have to leave town."

"Maybe, but in the meantime, he's going to wreak havoc on both of your lives. That's not right."

"I'll do my best to keep him at arm's length. Maybe he'll get bored and move on."

"I'm going to go check, anyway."

"Let me know If I can help in any way?" Javier asked.

"Thanks," she responded.

The kids returned, so they stopped talking about Butch. They finished up, paid the check and went their separate ways home. On the way home, Shannon told Kurtis that butch was coming over for dinner on Friday. He wasn't happy. He told her they just agreed to put space between them for a while, and she was going back on her word. She had no choice but to fill him in on what was going on. That Butch all but blackmailed her into a relationship, and that she had now enlisted the help of Dave.

"He did that? He stopped them in the street to fake ask for directions to scare them?"

"Yes."

"And he said he would hurt them if you didn't agree to let him come over and see us?"

"Yes."

"That's not right, mom. It's mean."

"That's why I didn't mention him all these years. He's not a good man, Kurtis."

"We don't need him. We've lived this long without him."

"I know, but we need to play nice on Friday. Do you think you can do that?"

"I guess I have to. But I won't like it."

"You don't have to. We just need to buy time until we can figure out what to do."

"Okay mom."

She smiled and ran her hand through his hair. "Thanks, sweetie."

5

Dave sat at the end of the bed while Gina brushed her teeth.

"This guy's bad news, Gina. I can feel it in my bones, and I dropped the ball on checking on him."

She came walking in from the bathroom.

"You didn't drop the ball on anything, Dave. You're doing all you can for that family. If there's something there, you'll find It. Do not beat yourself up. Let's talk about tonight."

"What about tonight?"

"You were great up there. How did it feel?"

"It was scary at first, and then exhilarating." He smiled and grabbed her hand. "All the anxiety completely left me when I started talking about the Lord. I asked him to speak through me, and He did, or at least calmed my nerves enough so that I could speak."

"That's awesome. You looked very natural at the podium. And very handsome."

"I know. Shawnee and Lisa told me so."

"Shawnee called you handsome?"

"No, but he said I looked like a natural up there."

"Do I need to have a talk with Lisa?"

She raised an eyebrow. He laughed.

"She's no threat to my one and only. Besides, she said it to be nice."

"Okay, but I'm going to keep my eye on her."

"Dave Jackson, playboy extraordinaire. I don't think so."

She laughed, sat down, and placed her head on his shoulder.

"How are you feeling?"

He paused. "Good."

She pulled her head off of his shoulder and looked at him.

"You paused."

"I didn't pause. I was clearing my throat."

"Silently. No, you paused. What's wrong?"

"Nothing. Just a little extra pain lately. Nothing to get excited about."

"You said you would tell me when..."

"When I had to take two pills."

"Are you there?"

"Not yet. I'll tell you."

He had only taken two twice so far. Dave wasn't even sure he was there yet full time. He would wait just a little longer to see if that was the case, but he didn't want to alarm her right now.

"Don't hold back on me because you know it will upset me. We're in this together. Please?"

"I won't. It's me and you, babe."

She cried.

"I don't want you to die, Dave. I need you here with me."

"If it were up to me, I would stay right here with you, but it isn't. We have to accept His will. If I hadn't gotten this diagnosis, would I have given my life to Him? I don't know. But since I have, I have felt reborn. I'm sorry, this is how it has to be. You and those kids mean everything to me, but your work here isn't done. We might be separated for a few years, but by His grace we will be in eternity together."

"That's the only comfort getting me through this." She managed a smile. "I know I asked you before, but are you scared to die?"

He faced her, ran his hands through her hair, and held her face up to his as he looked into her eyes.

"You can't scare me with heaven."

They wrapped their arms around each other and held on tight. She burrowed her head into his chest and he laid his cheek on top of her head and they cried together.

"Can we lie down and fall asleep like this?" she asked.

They pulled the sheets back, turned off the lights and laid down. He pulled her in close as she nestled into him and they laid there in silence. There was no pain that night. The last thing he remembered before waking up in the morning was thanking God for this beautiful woman.

Chapter 26

Thursday—September 16, 2010

Dave woke up with an intense pain in his stomach. He made it to the bathroom just in time to vomit blood into the toilet. It wasn't a lot, but it was painful. He stood up and surveyed the area. It was in the bowl and nowhere else. He flushed and everything looked fine. He walked over to the nightstand and swallowed two pills. Dave made his way down to the kitchen. He gulped down two glasses of water and then had a seat at the table. No bible in hand. He bowed his head and prayed.

"Lord. Thank you for allowing me to spend more time with my family. Please be with us all as we go through this together." Some tears fell from his eyes. "Thank you. Amen."

Dave sat at the table drinking coffee, lost in his thoughts all morning. He took the time to map out a plan. He would work one last weekend. Law enforcement was his passion. One of the true loves in his life. He would dedicate one more weekend to her before leaving to spend the rest of his days with his family. The true loves of his life. He would spend whatever time he had left with them. Dave just hoped that most of it would be quality time. He would tell Gina when she came home from work on Monday, and they would tell the kids together that afternoon. From there, they would figure out how to tell everyone else. He would apologize to her for not telling her about the amusement park incident, and for not telling her he had been taking two pills for a few days now. She would forgive him. He had it all mapped out in his head. He looked at the clock. It was 1:30 p.m. He decided he should go take a nap. He walked upstairs and laid down. He was awakened at 4:00 p.m. by the gentle caress of his wife's touch on his forehead.

"Wake up, sleepyhead."

He smiled.

"Hey babe."

"Hey."

"I woke up early this morning, so I laid back down around one thirty to take a nap."

"Naps are good," she smiled.

"How was your day?"

"My day was good. Nothing out of the ordinary, just good."

"Good. The kids home?"

"They are. I think Marc's playing guitar outside and Melissa is watching Tv and talking on the phone."

"Sounds about right."

They both laughed. She kissed his forehead.

"I wanted to run something by you."

"Okay."

He sat up and cleared his throat. She walked over and opened the blinds. The light filled the room and had him covering his eyes for a moment.

"Too bright?" She asked.

"No, leave it. I'll adjust in a second."

She came over and sat next to him.

"What do you think about Shannon and Kurtis staying in the apartment above the garage?"

He smiled.

"I actually thought about that last night while we were having dessert. I was going to talk to you about it sometime today."

"We really share one mind."

"Scary, right?"

She laughed. "Were you able to make it to work today to check on her ex?"

He rubbed his eyes and grimaced.

"I don't know what's wrong with my brain. I completely lost track of time and forgot today."

"It's okay. You can just do it when you go to work tomorrow."

"I'll call her later and let her know."

She leaned over and kissed him on the forehead again. "I'm going to head downstairs, grab a cup of tea and hang out with Marc outside if you want to join us?"

"I do, but I'm going to grab a shower first."

"Okay. Bring your guitar. I want to hear a good old-fashioned father and son jam session."

"I shall do just that, my love."

She watched as he walked into their bathroom and shut the door. She heard the shower spring to life. Gina stood by the door for a few seconds until she heard him singing in the shower.

Dave and Marc played while Gina and Melissa listened and talked. Eventually, they moved the session inside, and Melissa played the piano while they jammed on the guitar. Gina recorded it on her phone and played it back for Dave later.

"Wow. We sound good," Dave commented.

"I know. Who would have thought?" Gina responded.

"Man, that girl can really play the piano."

"I told you. She's good."

"Let's go show the kids."

They walked into the living room, where both kids were watching TV. Gina sat in between them.

"Hey guys, watch this."

They muted the TV and watched as they rocked out.

"Oh my gosh," Melissa stated.

"I know, right?" Gina responded.

"We should go on tour," Marc commented.

Dave laughed.

"We sound pretty darn good. Man, you guys can rock."

"Don't sell yourself short, old man. You can still jam pretty good yourself." Marc responded.

Gina looked over at Dave at busted out laughing.

"Your son just called you an old man."

"You'll be here someday, boy."

Déjà vu.

"But it won't be for a long time," Marc smiled.

They all laughed. Dave walked into the kitchen and Gina followed. The kids resumed watching TV.

"Tacos for dinner tonight?" She asked.

"That sounds good. Let me call Shannon really quick to let her know I dropped the ball again, and then I'll help you."

"I bought plenty of ground beef if you just want to call and invite them over for dinner? We can talk to her about the apartment as well."

"Okay then. That's what I'll do."

She accepted their invitation, and she also told him she had news of her own. They settled on 6:30 p.m. for dinner. At 6:25 p.m. they pulled into the driveway. Kurtis barely waited for the car to stop before he got out. Shannon came into the kitchen and Dave yelled at the kids to wash up. Dinner would be ready in fifteen minutes. The ladies sat at the table while Dave cut up the tomatoes and washed the lettuce.

"How did you train him to do that?" Shannon asked.

"A lot of years of work," Gina responded, laughing.

"Hey! I pull my weight around here," Dave stated. "I'm going to change the subject. Shannon, you said you had some news to share?"

"I do. Butch is gone."

"What? Just like that? What happened?" Dave asked.

"Butch called this morning and said that he had a deal brewing in Texas, and he had to go. He said that it was an opportunity to make some big money and he couldn't pass it up. He told me to tell Kurtis that he would try to get back here this year, but it might not be until next year, and to tell him he will miss him and see him as soon as he can."

"Well, isn't that a pleasant coincidence?" Gina stated.

"Yeah, too nice. Out of the blue, just like that?" he snapped his fingers.

"Yep. That's the Butch McCabe way?"

"It doesn't make sense. The guy comes here to connect with his son, threatens you to stay in his life by taking a chance on messing with a cop's family, and then poof. Gone for a deal in Texas."

"Butch has always gone where the money is. It takes priority over everything else in his life."

"Do me a favor. Continue to keep your head on a swivel. If you think you see him, call the PD right away. Do you remember what kind of truck he drove? The color? The license plate number or state?"

She closed her eyes for a moment to think.

"It was a rusted out faded blue truck."

They turned to see Kurtis standing there.

"How much of that did you hear, baby?" Shannon asked.

"All of it," He answered. "Marc had to go to the bathroom, so I came down to see if I could help with anything. So, Butch just left?"

"He did. I'm so sorry you..."

"He couldn't even say goodbye himself? I know he isn't a good person, but it doesn't take much to say goodbye to someone."

"He's just no good Kurtis...."

He turned and ran. She stood to go after him.

"I'll go talk to him, Shannon." Dave stated.

Kurtis ran out of the front door and onto the porch. He sat down at the top of the steps. Dave came out, closed the door behind him, and sat down next to him.

"Are you okay Kurt?"

"No. No, I'm not. My whole life has been just me and my mom, and I got used to that. She picked other dudes over me, she was drunk or high ninety-five percent of the time, and even though I know she loves me, she always made me feel second best. And then, out of the blue, she wants to be a mom. It was right after my best friend got murdered, but she started." He wiped his eyes. "And that's another thing. They murdered Ronnie in the middle of all of this. So, she buckles down and starts doing really well. She kicks the habits almost cold turkey, but now I feel like we have an actual mother and son relationship. And then here comes Butch, right on cue. He rolls into town and gives me hope that I just might have a dad who cares about me. Butch turns out to be a total creep. He uses false names, deals with shady people, threatens my mom and people that I care about, and then just disappears. What's wrong with me, Officer Jackson? Why can't I just have a normal life?"

Dave wrapped his right arm around him and pulled him in close. Kurtis hugged him and buried his head into Dave's chest, but it didn't contain the noise. He cried hard and loud. Dave sat there, holding him close, letting him get it all out.. Shannon and Gina looked out the front window and saw them sitting there. Shannon sat down on the couch and cried. Gina sat next to her, rubbing her back, assuring her that everything was going to be alright. The kids came down to see what was going on with dinner and Gina just mouthed, "Give us a minute." The kids went back upstairs. When the crying died down, Dave found his composure and spoke.

"Kurtis. I know it hurts now, but it will get better, and do you know how I know that?"

"How?" Came the muffled reply.

"Because you're a fighter. All those years, your mom was going through something, something that she couldn't even explain. You stuck right by her side. You were there for her. Loving her and taking care of her. And Ronnie's death had nothing to do with you. He knew the risks of what he was doing. I know that doesn't make it hurt any less, but he chose his path. And Butch has been the way he is his whole life. Before you were even born, he was a conman and a swindler. Some people rebound in life, and some refuse to see the writing on the wall. They chase power, fame, and fortune instead of love and happiness. They have a distorted view of things, and often their obsession ends in terrible choices that hurt the ones they love." He pulled Kurtis away from him and looked him in the eyes. "You're a fighter."

"What do I fight for, Officer Jackson? Because it doesn't seem like I'm winning."

"You fight for what's right. You fight for the ones you love, and you fight for a better life."

"All of those things are worth fighting for."

"Yes. But many people give up when the going gets tough. You don't. You didn't take the Ronnie rout, or give everything up just to be with your dad. Kurtis, you use your head. You persevered. The love for your mom outshined all the bad things you could have done."

"She's, my mom."

He hugged Kurtis and squeezed tight. Kurtis started tapping on his back and he eased up.

"Sorry."

"So, what now?"

"Your mom starts a new job on Monday. You still have school. I guess life goes on."

Kurtis smiled. "I guess it does."

"Now you have a support team to fall back on. Make sure you use them."

"I will. Thanks Officer Jackson."

Dave smiled. "You hungry?"

"Starving."

"Let's go destroy some tacos."

They stood and turned toward the door. As they walked into the house, Shannon stood and walked over to Kurtis. He gave her a hug. Dave looked at Gina and whispered. "Let's go get everything ready." They turned and went into the kitchen. She told him to go upstairs and grab the kids while she prepped. He went up and told the kids that dinner was now ready and explained to them that Kurtis and his mom were just having a moment earlier. When they all came downstairs, Gina, Shannon, and Kurtis were already sitting at the table, ready to go. The feeding frenzy began.

2

Friday, September 17, 2010

Dave woke up around 1:00 p.m. and made his way downstairs to the kitchen. He kept Gina awake until midnight talking about the past, watching old movies, and eating junk food. She finally told him she had to go to bed so she wouldn't be too tired to work in the morning. She gave him a kiss and went upstairs to bed. Dave grabbed his bible and made his way over to the lazy boy. He flipped to the Book of John, chapter ten. He had highlighted verses twenty-two to thirty.

"'Now it was the Feast of Dedication in Jerusalem, and it was winter. And Jesus walked in the temple, in Solomon's porch. Then the Jews surrounded Him and said to Him, "How long do You keep us in doubt?

If You are the Christ, tell us plainly." Jesus answered them, "I told you, and you do not believe. The works that I do in My Father's name, they bear witness of Me. But you do not believe, because you are not of My sheep, as I said to you. My sheep hear My voice, and I know them, and they follow Me. And I give them eternal life, and they shall never perish; neither shall anyone snatch them out of My hand. My Father, who has given *them* to Me, is greater than all; and no one is able to snatch *them* out of My Father's hand. I and *My* Father are one.'"

He smiled and whispered. "'And I give them eternal life, and they shall never perish; neither shall anyone snatch them out of My hand.'" His heart and soul rejoiced as he repeated those words. Jesus would not let anyone take him. He belonged to the Lord, and that comforted him. He closed the Word and sat in his chair, looking up at the ceiling. Dave thought about his life over the years. He could see every detail. His childhood. His marriage. His children. Dave got out of the chair and walked over to the closet. He opened it and rummaged through the top until he found what he was looking for. He took three photo albums over to the chair and sat back down. Dave went through all of them, page by page, smiling at each memory. As he closed the last book and sat it on the table next to him, he smiled because he knew everything was going to be alright. He looked over at the clock. It was 3:45 a.m. The time had just flown by. He turned off all the lights and went upstairs to bed.

He swallowed two pills and poured himself a cup of coffee. He wanted to go for a run, but that wasn't happening. Dave walked out onto the front porch and stood at the top step. He sipped his coffee and scanned the neighborhood. This was a wonderful street. The neighbors were good people who took care of their property and mutually respected each other. God had blessed them with living here. Dave knew the chaos that ensued when you didn't get along with your neighbors. He spent the day putzing around the house, cleaning up here and there, reading a little, and playing his guitar. When the kids got home from school, he helped them with their homework, well, the best he could, and then they watched TV until Gina got home. They all pitched in on dinner that night and enjoyed a nice family meal before he had to go to work.

The first thing that Dave did after loading up his squad car and grabbing a cup of coffee was head to the Torres Inn to check the status of one, Mitch Arnold. He rolled into the hotel lot around 7:20 p.m. He parked and went into the office. An older woman, in her early sixties, came from the back and greeted him.

"Well, hello their officer. What can I do for you today?"

"I was checking to see if you had a guest here by the name of Mitch Arnold?"

"Mitch was quite the popular guest."

"Was?"

"He left yesterday. Looked kind of in a hurry."

"Did he say why he was leaving?"

"Some opportunity. He's paid up through the weekend. Told me to give his credit to the gal next door."

"Do you keep a record of their vehicle registration by chance? Make and model? License plate number?"

"Heavens no. He drove a beat-up old truck. I couldn't tell you whether it was Ford or Chevy, let alone the license plate number or state it was from?"

"Do you have a copy of his ID?"

"I never saw it. The other gal checked him in when he arrived."

"And when was that?"

She opened the book and found his name. "Looks like, August 14th."

"The guys been here for a month? Did anyone see ID?"

"You'd have to ask her. He never used a card. All cash."

"What room did he stay in?"

"Let me check the computer." She turned to her computer and started clicking away at the keyboard. "Room 165."

"And that's..."

"Toward the back on the right."

"Thank you. Oh, what was the name of the 'gal' next door?"

"Erica. She's in 166."

"I appreciate your help."

She smiled. "We always like to cooperate with law enforcement."

He smiled and walked out the door. He drove to where she told him Butch had been and parked in front of door 165. There was no sign of the old pickup truck. He got out of his cruiser and walked up to the door, and knocked. Nobody answered. He turned to walk back to his car when the door to room 166 opened and a female came out. It startled her to see him.

"I'm sorry. I didn't mean to startle you."

She laughed, "That's okay, I just didn't expect to see anyone there." She lit a cigarette. "Are you looking for Mitch?"

"Yes."

"He's gone. Packed up and moved out yesterday." He stood there without saying a word. "He left in a hurry. I don't really know why."

"He didn't mention any kind of 'Opportunity.'"

She laughed. "No. He seemed spooked."

"How well did you know him?"

"Saw him every day for a month."

"Do you live here at the motel?"

"Kind of. They give me a better rate because of it. The owner says he enjoys having me around."

She took a drag. Dave smiled.

"Do you know why Mitch was here?"

"He was in town to reconnect with his ex-wife and kid."

"Do you know where Mitch was from?"

"All over, I guess. He didn't really say. He had a bit of an accent. Southern."

"He didn't say where he was going, did he?"

"No. Just that it was nice knowing me, but he had to split."

"Do you remember what kind of truck he drove? Or where the plates were from?"

"An old beater of a truck. North Dakota, I think."

"Thank you..."

"Erica."

"Thank you, Erica."

"Is he in some kind of trouble or something?"

"Something."

He smiled at her and got back into his squad car. He backed up and drove away. She waved. She couldn't be over twenty-one or twenty-two. Another wayward soul searching for acceptance. He drove around the complex looking for the truck, just in case, but he didn't find it. He eventually left and went back into his own city. The rest of the night was pretty tame. Dave and Javier had a coffee here and there. He made a few traffic stops and then made it back to the PD around 6:50 a.m. He checked all of his equipment in and then went downstairs to the locker room. The crew decompressed, and just before he left, Javier told him they had enough people for them to partner up tonight. He got home around 7:20 a.m. and was out by 7:30.

Chapter 27

Saturday—September 18, 2010

Dave's eyes popped open at 1:30 p.m. on the dot. He laid there for a moment, listening. It was perfectly quiet. He felt refreshed and well rested. There was no tossing or turning. No dreaming. Just sleep. He put on his robe and his slippers and went downstairs. The house was empty. He checked his phone. No missed calls or texts. His family had disappeared. He sat down at the kitchen table and opened his bible. Before he read, he got up, poured himself a cup of coffee, and then checked his phone again. Nothing. He sat back down and opened his bible to the book of Acts. His attention was drawn to a verse he highlighted and put an asterisk with the word "hallelujah" written by it. It was chapter four and verse twelve. "Salvation is found in no one else, for there is no other name under heaven given to mankind by which we must be saved." He smiled and whispered, "amen." Before he could read any further, he heard the front door open and the voices of his family. Gina walked into the kitchen and saw him sitting there.

"You're up," she smiled.

"I am. And where has my family been?"

Before she could answer, Marc and Melissa came walking in behind her. The aroma of breakfast was with them.

"Hey dad," Marc stated.

"Good morning, dad," Melissa stated.

"Hello my wonderful children. Do you come bearing breakfast?"

"We do," Gina answered. "We went to B&G and grabbed some stuffed French toast, applewood bacon, home fries, and, of course, some biscuits and gravy."

"I love you all so much." He smiled and closed his bible.

"You can finish reading. We'll eat when you're done." Gina responded.

"Lord knows with those smells I could not concentrate, and that would be an injustice to Him. We need to eat now so I can thank Him later."

"Amen brother." Marc responded.

They all laughed. Within seconds, there were plates and silverware on the table. Less than twenty minutes later, all that was left of the feast were Styrofoam containers and wrappers. Not a morsel remained. They were all sitting back in their chairs, rubbing their stomachs. He smiled.

"Simply awesome."

Gina laughed. "Wow! I don't think anyone came up for air."

"What good is air when you can shove bacon in your mouth," Melissa responded.

Dave pointed to her. "That's my girl."

Marc just sat back with his head resting on the back of the chair, looking up at the ceiling.

"I'm never going to eat again."

They all laughed again.

"Alright, you guys go relax on the couch. I'll clean up," Dave offered.

Before he could recant his statement, Marc and Melissa were out of the room. Gina looked at him and smiled.

"I don't think I've ever seen our kids move that fast."

Dave laughed. "Even when Marc was running track."

He walked over and grabbed the trash can. She started clearing plates from the table.

"How are you feeling today?"

He thought about it for a moment and realized that he actually felt great. There was no pain. He felt like his old self.

"I actually feel fantastic. How are you today?"

"I'm good." She smiled. "I'm glad you feel good."

He looked at her. "You know I meant what I said when I said that I would clean up. Go. Relax. I got this."

"Nope. Were a team. Even in clean up duty."

"Your way too good for me."

"I know," she smirked.

He smiled. They cleaned the table, and she loaded the dishwasher while he took out the trash. Dave put the bag in the can and stopped. He drew in a deep breath and then exhaled. He coughed.

"I probably should have done that away from the trash cans."

He just felt good. It was a pleasant change. He walked back into the house and Gina had already joined the kids in the living room.

"What's for dinner?" Marc asked.

"So much for 'I'm never going to eat again.' I don't know. What do you think, my love?" Dave asked.

"I am making a pot roast."

"Perfect," Dave responded.

It was one of his favorites. He loved her pot roast. It was not only so flavorful and good, but there was always enough left over to take for lunch. Melissa loved it too, and she reached over and gave her dad a high five.

"Cool," Marc responded. "I'm going upstairs to take a nap."

Melissa followed him up the stairs, phone in hand, already talking to one of her friends.

"Looks like it's just you and me, amigo," Gina stated.

"The two musketeers." He smiled. "I would call in sick tonight, but Javier and I finally have a chance to partner together. It's been a while."

"I like when you two partner. It makes me feel better about you going to work. Besides, Patty is coming over later and we're going to have some coffee, dessert, and girl talk."

"I'm sorry. I have to miss that."

"I'm sure you are."

"What are the kids doing?"

"Patty's bringing them. Frank has bowling tonight."

"I wish I had bowling."

"No, you don't. You hate bowling."

"I never said I hated it. I just said that I would rather watch paint dry."

They both laughed.

"Do you two have hijinks planned for tonight?"

"No. We'll handle our runs, make a few stops, and catch up."

"I don't mind that plan."

She threw her feet up onto the couch and laid her head on his lap. He ran his fingers through her hair over and over. Within a matter of minutes, she was out.

2

The day moved quick. Before dinner, the whole family went through those old photo albums, smiling and laughing at every page. The roast tasted amazing, as usual, and afterward he had some time to hang out with them on the couch and watch some TV. He took a shower and got dressed for work around 6:20 p.m.

"Usually, you're out the door by six to work out before your shift. Running a little late today, or just getting lazy?" Marc asked.

"Not at all," he answered. "I just felt like spending a little extra time with my family."

"And were happy you did," Gina stated as she gave him a hug.

He gave them a hug and a kiss and walked out the door. Gina followed him out onto the porch and gave him another hug.

"Stay warm. There's a chill in the air tonight."

"I will. Have fun swapping gossip with Patty."

She laughed. "It's not gossip. We're just talking."

"Sure," he said with a hint of sarcasm.

"See you in the morning."

"You bet."

She pulled away from him to go into the house, and he pulled her back in. He held her face as he kissed her passionately. They separated, and he kissed the tip of her nose and then pulled her in for another hug.

"Why David Jackson? What's gotten into you?" She asked in a playful southern voice.

"Why, I reckon you Miss Gina," he answered in his most southernly gentleman's voice. "I just want you to know that I know how very lucky I am."

"Ditto," she answered.

"I love you."

"I love you too."

With that, he walked down the steps and to his truck.

Chapter 28

Dave and Javier started the shift at DD. The inside was empty, but the drive through was hopping. People getting an after-dinner donut, or a head start on their breakfast for the morning. They often sat here and debated life's deepest problems. Will the Wings win the cup? Can the Tigers shake the cobwebs off of their 1984 World Series win and do it again? Are the Pistons in a rebuild, and will the Detroit Lions ever win another playoff game? But tonight, the conversation took a different route.

"What's your favorite book of the bible?" Javier asked him.

"John." He answered without hesitation.

"Why John?"

"Because out of the four gospels, it truly focuses on who Jesus is. In chapter three, Jesus specifically describes the way to gain eternal life through Him."

"Do you have a favorite verse?"

"I have many. One that is always at the forefront of my mind is in the book of James, chapter one, verse twenty-two. 'But be doers of the word, and not hearers only, deceiving yourselves.'" He smiled. "Short and sweet. You?"

"Hebrews. Paul gives us a blueprint for living the Christian life."

"What verse sticks out to you?"

"Chapter thirteen verse eight. 'Jesus Christ is the same yesterday, today, and forever.'"

"Amen brother."

They clinked coffees like he had just given a toast. Javier smiled.

"Did you ever think that you would sit in uniform at a booth in DD talking about the bible over sports?"

"I did not." He smiled and shook his head. "But seriously, do you think the Lions will ever win a Super Bowl in your lifetime?"

Javier laughed. "I'm not sure they'll win one in my unborn kid's lifetime."

They both started laughing.

"Favorite Old Testament character?" Dave asked.

"There are so many to choose from. But I have to go with David."

"Yeah, he's certainly top three. Very strong name."

"I knew that was coming," He smiled, "who else you got?"

"Joseph."

"Oh yeah. Good choice. The epitome of faith, wisdom, and forgiveness."

"Don't forget perseverance."

"That too."

"Hey, what do you think about..."

Dispatch interrupted them, "616."

"616," Dave answered.

"38012 Chester, 38012 Chester, the wife states that her husband just pushed her."

"616 on the way."

"She'll be waiting on the porch for officers. There are no weapons registered at the location and CAD shows that we have been there one other time for a DV in 2006."

"616 copy."

"I'll show you on the way at 1953 hrs."

"Well partner, it's time to get to work," Dave stated as he took a sip.

"Ain't nothing to it but to do it." He responded.

They stood up and made their way toward the door. They both deposited their cups into the trash can and waved to the worker at the counter, letting her know they would be back sometime tonight.

2

After dinner, Kurtis and Shannon watched a movie. It had been a long day, and she was finding it difficult to stay awake. He watched as her head bobbed forward and she caught herself from falling off of the couch several times.

"Mom. We can watch this some other time. You should go to bed."

"No honey, I'm alright."

"Mom. It's okay."

"Are you sure?"

"Positive."

"I just feel bad because it's a Saturday night and we should do something."

"You're tired. No big deal. I'll just watch some TV and go to bed later."

She was afraid that he would leave the house while she was sleeping and get into trouble. Things had been good lately, but sometimes old habits die hard. He and Ronnie used to hang out on the weekends by Pops downtown and do God knows what. She assumed they got into trouble, but she was always too high to know, or even care. She didn't want him reverting to those habits, even though Ronnie wasn't around anymore. Shannon feared he would find a new friend, another one that would try to entice him to sell.

"Okay, sweetie." She looked at the clock. It was 9:15 p.m. "Don't stay up too late. We have church in the morning."

"I won't."

She stood and gave him a kiss on top of the head.

"Goodnight."

"Goodnight mom."

She went into her bedroom and shut the door. He flipped through the channels, looking for something to watch. He found an old western. Kurtis remembered Dave told him how he and his dad used to watch all the old spaghetti westerns together. It was kind of their thing. He remembered some of the actor's names that Dave talked about. Most notably, John Wayne and Clint Eastwood. Right when he flipped it to the channel, he saw, 'Staring Clint Eastwood.' He waited to see what the title was. It was, *The Outlaw Josey Wales*. Ironically enough, Dave said that this was his favorite western. He put the remote down and settled in. He fell asleep halfway through. When he woke up, it was 1:27 a.m. The TV was on some infomercial. He sat up on the couch and rubbed his eyes. He walked into the kitchen to get some chips. There were none. He looked for something else of the junk variety. Nothing. There was a ten-dollar bill on the end table by the front door. He looked at the clock again. If he peddled fast enough, he could make it to Pops by the time they closed. A bag of chips, pop, and candy bar was within reach. He grabbed the ten and was out the door.

3

Dave was just finishing up the report on their second domestic violence arrest of the night. Javier had finished processing the suspect and was sitting in the command center talking to the sergeant on duty. Dave looked at his watch. It was 1:53 a.m. He stood up and stretched. Time for another coffee. He was getting ready to walk around the corner to the command center when his phone rang. This couldn't be good. He answered.

"Hello."

"Dave, he's gone."

"What? Who is gone?"

"Kurtis. I woke up and came out to see if he was still watching TV, and he's nowhere to be found."

She was frantic.

"Is he outside on the porch?"

"No."

"Did he leave a note?"

"No. I know he's back downtown. You don't think he's selling, do you?"

"Just calm down Shannon. Kurt's a good kid. He never did that, and I don't think he would start now."

"What else could it be?"

"I don't know, but me and my partner will head down and try to find him."

"Should I jump in my car and..."

"No. You stay home in case he comes back. I'll look for him."

"Okay. Please let me know when you find him."

"I will."

"Thanks Dave."

"Your welcome, and don't think the worst. He might have just gotten the munchies or something."

She looked over at the table by the door.

"The money is gone."

"What money."

"I left a ten-dollar bill on the table. Maybe he took it to get some food."

"That's probably what happened. Where do you think he might have gone?"

"The only place open would be downtown. The stores around here close at midnight now."

"Okay, then he probably went to Pops. I'll go check it out."

"Thanks Dave. I'm sorry to bother you."

"It's no bother. I'll call you soon."

He hung up the phone. He hoped he was right. Kurtis had a good heart, but with all that had happened to him recently, poor decisions were possible. He walked around the corner and grabbed Javier. He filled him in on the way downtown.

Kurtis came walking out of Pops at 1:57 a.m. with a little brown bag. He had a Mountain Dew, Chili Cheese Fritos, and an extra-large Pay Day bar. He parked his bike in the alley next to the store. The same alley where Ronnie was murdered. He set the bag next to his bike and walked halfway down the alley. He closed his eyes and took in a deep breath. Kurtis exhaled slowly as he pictured the scene in his head. Ronnie standing there with a knife in his chest. All for a couple of rocks. They hadn't found the killer yet. As far as he knew, they didn't even have any leads. He opened his eyes. Some tears rolled down. There was some movement to his right. He backed up when the man walking toward him spoke.

"Kurtis. Come here, son."

It was Butch.

"Butch?"

"Yeah, kiddo. It's dad."

"You're not my dad."

"It's okay kid. I just want to talk. Please."

Kurtis stopped backing away.

"I don't think we really have anything to talk about."

"Just give me a chance to explain. Then I'll leave you and your mom alone. I promise."

"Explain."

"Sometimes adults do things that are..."

Kurtis cut him off. "Criminal?"

"Technically, I guess. Yes."

"Why did you say you were leaving?"

"Mrs. Spader told me you stopped by. And she told me about the conversation you two had. I knew I had to leave at that point, because your police friend would probably come looking for me. I couldn't be a father to you from prison."

"From prison? What did you do?"

"I've done some less than honorable things in my life. That's why I came here. For a new start with you and your mom."

"I heard you. You came here to get money out of my grandparents. You were never going to stay."

"Kurtis, you heard wrong. I came here to be the father you needed. Maybe you and I could go somewhere and start over together. You've had it rough too. We could make a new start as father and son."

"What about my mom?"

"She can come if she wants." He was so focused on the words Butch said that he hadn't realized Butch was still moving slowly toward him. "I'm parked at the other end of the alley, kid. We can just get in the truck and drive. You want to be with your dad, right?"

"No. You're an evil man. I don't ever want to..."

Butch lunged forward and grabbed onto his arm. Kurtis tried to pull away, but it was no use. Butch was strong. He dragged the kid down the alley.

"Let's go. I know what's best for you. I'm your father."

As Javier drove by Pops, they could see that the lights were off and the store was closed. Dave had his window rolled down, and as they approached the opening of the alley, he heard someone yell, "Help!"

"That's Kurtis," he stated.

They looked down the alley to see a man pulling a boy toward the other end. As Dave was jumping out of the squad car, he shouted to Javier, "Drive around to the other end and cut him off!" Javier sped off down the street as Dave ran toward the figures. As he approached them, he could clearly see that it was Kurtis being pulled by an unknown man. Butch looked up to see Dave coming, and just as he let Kurtis go, Dave tackled him to the ground. Kurtis fell back and watched as the two men wrestled. They both got to their feet and Dave grabbed onto Butch's shirt and drove him into a wall nearby. Dave launched a forearm into Butch's chin that sent him stumbling backwards, falling to the ground. Dave started toward Butch again, but he raised his hands into the air and shouted.

"I'm done, I've had enough."

Dave stopped and looked down at him. Butch had propped himself up against the wall. His face was in his hands. He was a beaten man. Dave looked back at Kurtis.

"Kurt, you alright?"

All it took was a second. There was no planning involved. Just a single solitary second of losing focus. Twenty years of training undone. Butch used the wall as a springboard, lunged forward, and planted the knife on the inside of Dave's right thigh. He felt the blade enter his leg and immediately turned toward Butch again. He looked down to see Butch laying on the ground by his leg, and the knife firmly resting in his thigh. Dave stumbled backwards with a look of disbelief and shock on his face. Butch sprang to his feet and took off down the alley toward his truck. Dave grabbed his mic.

"Officer down radio."

He ripped the knife out of his leg and fell back into the wall. Kurtis had gotten up and was running toward him. He stopped dead in his tracks as he saw the large pool of blood that Dave was now sitting in. Dave had dropped the knife and was looking up at the sky. The radio traffic was heavy. Dispatch was shouting out directions, trying to get units to Dave's location. Dave heard none of it. It was background noise to him at this point. His life flashed before his eyes in slow motion. He could see Gina clearly. He could feel her warm breath on the nap of his neck as she gently whispered to him, 'I love you.' Dave could feel the softness of her lips as they kissed before he left home tonight. He smiled. Kurtis dropped down by his side and was now hugging his arm, screaming.

"Please don't die. Please."

He looked down at Kurtis.

"Everything's going to be okay Kurt."

Kurtis stared up at him, eyes puffy and red, tears flowing down them.

"It's not. Don't die. Please. This is all my fault. It's my fault."

In the background, the sirens were loud and getting closer.

"Kurt." His speech was soft and fading. "Look at me." Kurtis looked up at him. "This is not your fault. You didn't do any of this. Butch did this, not you." He coughed. He leaned down toward Kurtis and their foreheads touched. "Trust in God to do something great with your life."

His eyes were slowly closing, and he could feel his life slipping away. He was simply falling asleep, and when he woke up, he would be in the presence of the Lord. Kurtis just clung to his side. Holding on as if he held on tight enough, Dave would be okay. Officers from all over answered the call, but no one got there in time. The paramedics loaded him into the ambulance, but he was already gone. Butch didn't even make it to his truck. Javier took him to the ground and was cuffing him up when he heard the 'Officer down' call. Everything was over in an instant. The coroner's report would later state that the knife completely severed the femoral artery.

On Friday, September 24, 2010, Officer David Jackson was laid to rest at the Mount Zion Memorial Cemetery. The service took place at Faith Bible Church, with Pastor William Dunkirk delivering the eulogy. The procession went from the church, through the center of town so that the citizens could pay their respects to their fallen hero. The city streets were lined with men, women, and children. Javier stood in place as a member of the honor guard, tears streaming down his face as taps played in the background. Gina remembers nothing about that day. She sat in a fog as the officers fired the twenty-one-gun salute, and as the flag was folded and handed to her. She doesn't remember handshakes or hugs or any of the day's events. She just stared at a casket that carried the man she loved. His smile, his wit, his humor, and his touch were all gone now. She doesn't know how she got through that day, but she did. That night, as she sat in the lazy boy that Dave had all but worn out, she picked his bible up from the end table and opened it. The pages were filled with notes and insights, and as she read some of them, her spirit became fed. The pain of losing him was still there, but she knew that one day they would be reunited. She closed the bible and hugged it close to her body. She reclined back and turned off the light.

Epilogue

September 18, 2013

A slight breeze moved across the cemetery, sending the fallen leaves in different directions. The evenings were getting cooler as summer was winding down. Gina sat on a bench next to Dave's grave, sipping a cup of coffee. She had already laid a beautiful bouquet of bright red and yellow day lilies next to his tombstone. They were his favorite. She grew them every year just for this day.

"It's been three years since we lost you, Dave. There isn't a day that goes by that I don't close my eyes and see your smiling face. I miss you. The kids miss you." She paused and smiled. "But you sure left your mark on this world. Where to begin." She cleared her throat and took another sip. "By the way, this coffee has cream in it." She laughed. "Your children are doing well. They both stayed home for college. Marc started at Lawrence Tech this month in pursuit of his engineering degree. He still plays the dickens out of your guitar, and I'm not sure that he won't eventually choose music as his path. Melissa started at Madonna University this month in pursuit of her...drum roll please...nursing degree. She has the perfect temperament for it, Dave. She's sweet and kind, and somehow has developed patience." Gina laughed. "As you know, Kurtis and Shannon moved back to Texas two years ago. That apartment still seems empty without them. Kurtis and Marc text all the time, and he told Marc this week that he is going to follow in the footsteps of his grandfather and take over the ranch in a few years. Shannon and I talked on the phone the other day for about an hour, and she told me that Kurtis has fallen in love with ranch life. She also told me they are very involved in the local church there, and that Kurtis has talked about teaching Sunday school on Sunday mornings." She stopped to collect herself and shed a few tears. "Can you believe that, Dave? She said that he reads his bible daily, and has developed a taste for black coffee." She laughed. "Shannon is doing well, and told me that her relationship with her parents is better than ever. They all go to church together on Sundays now.

Still no man in the picture, but she's content with that, and that's good." She paused. "Butch is still on death row in South Dakota for murdering Trooper Post." She paused. "Marc and Kurtis visited him this summer and witnessed to him." She cried some more. "You would be so proud of those two boys, Dave. They had the strength to do something I couldn't. I know why they did it. You rubbed off on them. The mercy and grace of God is for everyone." She broke from crying to laugh. "When I questioned them about going, Marc actually quoted scripture to me. Can you believe that? I asked them why would you go to that prison to save that man. He said to me, 'Because mom, Jesus says in Matthew chapter nine verse thirteen, I did not come to call the righteous, but sinners, to repentance.' He's a chip off the old Dave. That's a quote from Javier." She took a tissue out from her sweater and wiped her eyes. "Butch told them that there was no God, but consented to future visits. So, there is hope for him, I guess." She took in a deep breath and exhaled. "On to happier topics. I just found out that Javier made sergeant. He's a good man. I think it was harder on him than anybody when you were taken from us that night. He was struggling with guilt and depression over not being there for you. He was blaming himself for your death. I eventually had to tell him about your diagnosis. That you were leaving us by the end of the year anyway, and that God spared you of the pain associated with what you were about to go through. It really helped him to know that. Javier could make peace with losing you after that. He's the only one I shared it with, and as far as I know, the only one that will ever know about it. He and Rita even go to our church now. They are currently expecting their second child." She wiped her eyes again. "Your mom calls and visits more now. The kids even spent some time with her in Florida this past summer. She misses you greatly, and she told me she doesn't want to lose contact with me or her grandkids. She's doing well." Gina paused again to think. "Pastor Dunkirk asked me to lead a women's bible study on Tuesday nights at six. We are in our fourth week now, and it's going well. I'm teaching on the book of John. I know it was your favorite. Pastor Dunkirk misses you too." She wiped the tears from her eyes once more, and a beautiful bright red cardinal landed on top of his headstone. She smiled. "I love you so very much, David, and I miss you so much. But I know that one day we will see each other again, and that comforts me. If you don't mind, I'm just going to sit here in silence for a bit. Remembering your beautiful smile." She watched as the cardinal took flight into the sky. He went straight up, and she could swear that it disappeared into the heavens.

The End.

Tragedy can strike at any moment. Without warning life can change in the blink of an eye. This book was written to give you comfort in knowing that God is with you when that blink happens. The assurance that we have in Jesus provides a lifetime of love and support. Accepting the free and perfect gift of salvation gives us a rock to lean on throughout this life, and an eternity to live with Him in heaven where there will be no more tears, and no more pain. Ever. He paid the price on the cross for us. Won't you let His grace wash over you today and transform your life. May God bless you and keep you in His loving arms always. Thank you for reading Salvation Blue.

I would like to take the time to thank a few people: First and foremost, God in heaven above for giving me the words to write this novel. My darling wife, Crystal for all of her love, support, and patience. My two wonderful daughters, Jessica and Alyssa, and my son, Chris, for their love and support. My amazingly cute and lovable grandson, Lincoln. His innocence and love are an inspiration. To my parents, Don and Irma, for always showing me the love and support I needed growing up, and throughout my life. Finally, to all of my wonderful family and friends who are way too numerous to list, but have all had a loving impact on my life, I say thank you.

Don't miss out!

Visit the website below and you can sign up to receive emails whenever Reese Barton publishes a new book. There's no charge and no obligation.

https://books2read.com/r/B-A-ELQW-LDANC

BOOKS 2 READ

Connecting independent readers to independent writers.

About the Author

Reese Barton grew up in Detroit, Michigan, with two loving parents who opened his eyes and heart to a gracious and forgiving God early in life. Faith, family, and sports were a big part of his life growing up. His love for reading and writing developed at an early age, but God had a different calling for him: law enforcement. After a rewarding 26-year career as a police officer, he retired on July 1, 2022.

The love of reading and writing never left his heart, so after retiring he took up the pen and paper and penned his debut Christian novel, Salvation Blue. It combines two of his greatest passions. God and law enforcement. It is the first novel in which he hopes will be many that outline the love, mercy, and grace of God. He knows the many difficulties that life provides, but during it all is a God who cares about you and what you're going through.

Aside from reading and writing, he enjoys golfing, watching movies (Horror at the top of the list), Detroit sports, going to the beach, and having BBQs. But what he loves the most is just hanging out with family and friends. God blessed him with two wonderful daughters, a son, and an amazingly cute and awesome grandson.

Reese and his wife live in a suburb outside of Detroit with their two rotten German Shepherds, Bullitt and Bristal.

Read more at https://reesebarton.com/.

About the Publisher

Cross of Grace Publishing was created in 2023 to publish quality Christian books that glorify the Savior, Jesus Christ. Books that communicate strong Christian values and focus on a fulfilling and rewarding life in His service.

Although the stories are fiction in nature, they are based on the very real truth that Jesus Christ is Lord.

www.ingramcontent.com/pod-product-compliance
Lightning Source LLC
Chambersburg PA
CBHW071643260626
47170CB00001B/211